HIGHLAND DEVIL

THE CLAN SINCLAIR LEGACY

CELESTE BARCLAY

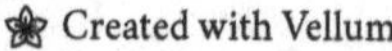 Created with Vellum

SUBSCRIBE TO CELESTE'S NEWSLETTER

THE CLAN SINCLAIR LEGACY

Highland Lion

Highland Bear

Highland Jewel

Highland Strength

Highland Devil

SINCLAIR FAMILY NAME GUIDE

Liam Sinclair m. Kyla Sutherland

    b. ***Callum Sinclair*** *m. Siùsan Mackenzie* (SH-IY-oo-san)

    b. Thormud Seamus Magnus Sinclair (TOR-mood SHAY-mus)

    b. Rose Kyla Sinclair

    b. Shona Mary Sinclair

    b. ***Alexander Sinclair*** *m. Brighde Kerr* (BREE-ju KAIR)

    b. Saoirse Sinead Sinclair (SEER-sha shi-NAYD)

    b. Nessa Elise Sinclair

    b. Mirren Louise Sinclair

    b. ***Tavish Sinclair*** *m. Ceit Eithne Comyn* (KAIT-ch En-ya CUM-in)

    b. Ailish Elizabeth Sinclair (A-lish)

    b. Tate Henry Sinclair

    b. William "Wiley" Matthew Sinclair

    b. ***Magnus Sinclair*** *m. Deirdre Fraser* (DEER-dreh FRA-zer)

    b. Maisie Blair Sinclair

    b. Blake Magnus Sinclair

    b. Torquil Lachlan Sinclair

   b. ***Mairghread Sinclair*** (Mah-GAID) *m.* *Tristan Mackay*
   b. "Wee" Liam Brodie Mackay
   b. Alec Daniel Mackay
   b. Hamish Kincaid Mackay
   b. Ainsley Maude Mackay

PREFACE

Laird Liam Sinclair married Lady Kyla Sutherland (*Their Highland Beginning*) to end a feud between the Sinclairs and Sutherlands. I took creative license in this historical event since the actual feud took place in the 16th century as opposed to what would have been the late 13th century in the world I'm building. This marriage has been the catalyst for all my other Highlander books. At this point, the family trees are a little complicated. I never imagined the six-book series, *The Clan Sinclair*, would launch so many more books. Oh, what a tangled web we weave when at first we practice to conceive. The following should help you better understand the intricacies of all the marriages and alliances.

Kyla Sutherland Sinclair was Laird Hamish Sutherland's younger sister. He married Amelia Ross in a book that is yet to be published. This marriage connected the Sutherlands and Rosses, whose feud is a product of my imagination. Amelia had several nieces and nephews, but two played roles in *The Highland Ladies Always* series and *The Clan Sinclair Legacy* series. The Sutherlands, through the Rosses, allied with the Campbells when Amelia's niece Laurel Ross married Laird Brodie Campbell in *A Hellion at the Highland*

Court. In that book, I introduced us to her brother, Montgomery Ross, heir and tánaiste to their clan.

In this book, we meet Montgomery again, but he is now the Earl of Ross. Laurel and Brodie had a son who they named Montgomery. The younger, or Óg, inherited the lairdship when the elder, or Mòr, stepped down because of age. I refer to Laurel's brother as Monty Mòr, and her son as Monty Óg. Monty Mòr remains the Earl of Ross while Monty Óg is Laird Ross.

Liam and Kyla's eldest son, Callum, married Lady Siùsan Mackenzie (*His Bonnie Highland Temptation*). Her mother, Rose, was a MacLeod of Assynt (died at her birth). Her stepmother was Lady Elizabeth Gunn. Her half-brothers Seamus and Magnus Óg (because Magnus Sinclair became known as Magnus Mòr) fostered with the Sinclairs. Magnus Óg married Saoirse (*Highland Rose*), the daughter of Alexander Sinclair (the second son) and Brighde Kerr (*His Highland Prize*). The Gunns are the villains in several of my books since they feuded with the Sinclairs, the Sutherlands, the Mackays, the Mackenzies, and the MacLeods of Assynt. Some of this is based on historical fact and some are the product of my imagination. You also encounter the Gunns in *A Devil at the Highland Court* (*The Highland Ladies Always*) and *Highland Strength* (*The Clan Sinclair Legacy*).

A shared ancestor related the MacLeods of Assynt to the MacLeods of Lewis. Laird Kieran MacLeod married Hamish and Amelia's elder daughter Maude (*A Wallflower at the Highland Court*). Kieran's younger sister Madeline married Fingal Grant (*A Sinner at the Highland Court*), and together they had Angus, Adelaide, Harry, Sarah, and Finley. When I named these children at the end of *An Angel at the Highland Court*, I had no idea I would later use them in a subsequent book.

Consequently, I've gone back and changed Magnus

to Angus (otherwise there'd be three of them in this book) and Adeline to Adelaide. I felt having a Madeline and an Adeline (even if pronounced Mada-lyn and Ade-line) was too similar. This meant I had to change the name of the MacLeods of Lewis siblings' mother in *A Wallflower at the Highland Court, An Angel at the Highland Court,* and this book since I wished our heroine to be named for Madeline's mother. As I said before: oh, the tangled web we weave when at first we practice to conceive.

Kieran and Madeline's younger sister, Abigail, married Laird Ronan MacKinnon (*An Angel at the Highland Court*). Abigail entered a handfast with Laird Lathan Chisholm before marrying Ronan. This failed handfast plays a role in this book.

Fingal Grant is the Clan Grant tánaiste and a distant cousin to Laird Edward Grant. Laird Edward and Lady Davina's daughter Cairstine married Eoin Gordon (*A Rake at the Highland Court*). Their other daughter, Fenella, married Kennon Campbell, cousin to Brodie (*A Hellion at the Highland Court*) and Domenic (*A Harlot at the Highland Court*) Campbell. While Edward and Davina's relation to Adelaide and her siblings is distant, she and the other Grant children refer to them as Aunt and Uncle since they were more like a great-aunt and great-uncle.

Because of these marriages, we find the Sinclairs linked directly to the Sutherlands and Mackays (Mairghread Sinclair married Laird Tristan Mackay in *His Highland Lass.*) Subsequent marriages allied the Sinclairs to the MacLeods of Assynt, the Mackenzies, the Frasers of Lovat, and the Gunns. Furthermore, additional marriages connected the Sinclairs, through the Sutherlands, to the Rosses, the MacLeods of Lewis, the Camerons, and the Lowlander Johnstones. Moreover, the Sinclairs, by way of the Sutherlands and Rosses, have a loose connection and alliance with the Campbells.

This wraps back around in this book since the Grants had an alliance through marriages with the Gordons, the Campbells, the MacKinnons, the Mac-Leods of Lewis, and Sutherlands. In this book, marriage creates an alliance between the Sinclairs and the Grants.

I realize this may prove difficult to follow as even I, the creator of this world, must pause to remember where the pieces go in this puzzle. I've included family trees in this book to help illustrate the Sinclair and Grant connections through marriage.

I hope you enjoy reading Tate and Adelaide's story as much as I did creating it.

Happy reading,

Celeste

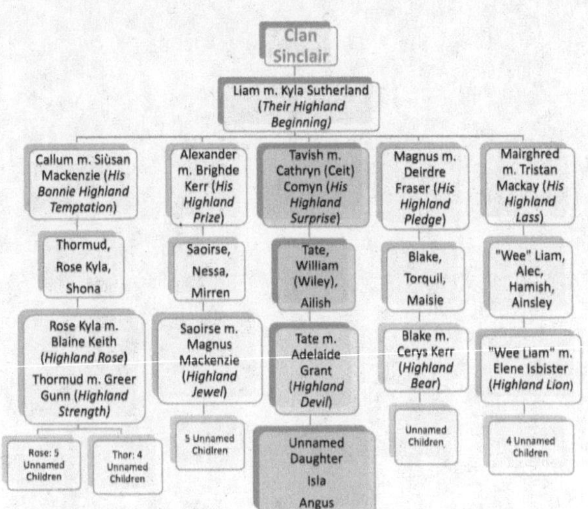

Clan Sinclair
Liam m. Kyla Sutherland (Their Highland Beginning)
Callum m. Siùsan Mackenzie (His Bonnie Highland Temptation)
Alexander m. Brighde Kerr (His Highland Prize)
Tavish m. Cathryn (Ceit) Comyn (His Highland Surprise)
Magnus m. Deirdre Fraser (His Highland Pledge)
Mairghred m. Tristan Mackay (His Highland Lass)
Thormud, Rose Kyla, Shona
Saoirse, Nessa, Mirren
Tate, William (Wiley), Ailish
Blake, Torquil, Maisie
"Wee" Liam, Alec, Hamish, Ainsley
Rose Kyla m. Blaine Keith (Highland Rose)
Thormud m. Greer Gunn (Highland Strength)
Saoirse m. Magnus Mackenzie (Highland Jewel)
Tate m. Adelaide Grant (Highland Devil)
Blake m. Cerys Kerr (Highland Bear)
"Wee Liam" m. Elene Isbister (Highland Lion)
Rose: 5 Unnamed Children
Thor: 4 Unnamed Children
5 Unnamed Chidlren
Unnamed Daughter, Isla, Angus
Unnamed Children
4 Unnamed Children

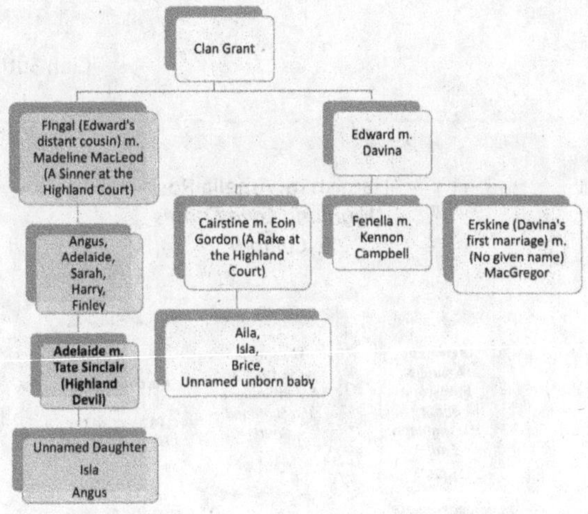

Clan Grant

Fingal (Edward's distant cousin) m. Madeline MacLeod (A Sinner at the Highland Court)

Edward m. Davina

Angus, Adelaide, Sarah, Harry, Finley

Cairstine m. Eoin Gordon (A Rake at the Highland Court)

Fenella m. Kennon Campbell

Erskine (Davina's first marriage) m. (No given name) MacGregor

Adelaide m. Tate Sinclair (Highland Devil)

Aila, Isla, Brice, Unnamed unborn baby

Unnamed Daughter
Isla
Angus

Clan Sutherland

- Dougal
- Murdoch
- **Hamish m. Amelia Ross** (*Highland Love Comes Calling*)
  - Lachlan m. Arabella Johnstone (*A Beauty at the Highland Court*)
    - Callen, Alasdair, Gavin
  - Maude m. Kieran MacLeod (*A Wallflower at the Highland Court*)
    - Amy, Graham, Mairi, Unnamed Child
  - Blair m. Hardwin (Hardi) Cameron (*A Saint at the Highland Court*)
    - Roddy, Unnamed Children
  - Callum m. Siùsan Mackenzie (*His Bonnie Highland Temptation*)
    - Thormud (Thor), Rose Kyla, Shona
      - Rose Kyla m. Blaine Keith (*Highland Rose*) 5 Unnamed Children
      - Thormud m. Greer Gunn (*Highland Strength*) 4 Unnamed Children

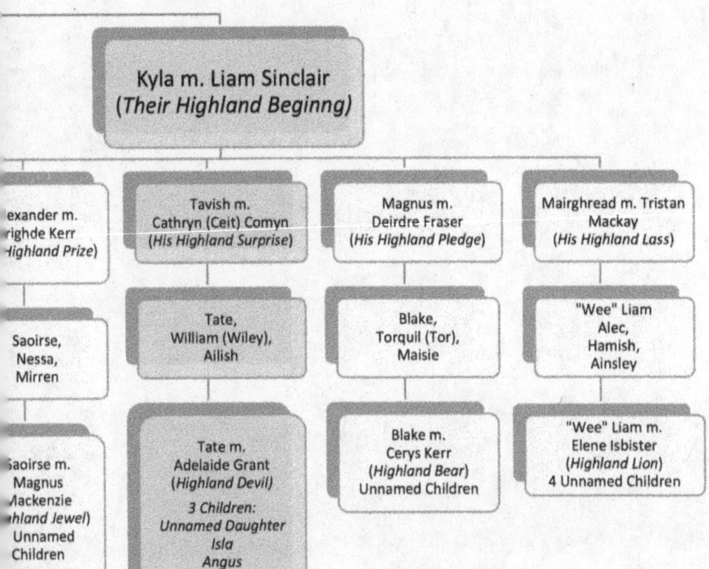

Kyla m. Liam Sinclair
(Their Highland Beginng)

Alexander m.
Brighde Kerr
(Highland Prize)

Tavish m.
Cathryn (Ceit) Comyn
(His Highland Surprise)

Magnus m.
Deirdre Fraser
(His Highland Pledge)

Mairghread m. Tristan
Mackay
(His Highland Lass)

Saoirse,
Nessa,
Mirren

Tate,
William (Wiley),
Ailish

Blake,
Torquil (Tor),
Maisie

"Wee" Liam
Alec,
Hamish,
Ainsley

Saoirse m.
Magnus
Mackenzie
(Highland Jewel)
Unnamed
Children

Tate m.
Adelaide Grant
(Highland Devil)

3 Children:
Unnamed Daughter
Isla
Angus

Blake m.
Cerys Kerr
(Highland Bear)
Unnamed Children

"Wee" Liam m.
Elene Isbister
(Highland Lion)
4 Unnamed Children

CHAPTER 1

Tate Sinclair reined in his horse as he drew close to the Grants' stables. He'd spotted the bonnie Adelaide Grant the moment he entered the bailey. He shot her a devilish smile, but it slipped only a heartbeat later. He hadn't predicted she would step forward when she did. He hadn't predicted how close it would put her to his horse's hindquarters. And he hadn't predicted that was the moment his horse would drop at least a stone's-worth of dung at the young woman's feet.

Adelaide jumped, releasing a slew of curses that made Tate laugh but only made her face a deeper shade of crimson. Anger, then embarrassment that anyone should hear her swear like a drunk man at a whorehouse, made her glare at Tate.

"Ma apologies, ma lady. Ma horse is an uncouth beastie."

Adelaide narrowed her eyes. "He matches his master."

Tate dismounted and handed off the steed that seemed to have the trots after trotting for so long. It left several more piles as the boy led the animal away. Tate placed his hand over his heart as he bowed to Adelaide, who refused to offer her hand for him to place an air kiss above it.

"How fortunate we are that yer fragrance is so refreshing."

"How much time do ye spend in the stables that smelling of horse is better than smelling like horse shite? Mayhap ye're in the stables, but too busy to notice the horses' stench."

Tate's chestnut eyebrows shot straight up to his chestnut hairline. He straightened as he gazed down at a woman who was surely a foot shorter than his nearly six-and-a-half feet. Her obstinate stare didn't waiver, despite how he continued to watch her.

"Ma lady, do ye nae ken yer plaids? I'm a Sinclair."

"Aye. Tavish Sinclair's son."

Tate gritted his teeth to keep from saying aught he couldn't take back. "Aye. And ma da has been unwavering in his faithfulness to ma mama for nearly a score-and-five years."

"He wasna always married."

"Lady Adelaide, I ken ma father's infamous past as a bachelor. I ken I am the spitting image of him. All the Sinclairs of ma generation look as much alike as ma father and ma uncles. They are wise men who taught us the lessons they've learned through the course of their lives. They made sure the sins of the father wouldnae pass down upon the son."

Tate's jovial nature disintegrated as he defended himself for the umpteenth time. That his father devoted himself to Tate's mother and had since they met seemed easily forgotten by so many. Plenty of people attributed Tavish's youthful habit of bedding different women to Tate and his younger brother, Wiley. Tavish had intended to remain a bachelor but fell in love with his wife almost immediately. The comparison usually happened when someone wished to be scornful toward the entire Sinclair family, or even the entire clan. But the Sinclairs and Grants were on good terms. Adelaide's disgust with him was unwarranted as far as Tate knew. He wanted to understand exactly why the young woman disliked him when they'd known each other since childhood.

"Have I erred, ma lady, and done ye afoul?"

Adelaide notched up her chin. "Ye have a wandering eye that landed on me a few too many times at the last Gathering. Da had plenty to say to me since yer clan left early for Lady Elene's lying in."

Tate's heart sank. "Ma lady, I'm sorry I got ye in trouble with yer father. That wasna ma intention."

"I ken that, and ye didna get me in trouble. He warned me away from ye."

Tate twisted to look farther into the bailey where Lady Madeline and Fingal Grant stood talking to Tate's parents, aunts, uncles, and grandfather. Clearly, Adelaide had heard of his parents. But he'd heard of hers, too. Fingal hadn't been eager to marry but was willing to. It wasn't until he met Madeline and fell in love that he welcomed marriage. It wasn't entirely unlike his own parents' story. He was certain Fingal had been as close to being a virgin as his father had been when both men wed.

"I am nay more ma father than ye are yer mother. I assume." He tacked on the last bit with a measured pause. Adelaide's eyes opened so wide Tate thought they might fall from their sockets. The jab met its mark.

"Excuse me. I must refresh maself." Adelaide made to step around Tate, but he shifted. His much larger frame meant Adelaide had to take a wider step. When she did, her foot landed in the pile of dung Tate's horse left. Both Adelaide and Tate looked down at the squelching sound.

"Ma lady, I truly am sorry for that!" Tate blurted before placing his hands on her waist and lifting her out of the offal. He knew if she'd tried to pull loose, she would have fallen and left her boot behind. Her hands went to his biceps to brace herself, though she had no need. He lifted her with ease. She felt the heat and the muscles tense through his leine.

She was at loss for words as her mind appreciated the feel of him beneath her palms and fingers. All she could muster was, "thank ye." He placed her on clean ground only a second later, but neither of them let go. However, they both looked in their parents' direction. Fortunately, no one paid them any attention. Adelaide's expression shifted when he put her down, and she no longer gazed at him with annoyance. She hoped she didn't appear too starry-eyed. But she'd gotten a better view of his whisky-hued eyes when he lifted her, and she was certain she'd get drunk from them if she looked into them for too long. Yet, much like liquor did to many people, they reached into her and addicted her before she knew what was happening. She wanted to keep staring, but she had no reason to.

"Ma lady—"

"Tate—"

They spoke at once, and they both smiled. They were soft lifts of the right sides of their mouths.

"Ye first, ma lady."

"I'm sorry for being such a shrew. I'm nae having ma best day, and the horse shite sums up ma afternoon. I shouldnae have spoken to ye as I did. I fear I've made a wretched impression of maself. It wasna yer fault, and ye didna deserve what I said."

"I accept yer apology, ma lady. We all have bad days and arenae always at our finest. I owe ye an apology, too. I tried for witty and failed."

"I accept yer apology, though I dinna think ye need to give it. I was in the wrong."

"I could have kept ma last comment to maself, and I regret even thinking it."

"I didna give ye much reason nae to think I'm like the reputation Mama had before marrying Da." Adelaide knew the story of her parents' meeting. Adelaide was familiar with the reason her uncle exiled her mother from court to a nunnery for years. Her mother's history didn't embarrass her. Her own behavior did that.

"Ma lady, I suspect we can go around in circles apologizing for the words we just exchanged." Tate peered into the robin egg blue eyes Adelaide inherited from her mother. They reminded him of gazing into the brightest blue sky in late autumn.

"I hope we have a better go of it the next time we run into each other." Adelaide offered him a heartfelt smile, wishing she could make a better impression than she had. While they'd known each other since they were children, things changed over the last few years. They'd noticed each other several times at the last Highland Gathering, and she'd hoped he might talk to her. But he'd never approached, and it wouldn't have been acceptable for her to approach him.

However, they'd exchanged glances enough times that her father took her to task about ogling men. It hadn't been entirely about Tate so much as being careful not to start rumors. He made sure Adelaide understood he held Tate as responsible for their exchanges as he did her. He admitted how unfair it was, both as a woman and as a member of the laird's family. She was some sort of cousin a few times removed from Laird Edward Grant, but her father was tánaiste and Edward's heir.

Their hands had already fallen away from each

other at some point neither of them had noticed. Tate bowed to Adelaide again, then stepped away. Adelaide moved past him and hurried toward the keep. She forced herself not to glance back at the far too handsome Highlander. While she hadn't meant all the barbs she'd tossed at him, she knew plenty of other women had their eye on him. She doubted after her less than stellar impression that morning he would look in her direction again.

She slipped her boots off at the top of the steps, knowing they were disgusting and needed cleaning before she could wear them again. She reconsidered her course and slipped them back on. She hurried to the garden, where she intended to knock the loose dung from them. She would find somewhere to wipe them before going inside. She searched for a rock just outside the garden that would work well for her. Once she found one, she continued to the vegetable patch. She took her boots off a second time and began fertilizing the garden with the manure.

She was in the middle of cleaning the first boot when she looked up and spied Tate with his arms around a beautiful woman with deep brown hair. She couldn't see their faces clearly, but she knew she shouldn't watch as they shared a kiss that must have left them breathless. Adelaide's heart dropped. She shifted her attention back to her shoes, but a shadow loomed over her. She looked up and furrowed her brow.

"I feel like I should do that since it was ma horse's fault." Tate squatted beside where Adelaide kneeled. He took the boot and the stone from her as she stared speechlessly at him. Then she turned her head toward the couple who were still kissing. Tate followed her gaze.

"Blake and Cerys are shameless. Learned it from his parents." Tate chuckled.

Adelaide's head whipped back toward him. "Blake and Cerys?" He was Tate's cousin.

"Aye." Tate watched a tinge of pink rise in Adelaide's cheeks. It was far subtler than the red they'd turned when they first encountered each other. "Who'd ye think it was?"

"Someone in yer family," Adelaide hedged.

Tate didn't press. "We all look a great deal alike. Ma only cousins who dinna look like me are Auntie Mairghread's lads and lass. Alec, Hamish, and Wee Liam look exactly like ma Uncle Tristan. Only Ainsley looks a wee like me because she could pass for ma aunt as easily as ma other cousins could pass for ma uncle. Uncle Callum's Thor and Rose Kyla look like me but have Auntie Siùsan's strawberry-blond hair. I ken it can be confusing at times."

Adelaide nodded, certain Tate knew she'd believed he was the man in the garden kissing someone. And she was certain he noticed she didn't care for that. Since she'd known all the Sinclairs and Mackays from childhood, she should have been able to tell them apart. At least his explanation saved her a modicum of embarrassment. She traded boots with Tate, who'd not only knocked the dung from her first boot but wiped it on a cabbage. They remained quiet while Tate cleaned the second one. When he finished, they both rose. Adelaide bent to slip her boots back on, and it wasn't until she straightened she realized she'd given Tate a view down her kirtle. She wasn't the most endowed woman, so she feared he'd seen clear to her belly. When she looked up, he was studiously looking away.

Bluidy hell. I'd go to bed and forget aboot today and start fresh tomorrow, but I canna.

"Thank ye for doing that. Ye didna need to, but I appreciate it. I really must tidy up since Mama expects me in the kitchens. She's likely to send Sarah to look for me soon."

Adelaide's younger sister would never let her hear the end of it if Sarah found Adelaide mooning over a man. She managed to remember to dip a slight curtsy as Tate bowed a third time that day. She hurried to the steps and inside the keep. She sped across the Great Hall and bolted up the stairs to the family chambers. She sprinted down the passageway and pushed open the door to her chamber, which she would share with Sarah during the Gathering. Their sister, Finley, shared with their Mackay cousin. The laird and lady of each clan with which the Grants had a close alliance would have a chamber in the keep.

She pulled the laces on her kirtle loose and shed it, along with her chemise and stockings, before pouring water in the ewer and dunking a linen cloth into it. She set it aside before plunging her hands into the cold water. She scrubbed them clean, then lathered soap onto the cloth. She swiped across her face and neck. She ran it beneath her arms, then over the rest of her until she no longer felt like she smelled of horse and dung. She wrinkled her nose at her filthy gown. She folded it, the dirty hem tucked inside, and set it aside for a maid to clean. She went to her armoire and pulled out a gown that was more appropriate for working inside the keep. From her chest, she gathered a fresh chemise and stockings. She donned those as quickly as she could before yanking the kirtle over her head. She hurried to tie the laces that ran along both sides.

Next, she swept a comb through her black hair and tied it back with a ribbon. She took a second ribbon, placing it at her hairline and tying it beneath the gathered hair. The wisps tended to stick to her forehead when she toiled in the overheated kitchens. She thought the hairstyle made her look like a little girl, but practicality prevailed. With her hair and clothes in place, she slipped on shoes before slipping out of her chamber, wincing when she closed the door a little too hard. She rushed to the kitchens as quickly as she had to her chamber. She arrived out of breath, but she grabbed a ball of bread dough and rolled it out. She started to help only moments before her mother came inside.

Lady Madeline Grant swept her gaze over the kitchen, surveying everyone chopping vegetables and preparing bread. She smiled at Adelaide as she stepped farther into the room and peered around a corner to the connecting kitchen. Several animals roasted on four spits. The fires from that portion of the kitchens made everywhere exceedingly hot. Madeline made her way to Adelaide's side. The younger woman appreciated the higher temperature in the room. She hoped her mother would believe the sweat on her brow came from the roaring fires nearby and not her mad dashes through the keep.

"Ye're in a different kirtle, lass." Madeline kept her voice soft, so their conversation was only between the two of them.

"Aye. I stepped in horse shite and got the hem dirty. That, along with riding this morning, meant I wasna fit for company. Definitely nae working around food we'll serve to at least fifteen clans' leaders."

"It was kind of Tate Sinclair to help ye clean yer boots after it was his horse that shat in yer path."

Adelaide forced herself not to cringe. "It was."

"He's a braw lad, much like his da was."

Adelaide heard the unspoken warning. It echoed the one Fingal gave her last year and was the basis for the accusations she'd hurled at Tate.

"Aye, Mama."

Madeline watched her daughter, who looked so much like her and so much like her own mother, for whom they'd named Adelaide. She rested her hand on her daughter's forearm. "I dinna ken the lad's past, only his da's. I would warn ye against him in case all he wishes is a dalliance. But besides yer da, there is nay finer mon to marry than a Sinclair. Everyone kens that. But that young mon doesnae strike me as the type looking for a bride."

"I ken that too. I will remember yer advice."

Madeline kissed Adelaide's cheek before moving on to speak to other women laboring to make the evening meal. The rest of the afternoon passed in a haze for Adelaide as she continued to help wherever their head cook sent her. She knew she'd need to bathe before attending the evening meal. The quick wash she'd done was to make her presentable enough to sweat even more in the kitchens. She caught a servant's attention and asked for the tub and hot water to be sent to her chamber. She learned her sister was already abovestairs bathing, so the servant offered to bring fresh water.

"Sarah?" Adelaide rapped on the door and called out before opening it a crack.

"Aye, come in. I've just gotten out."

Adelaide slipped into her chamber, glad to not see her sister. The younger woman was behind the screen to dress, so no one who might walk behind Adelaide could see in.

"Ye didna lock and bar the door while ye bathed," Adelaide admonished.

"Because I thought ye might get here, and I didna want ye having to wait in the passageway."

"Better that than someone coming in who doesnae belong in here. There are far too many men in and near the keep. Ye must bar the door while ye bathe."

Sarah stuck her head around the screen and nodded. She'd weighed her options and chose to leave it unlocked for Adelaide. She understood the risk, but she didn't like the idea of her sister being forced to linger alone in the passageway. She believed that to be as dangerous as someone intruding upon her bath.

"I will. Can ye help me with ma laces, please?"

Adelaide stepped next to Sarah and pulled the kirtle closed, tugging the laces tighter before tying them. She'd just finished when they heard a knock. Adelaide cast her eyes over Sarah, satisfied the clothes properly covered her.

"Enter," she called out. Six servants shuffled in, each with an empty bucket and one full of steaming water. She knew the servants kept an ongoing rotation of clean, hot water for baths since so many guests, along with the laird's large family, would need them. They bailed the dirty water and poured in the fresh. Adelaide was already stripping off her clothes behind the screen while the servants refilled the tub. Sarah sat on the bed, waiting for both the servants and her sister to finish their tasks. Adelaide sighed as she slid beneath the surface, wetting her hair and body. When she emerged, she looked toward Sarah.

"What did ye do this afternoon while I was in the kitchens?" Adelaide grabbed a fresh linen square and lathered the soap. She gave herself a far more thorough scrubbing than earlier. Between the warm water and the linen, she watched her skin pinken. She imagined her cheeks likely matched her arms when Tate caught her staring at Blake and Cerys.

"I went fishing with Angus and Harry." Sarah grinned. Angus was their older brother, and Harry was their younger. Between Sarah and Harry was their other sister, Finley.

"And I suppose ye caught twice as many as either of them. The only time ye're quiet is when ye fish. We should send ye out more often." Adelaide flicked water at the woman only two years her junior. She looked as much like their father as Adelaide looked like their mother. Their personalities were mirrors of their respective parents, too. Sarah was prone to annoyance faster than Adelaide but was also far more outgoing.

Adelaide tended to be more reserved like their mother had become after years living at a convent. However, once comfortable around people, Adelaide had a wickedly sharp and witty sense of humor. She'd behaved more like her sister around Tate than she did her usual self. She hid her smile as she poured fresh water over the hair she'd lathered while talking. She could only imagine what Sarah would have said to Tate if she'd been the one to have shite dropped at her feet.

"What has ye grinning?" Sarah leaned forward, as if to get a better look at Adelaide.

"I had a run-in with a horse's arse today."

"And what was his name?"

"I dinna ken. I didna think to ask."

"What clan's he from?"

"Sinclair."

"Aye, well, the list is a league long. Blake, Tor, Thor, Tate, and Wiley."

"The list isnae that long, but they do all look alike."

"Aye. Which mon do ye think it was?"

Adelaide laughed. "I meant a real horse's arse. Tate's horse practically shat on ma shoes. I didna think to ask the steed's name."

"Tate? Wasna he the one watching ye last year?"

"He wasna watching. We just—" Adelaide shrugged. "—Noticed each other."

"Noticed." Sarah snorted.

Adelaide pretended to be busy wringing out her hair and wrapping a drying linen around herself to respond. She patted her body before squeezing out the last drops from her hair. Once she dressed, and their hair was dry, the sisters took turns doing each other's coiffures. They chatted about the events they most wanted to watch at the games, and who they thought most likely to win each. Adelaide looked up at her sister through the mirror.

"We can speculate all we want, but ye ken it'll be a Sinclair, Mackay, or Sutherland who wins. They breed the men as well as their horses. Finest stock in the Highlands."

"Aye, they are." Sarah giggled along with her sister as they walked to the door.

They made their way belowstairs, but it wasn't Tate's flash of a smile that caught Adelaide's attention. That would have been nice. It was far worse than that.

CHAPTER 2

Tate noticed Adelaide and Sarah making their way down the stairs. Her eyes flickered toward him before something stole Adelaide's attention. He watched her gaze harden as it landed on someone she clearly didn't want to see. He followed her line of sight, but he couldn't be sure who she shot daggers at until one of the Chisholm men grinned.

"Give me a moment," Tate whispered to Wiley. He left before his brother could ask him anything. He wove his way through the crowd until he was close enough to hear the Chisholms speaking amongst themselves.

"The bitch is as haughty as her aunt was, and ma father dumped her on the steps of her brother's keep. Nay wonder nay one wants this one either."

Tate listened to Adam Chisholm speak about Adelaide. It took all his resolve not to push through the men and land his fist in the bastard's face. And a bastard he truly was. It remained no secret he was born before his parents married. His father entered a handfast with Adelaide's aunt, Madeline's sister, never intending to make it a permanent marriage. He did it for the dowry. He'd humiliated the woman by sending his

15

guards with her when he sent her back to the Isle of Lewis. The man had a mistress who he'd continued to bed once he'd handfasted. Somehow, the man convinced the church to recognize all his children as legitimate once he married his leman.

He wanted nothing more than to rush to her defense, just as he would any woman's, but he would start a brawl in the Grants' Great Hall if he did that. He would seek Adam out when they could be alone, then he would break the man's nose. Again. He'd done it last year during their wrestling competition. Tate won, making him the undefeated champion among his age group. His father remained the champion among the older men. Perhaps Tavish would lose if he ever wrestled one of his brothers. But the other three men stopped competing in the event when people claimed they cheated to keep winning. It had been a score-and-seven years since anyone else bore the title. Tavish won his first match and kept on winning. The same was the case with Tate. He'd held the title for nearly eight years. He didn't fear going up against Adam Chisholm in public or in private.

He drew away from the other clan and returned to Wiley, who now stood with Thormud, Torquil, and Kirk Hartley. Kirk's white-blond hair was as fair as the Sinclair men's chestnut hair was dark. Add in the Mackay cousins, with their raven-wing black hair, and the men drew endless attention when they gathered together.

"What's happening over there?" Kirk asked.

"I noticed something, so I went to listen." Tate hoped he sounded casual.

"What did ye notice, and what did ye hear?" Thor asked.

"Naught as interesting as I thought," Tate replied.

"Dinna trip over the pile of lies ye're leaving," Tor

quipped. Thor and Tor. The cousins had been unholy terrors as individuals when they were toddlers. They'd been the devil when they'd played together.

"They arenae lies. It didna end up being as big a deal as I thought." Tate shrugged.

"Then why did ye look like ye were ready to maul every mon over there?" Kirk wondered with false innocence.

Tate relented with a long exhale through his nose. "I noticed the way they were looking at Lady Adelaide and Lady Sarah as they came belowstairs. Something felt off. I went to listen. They insulted one of them."

Tor looked over his shoulder at the clansmen before looking back at Tate. "What'd they say?"

"That Lady Adelaide was the same haughty bitch as her aunt, and it was nay wonder his father sent her aunt away." He kept the last bit to himself since he didn't know who else saw him talking to Adelaide that afternoon. He wasn't in the mood for teasing.

"And ye said naught?" Thor wondered.

"This isnae the time or place. The Grants arenae going to look favorably at us if we start a melee right before the first evening meal. I will deal with it tomorrow during the wrestling."

His cousins and friend nodded, and the other men changed the conversation. Tate kept an eye on Adam, unconvinced the man wouldn't insult Adelaide to her face. He and Adelaide might have traded words that day, and they'd been hurtful for both of them. But Tate was positive anything Adam said would be a dozen times worse than Tate's insensitive comments.

"Let's get seats before they're all gone." Wiley nudged Tate and gestured to where their cousins and Kirk already stood at a table. He nodded and took a seat next to their father. Wiley sat to Tavish's other side, his mother between the large men. Their sister sat between Tate and Tor. The Grants' laird's table wasn't nearly as large as the Sinclairs'. Tate supposed few tables were. But there were nearly forty members of his family. Not all lived at Dunbeath Castle, but they visited often enough. Only his grandfather, uncle, and aunt sat at Laird Grant's table, along with a handful of other lairds and ladies, and tánaistes and their wives. He recognized his other aunt and uncle, Mairghread and Tristan Mackay.

He also recognized the Sutherlands, who were related to him through his father's mother. The Gordons sat there since Laird Grant's daughter married one of the twin brothers. Laird and Lady Fraser, who were indirectly related to him through one of his aunts, were at the table, along with Laird and Lady Campbell. He was even more indirectly related to Lady Campbell, since his father's mother's brother married a woman who was a Ross by birth. Lady Campbell was the current Earl of Ross's sister and Lady Sutherland's niece. There remained few clans in the Highlands to whom the Sinclairs weren't related in some way or another. It made for an enormous and intricate spider's web of alliances. It helped keep the peace—mostly. But when feuds inevitably broke out, it tested some alliances more than others. The enemy of my friend might also be my friend.

As the dais grew crowded, Tate watched Adelaide and Sarah ease into seats between their brothers Angus and Harry. Not long after, Tate's family drew his attention. He had two parents, two aunts, two uncles, two siblings, seven cousins, one cousin-by-marriage, and their family friends, the Hartleys, seated with him. It made for a crowded and noisy table. Behind Tate were the Mackays, so conversations stretched to that table, just as it did to the table in front of him, where the Mackenzies sat. A cousin married into that family, and the laird and tánaiste were one of his aunt's half-brothers. The Keiths sat at the table to Tate's left, and another cousin of his was now the lady of the clan. The Sutherlands were at the table to the right of Tate's. Without a family tree written out in front of someone, they were likely to get tangled in the branches.

The clan that bound Adelaide's clan to his was the MacLeods of Lewis. Tavish's cousin, a former Sutherland, married the laird, who was Madeline's brother. Fingal had also fought alongside Laird Liam Sinclair and his four sons—Tavish and his three brothers—against the English. Their clans helped place King Robert the Bruce on the throne and continued to champion their exiled King David II. Tate had ridden into battle beside Angus and Harry Grant. He trusted Adelaide's brothers as much as he did his uncles and his cousins. However, he doubted neither Angus nor Harry would appreciate how long Tate's mind stayed on Adelaide. It kept going back to her.

When the meal ended, and servants pushed the tables aside, musicians played. Tate partnered with his sister and cousins, while Adelaide partnered with her brothers and Gordon and MacLeod cousins. Such large families meant there was never a derth of partners. There were far too many people crowded together for Tate to catch sight of Adelaide. In turn, she never caught a glimpse of Tate. At least, not one she could be sure was him. Eight Sinclair men stood at six-and-a-half feet tall with the same chestnut hair, and almost all of them had the same whisky-brown eyes. Their features were so similar it would be easy to imagine only one man who moved through the dancers.

Adelaide didn't want to admit to herself that she kept trying to spy Tate. It annoyed her that she wanted to know with whom he danced and whether he looked for her. By the time the musicians finished, and people retired for the night, her head ached from the noise and heat of so many people moving far too close together. She'd been jostled and bumped too many times. It relieved her to make her escape abovestairs with Sarah. But as she lay next to her sister, listening to Sarah's soft and deep breathing, her mind wouldn't settle.

Cease yer curiosity before ye wind up with more trouble than ye can manage. The mon is braw and even kind. But Mama is right. That doesnae mean he's looking for a bride, and that doesnae mean I should look to him as a groom. I'm nae looking to go that far, but I dinna mind looking a wee. I'm certain I shall wake and have plenty to occupy maself with instead of thinking aboot Tate Sinclair. Naught good can come of that. We werenae even flirting today, so why do I think he might have any interest in me beyond cleaning some shite off ma boots? If I had any sense, I would be asleep right now.

She rolled over and adjusted her pillow. She closed her eyes and thought about the competitions the next day. She drifted off, imagining her brothers winning first and second place in the swim. It was a far more harmless dream than anything she might conjure about Tate.

* * *

ADELAIDE SLIPPED into the ale tent and tried not to curl her nose. Warriors who'd finished their competitions that morning packed the confined area from end to end and side to side. Some weren't competing at all, instead, wasting their time with ale and wenches. She slipped between men as best she could, but her elbow contacted more than a few sets of ribs. When she came to two men who simply refused to move, she looked around for another route. She froze when two hands shot past her ears, landing on the offending men's shoulders and shoved.

"Ma lady already asked ye twice vera politely to move. Now I'm telling ye to."

The men swung around but froze when they recognized Tate then Adelaide. Both men wisely decided it was far healthier to move aside. Adelaide was certain it was because Tate was a Sinclair, but perhaps it was partly because she was the hosting laird's cousin. She highly doubted the latter.

"Thank ye." Adelaide wasted no time offering her appreciation, then moving to the counter where a man and three women rushed to serve ale, mead, and whisky. She knew Tate followed her. She glanced at him as he positioned himself between her and the next man at the counter. The way he stood shielded her from most people's view.

"What are ye doing in here, ma lady?"

"Getting ale for Da and Angus." Adelaide caught the alehouse keeper's attention as she spoke and held up two fingers. She looked up at Tate, confused by the confused expression he offered her.

"Magnus? Do ma aunt or cousin ken ye're getting ale for their husband? Havenae ye heard aboot the women in ma family? Vera protective of their men."

Adelaide mockingly rolled her eyes but refused to take the bait.

"Ah, ye like to live dangerously. Dinna say I didna warn ye. Auntie Deirdre and Saoirse arenae the forgiving type to women who get too close."

"Do they think I'd approach their husbands and try to seduce them?"

Tate laughed. "Nay one is that daft. But Uncle Magnus is the largest mon here besides his sons Blake and Torquil. He always wins the caber toss, which I ken yer brother Harry intends to enter. Saoirse kens yer brother Angus is auld enough to compete against her husband, Magnus, in the throwing the weight over the bar. They wouldnae want ye putting a sleeping tincture or some such in their men's ale."

Throwing the weight over the bar was exactly as it sounded. The contestants hoisted the largest rock found in the area and tried to toss it over a bar that stood eight feet high. It was one competition with the fewest entries since only the largest men could even attempt the feat, let alone accomplish it.

"Ye ken as well as I do I mean ma brother Angus. It's nae ma fault yer family canna come up with more names, and ye canna hear."

"And ye ken that ma uncle and ma cousin's husband arenae related by blood. Besides, we call ma uncle Magnus Mòr, and ma cousin's husband Magnus Óg to keep from confusing them. Shall we call yer brother Angus Glè Óg?"

Mòr meant greater but signified older, and óg meant younger. However, Adelaide recognized Tate meant her brother was the least of the three.

"Vera lesser, indeed. Mayhap clean yer ears out. Their names arenae that similar. Wait until he beats yer cousin-by-marriage." After putting two coins on the counter, Adelaide picked up the two tankards and turned toward the way she came in. Somehow, in the space of five minutes, it had grown even more crowded. She would never get out without sloshing the drinks down the front of herself.

"Let me have ma pint, lass. Then I'll help ye outside." Tate accepted the one the alehouse keeper placed in front of him. He put down a coin of his own as he watched Adelaide. He could practically hear the debate waging in her mind. "I can carry the one for yer father and the one for ma uncle."

"It's nae for yer uncle."

"Then the one for ma cousin-by-marriage. I dinna ken if that's any better than getting it for ma uncle. Saoirse's as terrifying as Auntie Deirdre. Both are vera creative when making their point, and it'll be a memorable point to stay away from their husbands."

"Why do ye continue to play daft? Ye ken it's for ma brother."

"If that's the case, then why's he been sitting over there with that wench on his lap since before ye entered?"

Adelaide spun around, splashing ale over the rim and onto her hands. Her lips thinned as she spotted her brother. She practically shoved one tankard into Tate's chest as she muttered, "For ma father." She wound around the ends of the tables, leaning over to avoid the side of the tent. She came to stand beside her brother Angus.

"Ye look as overheated as ye claimed. Mayhap I should help ye cool off." Adelaide lifted the mug over Angus's head, and he knew his sister well enough to know she wasn't issuing a false threat. He stood so abruptly, the woman on his lap almost fell over. One arm went to brace her, while the other went for Adelaide's forearm.

"Ada, dinna." Angus tried to lower her arm, but she resisted.

"Ye miserly arse. Ye sent me to get the ales because ye didna want to pay for them yerself. How'd ye get that one?"

Tate came to stand beside her. "I bought that one."

Adelaide glared at him. "What?"

"Aye. I owed him one from last year, so I bought the one he has now. Can ye see why I was so confused?"

"Confused, ma arse. Ye kenned and made me have to defend maself." She poured the contents of the mug onto Tate's boots. "I willna be helping ye clean yer boots."

Tate stared at Adelaide, then his boots, before grinning. "I like the smell of ale."

"We'll see how much ye like it when the mice nibble through yer boots tonight." Adelaide knew Tate was sleeping in a tent like the rest of his family, except for his grandfather. His uncle—their clan's tánaiste—and his aunt offered their chamber to their daughter and husband, the acting Laird and Lady Keith, since she was expecting. They were sleeping in a tent too. Men would stand their boots upside down, and women would turn their shoes over to keep the mice from leaving presents in them during the night. The scent of stale ale would entice the vermin, and they could easily nibble through the leather. Adelaide wouldn't have done it if she weren't certain Tate knew how to clean them and keep that from happening.

"Ada!" Angus looked aghast at his sister, but she stared at Tate, who continued to grin at her. "Ye should go. Da is likely waiting for that ale. If ye dinna hurry, he'll come in here, searching for ye. He willna be pleased."

"I ken. He willna enjoy hearing ye swindled me." Adelaide dropped the empty mug on the table and took the one Tate still held for her. She leaned forward to whisper in her brother's ear. "I'd hide yer boots tonight lest ye wake with ants in them."

The wood ants were harmless when left alone. However, they instinctively defended wherever they were, as though every place they roamed was their colony. They'd bite, and it hurt. It wasn't the first-time brother and sister were at odds, and it wouldn't be the first time Adelaide used that weapon.

"Do that, and I'll let the hounds play with yer balls of yarn."

"Go right ahead. Then ye can explain to Mama and Da why ye wasted wool that will make our people blankets and coats this winter." Adelaide crossed her arms while holding the remaining tankard.

"Sister."

"Brother." Adelaide looked down at the ale before bringing the mug to her lips. She downed the entire pint in only a few gulps. She dropped the empty vessel on the table next to the other one she'd put down. "Ye'd best fetch Da an ale before he comes looking and finds ye here with a wench on yer lap. When he asks, tell him I've gone for a swim with our sisters."

That made her wonder if Tate had a woman sitting on his lap when she arrived. He'd clearly already been in the tent and made his way around to come up behind her.

"Nay, Ada. Nae unless Harry's going with ye. Ye arenae going to the loch with only guards."

"But I already promised Sarah and Finley." Adelaide smirked. She knew Angus wouldn't let her or their sisters go to the loch to swim without him or their brother. Not with this many men moving around the keep and the surrounding area. She'd planned to butter Angus up with the ale and convince him to take his sisters. Now she'd guilt him into it. Angus glowered at her as she turned a patently fake and falsely innocent mien toward him. He signaled for three ales, and only a moment later they arrived. He handed one to Tate.

"How'd ye ken?" Angus grumbled.

Tate's laugh boomed. "I have a sister and live with a passel of female cousins. I warned ye."

"Warned him aboot what?" Adelaide queried.

"I told him ye'd be fit to be tied when ye found him here."

Adelaide fisted her hands since she didn't trust herself not to lash out, and she pressed her lips together so hard that they burned.

"And I owe him an ale, since he was right."

"Ye wagered on me?"

Tate's heart tightened when Adelaide's voice came out barely more than a murmur. He didn't think she faked the hurt in her voice or the flash of sadness in her eyes.

"We meant it only in jest. But ma humor seems to fall short with ye. We didna mean any harm by it. I'm sorry."

Adelaide nodded before turning toward the tent's flap. Tate led the trio toward the exit. When it became too congested, he reached back and felt for Adelaide's arm. He slid his hand down until he could take hers. He was gentle, even though his grip was firm, which was a good thing. The crowd would force her from him otherwise, and Angus now had a tankard in each hand. But when a drunk man staggered into her and nearly knocked her over, Angus put both mugs in one hand and the other on her shoulder. They'd almost made it outside and were only a few feet from the flap when a fight broke out. Tate spun and pulled Adelaide against his chest, engulfing her. He shielded her as he felt elbows and arms jam into his back and ribs.

"Tate, are ye all right? We need to get out of here before they draw ye and Angus into this."

"Wheest. It's best we stay where we are. If we try to move, someone will injure ye."

"But they're—"

"Haud yer wheest, wee one. I barely feel aught." Which was as bold a lie as he'd ever told. He felt it all, and he would have the bruises to prove it in the morning.

"Enough! Cease!" Angus roared as he stood on a table. "All of ye out. The alehouse is closed. Go to yer clans and sober up before Laird Grant sends yer clans home. We dinna battle each other at the Gatherings. Ye ken the rules. Fight each other on yer own lands. We have peace at the Gatherings, and if we dinna, the violators leave. Now, out!"

Adelaide couldn't see Angus jump down, but she heard him land. Tate quickly let go and stepped aside, but he found he wasn't eager to yield Adelaide's protection to her brother. Angus pulled his sister into his arms.

"Are ye all right, lass?"

"Aye. I'm fine. But Da is going to be livid. Who was it?"

"All of them. I dinna ken who threw the first punch, but it didna matter. It was an excuse for enemies to claim they were just defending themselves. Let's get ye away from here." Angus kept Adelaide wrapped in his arms as Tate once again led the way, shoving drunken men who staggered into their path. They'd barely made it outside when the trio saw Fingal and Edward running toward them.

"Ada!" Fingal sprinted the last hundred feet and practically ripped his daughter from his son's arms. "What were ye doing in there?"

"I went to fetch ye and Angus ales. I saw how hot ye both were, so I thought to do something nice for ye. Angus was already in there by the time I made ma way inside. I ran into Tate and him. They helped me get out when the fight broke out."

She shot a pointed look at Angus and Tate. She didn't need to worry. Neither of them intended to share their conversation with the two older men. The man she always thought of as Uncle Edward patted Adelaide on the shoulder before making his way into the tent to inspect the damage.

"Thank ye, Sinclair."

"I'm glad Lady Adelaide is unharmed. I didna see any of ma clansmen in there, but I should tell Grandda right away in case any of them were. Good day." Tate didn't want to walk away. He didn't want to leave Adelaide behind, even though he knew she was safest with her father and brother. He reasoned it was his guilt for keeping her in the tent for so long. If he hadn't teased her and just told her Angus was there, she would have left sooner. She wouldn't have been there when the brawl began. He looked back over his shoulder, but the Grants were already walking in the opposite direction. He scanned the crowd he approached and realized it was much closer to the first round of wrestling than he thought. He jogged over to his father.

"I was aboot to send scouts out for ye," Tavish hissed. "Adam Chisholm has been spewing twattle for the past ten minutes. He claimed ye feared him too much to show up, so we may as well call it a forfeit."

"A fight broke out in the alehouse. I helped Angus Grant get his sister outside, then stopped briefly to speak to Fingal."

"Was the lass harmed?"

"Nay. I dinna think any of our men were involved, but I was going to tell Grandda. I dinna have time now."

"Wiley!" Tavish called out to his younger son. When he came over, he spoke while Tate stripped off his weapons and leine. "Tell Grandda there was a fight at the alehouse. Have Thor look over the men to see if any were involved."

Thormud was the eldest grandchild among the Sinclairs who lived at Dunbeath. Only Wee Liam Mackay and Thormud's three-minutes-older twin sister came before him. He was in line to inherit the lairdship after Tate's uncle and grandfather passed away. Thor was the clan's captain of the guard, so the responsibility fell to him to handle misbehaving warriors.

Tate's mother, Ceit, approached with a satchel in hand. She held it open to her son, and he placed his various dirks in the bag, along with his leine. He kissed his mother and embraced his father before stepping into the ring of stones that marked the wrestling space. A Grant councilman announced Tate's name and his opponent's. Then the man rattled off Tate's winning record as Tate stared at Adam. His expression was blank, and he knew that was more disconcerting than if he growled at his opponent. The signal was given, and Tate launched himself at Adam.

He knew his opponent had seen him wrestle before, and they'd had more than one round against each other. He knew Adam expected Tate to circle until Adam got impatient and made the first move. He caught Adam completely off guard by slamming into him only seconds after the match started. Tate was larger and bulkier than Adam, having inherited his father and grandfather's barrel chest. He pinned Adam to the ground and held him in place as Adam tried to buck him off. Tate shifted to put his knee on Adam's chest, pressing almost all of his weight onto that calf.

"I heard what ye said aboot Lady Adelaide last night."

Tate watched Adam's eyes widen just as he expected. Tate appeared to brace himself with one hand in the dirt, but he didn't need to. He scooped some as he brought his hand up as though he needed to reposition himself. He made sure it landed in his opponent's eyes.

"Ye're alive because I didna tell Fingal or Lady Madeline." Tate shifted again and yanked Adam to his feet only to flip him over his shoulder, following Adam down to the ground once again. This time, he placed his knee low on the man's abdomen. When he stood, he made sure his shin pressed on Adam's rod. His foot kicked the man's bollocks, but Tate knew he made it look like an accident.

"Are ye fucking her? Is that why ye care? She's a bitch like her aunt."

The second time Tate pulled Adam up, he twisted the man's arm so far back that he dislocated the shoulder. He grabbed the other arm that flailed and did the same thing, yanking it back just short of dislocating it before jamming his knee into the back of the other man's. When Adam's leg buckled, Tate kicked the man's ankle on the same side. They crashed to the ground. Because of how Tate held Adam, the man couldn't turn his head in time. He landed face down. Tate heard the crack and knew he'd broken Adam's nose.

"Stay down, or I will keep going until I kill ye." Part of Tate hoped the man would resist. But this was supposed to be a competitive but friendly match. He would only cause more trouble than Adam was worth if he killed him. The man refereeing the match came over and declared Tate the winner. He gracefully stood and raised his right fist over his head. He glanced around, catching sight of his beaming father and his reluctantly smiling mother. But he faltered when he spied Adelaide's horrified expression. She spun on her heels and dashed away.

He wanted to chase her, but that was impossible. Besides the fact his next match was in a few minutes, he would cause a scene if he did. But what scared her off? Did his tactics disgust her? Did she sympathize with Adam?

Bluidy hell. Does she want him when he thinks so lowly of her? Will she hate me for hurting the mon she wants?

He had no answers to those questions, but he planned to get them. If Adelaide pined for Adam

Chisholm, he would disabuse her of any romantic wishes she had.

Wait. I looked at Adam because I saw how she stared at him. There was nay longing there. More like—what? Distrust? Dislike? That was the entire point of why I went over there. What did the bastard do to her?

CHAPTER 3

$\mathcal{A}$delaide watched in horror as Tate practically pulverized Adam as they wrestled. The latter never stood a chance. The moment Tate bent low and charged toward Adam, the match may as well have been over. She was certain Tate had to weigh close to sixteen stone, and with momentum, it would feel like a bull rammed into Adam. She couldn't hear what either man said, but Tate clearly didn't care for Adam's response. The referee was wise to call an end to the match before Adam lost the use of all his limbs. He'd need his shoulder set. She watched as Tate raised his arm in victory, but she shifted her gaze as Adam clambered to his feet. The loathing he shot at Tate was unmistakable. Then he looked at her. She received the same stare. She needed to get away from the match before anyone noticed.

Adelaide called back to her sisters, who'd also stopped to watch the wrestling. When they were away from the crowd, Adelaide slowed her pace. She looked around and spotted their younger brother. Sarah and Finley came to stand beside Adelaide as their older sister called out and waved.

"What had ye tearing away like ye had wasps up yer skirts?"

"Ye saw how Adam looked at me." Adelaide kept her voice hushed. "Dinna say aught in front of Harry."

Sarah and Finley nodded, and the three sisters soon convinced their brother to go to the loch with them. They weren't the only ones with the idea of swimming on the warm summer day. They heard women's voices, then recognized the MacDonald guards. Harry issued his sisters a warning to be careful mostly because he felt obligated. He happily went to stand near the other guards, so his sisters could duck behind trees to undress.

"Clara!" Adelaide waved both arms over her head to her friend.

"Ada!" Clara MacDonald of Lochalsh waved back a few feet away from the shore. She swam closer as Adelaide, Finley, and Sarah pulled off their boots, stockings, and kirtles, leaving them in their chemises. It would prove practically pointless to keep them on since they would stick to the women like a second skin when they emerged. Then they'd soak their kirtles once they put their gowns on since they'd have nothing with which to dry themselves. Adelaide looked around to make sure no one but the women already in the loch could see her. She whisked her chemise over her head and ran into the water. Even though it was summer, it was brisk.

"Adelaide!" Sarah sounded aghast.

"Do ye want soaked clothes to put back on? Do ye want to battle yer kirtle to get it on over wet skin? I dinna. Nay one can see us. That's why Harry came. Even if the other guards didna ensure it, Harry would." Adelaide kicked off the bottom and swam out to where she could no longer stand. Clara, Finley, and Sarah swam alongside her. "Clara, how are ye? I didna see ye at the evening meal last night."

"We only arrived this morn. A spoke on one of our carts broke. It slowed us, so we arrived late. How're ye?"

"Fine as a Scottish summer day."

"What storm blew in?" Clara asked. Wait long enough, and a person could have all four seasons in one Scottish day.

"The Chisholms," Finley supplied.

"Is yer aunt here?" Clara wondered about Madeline's younger sister who wound up falling in love and marrying happily after her disastrous handfast ended.

"Aye. She and her clan are keeping their distance. Ma uncle had words with Laird Chisholm at the last Gathering. He told Laird Chisholm to keep his clan away, but I doubt they are. They love antagonizing ma uncle."

The tangled web of alliances only grew more complicated since her mother and aunt were MacLeods of Lewis by birth. They were the greater branch and distant relatives to the MacLeods of Assynt. It related the latter to Tate's aunt Siùsan Mackenzie, who'd married into the Clan Sinclair. Their shared Gunn relatives also connected the MacLeods of Assynt to the Mackenzies. After generations of animosity, the Gunns and Sinclairs were finally allies. Thor married the old laird's daughter. It was enough to make Adelaide's head buzz when she tried to remember how the Sinclairs connected to almost every clan in the Highlands.

"Just keep yer distance," Clara advised.

Adelaide recalled the venomous glare Adam shot her after giving Tate an even more ominous one. "I will. What are ye most looking forward to this year?"

Clara beamed. "Can ye keep a secret?"

"Ye ken we can," Sarah chimed in.

"Ma da is going to announce ma betrothal to Fergus!" Clara MacDonald and Fergus Matheson had been in love since they were barely adolescents. It would surprise no one that the couple was finally betrothed. At only a moon past her eight-and-tenth saint's day, Laird MacDonald finally consented to the marriage on her birthday. "We're marrying right after the Gathering. The Mathesons' priest has already read the banns three times."

"Felicitations," Adelaide, Finley, and Sarah said together.

"I'm so excited."

"I'm sure ye are. I ken for years ye could only see each other at Gatherings. Has Fergus courted ye, or did yer fathers settle the matter between them?"

"Mostly settled the matter between them through missives, but we've stayed at their keep for the past three sennights for the sake of the banns. It's been wonderful."

Adelaide cocked an eyebrow at Clara, mirth dancing in her eyes. "Just how wonderful?"

"I willna be cutting the head off a chicken, but—we've done things."

"Och, aye. Nay chicken, but what aboot a sheep?" Adelaide waggled her brow. She and Clara had been friends since they were old enough to make friends. They gravitated to one another at events, and they'd stuck to each other the last time their families were at court together. Angus stayed so close to Adelaide at court that she'd wondered if her older brother was keen on Clara. But Harry had glued himself to Sarah, so it turned out to be merely her brother's protective nature and Clara's coincidental company.

"None of that either." Clara winked. "It is tempting."

"Fergus is a braw mon, and ye are a bonnie lass." Sarah waggled her brow just as her sister had. She didn't want Fergus, but she could appreciate the man's good looks. However, he wasn't nearly as tall as she preferred. While she wasn't as tall as either of her brothers, or any of her uncles and cousins, she was above average for most women. She didn't want to appear like a giant alongside a husband, so she wished for a man who rivaled in height to the ones in her family.

"Mayhap, but he isnae a braw husband, and I am nae a bonnie wife. We're waiting."

Adelaide saw the apprehension in her friend's gaze. "Are ye worried yer father or his will call it off?"

"Aye. Ye ken how things are while our king is in exile. Alliances shift. Ma clan can afford to lose ma dowry. The Mathesons can afford nae to receive it, even if they are a smaller clan than mine."

Adelaide nodded. Clara spoke the truth. Most clans in the Highlands supported King David since most fought to place his father, Robert the Bruce, on the throne. But some hedged their bets and supported the English to make their clan's life easier, even if it antagonized their neighbors. The division of loyalty was far more prevalent in the Lowlands nearer the border.

"Fergus has been in love with ye since practically forever. He willna let his father break the contracts, and yer da wouldnae wish to disappoint ye."

Clara grinned, then giggled. "I am a wee spoiled."

Amongst a hoard of six brothers, Laird MacDonald had a soft spot for his two daughters. He'd lost two wives to illness. He hadn't loved either woman, but he'd been fond of both. Clara was the spitting image of her mother, the laird's third wife. He adored Clara's mother, and they were a happy couple.

The women swam for another half-an-hour until their fingers and toes were prunes, and the evening meal drew near. They swam back to the shore, and Sarah called out to her brother.

"Harry!"

"Aye!"

"Give us yer plaid!"

"Nay!"

The man's leine would reach close to his knees, so he would remain decent. He didn't wish to pleat a sodden length of wool when his sisters finished drying themselves.

"Who's out there ye dinna want seeing yer knobby knees?" Sarah enjoyed taunting her younger brother. With two older siblings, she received enough of her own teasing.

"Are ye decent?" Harry's voice drew closer, and the women could see his back.

"Decent enough," Adelaide answered.

Harry kept his voice low, so the guardsmen nearby wouldn't hear. "Ye should have taken yer chemise off like Ada. Then ye'd have something to dry yerself with. Nae ma fault ye didna plan properly."

Adelaide turned in a circle, panicked that someone else saw her naked. But Harry would have had a fit if anyone else had. There'd be dead bodies strewn everywhere.

"Calm down, Ada. I checked on ye twice. I could see yer bare shoulders but naught else." Harry still had his back to the women, but he knew his sisters. With a beleaguered sigh, he unfastened his belt and unpinned the extra length of plaid over his shoulder. He dropped the pin into his sporran and unraveled his plaid. When he had it free of his body, he stuck out his arm behind him, dangling the yards of material. The four women hurried to the shore, and Sarah grabbed it. They rushed back to where they'd left their clothes. Adelaide considered using her chemise to dry off like she'd intended, but she grabbed an end of the plaid and hurried to rub it over herself. She used it to ring out her hair, leaving a massive wet spot on the end she knew would be closer to her brother's body. Clara glanced around guiltily, but took the material when Sarah offered it to her.

Adelaide donned her chemise and other clothes before tugging on her boots. She was the first dressed, so she took the plaid back to her brother. She kept her expression neutral as she handed it back to Harry. He glared at her as he laid the yards of wool on the ground, annoyed he not only had to pleat it but put it in dirt. He positively glowered at her when he came to the section that was sopping wet. He hurried to wrap it around himself and grimaced as the wet wool soaked his leine.

"Ye shouldnae have taken the last tart at the evening meal last night. Ye saw me reach for it. Ye wouldnae even share. Ye ate it so fast Mama couldnae tell ye to." Adelaide notched up her chin and stared at her brother imperiously.

"I'm still a growing lad."

"Aye. Growing as broad as a barn." Adelaide poked Harry's ribs, where there wasn't an inch of fat to spare. If eating were a contest at the Highland Gathering, Harry would have no competition. Adelaide knew of no other man who could polish off a meal as fast as her younger brother, then ask for four more helpings right after. Even men larger than him couldn't eat as much as he did. "One day it shall catch up with ye."

"Aye, but nae today."

Sarah, Finley, and Clara emerged from behind the rocks. The latter grinned as she spied her betrothed. She stepped forward and offered Fergus her hand. He kissed the back of it before looking around. Satisfied no notorious gossip was within sight, he kissed Clara's cheek. Adelaide watched the couple, happy for them since they were a love match. Her aunt, Abigail, and her uncle, Kieran, had wed their spouses for love. But her parents hadn't had a love match, but a marriage arranged by King Robert the Bruce. Her parents fell in love on their way from court to their home at Freuchie Castle. Her distant cousin, Edward, had had an arranged marriage to his wife when he unexpectedly inherited the lairdship. They developed a deep love for each other. It made Adelaide wonder which she might have in her future. She nearly shrugged as she thought about it, but she caught herself before anyone noticed.

The group made their way back to the keep, a handful of MacDonald guards following them. Once they reached the postern gate, Clara, Fergus, and the guards broke off and went to the massive encampment to find their clans. Adelaide, Sarah, Finley, and Harry entered the bailey. Across from them, at the far end, entering under the portcullis, was a wave of giants moving toward them. Adelaide spotted the original giant with ease, but differentiating the man's replicas challenged her.

It was the Sinclairs. Nine men with deep chestnut hair and one with strawberry-blond, with the broadest shoulders Adelaide had ever seen, and bodies that towered at six-and-a-half feet surged toward them. Amongst them walked four men with hair as dark as her own, a midnight black. The Mackays. They made an impressive sight. Adelaide could only imagine what their enemies thought as that siege engine descended upon them. The Cairngorms must have sprouted legs.

Even from a distance, Adelaide could hear their lighthearted voices and laughter. She noticed Laird Liam Sinclair laughing at something his son-by-marriage, Laird Tristan Mackay, said. Men of all ages elbowed one another as they likely teased about their performances that day. They looked like a litter of gigantic puppies jostling one another.

"When ye see them like that together, ye would

never ken how terrifying they are in battle," Harry whispered.

"Oh, I can imagine," Sarah whispered back.

"So can I," Adelaide murmured. Her gaze swept over the men, but she couldn't tell one from another until she spotted Tate. She didn't know how she was certain it was him, but she was. Mayhap seeing him reminded her of the ale tent. He'd played a joke on her she didn't find funny. It waylaid her and resulted in her being trapped in the tent when the brawl began. She forced herself not to scowl as she and her siblings approached the massive family. Adelaide knew the family numbered nearly forty when they gathered with the Mackays. That was just immediate family since the youngest of the older generation of Sinclairs married into the Mackays.

She watched as the two lairds broke away from the group, tossing quips over their shoulders about being the only civilized ones in the group. The rest continued to approach Adelaide and her siblings. It was the clan's tánaiste who greeted them and stopped.

"Good day, Lady Adelaide, Lady Sarah, Lady Finley, Harry."

"Good day," Harry answered from behind his sisters. "What events did all of ye win?"

"Tate finally lost the swim to me this morning," Wiley crowed.

"By a bluidy fingertip," Tate groused. Adelaide watched him as he shoved his younger brother none too gently, but Wiley didn't even sway.

"Aye." Wiley grinned.

"Ye can see neither of ma nephews are gracious winners nor gracious losers. They get it from their father. Ma little brother doesnae do any better."

Tate's father, Tavish, was only a hair's breadth shorter than his two older brothers and one younger brother. He loathed being called the little brother because he knew his older brother didn't mean his age. Tavish shoved his older brother just as hard as Tate shoved Wiley, and just like the younger brother in that pair, Tavish's older brother didn't budge.

Their jesting made Adelaide smile until her gaze locked with Tate's. Her hackles went up, but she reminded herself it was Tate who sheltered her and protected her from the mob. She'd noticed the bruises forming when he'd stripped off his leine to wrestle. Tate's eyes narrowed as he watched her. He pushed past two of his cousins and stepped out of the crowd.

"If we wish to wash before the meal, we canna mill around clishmaclavering with each other." Tate dipped his chin toward the Grants, and his family soon followed.

"What was that aboot?" Sarah whispered as the siblings continued toward the steps.

"I dinna ken." And Adelaide didn't. Was it because she hadn't thanked him for protecting her? She thought she had, but perhaps she'd forgotten before he walked away.

"I thought he'd still feel a wee badly aboot his horse and yer boots from yesterday, but he appeared put out to see ye."

"Who kens what goes through a mon's mind beyond hot air?" Adelaide grinned as Harry harrumphed. Not long after that, the siblings left their chambers in fresh clothing to go belowstairs for the evening meal. They took their places at the high table, and Adelaide listened to the conversation swirl around them. It interested her to hear about the competitions she hadn't seen, but when the wrestling matches came up, she couldn't help but be extra attentive.

"Tate defended his champion title. Chisholm's already bawling over young Sinclair. Tate dislocated his son's shoulder, broke his nose, and nearly snapped the whelp's ankle," her father mused. "The healer tended his son despite the curses the arse spewed, which could be heard all the way to Stirling."

"If he wasna up to the challenge, he shouldnae have entered the ring against ma grandson," Laird Liam Sinclair stated in a matter-of-fact tone. The man took another bite of food as though he'd spoken the most obvious response, and it warranted no further consideration.

"But did yer grandson really need to injure him that badly?"

Adelaide didn't look at the opposite end of the table quickly enough to see which laird or tánaiste spoke. Tate's uncle, who'd greeted Adelaide earlier, answered.

"The Chisholm lad is lucky that's all that happened. It's nae Tate's fault the mon's bones are so brittle. He didna break a single rule with his moves." Just like his father's, the man's tone said as much as his words. Tate won fairly, leaving nothing to debate.

"But—"

"Would ye care for more of that—och, I beg yer pardon, Laird MacDonnell. I didna mean to speak over ye, but since the servant is here, would ye care for more pheasant?" Madeline interrupted the laird who didn't sound like he planned to retreat. Adelaide's mother wasn't interested in anyone antagonizing the Sinclairs. The Sinclairs would continue not to react, but the conversation would devolve into those who supported the Sinclairs, and those who didn't. Madeline gave the servant a pointed look before the woman piled more poultry onto the rotund laird's trencher.

Adelaide listened as Uncle Edward, as laird, tactfully redirected the conversation. But her gaze swept the crowd before resting on the Sinclairs seated at most of the tables, mingling with their extended family from other clans. Her mother and distant cousin were wise, and she hoped she had their aplomb one day. She didn't know if she would ever become lady of a clan like Aunt Davina or her mother in the future. She actually hoped she didn't, but she would if that was the marriage her father and Uncle Edward arranged.

"Do ye want the rest of the neeps and tatties?" Sarah whispered beside her.

"Nay, I'm full." Adelaide frowned at the turnips and potatoes left in their shared trencher. They'd both eaten almost all the potatoes and left the turnips. Neither young woman enjoyed them, but with so many people to feed at the Gathering, Adelaide felt guilty wasting any food that could feed someone else. But she might choke if she forced herself to eat the vile root vegetable, so she opted not to cause a scene.

She was certain her mother breathed easier when the servants cleared the trenchers and platters as the music began. Angus offered to dance with her, so he led her off the dais. The song required them to change partners more than once. They moved together until the first rotation happened, and Adelaide found herself with Fergus.

"Felicitations on the betrothal. I ken yer fathers havenae announced it yet, but Clara said yer priest has read the banns thrice."

"Aye. They're waiting a couple more days, then they'll ask Laird Grant if they can do it at the evening meal."

"How vera exciting. When do ye think ye'll wed?"

"As soon as we're home. The MacDonalds are coming to Shiness for the ceremony and feast before they return home."

Adelaide saw as much as heard Fergus's excitement as he spoke of his upcoming wedding. It matched Clara's earlier that day. She smiled at her close friend's betrothed, but that smile faltered when she switched partners again and found herself in Tate's arms.

"Felicitations on winning yer matches." Adelaide attempted to sound cordial.

"Thank ye." Tate wasn't quite brusque, but he was hardly as jovial as he'd been that afternoon in the alehouse.

"I owe ye ma thanks for protecting me. I canna remember if I said that when we made it outside. I hope I did, but in case I didna, thank ye."

Tate nodded. "Ye're welcome, ma lady."

Adelaide didn't understand the coldness from Tate. "Have I done aught wrong?"

"Nay."

Adelaide thought about letting the matter drop, but her mouth seemed to move independently from her brain. "Ye had plenty to say in the tent, but now ye can barely spare the seven words ye've said."

"Ye appear hale, so I dinna think ye are any worse for wear after the fight. Should I have asked how ye are?"

Adelaide stiffened as Tate now sounded flippant. "Nay. It isnae yer concern how I fair. But are ye well? I saw the bruises forming."

He might not have the manners to feign interest in her wellbeing, but she could pretend she cared about his. Tate tucked his chin to better look to Adelaide's eyes. He tried to interpret the stormy gale brewing in eyes that normally appeared like the brightest sky during the best Scottish weather.

"I'm hale too. I got more from wrestling than in the tent."

"That's good. I mean ye being hale."

The music forced them apart, and they both sighed with relief. But it proved temporary. Five minutes later, the next song brought them back together, and they wouldn't change partners until the end.

"Tate, have out with it. I've done something," Adelaide blurted.

"Ye appeared mighty concerned aboot Adam when they declared me the victor."

"Victor? It wasna a battle, but ye treated it like it was."

"It was a competition to prove which clan was better. They're all competitions to prove that. They havenae been aught else since I stopped competing in the weans' games. We arenae supposed to battle each other outright here, but dinna believe for a moment that we arenae proving who's the mightiest." Tate clenched his jaw, not having planned to say as much nor say it so harshly.

"Because the Sinclairs must always be the best at everything. Ye dinna ken Adam Chisholm, and ye will wish ye werenae aboot to ken him as well as ye will."

"Worried aboot him?"

Adelaide's entire demeanor changed while Tate watched her. He was ready to let go and walk away if she preferred Adam so much more than him.

"Hardly," Adelaide hissed. "He and his brothers are cut from the same cloth as their father. The mon is horrid and unrepentant. His sons are nay better. But, while their father is content to live in the past, they live in the present. Adam willna forgive ye for the slight. He will retaliate. Ye'd do well nay to go anywhere alone in the dark lest ye find a dirk in yer back."

"And how do ye ken so much aboot Adam Chisholm?"

"Because Laird Keith, as the Marischal, tried to betroth me to him when we were weans to end the animosity between our clans. Mama can barely stand the mon after what he did to Aunt Abigail during and at the end of their handfast. Laird Chisholm still speaks ill of ma aunt even a score of years later. Mama and Da refused to consider the betrothal. Uncle Edward made it clear to Laird Keith that forcing his hand would cause the Grants to draw back their support for the Keiths against the Gunns. Adam Chisholm has been a smug bastard since he could talk. He's taken every opportunity to insult me since we were children, as though it was his father who refused the betrothal. The Chisholms need the Grants. The Grants dinna need the Chisholms."

Tate listened to Adelaide, vaguely aware of the history between Adam and her. "Then why did ye run from ma match against him, looking as though I'd killed yer favorite hound?"

"Because I didna trust him nae to pull a knife from somewhere and gut ye. I didna want to see that."

"He wouldnae dare with so many people watching."

"Mayhap nae something so extreme, but I didna trust him nae to start a fight once ye stepped outside the rocks. He wouldnae fight by any rules if he did. Even if ye defeated him, he would have injured ye. I didna want to watch that."

"Ye looked like I horrified ye with what I did to win. I—" Tate snapped his mouth shut.

"Ye?"

"Naught. I will keep ma eye out for him and nae give him ma back."

"I hope ye heed ma warning."

"With a dislocated shoulder, a broken nose, and an injured ankle, he willna come after me during this Gathering."

"He might send someone after ye. Just be careful, Tate. Dinna underestimate his willingness to hold a grudge."

The music ended, and they let go of each other,

stepping apart. Neither turned to find another partner as people began to move around them.

"I think I will sit out the next set and have some ale," Adelaide explained.

"Same."

They walked away from the dancers, and Tate signaled a serving woman with a tray of tankards. He took two and offered one to Adelaide. She glanced down at his boots sheepishly.

"Dinna fash. They're clean. I had to since they were dusty and filthy from wrestling."

"I shouldnae have done that. I dinna ken what came over me. It was shameful."

"Nay. I found it humorous. I'm fortunate ye didna dump it over ma head."

Adelaide's face flushed. "I would never humiliate ye like that. Nae in public nor in—where anyone could see."

"I ken, lass. I teased ye, and ye found out I wagered with yer brother. A little ale was naught to cry aboot. All's well."

"Thank ye. And now ye ken I am nae interested in aught aboot Adam, unless it's him leaving."

Tate raised his mug to her and nodded. "Have a good evening, ma lady."

"Ye too."

They parted and went in opposite directions. Rather than make it to the dais, she stopped to speak to her MacLeod and MacKinnon cousins. They made plans to go riding in the morning, and Adelaide looked forward to it.

CHAPTER 4

"*T*ate!"

Tate turned around as Fergus rushed toward him, waving. He stopped and waited for his friend to join him outside the stables.

"What has ye in such a fit?" Tate laughed as he took in his old friend's ruddy cheeks and tousled hair. It looked like he'd been pulling at it in frustration. It stuck out in all directions. "Yer bonnie wee bride twisting ye in knots?"

"Nay." Fergus smiled almost bashfully. "We were planning a picnic, but her sister got too much sun yesterday and isnae well today. Ma brothers are too young to accompany us without Clara's sister. Would ye and yer sister chaperone our picnic? It's the only chance we've had to be away from the crowds."

"Ailish and Ainsley are helping Mama and Auntie Mairghread with the laundry today."

They both turned toward approaching riders. Tate recognized Adelaide immediately. Her hair and eyes made her stand out among any crowd. She was with her brothers and two women Tate only vaguely knew from another clan, which he couldn't remember. Fergus stepped forward as Adelaide dismounted.

"Perfect. Will ye come with us, Lady Adelaide?"

"With ye and Clara? I thought her sister was going along with yer brothers."

"She's nae feeling well, and ma brothers canna chaperone. They're too young, and a lass must go too. Clara canna ride out with a group of lads and me. People would talk."

Adelaide nodded. It wouldn't matter to some that she would ride with her future brothers-by-marriage. It would be one woman with young adolescent men and her betrothed. Chins would wag, and Adelaide didn't want that for her friend.

"Aye. I'll go."

"Thank ye. Tate's coming too."

Tate didn't recall saying yes. He'd said why his sister couldn't go, but he hadn't agreed. But he would help his friend. He had no competitions that afternoon, and none that his family competed in were finals. He could spare an hour. He waited for Adelaide to look at him, but she looked around until she spotted Clara. Fergus hurried to help the petite woman with the basket she carried.

"Did Cook pack the entire larder for ye?" Adelaide asked as she peeked into it.

"Nay. The woman thought Fergus's brothers were coming, so she kenned the lads would complain they were starving. I tried to talk her out of it once I said they weren't joining us. But she said it was better to have too much than too little."

"I'll get yer mounts," Tate offered, ducking into the stables before anyone could say something. He asked stableboys to prepare Fergus's and Clara's horses while he saw to his own. When he heard hooves outside his horse's stall, he turned to see Adelaide leading her steed past him.

"Misty needs the blacksmith to check a shoe. I fear

it's coming loose." Adelaide named the mare because she was a dappled gray much like the mist that hung low many mornings. She'd been eight at the time. She didn't think the name was so unique now that she was twenty. "I'll take Harry's."

"Ye ride that beast?" Tate knew which horse that was, and it rivaled his own warhorse in size. He couldn't imagine how she would mount, let alone manage the animal. Much like most animals trained for battle, Harry's horse didn't like anyone but his owner.

"Who do ye think trained him? It wasna Harry who broke him in." Adelaide handed off Misty to a boy and moved to the stall across from Tate. She crooned to the horse, who nickered and nodded his head. Tate watched from the corner of his eye as the beast turned docile and barely moved while Adelaide saddled him. The enormous steed rested his massive head on her shoulder as she passed the bridle over his ears. He turned that head to watch her as she gathered the rest of the tack and prepared him for their ride. Tate knew his own steed and made sure he left the stalls first lest his horse nip Harry's.

He mounted and watched Adelaide lead the animal to a trough. She stepped up and onto the ledge before swinging into the saddle. He'd worried for a moment that she would fall into the water, then he regretted not offering to help. Their horses stood at the same height, but Tate stood a foot taller than Adelaide. His legs were longer and stronger to propel him upward.

Only a moment later, Clara and Fergus mounted with the basket tied to Fergus's saddle. Adelaide led the way to the portcullis, but she slowed when they came to the massive gate. Tate and Fergus guided their horses past the two women and left the keep first. Adelaide and Clara followed until the men separated enough for the women to ride between them.

When Adelaide came abreast with Tate, he glanced at her.

"I appreciate ye letting us go first. With so many people around, I felt better checking the path before ye or Lady Clara came out."

"I ken. Ma brothers do the same. I appreciate it too." Adelaide shot him a smile just before the riders spurred their mounts. They rode northeast and away from the village made of tents that surrounded half the castle. Eight guards followed them, two from each clan. It seemed Fergus had already inquired about them before he asked Tate or Adelaide to come. He merely shrugged when Adelaide looked behind her and recognized her clansmen. She'd assumed her friends and Tate arranged for guards for themselves, not knowing Tate was a late addition like her.

Their horses cantered for twenty minutes before they found a spot with shade. It was a warm day again, and the shade would be a welcome respite after riding in the sun. They hadn't been out long, but all four riders and their mounts noticed the heat. When they reined in, Fergus immediately went to help Clara from her mount. Adelaide didn't expect hands to wrap around her waist as she twisted to draw her right leg over the saddle. Tate lifted her as easily as he had when she'd become mired in dung. He placed her gently on her feet and pulled away.

"Thank ye. It is quite a long way down."

"Ma pleasure, ma lady."

"Out here, canna we be Clara and Adelaide?"

Tate looked past Adelaide to where Clara and Fergus chatted as they spread out the blanket and food. "I dinna ken Lady Clara well enough to be so forward. If yer guards hear me address ye without yer title, they'll speak to yer father. I believe he warned ye away from me."

"Try nae to boom everything ye say." Adelaide grinned. Tate had a deep voice that carried when he spoke in anything but a whisper.

"I am nae that loud."

"Sort of." Adelaide smiled as she led her horse into the shade and dropped her reins over a bush that would tangle them if the animal tried to leave. Tate followed suit, and they joined the blissful couple on the blanket. Clara handed food to them both, and there were a few minutes of quiet as everyone ate the cold chicken, cheese, bread, and pears. Tate soon realized they'd be gone longer than an hour. They passed a wine skin filled with summer ale before talking.

"What's the best event ye've seen so far, Clara?" Adelaide asked between bites of her second pear.

"I dinna have a favorite. I enjoy watching them all." Clara didn't look at Adelaide as she spoke, instead, beaming up at Fergus. He rested back on his hands, and Clara sat close enough that she could lean almost inconspicuously against him. Fergus wasn't competing that year, so he and Clara watched the competitions together.

"What aboot ye, Lady Adelaide?" Fergus asked as he offered Clara a plum he spotted in the cheesecloth that held the last pear.

"I enjoyed watching Lady Mackay trounce her brother yet again." Adelaide grinned at Tate.

His aunt Mairghread was infamous for her skills with a dirk. She had four older brothers she played with when the Sinclair siblings were children. When she got to three-and-ten, her brothers no longer knew what to give her for her saint's day, so they gave her dirks. They wished to make sure they prepared their beautiful younger sister to always protect herself. However, none expected her to become the best competitive knife thrower in all the Highlands. The only man who came close to her skill was the Sinclairs' tánaiste and Tate's eldest uncle, but he hadn't beaten Mairghread since they were adolescents. Mairghread's skill made it unfair for her to compete against other women. It was the only competition each year that made a special dispensation for a woman to challenge the men. Tate assumed it wasn't his aunt's skill so much as the humbling experience for his uncle that convinced everyone to allow her to compete. His uncle always came so close to winning, but Mairghread's patience inevitably paid off.

"What aboot ye, Tate?" Fergus asked.

"Watching Uncle Magnus, Blake, and Tor compete against each other in the caber toss." While the Sinclair men all stood at almost exactly the same height, Magnus and his two sons were the biggest in the family. Their legs were like mighty oak tree trunks, and their chests were so broad Adelaide once heard there was room to draw the world across them. Magnus and Blake dwarfed their wives, who they doted on.

"They are merciless in their teasing. I dinna ken how any of them concentrate with the things they say to one another," Clara marveled.

"I can only imagine what they're taunting back in their heads that keeps them focused." Tate knew what he thought when his brother or cousins turned their attention to him before and during his matches. Those responses weren't fit for anyone's ears.

The conversation moved away from the games and to their observations about various clans. They discussed which clans were at odds with one another and recent battles, but now had to pretend to be friends. They discussed news from their own clans. It surprised Tate how well-informed Adelaide was about the situation with King David's exile. Clara remained quiet and listened, but Adelaide engaged in the conversation with

Tate and Fergus. She watched as Tate listened to what she said. When he disagreed, he did it with politeness. He didn't discount her opinions or belittle them. He gave reasons he thought otherwise.

"I think King David will return one day, but I dinna ken that he'll rule Scotland as he should," Adelaide mused.

"I agree. He is still barely more than a wean. When he returns, King Edward willna let him rule Scotland. I think he will either kidnap our king or trap him in England if King David wishes to end his exile. Mayhap one day he will rule as his father did, but I dinna ken if I'll live to see the day," Tate explained.

"Ye dinna think he'll be that auld, do ye?" Adelaide asked.

"We arenae at peace with England. I've survived the battles so far, but there's nay guarantee aboot the next or the one after that." Tate stretched out his long legs as he watched Adelaide listen to him. Her voice was softer when she responded.

"Ma brothers and Da fight in those same battles. I hope for yer family and mine that ye all live to be auld men who've seen King David return and rule for many years."

"As do I, lass." Tate offered her the last pear, but she shook her head. He watched her grow quiet and almost withdrawn. He hadn't wished to upset her. "Lady Adelaide, nay warrior can guarantee his future. But yer brothers and father are among the finest fighters in the Highlands. Dinna fash for them."

Adelaide nodded. It wasn't just her family she thought aboot. As Tate flashed smiles and looked so relaxed compared to when he was among the other clans, she couldn't imagine not seeing him again. She didn't know what to make of the sadness that settled in her chest at the thought.

"It's never easy to be left behind when they ride out, but I dinna envy them the job they have when they do." Adelaide handed the wineskin she'd rested in her lap to Clara. She no longer felt hungry or thirsty. She looked at her friends as they whispered together. She knew they wished to be alone, but she couldn't just wander off.

"Lady Adelaide, would ye care to walk? I think I need a wee stretch of the legs after eating so much."

Adelaide nodded. Tate ate a scant amount compared to what she was sure he could. But it served as an excuse to give Clara and Fergus time together. They rose, and Adelaide shook out her skirts. She peeked at the guardsmen, who'd spread out into a wide circle around the four nobles. They'd turned their backs to the two couples and stared outward, scanning for any threat. The circle was wide enough for Adelaide and Tate to walk away from Fergus and Clara. But not so wide that they could go anywhere out of earshot of either their friends or their guards. Someone was bound to overhear them.

"Lady Adelaide, I feel I still owe ye an apology for the alehouse. It was a poor jest at yer expense, and it kept ye there long enough to be caught in the brawl."

"Dinna fash. I feel I still owe ye ma thanks for shielding me. Ye didna fare as well as ye claimed."

"It wasna any worse than what ma brothers, cousins, and I used to do to each other when we were weans. We were like a litter of puppies tumbling over each other, all elbows and knees going in every which direction." Tate grinned. Dunbeath Castle might have felt like it was bursting at the seams most days. However, Tate wouldn't deny he had mostly happy memories of growing up in an enormous family. He'd always found someone to play with. Someone to get into trouble with, and someone else to blame.

"I can only imagine. Ma brothers, sisters, and I always played together when we were weans. But I ken there were times Angus wished he didna have three little sisters trailing after him. He didna mind Harry so much because Harry thought Angus was perfect. I'll never forget when Angus gave our brother his wood sword. Harry thought he'd earned Angus's most prized possession. He didna ken Angus did it to try to convince Da to give him a real sword." It was Adelaide's turn to smile as she remembered her older brother arguing his case. He insisted that since he no longer had a sword but needed one as a Grant warrior, he may as well get a new one that was made of metal, not wood. He'd been three-and-ten, and Harry was five.

"We all had duties around the keep from when we could walk. But the lasses played alongside the lads until they could nay longer match our strength. The moment our parents kenned a lass would wind up injured if she kept wrestling and fighting, it turned from fun to ensuring they can defend themselves. And by that time, each of us had more responsibilities than we had time to play. I can remember wishing Ailish didna always have to come along, but that's because ma sister was faster than me until I was three-and-ten, and she was nine. I'm faster than her now, but the lass could run from sunrise to sunset without needing to catch her breath."

Adelaide heard the pride in Tate's voice as he spoke of his younger sister. She didn't know Ailish well, but she'd always admired her. She was like all the other Sinclair women: fearless. Some were quieter than others, but no one ever doubted that a Sinclair woman was just as brave as any man or boy in that clan. Four sisters-by-marriage ran the keep when the men rode out. No one in the Highlands had the will to raid Dunbeath Castle with Siùsan, Deirdre, Brighde, and Ceit left in charge. Their daughters were no different. Adelaide suspected most warriors would prefer to meet the Sinclair men in battle than face those four women staring down at them from the battlements. As loyal servants to both King Robert and King David, the men were often away fighting. It would have been easy for rivals to target them, but few did. And none survived to tell the tale of their foolishness.

Adelaide looked in her home's direction. While there weren't as many women in her family, she knew her mother's and Aunt Davina's reputations. She could only remember two times in her life that anyone tried to raid their keep while her father and Uncle Edward were away. Fingal and Edward came home to a mound of fresh graves a league south of the keep. They'd feared sickness had wiped out most of the clan. Instead, they found Madeline and Davina working in the gardens, unfazed by the battle that had raged only the day prior. The warriors who had remained to guard the keep were as loyal to those two women as they were their laird and tánaiste.

"I suspect the women of yer clan arenae that different from the ones in mine," Tate mused.

"To survive life in the Highlands, we canna be weak." Adelaide shrugged as she turned to look at Tate. The sun shone in her eyes, making her squint. He stepped in front of her, blocking the brilliant light. The sunlight illuminated the gold and cinnamon-hued highlights in Tate's hair and made it appear as though he had a fiery halo. An avenging angel popped into Adelaide's mind.

"That's true. But some people's dispositions are braver than others. I heard the tale of yer mother riding out with nay one to accompany her when yer da was injured. She refused to believe he was dead, and she wouldnae accept his body being left behind."

Adelaide smiled. Her mother's infamous past was a source of pride and regret to Madeline, but Adelaide respected the older woman for all of it.

"I suspect ye are yer mother's daughter, ma lady." Tate peered down at Adelaide, whose vibrant blue eyes with a tinge of green seemed to see inside him. It was most disconcerting.

"If I am, I'm a lucky woman. I hope to be so one day." Adelaide shrugged, not comfortable with the attention entirely on her. She often worried she wouldn't be as strong a leader as Madeline or Davina. She'd hoped to marry a second or third son instead of a laird or tánaiste because she feared she wouldn't make an adequate lady of any clan.

"Ma lady, I believe ye already are. A clan will be fortunate to have ye lead alongside their laird." Tate watched the uncertainty in Adelaide's expression as she spoke, and he wondered what made her doubt herself so obviously. He knew any man she married would count himself fortunate. She was intelligent, insightful, witty, and stubborn. All the qualities he knew so well from the women in his family.

"Are ye ready to return?"

Adelaide and Tate turned toward Fergus as he called out to them and waved. They walked back to the couple who were repacking the picnic. Adelaide glanced toward the sun and realized they'd been away from the keep for at least two hours. She hadn't told her parents or siblings where she was going. She prayed a guardsman would inform them if anyone looked for her. She and Tate helped their friends clean up, and Tate lifted her into the saddle. Her waist tingled where his hands touched her, and she felt a moment of shyness when she looked down to thank him. He'd touched her twice before, lifting her out of the mud and off her mount. He'd touched her when he wrapped himself around her to protect her during the brawl. They'd danced together. None of those times stirred the reaction this time did. She watched him turn his horse before mounting. She saw how his calf and thigh flexed between the bottom of his plaid and the top of his boot as he hoisted himself into the saddle. She glanced away when he turned his head in her direction.

Tate was certain he'd spied Adelaide watching him. But she'd averted her gaze by the time he looked at her. He wondered what she thought when she saw him. She'd been enjoyable company while they walked, then stood talking. She'd intrigued him while they shared the meal with their friends. He'd admired her from afar for years. However, he couldn't tell what she thought of him. Not that it would matter since she was a tánaiste's eldest daughter and would likely marry a laird or tánaiste from another clan. He maneuvered his horse and turned his attention to the evening meal, his stomach growling since lunch had been little more than a snack for the braw warrior. He kept his eyes straight forward lest he have inappropriate thoughts about what he might like to nibble on. If Adelaide's father even caught a hint of what he'd just thought… Suffice it to say, Tate kept his eyes forward for the entire ride back to the keep.

CHAPTER 5

The next two days passed in a blur. Tate continued to compete in other contests, but he was never the favorite to win. If a Sinclair didn't win, it was usually their extended family. He enjoyed himself and fell into an exhausted sleep each night, despite using a bedroll on the ground. Riding patrol on his family's land conditioned him to it, even if he didn't enjoy it. He loved seeing his second cousins, third cousins, and cousins however many times removed during the Gatherings. The only other time so many gathered together was at Christmastide. The clans rotated hosting. But foul Highland weather often meant people missed the festivities when travel was impossible.

That evening, Fergus invited him to eat at the Mathesons' table, so Tate found a seat beside his friend. It was almost as crowded at his own family's since Fergus had several younger brothers. The boys shifted to make space when Clara and Adelaide appeared. Tate didn't miss the longing looks exchanged between Clara and Fergus, but his friend's intended sat across from Fergus rather than beside him. It meant Adelaide sat across from Tate. They exchanged pleasantries, but they'd barely passed one another since their picnic. That didn't mean Tate hadn't spied Adelaide several times. And each time, he reminded himself he wasn't an heir, and her father already warned her away from him.

Adelaide stepped over the bench and settled into her seat as a servant arrived to place a trencher in front of Clara and her. She smiled at the woman who was close to her age and someone she'd played with as a child. She turned her head and shot a Matheson guardsman a glower when she heard his comment about the woman's breasts. She watched Tate lean past two men to whisper something to the offender, making the man flush. Tate's expression told her what she couldn't hear. He didn't approve of the comment and said as much. When Tate sat up, she offered him a soft smile. He dipped his chin in return.

The conversation swirled around Adelaide. She listened to Tate and Fergus banter with one another, and her heart warmed at Fergus's solicitousness to Clara. She was happy for her friend, but she couldn't help but feel a sense of longing. Her parents were adamant that she and her siblings would choose their future partners. That's why the Great Marischal's attempt to betroth Adelaide to Adam met with such resistance. While her own parents' marriage began as one of convenience, it had taken no time for Madeline and Fingal to fall deeply in love. She wanted to believe her parents were right, but she feared the king might decide for her, like his father had for Madeline and Fingal.

She focused on her food for most of the meal, always polite when the servants brought her dishes to choose from. But she wasn't nearly as talkative as she was when she sat with her sisters and brothers. She felt out of place in her own home when the music began after the servants moved the tables. Fergus and Clara immediately partnered. She noticed Angus and Finley, and Sarah and Harry joined the other dancers. Usually, she danced with her brothers before anyone else.

"Lady Adelaide, would ye dance?"

Adelaide's eyes narrowed when Adam came to stand before her, his hand outstretched. His mangled face, the evidence of his failed attempt to best Tate, tempted her to grin. His injured shoulder drooped, and she wondered how he planned to dance with only one arm. He limped from a strained ankle. She glanced around, knowing he intended to back her into a corner, both literally and figuratively. He'd done it the year prior when the Gordons hosted. He'd forced her to accept his offer because so many people saw him. When she had, he maneuvered her toward a corner and berated her for anything he could think of, which was mostly being related to his former stepmother of some sort. Adelaide's aunt had endured a yearlong handfast with Lathan Chisholm, Adam's father. Adam had been alive and illegitimate then. Lathan tried to keep the dowry that came with Adelaide's aunt while repudiating their handfast. Adelaide's uncle petitioned King Robert and received the majority back. But it left animosity among the clans that lasted more than a score of years.

"I'm afraid Lady Adelaide already promised me this dance. Move." Tate stood beside Adam and reached between them for Adelaide's hand. She didn't hesitate to place hers in his. Tate stepped forward, practically ramming into Adam, forcing him to step aside lest he fall on his arse. Tate kept walking as though the man never stood in his way. He led Adelaide into the crowd as people swirled around them. It was a tune that would keep them together for the entire dance.

"Thank ye. That would have been most unpleasant." Adelaide wondered how Tate knew Adam approached her. He was an exceptionally tall man, but the Great

Hall was bursting at the seams. He had to have been watching either Adam or her.

"I warned him to stay away from ye, Addy. He should have listened. I dinna enjoy repeating maself, and he shall understand that by the nooning tomorrow." Tate looked over her head and shot Adam a menacing glare. He didn't notice what he'd called Adelaide, but she did.

"Ye warned him?"

"Aye. I thought I made maself clear when I ground his face into the dirt and dislocated his shoulder. Apparently, I didna speak clearly enough."

"While ye wrestled?"

"Aye. I'd overheard him ma first night here. I told him as much during our match. He didna take ma hint. I thought he'd understood when I left him on the ground. Apparently, he didna."

"Tate, he's a prideful mon. He'll only be worse to me now. He'll do it to spite ye as much as he does it to spite me. Dinna do aught else. Please."

Tate gazed down at Adelaide as she pleaded with him. It was against his better judgment, but he nodded. He would respect her request, but only to a limit. He wouldn't let Adam force her into being his captive dance partner. He released her as she twirled away for four steps, but his steely arm wrapped back around her as she stepped toward him. When she tilted her head back again to look him in the eye, he couldn't read what he saw. Was she angry with him?

"Lady Adelaide, I didna mean to overstep. I would have done the same for ma sister and cousins." Tate's brow furrowed for a moment. Now he truly didn't understand her expression. But she nodded, and the song drew to an end. They released each other and stepped away. Adelaide's own cousin approached and asked her to dance. Tate moved to the side of the Great Hall, unsettled by what Adelaide hadn't said. It was only as he reflected on his conversation that he realized he'd called her Addy. He'd offended her. Again.

* * *

ADELAIDE LAY in bed beside Sarah, who was fast asleep. She dozed off easily, but her eyes snapped open in the middle of the night. She tried rolling over one way, then the other, but she couldn't settle her mind. If it were any night other than when dozens of clans gathered on her family's land, she would have sneaked down to the kitchens to nibble on something. But she didn't dare prowl through the keep with so many men under the same roof. Her thoughts jumped from one thing to another as she recalled the various competitions she watched. She forced herself only to think about that and not a particular warrior that she'd admired from afar for years.

By the time the sun peeked through her window embrasure, she was exhausted and starving. She estimated she'd been awake for four hours and only slept for two. Her stomach growled as she went through her morning ablutions. She impatiently waited for Sarah, and the passing minutes tempted her to leave her sister behind. She knew Finley was an early riser and would be on her way to the Great Hall with Harry and Angus. But her parents had insisted the sisters not move around the keep alone in the early morning or at night.

"Did the Mathesons starve ye last night?" Sarah asked as she pulled her kirtle over her head. "Did they nae leave ye any food? I can hear yer stomach from over here."

"I couldnae sleep." Adelaide turned her back to Sarah and waited for her sister to tie her laces. Then she did the same for Sarah.

"Yer mind so busy that ye worked up an appetite? What were ye thinking aboot?"

"I dinna ken what woke me, but I kept replaying Angus and Harry's games." That wasn't a lie. But she only thought of the ones in which Tate competed against them. Both her brothers and Tate were in the archery competition that afternoon. When she found out, she'd teased her brothers that they may as well stand beside her and watch since three Mackays also competed. There was no point in anyone else joining them. Neither Harry nor Angus appreciated her advice.

The sisters chatted as they made their way below-stairs, the noise greeting them at their door. Sarah led as they walked up the dais's steps. They slid into their seats just as the meal began. Adelaide forced herself not to gobble down her food lest she give herself a stomachache.

"Are ye three coming to watch the games? Or does Mama have chores for ye?" Harry asked around bites of porridge.

"We're coming," Finley answered. "But it's Ada's day to help in the buttery. Mama's making her do inventory and calculate the cost of serving ale to all these people. Then she has to figure out how long it'll take the brewers to replace all of it, plus the cost of that too. Glad nay one expects me to marry a laird." The youngest Grant sister grinned at the oldest.

"Dinna be so certain of that," Angus chimed in. "Da willna be marrying ye off to some farmer or shepherd."

"Mayhap nae. But I'm happy with a fourth or fifth son. Someone nae likely to inherit. I dinna want to be responsible for so many lives as Mama and Aunt Davina are."

Adelaide kept her thoughts to herself, but she felt the same way as her sister. She couldn't guarantee any clan she married into would enjoy the peace and prosperity the Grants did. If she married into a clan that faced frequent raids, then she would be responsible for all the servants' and villagers' safety. She'd be responsible for providing plenty of food for the men to ride out with since the men couldn't guarantee they'd be able to hunt. It terrified her she might fail at such vital duties, not only harming her new clan but disgracing her mother and aunt. People would believe Madeline and Davina failed to train Adelaide properly.

"Ada?"

Adelaide looked over at Sarah, who'd watched her sister grow quiet. She knew Adelaide's fears since her older sister had confided in her several months ago.

"Aye. Just thinking aboot what I must do today. I hope to have time to watch this afternoon. I must go now if I'm to have that luxury." Adelaide pushed back her seat, leaving her half-eaten porridge. She didn't wait to hear if her siblings had anything else to say. She wound her way through the keep to the undercroft after retrieving the ledger she needed from her aunt's desk in the solar Davina and Edward shared. She'd only counted a dozen barrels when she heard male voices approaching. She glanced around and placed herself behind a table with her back to the wall. She pulled the *sgian dubh* from her boot. Neither the brewer nor the vintner had arrived, so she was alone in a small space. But it was only a moment later that she recognized the third male voice, allowing her to relax.

Tate and two other Sinclair men stopped at the door, all peering inside at Adelaide, who still clutched her knife. It hung from her hand beside her thigh instead of being raised like it was only a moment earlier. Tate was at the back of the trio, looking between the shoulders of his two cousins.

"Adelaide?" Tate pulled Blake back and shoved the rundlet, a small cask he'd been carrying at his cousin, who nearly dropped it in his haste to grab it. Tate pushed past Blake and Torquil. He hurried forward but stopped several feet from Adelaide, worried at the last minute that she might point the weapon at him. "What happened?"

"Naught." Adelaide shook her head, her gaze darting to the two colossi in the doorway. Blake had arrived first, and Tor was only half a step behind. "I heard yer cousins but didna ken who was coming."

Tate approached until Adelaide was within arm's reach. "Why are ye in here alone? If ye were fearful enough to draw yer dirk, then ye ken it isnae safe to be alone in the undercroft with the door open." He didn't care for the fear he'd seen flash in her eyes when they first arrived, or that they'd scared her enough to believe she would have to defend herself. He knew where she stood was a defensive position, so no one could sneak up behind her. However, she'd picked the wall farthest from the door, which would have made it difficult, if not impossible, to flee.

"I didna ken I'd be alone. I thought our brewer would be down here. I wanted to finish ma work, so I didna have to stay down here any longer than neces-sary. What are ye doing here? What're those for?"

"We're a large family and clan to feed and provide drink for. We ken that. We figured by now there would be room in here for the ale we brought. We appreciate yer family's gracious hospitality, and we wish to say thank ye," Tate explained. "We couldnae bring these into the Great Hall each night for ma family to drink from. But we can offer to replace what we must be taking."

"Thank ye. That's vera generous of yer family."

"Our relatives are bringing more," Blake added from across the room.

"Yer relatives?"

"Aye. Our Mackay cousins will bring theirs to-morrow morning," Tor explained. "The Sutherlands and Camerons will bring the next ones the day after tomorrow. The Mackenzies and MacLeods of Lewis said they'd bring theirs the day before the Gathering ends. I think the MacLeods of Assynt and the Rosses have some too."

Adelaide could only nod. She'd heard these clans had done the same in the past, but she'd never worked in the buttery during a Gathering before. She looked around before pointing to a set of shelves.

"Could ye put yers there, please?"

Tate returned to the cask he'd carried. Adelaide silently marveled as he hefted it onto his shoulder just like his cousins continued to hold theirs. They weighed just over ten-and-a-half stones, much like Adelaide believed she did. The trio moved with ease, looking like they barely hefted any weight at all. Blake and Tor were slightly broader across the chest and back than Tate, and Adelaide could tell their legs were stouter. Tate was also a hair's-breadth shorter than the two brothers. But he'd inherited his father's and grandfather's barrel chest, making him just as impressive as his cousins. She recalled seeing Blake kissing his wife in the garden the day the Sinclairs arrived and how she'd thought it was Tate. Now she could tell the difference between them with ease, but she recalled how disconcerted she'd felt thinking Tate was already married.

Tate came back to stand in front of Adelaide while the other two men went to the doorway. "How much more work do ye have?"

"At least an hour."

"And ye ken the brewer or vintner will come?"

"I thought they would. Now I dinna ken."

Tate twisted to see his relatives. "Go without me. I'll

wait outside until either the men come or Lady Adelaide finishes."

It shocked Adelaide when Blake and Tor simply nodded and left. Tate turned back to Adelaide, who only then realized she still had her *sgian dubh* in her hand. She lifted her skirts to the top of her boots and slid it back in its sheath.

"I'll be outside. If ye need help lifting aught, tell me. I'll do it for ye."

"Ye dinna have to stay, Tate. Ye have other things to do."

Tate merely stared at her for a moment then shook his head. "Ye arenae staying here alone. Ye drew a dirk because ye feared men coming in here. Unless I spy Angus or Harry or one of yer cousins, I'm staying." He turned on his heel, his plaid swishing against the back of his thighs. He posted himself with one shoulder visible from inside the room. Adelaide knew he did that to reassure her he hadn't left. It would only take one step sideways for him to block the entire entryway.

Adelaide stared for another moment before turning back to her work. It wouldn't get done if she didn't do it, so she focused. It took her an hour and a half to tabulate the number of barrels and the quantity she estimated was in each, then to calculate the costs. She ran through her column of numbers thrice before her precision satisfied her that her computations were accurate. She closed the ledger and tipped her head from side to side, stretching the kinks from it. She'd glanced at Tate several times while she worked, and he hadn't budged once. She walked up behind him and laid her hand on his back for only a moment, letting him know she wished to step out. She was certain he'd known exactly where she was the entire time without having to look inside.

"Are ye finished, Addy?"

"Aye. Why do ye call me that?"

"Call ye what?" Creases formed across Tate's brow, and Adelaide wished she could run her fingers over his forehead and smooth them away.

"Addy. Ye've done it twice." As she spoke, she also remembered he'd called her wee one in the ale tent when he blocked punches and kicks from striking her.

"I hadnae noticed that I did." He paused for a moment, then shrugged with forced nonchalance. He recalled doing it the previous night and how he feared he'd insulted her. "I suppose it's a habit to shorten people's names. Plenty of us have nicknames in ma family."

"Us? It Tate nae yer full name?"

"Nay. It's Tatum, but I dinna remember the last time anyone called me that. Mayhap ma christening." He grinned.

"Ma family calls me Ada. They named me for Mama's mama."

"I wondered aboot that."

He did? Adelaide didn't know what to say to that. It meant he'd thought about her outside of their conversations. Unless... Perhaps he'd wondered about it during one of the times he'd spoken to her. She'd thought about him, but it hadn't occurred to her he might think about her too.

"Aye. Most of the time I go by Ada, and Da calls Mama Maddy. So, we both have nicknames. Only Aunt Davina and Uncle Edward call her just Madeline. Everyone else calls her Lady Madeline."

"Maddy?"

"Aye. Da said she'd nearly driven him mad when they met." Adelaide grinned. "She wasna as demure as he'd believed."

"They say men marry their mothers."

"I'm certain nay woman wants to be compared to her groom's mother." Adelaide's nose crinkled. "Ma da's mother died when he was a wean. He remembers her, but he says it's gotten harder with age. I suppose there are some things that are similar between Aunt Davina and Mama, but in a lot of ways Mama is more like Uncle Edward. They both thought they'd commit their lives to the church and are still vera devout. But Mama's sense of humor is far more wicked than anyone else's."

It surprised Tate to hear that about Adelaide's mother since he'd heard about the woman's past because of how she'd treated his father's cousin. He knew she had a wicked tongue, but he didn't know that she now used it with humor. She seemed so reserved now compared to how she'd been as a young lady-in-waiting.

"Ye remind me of Mama and Ailish," Tate stated. The moment he did, he wished to suck the words back in. Did he just make it sound like he considered Adelaide as a candidate to become his wife? "They're both intelligent, witty, and vera independent. But they're also kind and loyal."

"Ye make them sound like yer favorite hound. Do ye scratch either of them behind the ear?" Adelaide arched an eyebrow. It felt like he'd described her as a hound too if he thought she was so similar to the women in Tate's family. She had a flash of an idea. What would be like to have him scratch behind her ear or anywhere else on her body?

"Mama would look at me as though I'm daft, and I'd likely come away less a hand if I tried that with Ailish." Tate pretended to shiver as he finished. He'd put his foot in it, and he wasn't doing much to get himself out of it. "If ye're finished, I'll escort ye to the keep."

Tate opted to change the subject, and he hoped they passed a Grant guard or one of Adelaide's family. He doubted she was enjoying his company and was likely as eager to get away as he was. He watched as she pulled the door shut and locked it before pocketing the key. She carried the ledger against her chest, and he wondered if she realized she looked like she carried it as if it were a shield.

They turned toward the keep, but they hadn't gotten far before they recognized Adelaide's oldest cousin, the heir to the MacLeods of Lewis. That cousin indirectly connected the Sinclairs and Grants. Graham waved to them and waited for them to reach him on the path. Adelaide spoke first. "Are ye headed to the keep?"

"Aye. Da wants me to get something from his chamber. Are ye going that way, too?"

"Aye." Adelaide glanced up at Tate, who'd grasped Graham's outstretched forearm in a warrior handshake.

"I will leave ye then," Tate nodded to the cousins. "I'm going to watch ma brother try to trounce our Sutherland cousins in the hammer throw."

"Thank ye, Tate." Adelaide offered him a warm but brief smile. He changed course and headed to the wide field where they played the games. He forced himself not to look back at Adelaide. It bothered him more than he wished to admit, finding her alone in the storage room, fearful enough to hold her dirk. He didn't approve, but it wasn't his place to say anything. He would have admonished his sisters and cousins if they'd taken such a risk.

It was three hours later when he noticed Adelaide standing at the edge of the archery field. It was a pasture the Grants turned into the competition area since it had a fence that ran all the way around it. They never wanted to risk a child running into the line of fire. Her arms hung over the top rail, and he followed her line of sight and spotted Angus and Harry. As he stepped up to the line along with her brothers, he noticed her attention shifted to him. Their eyes met, but hers darted away.

The official called for all the archers to take their mark. Tate's focus tunneled, and nothing existed around him. He pulled the bowstring back as he raised his elbow. He drew in a deep breath, and once the official announced the contestants should fire, he exhaled and released the arrow. It streaked through the air and landed with pinpoint accuracy in the middle of the target. It hit the hay bale with such force that the bale shook. He looked around and noticed Harry was his closest rival. Angus's arrow landed slightly to the left of the exact middle of his target. He couldn't see far enough to judge accurately where his Mackay cousins' arrows landed. All three—Wee Liam, Alec, and Hamish—competed too. He suspected it would be a four-way tie like it had been the last six years. When the official said it was safe, the archers retrieved their arrows.

Tate walked back past the firing line and out of the way for the second round of contestants. It was an elimination match, so the better of each archer who used the same target moved on. His cousins joined him, but he watched Angus and Harry walk over to their sisters. Tate hadn't noticed Finley and Sarah standing with Adelaide. He'd noticed none of the other spectators.

"Who's buying the first round of whisky?" Wee Liam asked. There was nothing wee about the man anymore. But he was the eldest grandchild and named for their shared grandfather, Laird Liam Sinclair.

"I believe it's Hamish's turn this year." Tate jutted his chin toward his cousin who his parents named for Laird Hamish Sutherland, their shared grandmother's brother. They took turns each year buying the victory drinks.

"He has to win first," Alec jested. "He's too busy eying the lasses instead of his target."

"And who do ye have yer eye on this year?" Tate wondered aloud, but he didn't care for the gleam that entered his cousin's eyes as Hamish grinned at him.

"I think Adelaide Grant looks quite fetching today." Hamish crossed his arms. While the stance, with his legs hip-width apart, broadened his chest, it also protected his middle. It was the innate posture to any man with an ounce of Sinclair blood in him. He didn't trust Tate not to jab him in the belly.

Tate shrugged and nodded. He wouldn't allow Hamish to goad him. "She's a bonnie lass," he conceded.

"A bonnie lass who keeps looking at ye. Breaks ma heart." Hamish placed his right hand over his chest. "I canna imagine why she'd strain her eyes on a sight like ye. Is that steam coming from the top of yer head?"

Tate gritted his teeth, but he still refused to take the bait. "Aye. It's a warm day. Ye're sweating too."

"Ye could do worse," Alec mused.

The official called out the names of the men who would continue to the second round. Tate and his cousins returned to their spots, having advanced as they knew they would. When given the call, they fired. Tate's arrow struck the same spot it had the first time. The official walked along the line, tapping the men on the shoulder who would advance to the third round. There were six. Tate and his cousins, along with Angus and Harry. The men moved to the center six targets, and Tate prepared to draw his next arrow. He fought the urge to look toward Adelaide. Between Hamish teasing and standing beside Angus, Tate wanted to admit to no one—not even himself—that he wished Adelaide cheered for him along with her brothers.

"Archers, to the ready," the official boomed.

Tate couldn't help himself. His gaze jumped from

the target to Adelaide. She was watching him. He was certain. She shot him a smile and a nod. He returned his attention to where it should be.

"Fire!"

He hadn't realized he'd released his arrow with the same strength he used in battle or to take down a stag. It impaled the target, pushing the top bale backward, which then tumbled off of the two bales stacked beneath it. People stared. Tate stared.

"This year, we have only one winner," the official announced. "We havenae seen aught like it since the last year his father competed. Tate Sinclair is the archery champion."

Tate recalled that event. It was the first time he'd competed, and the year before his winning streak began because his father bowed out in favor of his son. His mother was a Comyn before marrying into the Sinclairs. The enemy of Robert the Bruce, thus the enemy of most Highland clans, the Comyns were welcome nowhere. A MacLaren insulted Ceit, but Tavish couldn't defend his wife as he wished since there was supposed to be no fighting at the Gatherings. He'd been so irate that he'd hit the target so hard it sailed off the back of its stack and landed three feet behind where it had stood only moments earlier.

Tate had overheard the comment too, and he'd hit his own target hard enough to knock it sideways. Laird Rab MacLaren was there and learned what his warrior said. Tate didn't know what happened to the warrior, but he'd never seen him again. Not even during those same games. Rab had apologized profusely and assured Tavish that the man would never run afoul of the Sinclairs again.

The crowd cheered, drawing Tate back to the present, and he looked around. He noticed his parents stood beside Aunt Mairghread and Uncle Tristan. All four looked at him aghast. Wee Liam, Hamish, and Alec came to stand beside him.

"Was it something I said?" Hamish elbowed his cousin.

Tate ignored him and swept his gaze over the rest of the crowd that continued to cheer. He noticed Adelaide clapping with excitement until Angus and Harry stalked toward her. It was a foregone conclusion that neither of them would win, but they didn't appreciate their sister's hearty support for a Sinclair. Tate and his cousins joined their parents as they bent and stepped through the gap in the fence railings.

"Well done, laddie." Tavish pulled his son in for an embrace that cracked Tate's back.

"Move over, ye beast. Let me hug ma son." Ceit jostled between Tavish and Tate, pushing Tavish out of the way.

"As ye say, *seillean beag*." Little bee. Tavish had called his wife that since they courted. It was only a moment later that they squashed the petite woman like the center of a sandwich. The men embraced again with her between them, her arms wrapped around her son's middle.

"We're vera proud of ye, but nay one expected ye to shoot like ye intended to kill the poor bale." Ceit gazed up at Tate when his parents let go of him. He saw her worry, but he offered her a crooked smile.

"I was tired of letting ma cousins think they're better than they are. Hamish, I shall have two rounds of whisky, nae one. Ye owe me." Tate grinned at his cousins, but he shot them all a warning glare when all three Mackay brothers opened their mouths. The family's conversation ended when Angus, Harry, and their sisters walked over to them.

"Felicitations," Angus offered as he stuck out his arm. While it was a congratulatory offer, Tate returned the squeeze as tightly as Angus began it. There was rivalry between them, but it seemed like something more to Tate. They released each other when Wee Liam spoke.

"Lady Adelaide, what did ye think of the competition? Ye seemed to enjoy it the most."

Tate would have words with his cousins later. It was one thing to tease him. It was another to bring Adelaide into it. But he knew they were goading him, and that was exactly what they wanted.

"I thought ma brothers gave ye a true challenge." Adelaide answered without hesitation, but everyone knew it was a weak answer. People's gazes shifted between Adelaide and Tate, but Adelaide stared at her brothers, and Tate stared at his cousins.

<h1 style="text-align:center">CHAPTER 6</h1>

"**I** heard the archery competition was vera lively." Clara ambled beside Adelaide as they wound their way to the loch to watch the races the next morning. Adelaide didn't believe Clara's casual tone. The clans had been abuzz about Tate's performance, and plenty speculated about why he shot his arrow with such force. Some said he wished to show up the hosts' family. Some said a rift had developed between the Sinclairs and Mackays—an idea that was laughed at each time someone mentioned it. A few said Tate was arrogant and boastful.

Adelaide didn't believe any of those reasons. She assumed he was merely better than the rest of the men and was tired of letting his cousins win, too. She'd heard his jest about his cousins. But she didn't think it came from arrogance so much as wishing to stand out among the men in his family who excelled at everything they did.

"Aye. Angus and Harry made it to the finals. They both had nearly perfect aim."

"I dinna doubt that. I'm talking aboot Tate Sinclair knocking his target over. Ye'd think the mon believed he was in battle or hunting that hay bale." Clara chuckled.

"He's a large mon, so it's nae surprising he's strong." Adelaide shrugged.

"Aye. Strong. That's it." Clara's tone made it obvious she thought Adelaide's explanation was lacking. "I heard he was trying to impress a lass in the crowd. One of the Gordons."

Adelaide's stomach cramped, forcing her to breathe through the sharp pain. She and the Gordons were related through her father. Aunt Davina and Uncle Edward's elder daughter married one of the Gordon twins, and they had a daughter of their own. Did Clara mean Adelaide's distant cousin?

"There are a few eligible women in that clan." That was as much as Adelaide could muster.

Clara glanced at her friend, the temptation to roll her eyes almost overwhelming. She knew Adelaide to be one of the most astute people of her acquaintance, but her friend was as blind as an old woman with no teeth left. They arrived at the loch as the competitors waded in. The shorter men were waist-deep, but the taller men were still in water that was only mid-thigh. Nine heads with chestnut hair and one with strawberry-blond walked in a line, bare arses to the breeze. Laird Liam, along with his four sons Callum, Alexander, Tavish, and Magnus, waded in with Liam's grandsons Thormud, Tate, Wiley, Blake, and Tor. Liam's other grandsons, Wee Liam, Alec, and Hamish Mackay along with their father, Tristan, splashed interspersed with the Sinclairs. Their raven hair barely stood out against so many deep brown heads of hair.

Adelaide took in the sight of at least two and a half score of men. All had sun-kissed torsos and arms. But from waist to mid-thigh, the skin was stark white. It was comical until Adelaide recognized Tate. She didn't know how she could since none faced her, and the Sinclair men and Mackay men were mirror images of each other from the back. But she just knew. She watched the muscles bunch and ripple in Tate's back, arse, and legs as he entered the water farther.

If the men faced the crowd, Adelaide and Clara would have turned away. But no one would consider seeing the men's backsides too inappropriate, so she stared. She heard her father call out to the contestants before he released an ear-piercing whistle. The men took off with water spraying everywhere, a jumble of arms and legs trying to pull ahead. It was Tate, Tristan, and Wee Liam who soon led the pack. She watched as Tate adjusted course as they approached the rowboat that marked the turnaround point. Staying close to the tiny vessel, Tate completed the turn first. Tristan and Wee Liam were soon even with Tate's waist.

Adelaide couldn't look away, couldn't blink as Tate suddenly burst forward. She didn't understand how he had the energy at the end of a nearly two-mile swim to sprint to the finish. He swam to victory, only stopping once he was entirely past the end of the course. He stood but quickly realized that he'd reached a shallower point than he realized. He sank back into the water before it could drop below waist level. He was looking straight at Adelaide. She knew she should turn her head, but he was too magnificent a sight, with his golden skin and water dripping from each defined muscle. She finally came to her senses as Tristan and Wee Liam finished, the rest of their family on their heels. She looked away before turning with Clara. The men wouldn't wait for the women spectators to avert their eyes, so all the maidens rushed to face the other way.

Tate had sensed Adelaide and Clara arrive before Fergus called out to his betrothed. Tate bumped shoulders with his father as they teased one another, but it allowed him to glance back and confirm Adelaide was among the crowd. He usually wasn't the strongest swimmer in his family. He'd lost the shorter race to Wiley days ago, so he hadn't expected to beat his brother, who'd been the victor of the sprint. He'd hoped to come in fourth behind Wiley, Tristan, and Wee Liam. He looked at Wiley and noticed his brother had a bloody nose. He pushed past other men to stand in front of Wiley.

"What happened?" Tate tipped Wiley's head back.

"Uncle Alex's foot," Wiley responded nasally as his fingers pinched his nose.

"I didna mean to, lad," Alex, the second eldest son of the older generation, said. "I'm sorry I hurt ye. It'll teach ye to move yer arse faster next time."

Wiley narrowed his eyes at his uncle, but anyone could see the humor in his expression. "If ye didna have feet the size of a seal's fin, then there wouldnae have been a problem."

Much like everything else among the Sinclairs, they could all share clothes and boots. Alex's feet weren't any bigger than his nephew's. Tate wasn't concerned about his uncle's feet so much as whether he'd broken Wiley's nose. But their father stood off to the side talking to his other brothers, so Tate knew it couldn't be that serious. If it were, Tavish would fuss worse than a mother hen. It was the mothers in Tate's family who healed their illnesses and their injuries but were far more stoic than any of the fathers. It used to embarrass him when he was younger. Now he appreciated how rare the fathers' concerns for their children were, so he no longer took it for granted.

"It's nae broken," Tate concluded.

"I ken. The lasses love war wounds. Mayhap one of them will show me some love." Wiley's eyebrows waggled, but all seriousness returned when Tavish shot him a reproving look. "He has ears like a bluidy dog."

"Aye, and ye should remember the stories aboot Mama when they married. Da doesnae find those jests funny. Ye ken he regrets how he spent many of his days before they met. He doesnae want us repeating his woebegotten youth."

"I ken. It's all bluster."

"But other people dinna."

"All right." Wiley nodded as he wiped his nose with his forearm then leaned forward to rinse the blood from his arm. Their father and one of their uncles had a checkered past with women, and they made sure their sons and nephews learned from the error of their ways. The second generation of Sinclair men were far more restrained and circumspect. Neither Wiley nor Tate were innocents, but they figured they had enough experience not to embarrass themselves in front of their future wives.

Tate glanced over his shoulder to where Adelaide stood with a group of other women, all facing away from the water. In his hurry to check on his brother, Tate hadn't thought about his nakedness. He and Wiley were the only men left unclothed. He rushed to don his leine before moving farther away from the group with Wiley to pleat their plaids. Fingal waited until Tate was fully dressed before announcing him as the official winner.

"Well done, Sinclair," Fingal said to Tate as they stood side-by-side after the proclamation. "Is yer brother hale?"

"Aye. It was an accident and nae as serious as I feared. It bled a lot but isnae broken."

"Mayhap next time ye could dress while ye clishmaclaver, then." Fingal stared at Tate before looking in the unmarried women's direction.

"Ma apologies for keeping the lasses waiting, but I dinna apologize for making sure ma brother is uninjured."

"Aye, but ye had a nice chin wag once ye kenned yer uncle hadnae done any real damage."

"So ye say." Tate locked gazes with Fingal, and it took a concerted effort not to cross his arms and broaden his stance. He knew to many it made the men in his family appear sullen, stubborn, or brooding. It just felt natural to him, but he didn't want to antagonize his host. The men stared at one another until Sarah and Finley approached.

"Da, Mama needs ye. She's in the undercroft," Sarah stated. "She said something aboot ye being late to meet her."

Tate watched as both women crinkled their noses and looked away. Fingal gave Tate one last glare before nodding and rushing away. He suspected he knew why Madeline needed Fingal, and it had nothing to do with the contents of the storerooms. His parents were just as bad, even after more than a score of years together.

He and Wiley walked back to where his entire family now gathered at the crest of the hill near the loch. Adelaide and Clara stood with four of Tate's female cousins and his sister. He watched Adelaide laugh so hard she covered her mouth and nose. Then she swiped at the tears that rolled from her eyes as she continued to enjoy whatever Ailish was saying. Tate could only imagine what she'd shared, and he was fairly certain it was at his and Wiley's expense.

"Should we stop her?" Wiley whispered.

"Aye." Tate waved Fergus over to join the brothers as they approached the women.

"There he is," Ailish crowed. It set off another round of giggles among the women.

"What did ye tell them?" Now Tate crossed his arms

and moved his legs hip-width apart. That only made the laughter uproarious.

"I told ye," Ailish hooted.

Tate looked around until his gaze met Adelaide's. He cocked an eyebrow, but she just shook her head, unable to speak around her laughter. It was his cousin Nessa who finally composed herself enough to explain.

"Remember two years ago when ye and Wiley thought to ride that bull?"

Tate's face immediately flushed. Adelaide turned her head but sneaked peeks at him that Tate saw. "I remember."

"We just mentioned—"

"Nay, Ailish. Dinna have yer brother mad at us. *Ye* mentioned," Nessa corrected.

"Fine. *I* mentioned the scar on yer arse and how it looks like a heart after Saoirse stitched it for ye. I'm pretty sure the bull didna love ye as much as that scar says. I didna think ye'd ever get off that horn. I was certain that horn was going to go clean through ye, which meant—" Ailish couldn't finish. She started laughing again.

Tate looked at Nessa, who just shook her head. He looked at the other women, most of whom were related to him, but they giggled and shook their heads, too. It was Adelaide who took pity on him and stepped beside him. She went onto her toes. When he leaned sideways, she cupped his ear.

"She said it meant ye'd sprouted the greatest horn of all the men in yer family. She said at least ye would have been sure to—to—basically, that the horn would make sure ye at least had something to poke with." Adelaide lowered her heels to the ground, stumbling backward when Tate launched himself at his sister. He hefted her over his shoulder and spun back around to the loch. He pulled her from his shoulder and lifted her over his head before launching her into the loch. He stomped in and pulled her out when she emerged, spluttering. He carried her back to the shore and put her on her feet.

"Ye looked like ye needed yer mouth cleaning out. Be glad Mama isnae here. She'd do more than just dump ye in the loch. She'd hand me the lump of soap."

Ailish pushed her sopping hair from her face, smiling unrepentantly. "But I wasna wrong, was I?"

Tate moved to bend forward to grab her again, but with a shriek, Ailish lifted her skirts as best she could and took off. Tate was hot on her heels, but Tavish stepped in front of him.

"What wicked thing did yer sister say this time?" Tavish chortled.

"Nae only did she tell the story aboot the bull, but she implied—she said—bluidy hell. I'm glad she's only ma sister and nae ma daughter. She said at least I could have given a lass a good poke if the horn had gone through me."

Tavish stared at Tate for a moment before roaring, "Ailish!"

"Aye, Da." Ailish stopped at the top of the hill. She clasped her hands in front of her, the image of innocence.

"See Mama and tell her what ye said."

Ailish shook her head, walking back down the hill like she was making her way to the gallows. "Canna ye punish me instead? Or Tate can throw me in again. Please nae Mama."

"Ye should—"

"Wheest." Tavish cut off Tate before both his children would wind up in trouble with Ceit. He towered over Ailish when she came to stand in front of him sheepishly. "If ye thought it a funny enough story to share with people outside yer clan, then it must be a funny enough story to remind Mama."

"Aye, Da." She spun on her heel and marched back to the top of the hill, but she just couldn't resist. She called down to Tate, "Just because I'm in trouble doesnae mean it isnae true!"

"God have mercy on the mon's soul who marries her," Tate muttered.

Wiley and Tavish laughed, but Tate glowered at his brother. It had been the younger man's idea to attempt bull riding. Wiley came away with a nearly matching scar from his failed attempt after Tate. But Ailish hadn't seen fit to mention that part of the tale. No, she'd chosen to embarrass only him. She would say it was to keep his head from swelling after two major victories, but she'd been a troublemaker since she was a wean. Tate and Wiley never said she couldn't play with them, but once they were old enough, they made it hard for her to keep up. Tate was certain that's why she'd become such a strong runner. But until she'd built that endurance, she'd had to rely on her words to rally against her brothers. She had a wicked sense of humor, and he knew he'd gotten off easy. When it wasn't directed at him, he usually laughed the hardest.

Tate looked around and noticed several stunned expressions, and he wished to groan. People outside his family disapproved. Some shook their heads and chalked it up to Sinclair family antics. Others cast him disdainful glances for both making a public scene and soaking his sister—soaking a woman. The rest of his family paid him no attention since they were all accustomed to sibling rivalry. None ever fought in earnest, but they bickered. When they were much younger, their mothers would send them outside to spend their pent-up energy, and that usually resolved the short-lived disagreements. Tate hadn't thought twice about tossing her in, knowing Ailish wouldn't mind. It was better than him saying aloud what he thought. He wouldn't be able to take those words back, and that was a lesson all the parents instilled in all their children. He shrugged and looked for Wiley and Fergus.

Fergus stood with Clara, her sister, and Adelaide while Wiley had wandered away and now jested with their uncles. Tate could hear something about the swelling across the bridge of his nose being an improvement. Wiley was just as handsome as any of the Sinclair men, and he could pass for most of his male cousins' twin. Such was the case with the young women in the family. They all bore striking resemblances to each other, but several favored each mother's hair color. As Tate continued to look around, he realized they'd left him standing alone. He opted to retire to his tent rather than continue to socialize. He was exhausted and hoped to nap before the evening meal. He didn't care to reflect on why he'd pushed himself so hard in both the archery and swimming competitions. He trudged back to the tent village and found his clan's section.

"Tate."

He looked up as his mother called to him. He tried not to cringe as he changed course and walked to where Ceit and Ailish stood. "Aye, Mama."

"Yer sister has something she wishes to say." Ceit cocked an eyebrow at her youngest child.

"I'm sorry for what I said in front of the others, Tate."

"Are ye sorry for saying it in front of other people or saying it at all? Or are ye sorry ye got caught?" Tate crossed his arms and cocked his own eyebrow, but he knew he didn't look anywhere nearly as intimidating to Ailish as their mother did.

"Mmm."

"Ailish," Ceit snapped.

"For saying it at all and for getting caught." Ailish winked at Tate.

"Tate, what do ye have to say to yer sister?"

"Ye deserved it."

"Tatum," Ceit's stern tone warned he'd pushed as far as he could before finding himself in trouble. It mattered not at all that Ceit's children were in their twenties. None wished to find themselves on the wrong side of her temper. She'd be offering their skills to muck out the garderobes.

"I'm sorry—" Tate paused to consider for what he was willing to apologize. "For tossing ye in the loch in front of so many people."

"So ye're nae sorry for throwing me in and soaking me." Ailish crossed her arms and broadened her stance to match her brother's. "Ye had me walk through the camp with ma kirtle stuck to me like a second skin."

That gave Tate a moment of pause. His gaze scanned the hundreds of tents, noticing the men milling around.

"I'm sorry, Ailish. I didna think that far ahead. Did anyone say aught? Look at ye wrong?"

Ailish shook her head. She knew that if anyone had, her brother would run them through. She could accept she'd deserved his retribution, but it wasn't the same as when they were children and wet clothes meant nothing. Now that she was a woman, her sopping clothes drew attention. Fortunately, she took a route that kept her away from most people.

"Embrace."

Ailish and Tate looked at their mother before they nodded. Tate opened his arms, and Ailish stepped into them. He engulfed her, and all was back to normal. He cherished his little sister even when they bickered, and Ailish knew no place was safer than with Tate.

"I really am sorry, Ailish."

"So am I. I'm sorry too."

Their parents had always made a point of teaching them that agreeing with an apology wasn't enough. They had to speak the words. They also taught that there was no weakness in admitting when they'd wronged someone. It showed far more integrity to accept fault where it was due than trying to avoid taking responsibility.

"Go in and change yer gown. Then I shall try to get some shut eye."

"Och aye, impressing her takes a lot of energy." Ailish waggled her eyebrows.

"Who?" Tate forced himself not to swallow, not wanting his Adam's apple to bob and make his trepidation obvious.

"Ye ken." Ailish stepped back and ducked into the tent that she and her siblings shared with their parents.

"Ye ken ye can solve yer differences like that at home, but ye must rein in that temper. She will needle ye because she can. What she said was wrong, but ye overshadowed her sin by committing a bigger one on yer own," Ceit whispered.

"I ken, Mama. I didna want to scold her in public, and that's how we've solved our differences in the past. She's pushed me into the loch, the sea, and horse troughs before. I should have thought better of where we are. I embarrassed the family. I'm sorry."

"I ken ye are, wee one. All will be forgotten by the evening meal. Someone else is bound to do something more gossip worthy." Ceit strained onto her toes, and Tate leaned forward. She ruffled his hair and kissed his cheek. She'd been doing and calling him the same thing to solve the world's problems since he was a bairn. He prayed that never changed.

Once Ailish left the tent, he settled into his bedroll.

He rolled from one position to another, unable to get comfortable. He may have made up with his sister, but he worried he'd tarnished his reputation and cast his family in a poor light. Loyalty to his family and clan was one of the most important values ingrained in Tate, so he didn't take it lightly when he acted against their best interests. As he drifted off to sleep, he wondered if his mother would be right. He doubted it.

$\mathcal{A}$delaide observed Clara and Fergus as they gazed at one another during the evening meal. She took her spot on the dais just before the meal began. She supported her friend's love match, but at the heart of it, for anyone who wasn't Clara or Fergus, it was a political alliance for their clans. Adelaide glanced at her father and wondered when he would suggest she take finding a suitor more seriously. The Grants were among the most dominant clans in the Highlands, so there were few Adelaide could marry into that would improve the Grants' position. But there were certain clans that would eagerly ally themselves to hers, and she wasn't interested in men who saw her as means to get to her father and uncle. She hoped she would truly find a love match, but she accepted she might have to settle for a mere fondness for her husband. Perhaps such a relationship could grow into love.

Her parents married because the king ordered Madeline to wed, and Fingal wished for a demure wife who would leave him in peace. It began as a marriage of convenience, but they were in love by the time they'd traveled from Stirling to their home. She knew neither admitted their feelings until sennights later and several miscommunications. But once they had, they were a formidable couple that no one underestimated. Their devotion to one another was clear to anyone who merely glanced in their direction. Adelaide longed for that, but she knew, as the future laird's daughter, no one could guarantee that. Her parents promised it, but she would commit to her duty if the right prospect came along.

"He came."

Adelaide turned to look at her sister as Finley jutted her chin toward the keep's massive doors. From the raised platform in the Great Hall, Adelaide's belly churned to see yet another Chisholm arrive. Peter Chisholm was Laird Lathan Chisholm's heir. He was Adam times ten. He was arrogant and foul tempered at all times. He never had a nice word for anyone, and he was known to abuse the women in any keep in which he stayed. As though her father thought the same thing, he leaned forward.

"Lathan, keep yer son away from ma servants. I'll cut off his cods if he goes near a single one. If any woman reports he molested her, I'll put him in ma dungeon until ye leave. I warn ye now and only one time."

"That is hardly hospit—"

"Lathan." Ronan MacKinnon, Adelaide's uncle, growled. He was married to Abigail, Madeline's younger sister. Despite her miserable handfast only lasting a year, even a score of years later, she remained the butt of many poor jokes among the Chisholms. Peter was only a young lad when Abigail lived amongst his clan, and he'd been a bastard then. Ronan laid down his eating knife and covered his wife's hand with his on the table.

"The lad hasnae done aught wrong."

"Yet," Fingal snapped. "He has his evening meal here

and leaves immediately after. That is ma only compromise."

"Ye arenae—"

"I am, and I agree with ma tánaiste." Edward rested both fists on the table as he leaned back in the laird's chair. He knew Lathan's temper, and the man wouldn't remain quiet if he was interrupted a third time, but neither would Edward countenance Peter Chisholm raping any woman in his keep or accosting a woman from one of his visiting clans. As host, he bore the burden of ensuring everyone's safety on his land. He wouldn't have the Gathering disturbed for one man's perverted pleasure.

Adelaide surveyed the Great Hall as the men spoke, and she noticed more than one person sneer at Peter. That wouldn't engender warm feelings from the new arrival and was more likely to cause him to act out. She barely noticed the woman who walked behind Peter. His wife had been a Fraser of Lovat before she wed, and Adelaide didn't envy the poor woman. She knew she'd escaped the browbeaten existence the woman suffered when her parents refused to consider Adam.

"Everyone kens the type of mon he is, yet nay one stops him," Adelaide mused to Finley. "Da and Uncle Edward have warned Lathan, but do ye really believe Lathan will mention any of this to his son? Do ye really imagine any woman he accosts will step forward? He should be banned from the Gatherings altogether."

"Would that someone could. But he'll be laird one day, and then there really willna be aught anyone can do." Finley turned away from Adelaide when Sarah spoke on Finley's other side. Adelaide continued to watch Peter make his way to his clan, leaving her unsettled as though her anxiousness was a premonition waiting to present itself. She waited through three more courses before servants cleared the tables, pushed them toward the walls, and tipped them on their sides. The musicians began a lively tune, and Angus offered to dance with her. She accepted with a grin, and they joined the crowd.

"What did ye make of the Sinclairs' spectacle today?" Angus whispered.

"That they arenae any different from our family. If I'd shared such a story aboot ye or Harry, ye would do far worse than dunk me in the loch."

"We wouldnae," Angus retorted indignantly.

"Aye, ye would. Ye have. Ye left me to walk home in the rain from the far end of the village nae three sennights ago because I told the tavern wenches to water yer whisky if they wished for ye to remain up long enough to—"

"That's enough, lass. I remember just fine."

Adelaide still shot him a smirk despite him interrupting her innuendo. "Ye shouldnae have let the kitchen door slam in ma face when ye kenned I had a basket of turnips and potatoes in ma arms. I dropped the whole thing to keep the door from hitting me in the nose. Then, ye opened the door and told me nae to be so clumsy. Ye didna help me at all."

"And do ye remember, oh fair sister, why I did that?"

Adelaide grinned. "Because I slipped a heavy dose of hyssop into yer ale and left ye trotting to the garderobe every ten minutes for a day and a half. I still dinna ken how ye didna taste it."

"Aye. Granted, I might have deserved that for encouraging Harry to hide yer prayer book before Mass the Sunday before."

"Exactly."

Brother and sister grinned at one another. All five siblings had ongoing pranks they pulled on one another despite their ages. None of them wished to be outdone, and they all still enjoyed the challenge. She knew she and her sisters would miss the antics once they married and moved away. They knew the inevitable, and it further saddened Adelaide to think she would have to give up the close-knit family for a man she might only like, not love.

The music had them switching partners, and Adelaide took the time to consider each unwed man who twirled her. The Campbells had at least seven eligible men between the laird's and tánaiste's sons. The MacLeods of Assynt had a handful of bachelors who would make more than acceptable matches for Adelaide. Her blood relations to the MacLeods of Assynt were so distant that they weren't easily traceable, but they were a cadet branch of her mother's clan of birth, the MacLeods of Lewis. There was no issue of sanguinity, so she could consider the men as prospects. There were eligible men in the Mackays, the Sutherlands, and the Sinclairs.

Her next partner sneered at her as she met Peter Chisholm's gaze. Having a million biting ants crawling up her skin was more appealing than even one dance step with him. She kept her expression neutral, not offering a smile, but neither did she scowl.

"Lady Adelaide, fair as ever."

"Thank ye."

"A lady of few words. An admirable trait."

I prefer to save them for someone who matters.

Adelaide nodded.

"Ma brother says ye have a champion this year."

Adelaide's mind jumped to Tate. She appreciated him defending her honor, but she still worried what Adam would do for retribution. Now that Peter was with his clan, she knew the older brother would compound the damage. She opted to keep her thoughts to herself.

"Naught to say aboot that? If I didna ken ye better, I

might think ye're being awkward, Lady Adelaide. But ye would never be so ungracious to a guest."

"Until now, ye hadnae asked a question, so I had naught to reply."

"Why is Tate Sinclair so quick to defend ye? Are ye bedding him?"

"Release me now." Adelaide tried to pull away, but Peter only tightened his hold. He counted on her not making a scene. She stomped on his foot.

"Ye cunt. Ye will pay for that. I will do whatever I wish, and ye are too weak to stop me."

Adelaide glanced around before catching sight of her father dancing with Aunt Abigail.

"Da!" Adelaide screamed as loudly as she could, and everyone froze. She pushed against Peter's chest and brought her arm back, making it obvious she would swing.

"Ada!" Fingal pushed through the crowd. "Lass?"

"Da, let me whisper it." Adelaide's murderous expression told Fingal whatever she had to say would soon have his expression matching hers. He leaned toward her. Much like she'd done earlier that day with Tate, she cupped her hands around her father's ear. "He asked me why Tate defended ma honor when Adam insulted me among his clan members, and Tate heard him. Then he asked if Tate was bedding me. When he wouldnae let go after I told him to, I stomped on his foot. He called me a cunt and told me I would pay for it, and there was naught I could do to stop him because I'm too weak."

She leaned away from her father, flinching at the rage radiating from him. She questioned whether she should have said anything at all, let alone in the crowded Great Hall. But Peter frightened her more than she wished to admit, so her instinct was to cry out for her father. She'd caught herself before hitting Peter, knowing he had no limits to the pain he would cause her if he caught her alone. And she knew he would make sure he did.

"Get out of this keep and get off this land," Fingal growled.

"Now just a moment, Fingal." Lathan elbowed his way over to them. "Ye arenae the laird yet."

"I'm the bluidy tánaiste, and it's within ma control to order someone off this land. Yer son nae only insulted ma daughter but threatened to molest her. He goes, or the moment this Gathering is over, I will challenge him to single combat. Ye ken as well as I do that ye will lose yer heir if it comes to that. I'm giving ye the chance to keep yer son alive. I warned ye. He leaves now."

Edward walked toward them, people stepping away to make space for the laird. He angled himself to stand behind Fingal, the significance clear. He said nothing, merely looked at Lathan then Peter. He wouldn't undermine Fingal by being the one to pass judgment. But he would prove Fingal's word was law, and Edward agreed.

Madeline wrapped her arm around Adelaide's shoulders and shielded her from Peter's venomous mien. However, Adelaide knew how he would appear since she'd seen his mulish attitude too many times. It made her count her blessings that she would never marry into the family. She knew she wouldn't survive untouched by the foul man. She watched as the crowd shifted, people naturally moving to stand with their clansman. Clans moved to stand with their allies.

It didn't take long to make it clear that the Grants not only had more allies, but they were the mightiest in the Highlands. She noticed the Sinclair men had hands on dirks at their waist. The women had hands in their pockets, which she suspected held dirks too. The

Sutherlands were the same, and Mairghread Mackay had the handle of her dirk peeking out of her pocket. She prayed Mairghread didn't feel compelled to get involved because Peter wouldn't survive. The woman could lead an army into battle, and she'd defended her title again that year as the best knife thrower in the Highlands, which likely meant the best in Scotland. Adelaide's lips twitched as she changed her mind. She would love to see a woman like Mairghread bring the Chisholms low.

"How do ye ken the lass isnae lying?" Lathan questioned.

"Because I heard him."

Alec Mackay and Torquil Sinclair spoke at the same time. Adelaide twisted in her mother's arms to look at the cousins. They'd both danced with women beside Adelaide and Peter. The odious man had done little to lower his voice and keep his threat just between the two of them. The two men pushed forward until they stood beside Fingal. Adelaide noticed the other Sinclair and Mackay cousins inched closer. She knew it was only slightly in part to support her family and mostly to ensure their defense of Alec and Torquil. Mairghread and Tristan moved to stand directly behind their son. Tension rapidly rose among the clans, and Adelaide feared not only would they trap her in the middle of another brawl, but she'd also cause this one.

Fingal fixed his gaze on Alec. "What did ye hear?"

"Peter asked an inappropriate question to a maiden, then he called her a vile name that I willna repeat in front of a crowd." Alec stared at Peter until the man looked away.

"And ye, Sinclair?"

"The same as ma cousin. He accused her of nae behaving as a maiden should and called her a word ma mama will thrash me for repeating. I fear Lady Deidre

Sinclair far more than anyone but ma other aunts. So ye ken the word is vulgar if I'd rather face the English imposter's full army than speak it aloud." No one in the Highlands accepted King Edward III as the rightful King of Scotland. Their king, David, was still in exile in France.

While the Sinclair women's bark might have been worse than their bite when it came to their own children, there wasn't anyone who wanted to cross them. They defended their land and keep when their men rode out to fight the English, and they'd each earned their reputation for tenacity.

"Bah. They're family. Of course, they'd defend one another," Lathan scoffed.

Mairghread and Tristan bracketed Alec as Tristan leaned forward. "Are ye calling ma son a liar?"

Adelaide was certain there was a collective gasp among every person in the Great Hall. Now she truly regretted saying anything to anyone. She should have brought it to her father's attention when most people had retired.

"Ye did the right thing."

Adelaide turned her head to find Tate standing behind her, his hands on dirk hilts. "There is going to be a battle in ma home I caused."

"There willna be a fight. The Chisholms willna dare. And there are too many on yer side, willing to defend ye, for Lathan or Peter to challenge."

"I'm nae so sure." Adelaide glanced up at her mother as Madeline released her with a reassuring expression.

"If aught happens, ye come with me. Wiley, Thormud, and I will get ye out of here."

Adelaide noticed Tate's brother and cousin—the man second in line to inherit the Sinclair lairdship—behind Tate. Both men nodded confirmation of Tate's offer.

"I willna believe a word of this until the lass admits it aloud. For all we ken she's making something out of naught." Lathan sneered at her, and she felt Tate step closer.

"There is nay one here who doesnae ken yer son's reputation. Nay one here thinks it impossible or even unlikely that he said something vile to ma daughter," Fingal stated.

"I didna—"

"He tightened his arm around me when I tried to step away," Adelaide interrupted. "He claimed I was bedding a mon I am nae. Any midwife here can check to be sure I'm speaking the truth. When I stomped on his foot because he wouldnae let go of me, he called me a cunt and said I would pay for that. He said I am weak, and there is naught I can do to stop him."

Adelaide's voice remained calm as she told more than a hundred people how he'd humiliated her. She didn't cringe, and she didn't back down. Instead, she kept her gaze locked with Peter's. Whether she'd shared what he said, she already knew she would never leave her chamber without at least two guards with her at all times until the Chisholms left. She figured she might as well defend her honor before the Chisholms be-smirched it further.

"Dinna go anywhere without yer brothers or guards until they leave," Tate whispered.

"I ken. Tate, he claimed it was ye. I dinna mean to be unappreciative, but mayhap ye could nae stand so close right now."

She pulled her lips in as she looked up at him, and she wished she had said nothing. But if Peter named him, they would both be in far more trouble if he was standing at the ready to defend her. Tate faded into his family, and Blake stepped forward to take his place. She couldn't believe she'd ever mistaken him for Tate, even

at a distance. Now she could tell them apart immediately.

"I warned ye. He leaves, or he takes up residence in
the dungeons until the Gathering is over," Fingal
declared.

"I will compromise." Lathan's condescension hung
in the air.

"How magnanimous," Madeline replied. Her pa-
tronizing smile matched Lathan's smugness.

"Peter agrees to remain away from the keep and
outside the bailey walls, but he remains at the Gathering. We maintain the peace at the Gatherings, and clans
dinna fight one another. Therefore, ye canna expel
him."

Grumbles went through the crowd as no one but a
few of the Chisholms' staunchest allies stood unwaver-
ingly behind the troublesome clan.

"Ye ken that isnae how that rule works," Fingal responded. "He remains outside the walls; he's banned
from competing; and if he looks in any woman's direction, he goes into the dungeons. That is the only compromise ye shall get."

"Vera well." Lathan knew to cut his losses. He didn't
doubt the accusations were true, but as Peter's father
and laird, it forced him to defend the blighter.

The crowd broke apart, and the musicians played a
lively reel when Madeline signaled them to begin again.
Adelaide looked at her parents.

"I shouldnae have screamed like that. I should have
been more circumspect. I'm sorry."

"Dinna apologize for aught," Fingal embraced her.
"Ye are nae prone to hysterics. He truly terrified ye if ye
screamed like that. Ye did the right thing. Peter proved
exactly what I warned Lathan aboot."

"He's nae the first mon to say something inappropriate, but there was a note to his tone and words that

truly made me fearful that he wasna just bluster. I kept maself from striking him, but ma fear and anger tempted me. Da, can I have guards with me until everyone leaves?"

"Aye. I was aboot to say the same thing, and if I hadnae, Mama would have." Fingal wrapped an arm around Adelaide and his other around Madeline. He kissed the tops of each of their heads before releasing them. "Stay away from Tate. I warned ye last year, and I'm warning ye again. Obviously, people have noticed ye're around each other too often."

"Clara is ma best friend, and Tate is one of Fergus's closest friends. I canna be with Clara without Fergus and Tate. If I have guards to chaperone me, then nay one can claim aught that isnae true. Da, Tate hasnae done aught questionable. He's defended me and protected me, but he'd do the same for any woman."

"Mayhap." Fingal sounded unconvinced. Adelaide might have wished Tate's concern was unique to her, but she knew it wasn't. She refused to make something of it that wasn't true. "I'll arrange the guards now."

"Are ye all right now, *nighean*?" Daughter. The way Madeline said it to her daughters never made it sound distant. Instead, pride and love resonated in the single word. Adelaide nodded and accepted another embrace from her mother. Relief coursed through her.

"Aye. I'm all right. I wish to finish the evening laughing." Adelaide smiled when her younger brother thrust forward his hand. Angus and Harry had stood silently beside Edward, who'd remained just behind Fingal. Her brothers had been riding into battle for several years, but she'd never seen the expressions they must wear while killing their enemies until only moments ago. She might not need any guards assigned to her. It was unlikely Angus or Harry would leave her alone until the last guest was all the way off Grant land.

Adelaide accepted Harry's offer, and they joined the other dancers. The incident remained with Adelaide, but she enjoyed herself. No one looked at her askance. She saw concern and sympathy, but no one appeared to pity her or distrust her. She was heartened by that. When she stepped aside after four dances and snagged a mug of ale, she stood with Sarah, Finley, and Clara. Her brothers were unobtrusive but still nearby.

"What do ye wish to do tomorrow?" Clara asked, skirting the topic no one wished to discuss.

"The caber toss is the first event. I'd like to see that," Sarah answered.

"Me, too." Adelaide never grew tired of watching the men heft and throw the massive tree trunks. She couldn't imagine having the strength to do that, so it kept her in awe each time she witnessed the feat.

Finley shook her head. "Ada, dinna go to that. Peter and Adam were competing. Peter will watch instead. I dinna think ye should be anywhere near that field."

"They are?" It surprised Adelaide since neither had taken part in that event in the past, and neither of them stood a chance against their competitors. Magnus, Blake, and Tor were the front runners, and it was merely a question of who would place first. Tristan Mackay was also a contender, but less likely to beat his relatives-by-marriage. She also knew several Campbells would be there and would put on a good showing. It was a shame she would miss it, but she would take her sister's advice.

"I dinna ken what else I wish to watch then. The weans' games?" Adelaide shrugged with a smile.

"Nae a bad idea. Fergus's youngest two brothers are competing in the foot races," Clara mused.

"Ye dinna have to give up watching the toss on ma account. I'm certain I'll find someone to watch with, and even if I dinna, I dinna mind being there on ma own." Adelaide didn't exaggerate. She wouldn't be self-conscious about going to anything alone, especially since she would have guards with her. She doubted she could rope Angus or Harry into coming with her to the children's competitions.

"Mayhap the Chisholms will compete last, and we can leave before they start. Or better yet, they go first, and we can arrive late to miss them," Finley suggested.

"We'll see," Adelaide hedged as her gaze swept the crowd once more.

ate woke with a start, unsure what roused him. He looked around his tent, but his family was sound asleep. He strained to hear anything that might have disturbed him, but he couldn't distinguish anything from the rowdiness coming from the alehouse tent. Perhaps that caused it. Mayhap a particularly noisy and inebriated drinker yelled. He rolled over and tried to fall back to sleep, but he was fully awake. His mind jumped directly to the scene from earlier that night in the Great Hall. He'd overheard Peter too while he danced with his youngest Mackay cousin. He'd held back from saying anything since Peter had named Tate in his accusation. He feared he would only make it worse if he tried to defend them both.

He didn't want to admit to anyone, least of whom himself, why it bothered him to hear Adelaide ask that he leave her alone. He'd seen Fingal look in his direction several times, so he knew Adelaide admitted who Peter referenced. He also recalled his run-in with Adelaide when he arrived. She told him Fingal warned her away. He sensed her father did the same thing again that night. Fortunately for Fingal, his warning proved unnecessary. Adelaide seemed no more interested in

Tate than she had the previous years. If he wouldn't concede how much he disliked Adelaide telling him to stay away, he wouldn't consider how much it unnerved him that her disinterest stung.

He'd danced with plenty of unwed women since arriving at the Gathering, and some of them were even unrelated to him. But none caught his fancy or even his attention. He'd mentioned in passing to his cousins that he'd looked forward to seeing Adelaide this year, but he'd kept his comment flippant. He wanted to confess to no one how attracted he'd been to her last summer and how his admiration only grew each day that he attended this year's games. He'd spent years wishing far more—something permanent—might come of the casual friendship they'd had since childhood.

"Did ye hear something?" Wiley whispered.

Before Tate could answer, his father whispered back. "I did. Some eejit just fell against a tent. Lucky the bastard didna knock it down. It was Alex's."

Tavish's next oldest brother had three daughters, two of whom still lived with their family at Dunbeath. With no sons, he was the only man in the tent and highly attuned to anyone coming too close to his wife and daughters.

None of the men in his family were light sleepers, so it didn't surprise him that his father and brother woke too. But it also meant they noticed him tossing and turning while his mind wandered. It was likely why Wiley asked instead of merely going back to sleep. He couldn't see his father's face in the dark, but he sensed the older man looking at him. He vowed to himself he would keep still and pretend to be asleep if he had to.

It wasn't long before he heard Tavish's and Wiley's light snores, but Tate was no closer to being asleep than he had been minutes ago. The longer he remained awake the more he realized he needed to relieve himself. He crept from the tent, certain he woke Tavish and Wiley again, but neither said anything. Tate wound his way past the other Sinclair tents until he came to a spot away from where anyone slept.

"Ye'd do well to stay away from all of them."

A man's voice Tate didn't recognize wafted to him. He couldn't guess who the warning went to since so many briefly paused feuds existed among the gathered clans. They would resolve slights that happened there once the clans went their separate ways. The number of raids and razed fields often soared after the Gatherings when perceived wrongs were set to rights.

"I dinna give a shite what the bitch or her father says. I ought to slip into her chamber right now and fuck her. She was supposed to be mine years ago."

Tate immediately recognized Adam's voice. He inched closer and recognized not only Adam but Henry Rose, Laird Rose's youngest son. Tate waited for Henry to disabuse Adam of the idea, but Henry said nothing more to dissuade his friend. The hair on the back of Tate's neck stood up when Adam continued talking. Tate could tell the man was so far in his cups that it was more likely he'd licked the bottom of a barrel.

"The king wanted it, and if I fuck her, she'll have no choice. Neither will her bastard father."

Tate didn't like the conviction in Adam's voice. He didn't sound like a drunk man pontificating. He sounded like a drunk man who would feel the same way even after he slept off the alcohol.

Henry spoke up. "King Robert is dead. Nay one is going to force Lady Adelaide to marry ye. The king is in France and couldnae care less aboot something like yer marriage or Lady Adelaide's, so ye willna find help from that court. The one in Stirling isnae going to favor ye either. Andrew Murray is more concerned with defeating the English than yer nose being out of joint over someone like Lady Adelaide. Ye'd do better to marry ma sister and strengthen the alliance we already have."

Tate felt sorry for Henry's sister should Adam or Lathan take the suggestion to heart. He didn't wish the woman harm. She was barely three-and-ten, and Adam was beastly. He wasn't the sort of man to wait for a child bride to become a woman.

"I'll have what they promised to me. I'm of a mind to have it now."

"Ye're alone in that mission, Adam. I'm nae dying for ye to have a rut."

Tate listened, then watched Henry hurry away. He knew where the Chisholms had made camp, and it was next to the Roses and the MacDonalds of Lochalsh. He didn't know why either man was so far from his clan, but they'd ventured into enemy territory. The Gordons, Frasers of Lovat, and Campbells were all camped nearby. They were both fortunate it was Tate who overheard and not a member from any of the other three. He observed Adam watch Henry walk away before turning to peer at the keep. When he took five steps forward, Tate spun on his heel, his need to pish forgotten. He weaved and wound through the tents; certain he passed Adam, who staggered more than walked.

When Tate emerged from the tent village, he scanned the area and caught sight of Adam's shadow. Tate sprinted to the postern gate and waved to a guardsman on the battlements.

"Urgent message for ma grandda, Laird Liam Sinclair. It canna wait till morning."

"We dinna open the gates after dark, Sinclair."

"I ken, and I will speak to yer laird and take full responsibility. But this simply canna wait."

Tate watched the man, knowing Adam was far less

likely to be admitted than he was, but he didn't put it past the man to find some way in. The guardsman spoke to someone else, and soon the gate inched open. Two Grant warriors stood on either side. They escorted him in, one locking the gate behind them. They walked alongside him into the keep and up the stairs to the third floor, where the guest chambers lay. They stopped at Liam's door, and Tate rapped on it.

"Grandda, it's Tate." He heard movement almost immediately. Liam flung open the door, his plaid wrapped around his waist. "I need to speak to ye."

Liam nodded to the Grant men, and Tate stepped inside. Tate looked sheepishly at his grandfather before he explained.

"I really need to speak to Laird Grant, but I thought saying I needed to speak to ye was more likely to get me inside. I may need ye to come with me."

"And this canna wait until morning?"

"Mayhap, but if it canna, and I dinna say aught, I wouldnae forgive maself for nae speaking up."

"Does yer da ken ye came here?"

"I didna have time to tell him. I left the tent to pish, but I overheard something that alarmed me."

"Aye. What was that?"

"Adam threatened to find his way into the keep and attack Lady Adelaide. After what happened this evening, I dinna think it's an empty threat. He said that if he—bedded—her, then the Grants would have nay choice but to marry her to him."

"Daft sod. Fingal would have nay choice but to kill him."

"I ken that. Ye ken that. The rest of the Highlands ken that. But Adam isnae a mon to trifle with. I warned him away, and I fear that did more harm than good. If he's willing to stand against me and nae heed ma words, then he willna be easily thwarted. I truly fear for Lady Adelaide."

"Fingal intends to post guards with Lady Adelaide until everyone leaves. She's sharing a chamber with one of her sisters."

"That's more likely to get Sarah or Finley murdered and Adelaide still raped." Tate didn't notice that he'd dropped the women's honorific, but Liam did. He nodded as he turned toward the bed.

"Let me dress. We'll go to Fingal's chamber together. Stand behind me. He's more likely to speak to us if he sees me first. And he willna lob yer head off for spying Lady Madeline." It was no secret Liam hadn't looked in any woman's direction since his wife died nearly forty years earlier.

"Thank ye, Grandda."

Liam nodded and hurried to don his leine, then pleat his plaid. He forewent stockings and slipped on his boots. Tate followed his grandfather in silence as they made their way down to the second floor. Liam barely touched the door before Fingal flung it open.

"Sinclair?" Fingal looked over Liam's shoulder. "Tate. Why are ye here?"

"Ma grandson overhead something when he went to pish that alarmed him enough to seek me in the middle of the night. I agree that it's concerning enough to wake ye."

"What is it?"

Tate looked around before he shook his head. "Is there a chamber we can go to? Or mayhap yer solar? I dinna want yer daughters to hear or anyone else."

Fingal squinted at Tate before nodding his head. He looked over his shoulder. "Maddy, we're going to ma solar. We'll wait for ye in the passageway." He stepped through the doorway and shut the portal behind him. It was only a few minutes later that Madeline opened the door. Fingal wrapped his arm around his wife's waist before leading the way downstairs. No one spoke until they reached the chamber belowstairs.

"I assume this has to do with one of ma lasses if ye dinna want them or anyone else to overhear," Fingal stated.

"Aye." Tate kept his voice low, not trusting that the walls didn't have ears even this far from the bedchambers. "Someone stumbled into Uncle Alex's tent and woke ma da, Wiley, and me. I couldnae fall back to sleep, so I went to pish. I overhead Adam and Henry Rose talking. Both men are sotted, but Adam was vera clear that he plans to force himself on Lady Adelaide. He claims she always should have been his, and that if he beds her, ye'll have nay choice but to let him wed her. He plans to do it tonight. When I saw him walk toward the keep and away from his clan's camp, I hurried to get here first. I dinna doubt yer guards will turn him away, but neither do I doubt he'll find some way in and up to Lady Adelaide's chamber before most people stir."

"And how did ye get through the gate?" Fingal's casual tone belied his rising anger toward all things Chisholm.

"I said I had an urgent message for Grandda, which I did. I didna think ye would listen to me without him. And I wished to make certain disrupting ye was wise. Mayhap this could wait till morning, but I didna want to risk being wrong and wished for Grandda's advice. Yer guard wasna eager to let me in. I believe he would have denied me if I were from any other clan but the Gordons, MacKinnons, or MacLeods."

Fingal and Madeline exchanged a look before Fingal nodded. Tate didn't know what it meant, but he hoped one day he would have a relationship like theirs and the other couples in his own immediate and extended family. He'd tried to imagine that with each woman he'd danced with that evening and the ones before, but none felt right. None but one.

"Thank ye, Tate. We will warn our daughters and ensure Adelaide is always with her brothers, cousins, or guards," Madeline said with a smile.

"Lady Madeline, he meant he would enter Lady Adelaide's chamber. Ma fear is he will kill Lady Adelaide's sister before assaulting Lady Adelaide." Tate didn't know how else to say that, but bluntly.

"Adelaide and Sarah willna like it, but they'll understand it. I'll post two guards outside their chamber every night." Fingal sighed. He knew neither daughter would be keen on the arrangement, but they wouldn't argue against it.

"Thank ye for listening to me," Tate said as he rose. The others followed him, and he offered his hand, palm up, to Madeline. He leaned over it, proffering an air kiss. When he straightened, he thrust out his arm to Fingal, who didn't hesitate to grasp Tate's forearm. He sensed the man was still wary of him, but Fingal no longer suspected Tate was all charm and no substance. "Goodnight, Lady Madeline, Fingal."

Tate followed Liam out of the solar. Fingal and Madeline stayed back, presumably to discuss what Tate shared.

"Did I do the right thing the right way, Grandda?"

"Aye, lad. I'm proud of ye for speaking up. Fingal isnae an easy mon to approach on the best of days. He softened when he wed Lady Madeline, but he can still be pricklier than a porcupine during winter. Are ye worried ye didna represent the family well? Ye sound a wee off."

"After the way I reacted to Ailish teasing me, I fear I painted the family and the clan in a poor light. I dinna want anyone to think Mama and Da didna raise me properly. Since ye raised Da, it would make ye look bad, too."

"Lad, dinna fash. Nay one thought more of it than it was. Two siblings jesting with one another. Mayhap nae the best way, but neither of ye exchanged harsh words ye canna take back. Be more circumspect in the future, but nay harm came from it." Liam embraced his grandson, who bore the closest resemblance to him of all the young men with his barrel chest. He suspected Wiley would soon rival Tate for that position, but his younger grandson still had a more youthful face. Tate gladly returned the affection before Liam headed back upstairs, and Tate made his way to the bailey. When he stepped outside the barmkin, he swept his gaze over everything he could see. He didn't spy Adam, but intuition told him the man was nearby. He could only imagine the lies the man would devise to spread if he saw Tate leaving the keep after already claiming Tate was bedding Adelaide. He'd already prayed that if Adam saw him going into the bailey, he'd also heard Tate claim he had a message for Liam. He prayed for the same thing again. Otherwise, there would be nothing left of Adelaide's reputation.

CHAPTER 9

delaide watched her cousins and their extended family walking toward the caber toss. She wished she could spend the time with them, but her brothers refused to consider it once they learned Adam was still competing. She put up no argument since her interest in watching the competition waned the more she thought about it. She and her three guards wandered toward the children's races. She recognized Fergus's younger brothers with their shock of red hair and freckles. She waved as they ran toward her.

"Is Fergus coming to watch ye?" Adelaide asked.

"Nay, but Mama and Papa are." Adelaide couldn't remember the lad's name, but he was the second youngest.

"Aye. And Papa's announcing Fergus and Lady Clara's betrothal this eve," the youngest Matheson proclaimed.

There were still a few more days left to the gathering, so Adelaide hadn't realized they would make the announcement so soon. But she supposed it was no secret to anyone that the couple would wed since they were practically inseparable. She was certain Laird

MacDonald likely thought it was better to make it official than have speculation spread through the clans.

"That's exciting." Adelaide nodded her head along with the children. They turned and ran back to the starting line for the upcoming foot race. She spied Laird and Lady Matheson, but she didn't know them well enough to mingle or watch alongside them as their sons raced. As she glanced around, she realized she only knew the other spectators in passing. She'd told the others she would be fine watching the races alone, and now she would prove that to herself, hoping to convince herself that it wasn't as lonely as it likely looked since she had no family in the races.

She could hear the cheers from the people watching the caber toss, but she forced her attention forward. As the children's races began, she found herself waving and calling out encouragement, just like everyone else. It reminded her of her childhood and how carefree the world seemed. Now she wondered what her future held. The more she thought about it, the more uncertainty clawed at her belly. Her parents would push her into nothing, but she knew she needed to turn her attention to finding a husband.

As if conjured by her daydreams, she watched Tate and Wiley sprint toward the caber toss area. It was only then that she noticed the noise coming from the crowd no longer sounded like cheers. It sounded like a fight was about to erupt. Adelaide warned herself to stay away, but curiosity—the devil on her shoulder—was far louder than common sense—the angel on her shoulder. She hurried forward, and it only took one glance to see the problem. It wasn't a fight, after all.

A Campbell competitor must have lost his balance and fallen backward. The caber, which landed on top of him, trapped him beneath it. She watched as Magnus, Blake, and Tor lifted the massive log as though it were merely a twig. Laird and Lady Campbell rushed forward, and Adelaide spotted her clan's healer running toward the injured man. She scanned the crowd and spotted her brothers. She asked politely for people to move, and when that didn't work, she pushed through the crowd.

"One of ye needs to find Da. The other needs to organize a litter to carry the mon to the Campbells' tents. Dinna stand there gauping like a beached fish." Adelaide tipped her head away from the crowd. Angus and Harry forced their attention away from the scene before them and hurried to follow Adelaide's suggestions. She continued to look around until her gaze met Tate's. She saw relief in his expression, and she realized he must have heard about the accident and feared the wayward caber injured his uncle or cousins. She observed his exhale, then his slight nod to her. She broke their stare when she felt someone wrap their arm around hers. She looked to her left to find Clara following where her gaze landed only moments ago.

"With all this distraction, ye shouldnae be here, Ada. Peter and Adam are watching ye. This would be the perfect chance for them to approach ye since nay one is paying attention to aught but that poor warrior." Clara tugged on Adelaide's arm before they both turned around. Adelaide found Finley and Sarah right behind her. They were watching something over her shoulder, but it wasn't the injured competitor. She glanced back and found Peter and Adam glaring at her. A vise tightened around her, and she recognized it as fear. She put up no resistance when her sisters and friend led her away from the crowd.

"I'm going to the kitchens. I'll find something to do there," Adelaide explained.

"There arenae any more games until tomorrow. I'll come with ye," Finley offered.

"Mama wants me to help in the storerooms. I need to find guards to come with me." Sarah pointed to two Grant warriors and hurried along the path toward them. The other two Grant sisters walked with Clara until she found members of her clan, then they made their way to the kitchens with their own guards in tow. The rest of the day flew by, and Adelaide found herself rushing to refresh herself and change before the evening meal. As she chose her kirtle, she remembered the menacing expressions the Chisholm brothers wore. She recalled her visceral reaction. She was certain they were about to act on their anger toward her, but she couldn't guess how.

I wish I kenned where Tate was.

That thought shocked her. It shocked her even more when her reaction was to tell herself that it shouldn't shock her. He'd taken up residence in her mind far more often than was wise. But whenever he was near, she felt calm. Even the first day of the Gathering when they encountered one another outside the stables, and he'd irritated her. She'd felt comfortable with him, and for the brief moment he'd had his hands on her to lift her out of the muck, she felt protected. When they'd ridden out with Clara and Fergus, she'd enjoyed his company while they spoke. He'd lifted her into the saddle as though she were as light as a child, the muscles tense beneath the leine that stretched across them.

Foolish. Foolish. Foolish. Even if Da didna warn me away, he isnae any more interested in me than any of his married cousins would be. I've seen him chatting and smiling at the other unwed lasses he dances with. Some are even outside his family. He jests and smiles often. The times we've stood or danced together havenae meant aught to him. Even if I've thought him the funniest, kindest, most trustworthy, most loyal, and brawest mon for years. Even if I have har-

bored these thoughts since I was a lass, and they only grow stronger each day. Useless.

She glanced at herself in the looking glass before meeting her guards in the passageway. She resolved not to dance that night. She didn't want to encounter Peter or Adam, nor did she want to dance with Tate. She feared she'd appear like a lovesick calf if she went near him. She arrived in the Great Hall just as Fergus burst through the keep's main doors. Tate and Peter were close behind. Tate appeared ready to murder someone, and Fergus's face was flushed magenta. Peter sneered at everyone.

What the bluidy hell happened?

* * *

"Fergus, hurry up. Ye're going to be late to yer own betrothal announcement." Tate tried not to tap his toes in annoyance. His belly rumbled, and he wished to get to his family's table before they left only scraps. "Ye're bonnie enough already."

"Bonnie? Arse." Fergus stepped out of the tent. His hair was freshly washed and still damp. He wore his best leine and plaid, and Tate admitted the man looked better than usual. His friend practically vibrated with excitement.

"Let's go." Tate led them toward the keep, taking them past the MacDonald tents. He came to an abrupt stop when Peter hurried toward them, then blocked their path. The man didn't look at Tate, instead focusing on Fergus.

"Uh, ye dinna want to go this way. A Chisholm was ill and—uh—ye dinna want to see or smell it. He drank too much with one of the MacDonalds." Peter grimaced and pointed to the other side of the tent they stood near.

"Fine," Tate huffed. The sun hadn't set since it was summer, but evening approached. If Tate couldn't tell from the waning daylight, then his stomach reminded him as it rumbled again. They changed course and walked toward a tent with a candle lit within. It cast the occupants in a shadow that made it clear exactly what was happening between the man and woman. The sounds coming from it didn't help.

"What the fuck?" Fergus bellowed. The people in the tent froze. But Fergus's bellow didn't stop them for long. A long feminine moan filled the air before a deep grunt punctuated the couple's finish.

Tate looked over at Fergus, shocked with the rage in his normally even-tempered friend. Fergus stormed forward, a slew of curses spewing from him, directed at the couple inside the tent. When Tate heard Clara's name mixed into Fergus's rant, he realized whose tent they passed. He couldn't—wouldn't—believe Clara was unfaithful to Fergus. But his friend clearly believed that was what he'd just witnessed. Tate glanced back at Peter, catching smugness in the man's expression before false concern replaced it.

"I—I didna ken—I wouldnae—" Peter stuttered. Tate didn't believe for a moment that Peter hadn't orchestrated them passing the tent.

When Fergus burst into a run, Tate and Peter picked up their pace to keep stride of the furious warrior. He couldn't understand why Fergus's reaction was to run toward the keep rather than confront whoever was inside the tent. It made no sense to him. Tate looked over his shoulder toward the tent, but no one was there. He hadn't seen the man or the woman, so it tempted him to go back and discover who was truly there. But he didn't trust Fergus alone with Peter. He'd seen his friend angry before, but he'd never seen Fergus in the state he was in now. When they reached the top of the keep's steps, Tate was unprepared for how Fergus would fling the doors open. One hit the inside wall and flew back toward Tate. He barely caught it before it crashed into his face.

"Ah! Here's the groom just in time for the announcement." Laird Matheson stood on the dais beside Laird MacDonald. Fergus stormed forward, taking the steps two at a time. Tate looked around and spied Clara rushing forward, having come inside right behind them. He cringed inside, since she was smoothing her hair back as she hurried to take her spot on the dais.

"The only announcement being made is that I willna marry the harlot. Give nae this rotten turnip to me and mine. She has played me false, and I will nae take her to ma bed for her to bear me a bastard." Fergus stopped before his father and the man who was to be his father-by-marriage until only a second ago.

"What do ye mean, lad?" Laird Matheson's brow furrowed.

"Aye! What do ye mean, Fergus?" Clara lifted her skirts as she stumbled up the steps. Fergus watched her, doing nothing to help as she lost her balance. Tate caught her elbow as he hurried to reach her.

"I saw ye, ye—ye—whore."

His mind scrambled to catch up with the scene before him. That morning, Fergus would have murdered anyone who dared call Clara a harlot or a whore. Now he flung the words will malice.

"Fergus!" Laird MacDonald stepped between Fergus and Clara, reaching for the man who insulted his daughter. Clara latched onto her father's arm, tugging as hard as she could. It pulled her onto her toes, and her irate father still managed to grasp the front of Fergus's leine.

"Da, nay. Dinna hit him," Clara begged.

"I'm nae going to hit him. I'm going to kill him for his lies," Laird MacDonald growled.

"Fergus, what are ye talking aboot? What have I done?"

"I saw ye. Tate saw ye. Even bluidy Peter saw ye."

"Saw me doing what? Fergus, I dinna understand."

"We saw ye fucking," Fergus announced, and Tate doubted the man could speak any louder if he tried.

"Nay!" Clara screamed. "I wasna!"

Tate watched Adelaide push back her chair hard enough it almost toppled off the back of the dais. She ran around the table and wrapped her arms around her friend as Clara sagged.

"I saw ye in yer tent with another mon. I'm certain it was yer tent. Ye had a candle lit, and I could see everything. Like a maiden, ye blush now, but ye canna cover yer conniving sin." Fergus looked out at the silenced crowd. "Her blush is guiltiness, nae modesty." He turned back to Clara. "Ye come rushing in here after me, smoothing back yer hair and shaking out yer skirts. Ye ken what ye did."

"Nay. I wanted to look ma best for ye and in front of everyone. I didna do aught of the sort."

"Ye have with me already," Fergus hurled at her.

Laird MacDonald reared back his fist, and it took Tate, Laird Matheson, and Peter to keep the Mac-Donald from launching himself at Fergus. "Ye defiled ma daughter!"

"And she loved every moment of it, every time."

"Fergus," Adelaide hissed. She shot Tate a beseeching look, but she didn't know what he could do. She held Clara as sobs wracked her friend's body.

"Tate, tell them what ye saw," Fergus demanded.

Tate looked at Adelaide before looking out at the stunned crowd who barely breathed. "I saw a couple in

Lady Clara's tent. But I dinna ken who it was. I didna see a face, hear any voices, or hear a name."

"Ye heard the bitch moaning like a common wench. I willna stitch ma soul to such a proven wanton." Fergus glowered at Clara. Tate shook his, disbelief at his friend's actions pulsing through him along with growing anger of his own.

"I heard a *woman*, but I dinna ken who. Fergus, it couldnae be Lady Clara. She would never betray ye like this." Tate spun toward Peter. "Ye. Ye wanted us to go that way. I'd wager ma best dirk there wasna a Mac-Donald who was ill near where we walked. Ye blocked our way to force us near that tent."

Peter crossed his arms and shrugged. "The mon should ken the woman he was aboot to marry."

"Fergus," Adelaide interjected. "Tate is right. Clara would never do such a thing."

"So ye say. But it's too bad a midwife canna prove it."

Clara lurched out of Adelaide's arms and flailed at Fergus. "That's nae true. Ye ken we never. I've never."

Her father had to lift her off her feet and turn away from Fergus to keep her nails from sinking into the man she loved until only minutes earlier—minutes before he hurled false accusations that would ruin her life. It wouldn't just prevent a marriage to Fergus. It would keep her from marrying anyone. No reputable nobleman would agree to marrying an allegedly unchaste woman.

"Come, Clara. Let's go to ma chamber," Adelaide whispered as she tried to pull Clara from her father's arms.

"Nay. I wish to ken which mon it was ye claim I was with." Clara turned toward the crowd. "Who laid with me?"

"Ye werenae lying down. He was fucking ye from behind like a bitch in heat."

Tate stepped in front of Fergus, his disgust no longer in check. He kept his voice low, but it was a tone that brooked no refusal. "Enough. Ye've destroyed the lass's life. Now ye're aboot to do the same to yers. Nay father will marry his daughter to a mon who speaks this way aboot a woman. Cease."

"She destroyed mine. I loved her. I trusted her. I was prepared to give her ma clan's name. Better I found out now than after some other mon sired a child she'd pass off as mine." Fergus didn't lower his voice like Tate had.

Clara wailed before her knees gave out. Adelaide and Tate both saw Fergus waver as he nearly stepped toward Clara. Pain and fear replaced the rage. Clara saw it too because she reached for him. In her despair, she still wanted Fergus before anyone else. But he caught himself and sneered at her. Adelaide struggled but maneuvered her friend toward the dais stairs. Finley and Sarah rushed forward to help Adelaide as they half dragged, half carried Clara up the stairs to Adelaide's chamber.

Tate watched the women, catching Adelaide's gaze when the women reached the landing, and she looked back down. She shrugged with eyes wide in shock, utterly unsure what to make of the scene. He shot her a brief frown, as uncertain as she was. Tate clutched Fergus's arm as his friend's fists furled and unfurled. Not a word of it made any sense to Tate. None of Fergus's actions made sense. Not just his words but his rationale for storming inside rather than investigating. Tate wondered if Fergus's mind knew he couldn't manage seeing Clara in such a damning action if it had been her. He'd chosen flight over fight. This wasn't the man Tate had ridden into battle with.

"Let's go." Tate yanked on Fergus's arm, then led

him off the dais. He looked for his family, spotting them easily. Their shocked expressions mirrored how he felt. He caught his father's attention, then his grand-father's. Both men nodded as Tate hauled Fergus to-ward the doors. Just before they stepped outside, Tate looked back at Laird Matheson and Laird MacDonald. Neither spoke. Both men were too in shock to do or say anything. Their children were miserable, and the alliance had crumbled.

Tate scanned the crowd and spied Peter whispering to his father. He was certain they gloated. Nothing about the situation felt right to Tate. Peter got involved for a reason, and it wouldn't surprise Tate if Peter engi-neered the entire thing. But he had no way to prove it since he didn't know either person who was in the tent. The only thing he was positive about was that it wasn't Clara.

CHAPTER 10

" *How* could he say such wretched lies?" Clara whispered, curled on Adelaide's bed. She'd repeated herself at least a dozen times as Adelaide stroked her hair. Sarah kept dampening and applying a cool compress to Clara's forehead. Finley did her best to stay out of the way. None of the women knew what to say to ease the gut wrenching sobs Clara produced. Adelaide shrugged at her sisters when they looked to her for guidance. It was the same response she'd given Tate since she was at a loss for what to do.

All four women froze when someone knocked. Finley looked to Adelaide, who nodded. The youngest Grant daughter opened the door an inch to look outside, then opened it wide enough for Madeline and Lady MacDonald to enter. The latter went to her daughter and scooped Clara into her arms. Madeline and her daughters watched as Lady MacDonald cooed and comforted Clara. Adelaide leaned against Madeline, feeling utterly adrift by the turn of events. Never could she have imagined the night unraveling as it did.

She'd heard what Tate said to quieten Fergus, and he'd been entirely right. Fergus had ruined Clara's life.

They all knew it as though it were a leaden weight pressing down on all six women's shoulders. The unfairness that men could act as they pleased before they married, and women couldn't, settled in Adelaide's heart. She wondered if the man she married would have already sired any bastards.

Tate hasnae. I dinna need to ask to ken that. Nay mon in his immediate or extended family would. I canna consider his brother or cousins. But mayhap a Sutherland or MacLeod. There arenae any Mackenzies of an age to marry. Mayhap a Cameron. There are still two unwed Mackays. But none of them are Tate. Bluidy hell, Adelaide. Ye're fantasizing aboot who ye might wed when yer best friend just lost the one mon she wished to marry. Selfish.

Adelaide turned her attention back to Clara and Lady MacDonald. She watched them before looking up at Madeline. She whispered to her mother. "Clara must leave. Who kens what some mon'll get in his head now that everyone believes she's loose with her favors. She needs to get away from Fergus before the mon says aught else. I dinna trust her mind nae to tell her to leap from a parapet."

"I ken. Emily." Madeline tilted her head to a corner as Lady MacDonald looked up. She nodded tiredly, having seemed to age in the five minutes she'd been in the chamber. Adelaide slipped into her place and held Clara, who continued to cry but no longer sobbed. She stared blankly into space, and that frightened Adelaide more than anything else had.

"Ada."

"Wheest, Clara. It'll all come right."

"Nay, it willna. I canna stay here."

"We ken. We'll sort it out."

"I want to go to a convent."

"What? Nay. Dinna decide something so rashly. Ye

go home, where ye are safe and loved. Then ye decide yer future." Adelaide shook her head, displeased by her friend's announcement. While it might very well be where Clara wound up, Adelaide didn't want her friend trapping herself in a life of silence and solitude without fully considering the ramifications.

Madeline and Emily whispered back and forth before approaching the bed. Madeline came to stand beside Adelaide and rested her hand on her daughter's shoulder. "After everyone retires, we'll smuggle Clara out of the keep. Angus, Harry, and Da will get her out of the gate. Lady MacDonald is going to tell Laird Mac-Donald to send out their sons right now before the portcullis closes. They'll meet our men, and all of them will stay with Clara. We tell everyone else that Clara has taken ill and remains in the keep to recover. The Gathering will be over in four days' time. The Mac-Donalds will ride out after everyone else leaves that way nay one can ask why Clara isnae with them."

"What aboot the alliance, Mama?" Clara finally sat up.

Lady MacDonald sighed, clearly not wanting to tell her daughter whatever came next. "Yer father and Laird Matheson already agreed Agnes will marry Fergus."

"Ma sister?" Clara sounded as though someone strangled her as she choked out the two words.

"Aye. But Agnes willna go through with it. It saves face for us, but Laird Matheson must ken we'd never truly agree to it. We'll pay the dowry if we must, but we wouldnae wed yer sister to yer mon."

"But he's nae ma mon anymore," Clara wailed. "If nae Agnes, then he'll marry someone else. He'll love someone else. He'll sire bairns with someone else. He'll grow auld with someone else. And I will have naught. I wish I were dead."

"Wheest!" Adelaide held Clara again. "Dinna ever say that again. Nae because it's a sin to do such, but because none of us can imagine ye nae being with us. I would miss ye, and ye'd create such a hole in so many hearts."

"I have nay heart left. It stopped beating the moment Fergus accused me. I have naught but a body to drag around. What's the point of that? None. I'd be better off in true hell than the one I'll live in here."

Adelaide's heart beat with such speed that her ribs ached, and she was certain her chest needed to open to let it escape. Nothing about Clara's voice made any of them think she exaggerated her feelings. The women looked at one another, and it was clear none would allow Clara to be alone.

"Dinna bother telling Fergus that I feel ill. Tell him I'm dead. I'm sure I am to him, so I may as well be in truth."

"Enough, Clara," Lady MacDonald barked. Tears streamed down her cheeks as she listened to her child and witnessed the sheer agony Clara experienced.

"Tell Fergus that. Tell them all that," Adelaide whispered.

"What?" Madeline demanded.

"Tell Fergus she killed herself. Let him live with that guilt for what he's done. He's ruined her life." Adelaide rose from the bed after easing Clara away from her. She crossed her arms and raised her chin mulishly.

"Ye canna lie aboot something so serious," Lady MacDonald protested.

"Clara's already said she should go to a convent. Even if she goes home with ye and has time to think things through, we all ken there's a good chance she will go to one. Nay one will see or hear from her again. Same as being dead. Except Fergus willna have to take any responsibility for what he's done if people ken

Clara went to a nunnery. He did this, nae Clara. Let the shame rest with him."

"Adelaide, this isnae the solution," Madeline countered. "Ye canna lie aboot something so grave."

"Mayhap ye canna, Mama. But I can and will." Adelaide stared at her mother. Neither woman backed down. Adelaide's lips flattened before she walked back to her mother and drew her aside while Clara lay on the bed with her eyes closed. "Ye ken she isnae as strong as ye were. She will wither away in a convent, nae figure out how to thrive like ye did. Ye went there angry and had that to keep ye going until ye realized there was a better way. Clara doesnae have any anger, and even if it comes, she willna be like ye. She's a strong woman and would have made an excellent Lady Matheson one day. But that's nae the same type of strength that an unwilling person needs to survive a religious cloister. We still sneak her out, but that's so she can go home. She can be a recluse among her people, where she can still be herself. We tell everyone else that she died."

Madeline recognized the truth in what Adelaide explained, and she saw the merit in the suggestion. The thought of lying sat poorly with her, but she convinced herself that enough time in the kirk, praying would be her penance. She and Lady MacDonald locked eyes before they both nodded.

Adelaide exhaled as slowly as she could, hoping it would calm her. It didn't. But she pressed on with her idea. "Mama, ye and Lady MacDonald go back down belowstairs and make it kenned that Clara isnae well enough to go anywhere and is spending the night with me in here. After everyone retires, we sneak Clara out like ye suggested, Mama. Her brothers will already be beyond the walls to meet Da, Angus, and Harry. In the morning, I scream. Once Mama and Da have checked on me. We call Laird and Lady MacDonald to ma chamber. We three emerge from the chamber crying, and Da and Laird MacDonald appear shaken. We announce Clara is dead. We say she killed herself with one of ma dirks while I slept. I didna ken until I woke to find her beside me, ma dirk through her heart."

"Nay. People will question how she had the strength to do that. It isnae easy to thrust a dirk through bone, and it would be even harder to do it to yerself," Madeline stated. "We say she slashed her wrists and cut her throat. Between those two types of wounds, she bled to death."

"Finley, Sarah, can ye keep that secret?" Adelaide asked.

"We're offended ye should even need to ask," Finley replied.

"Nay one can stray from this lie," Adelaide insisted.

"Then dinna tell Tate," Sarah muttered.

"What's that?" Madeline asked.

"Tate Sinclair," Sarah stated. "Adelaide will tell him."

"Why would I do that?" Adelaide's head felt like it floated above her, and her ears felt like they'd become church bells.

"Ye're in love with him." Sarah's tone was so matter of fact that Adelaide could only blink.

"It's true, Ada," Clara whispered her agreement.

"How I feel isnae the issue right now. But I do trust Tate. If aught goes wrong with this, I ken we can count on him. He's Fergus's friend, but he's also reasonable. He's the one who made Fergus stop talking."

"And he's likely to tell Fergus this is all a ruse," Sarah argued.

"Nay, he willna," Madeline interjected. "Tate is an intelligent mon. He will figure out something is amiss. It's better he kens the truth than he speculates and searches for it. Ada, ye can tell him in the morning."

Adelaide nodded. She swept her eyes over everyone in the chamber. There didn't seem to be much left to do but wait for when Clara could slip out, then wait for when Adelaide would scream the roof down. She prayed God would be on their side for this, since it hadn't felt like he was on Clara's tonight.

CHAPTER 11

Tate could barely see straight as he stumbled toward the Sinclairs' tents. He'd shoved Fergus out of the Great Hall and out to the ale tent. He'd filled his friend with enough whisky to keep them both drunk for a sennight. He also kept his friend from tupping any of the wenches, which Fergus suggested more than once. Tate watched as the same woman approached his friend four times, and something felt amiss with the woman. He couldn't tell what it was, but the woman's eyes gave away something.

He'd already dumped Fergus in his tent, and now he tried to weave his way to his own tent without knocking down anyone else's. He concentrated on one foot in front of the other until he believed he was at his temporary home. He debated sticking his head in to be sure he was in the right place, but he feared that would only get it lobbed off if he wasn't. He crouched, then fell onto his side. With a groan, he managed to pull the extra length of plaid over both shoulders and his head.

He'd been certain the moment he was horizontal he'd be asleep. But his mind replayed the scene in the Great Hall over and over. If he'd even remotely conceived what Fergus would say in public, he would have wrestled his friend to the ground and knocked him out before letting him set foot within the bailey. He understood his friend's pain, and he wished he could say he felt it too. But the vile things Fergus hurled at Clara made Tate question how the two men were friends.

If a woman I loved played me for such a fool, I ken I would feel as Fergus does. But I canna imagine ever venting ma spleen in a such a public way or hurting someone I claim to love. Mayhap, it was an eye for an eye, but could Fergus truly love Clara that much if he could be so cruel? I canna imagine speaking to Addy that way.

He pictured himself in Fergus's shoes with Adelaide standing before him on the dais just as Clara had stood before Fergus. Hatefulness wasn't what came to mind. Soul deep sadness did. He didn't think he'd be able to say a thing if he found himself in Fergus's place. That a woman like Adelaide could or would betray him stole his breath and left him with no words.

Why am I picturing her?

"Because ye love her. Now can ye haud yer wheest and come inside before ye wake the entire camp and nae just me?" Wiley stuck his head outside the tent flap.

"What?" Tate struggled to sit up.

"Ye were speaking out loud, ye daft sod."

Tate felt the heat in his cheeks rise as his eyes suddenly cleared from what must have been the top of the whisky line he'd created by filling himself with more alcohol than a barrel could hold. That anyone heard his private thoughts sobered him. But to have Wiley claim he loved Adelaide was disconcerting.

"Ye can think aboot how right I am once ye're inside. Come on." Wiley held the flap open, and Tate crawled in. Tavish, Ceit, and Ailish all sat, watching him. He groaned, not from feeling ill from the whisky —though he did. He couldn't believe his whole family heard him talking to himself. He wondered what members of his extended family heard him, too.

"Where's Fergus?" Ceit whispered.

"In his tent, passed out, Mama."

"Good." Ceit laid back down and rolled over.

Tavish nodded to his son before wrapping himself around his wife and settling back to sleep. Ailish crawled to her brother and whispered to him. "We all see it, but neither of ye do. Dinna waste a chance like Fergus is with Clara." She turned around and returned to her bedroll, leaving Tate's head spinning.

* * *

"CLARA, Da and ma brothers will keep ye safe until ye get to yer brothers." Adelaide wrapped a Grant plaid around Clara's shoulders and head. "Then they'll all ride together. Da's already sent a message to a widow with a croft several leagues from here. She'll let ye stay there as long as ye need. Yer brothers can return here, so nay one questions where they went. I ken the woman, so I'm sure she'll take fine care of ye. Mayhap fed a little too much, but nay worse for wear."

"Thank ye," Clara mouthed. She mounted behind Fingal before the small party left through the postern gate. Finley and Sarah had collected a few food items, and Adelaide packed four of her kirtles for Clara to borrow. The food was enough for the riders to snack upon while they traveled. Adelaide suspected Clara wouldn't eat since she'd refused everything Adelaide offered her before she left. But the men would likely be hungry on the way back.

Adelaide watched them ride out, the stars the only light since it was a new moon. She prayed they reached the croft without trouble. They all hoped Clara would only be sequestered there for four, maybe five days.

Adelaide suspected it might be less since the MacDonalds would claim they wished to bury Clara on their land. She climbed the steps to the battlements and watched her family and Clara ride away.

Instead of returning to the steps, she contemplated the veritable village laid out before her. She watched two men weave as they tried to walk away from the alehouse tent. Immediately, she knew one man was Tate. She couldn't possibly see their faces or their plaids, but she didn't question her belief. She observed as the man she labeled at Tate pushed the other man into a tent. It was a Matheson one, so it confirmed her suspicions. Tate tripped over his own feet several times before he disappeared among the tents. She assumed he'd made it to the correct one since he didn't reappear.

She'd been bone weary before mounting the steps, but felt far better now, seeing Fergus and Tate leave together. She'd feared how Fergus might console himself and that he would do something he couldn't take back once she cleared Clara's name, which she was committed to doing. If he was so inebriated that he could barely stand upright, she felt confident that he hadn't the means to keep something else upright. She also felt confident Tate wouldn't allow Fergus to make such a mistake.

She returned to her chamber for a few hours rest before her eyes sprang open at dawn. She suspected Tate would go to the loch to bathe if he'd spent the night drinking. She hurried to dress before rushing across the bailey to knock on the barracks door. The sentry opened it a crack before recognizing Adelaide.

"Tomas, I need a guard to come with me, please."

"Where are ye going, Lady Adelaide?"

"To the loch."

"Ye canna go there." Adelaide tried not to laugh at

the man's scandalized tone. "There will be men bathing in the altogether."

"I ken. Ma guard can go ahead of me. I willna be able to see around whoever it is. He can stop me before I encounter anyone unclad."

"Why do ye need to head there? Yer da will skelp me alive for assigning anyone, and the poor bastard willna survive the duty."

"I'll make sure Da does naught to either of ye. I promise. There's someone I need to speak to without everyone and their mother kenning."

The guard looked at her speculatively, and she wondered who he suspected she wished to see. She had her answer a moment later.

"Jamie, accompany Lady Adelaide to the loch. Look for the Sinclairs." Tomas cocked an eyebrow, and Adelaide nodded. It frustrated her that everyone seemed to believe something existed between Tate and her when it didn't. She refused to believe any of them because she knew it would only disappoint her. She trailed after Jamie and through the postern gate, then along the path.

"Sinclair," Jamie called out in a stage whisper.

"Aye?"

Adelaide recognized Tate's voice and was about to step around Jamie, but his arm shot out.

"Nae here. Someone wishes to speak to ye, but it canna be near all the men."

Adelaide heard Tate's feet on the path until he came to stand before Jamie. He was half a head taller than her guard, so he easily spied her. His eyes widened before he nodded. She turned around, and when Jamie was certain Tate concealed her from the back, he stepped in front of Adelaide. He led the trio to the far corner of the keep that sat on a ledge above the loch. Before they reached the wall, Jamie stopped. Adelaide gestured for Tate to follow her.

"We arenae going out on that ledge, Addy. It's nae safe for ye."

"I've been out here plenty of times. I'm nae scared, and I'm certain ye arenae either."

"Mayhap that's true, but that doesnae mean it's wise to tempt fate." Tate refused to budge, and he snagged Adelaide's arm when she continued to walk away. He pulled her back. She spun straight into his chest. His free hand rested on her waist as she gazed up at him. "What do ye need, lass?"

Did his voice sound huskier?

Their thoughts matched, even if neither of them spoke it out loud. Adelaide's hands rested on his chest. As much as she didn't want to pull away after feeling the heat of his damp skin, she knew she had to. Not for propriety's sake, but so she could think straight.

"Fine. We can stay here, but we must whisper. I need to tell ye something, and I need ye to swear ye willna tell anyone."

"If I can, I will swear to that."

"I need ye to swear before I tell ye."

"Nay. I canna do that. I willna give ma word to something without kenning what it is."

Adelaide's admiration soared. She knew he took his integrity seriously, but it also meant he took whatever she had to say seriously. "I saw ye and Fergus from the battlements last night. I saw ye shove him into his tent, then ye must have found yer tent, too."

"Why were ye up there so late? That isnae safe either, Addy."

"I often go up to the battlements."

"At night?" Tate pressed.

"Nay."

"Good. Even with torches up there, it's nae easy to

see. Someone could spy ye up there and shoot ye with an arrow before the men could spot the archer. The stones get slippery even in summer. It's easy to slip in the dark. Ye could hurt yerself or go over the side. Please dinna go up there at night anymore." Tate didn't notice how his hands tightened on her arm and waist until their bodies brushed together.

"Does it really bother ye that much? Ye sound—I dinna ken. Worried, I suppose."

"Frightened. Kenning ye go up there at night when ye arenae used to where to stand and how to move aboot scares me."

"It's hard to believe aught frightens ye."

"I dinna like picturing ye coming to any harm, Addy."

"Ye call me that when we're alone."

"What?"

"Addy. Ye still call me that. Everyone else who doesnae use ma title calls me Ada."

"I'm sorry. I dinna have the right to be so forward. I willna do it—"

"I like it," Adelaide blurted. She pulled her lips in for a moment before continuing. "Tate, Clara left last night with Da, ma brothers, and her brothers. The men have already returned, but she's at a croft a few leagues away. Our families dinna feel it's safe for her now that Fergus ruined her reputation. She said she wanted to go to a convent, but she also said she wished she wasna alive. I dinna think she exaggerated."

"Ye think she would kill herself?"

"I think she could. And we believe other people think that too. Tate, the MacDonalds and ma family are going to say she killed herself. I must go back inside in a moment and begin the roleplaying."

"Why lie? And such a horrible one?"

"We thought aboot saying she was ill until the Mac-

Donalds leave. But this will allow her to live in peace at home with her family. She can go to a convent if she chooses, but nay one will expect it of her. If she goes, it's because it was her choice. Plus..." Adelaide trailed off as she shifted her focus toward the camp.

"Plus, Fergus should pay for what he's done. Ye wish him to suffer the guilt and shame just like Clara does."

"She only suffers the shame. She isnae guilty of aught. I'm certain of it."

"I'm almost certain, too. Addy, it looked like her. The woman was the right size. Her sister is taller and thinner than her. What other woman would be in her tent?"

"I dinna ken. But it wasna Clara. She wanted to marry Fergus too much. They've talked aboot it for years. She wouldnae throw that away. And what I saw in ma chamber wasna guilt from being caught. It was utter despair." Adelaide shifted her focus back to Tate before she continued. "I told ye, I saw ye leave the ale tent. Did Fergus rut with another woman last night?"

Her bluntness made Tate stare before he shook his head.

"Nay. Between the two of us, he considered it. A wench kept offering, and I think he wished to console himself and feel like he had revenge, but I made certain he didna. I kept plying him with whisky until he could do little more than breathe. We had to wait until we both sobered enough to attempt the walk back to our tents."

"Do ye think he went back after ye left?"

"Nay. I checked before I went to the loch. He was still asleep, and I asked the alehouse keeper. He said the woman left with someone else. None of his wenches left with Fergus."

"Is this a secret ye can keep?"

"Ye mean, is it a lie I will tell?" Tate's whisky-agedin-the-barrel-colored eyes peered into Adelaide's robin egg blue ones. "I will tell the lie and keep yer secret."

"Thank ye." Adelaide had never wished for a man to kiss her more as she stood with Tate. But he let go of her instead of pulling her closer. Disappointment greater than she expected coursed through her. But he didn't look any happier than she did when he took a step back.

Tate nodded before they moved into the open. He wondered if he should have taken the chance and kissed her while they were alone and out of sight, but he knew the guard was nearby. He didn't want the man to report to Fingal that not only had Adelaide been alone and hidden, but her lips were puffy, or her cheeks were pinkened from his beard. He wished to live long enough to help Adelaide.

"What happens next?" Tate wondered.

"I'm slipping back into ma chamber. I will scream, and Mama and Da will rush into ma chamber. Da will fetch Laird and Lady MacDonald, who will come in too. Lady MacDonald will scream and pretend to collapse. Laird MacDonald will take her to their chamber, where she will remain for an hour. Then she will lock herself into ma chamber. Da and the MacDonald will shut themselves into Da's solar with Uncle Edward. Tate, I need ye to be the one to tell Fergus. I want to be there."

"Addy—"

"Nay. I want to see his face when his world falls apart." Adelaide's voice was harsher than she expected, and she flinched. "I am nae someone who usually wants revenge for a wrong. But this—this is so heinous. He should ken what he's done to her life. That he's hurt her as badly as this will hurt him. At least it should hurt if he loved her as much as he claimed."

"I believe he does."

"Did ye ken he's now to marry Agnes?"

"Nay." Tate's head whipped toward the tent village. "He willna marry her sister. That's—that's—"

"Wrong. Aye. But their marriage wasna just for them. It was for the alliance. Their fathers still need that. Since Clara is nay longer an option, Agnes is."

"Does she ken this? Does she ken aboot her sister?" Tate stood aghast.

"Aye to both. I doubt she's pleased, but she'll do what she must."

"Ye canna seriously believe that marriage should happen. It's nae fair to Agnes to live the rest of her life with a mon who loves her sister."

"Mayhap he doesnae love Clara, after all. Mayhap, he'll be happier with Agnes."

Tate stared at Adelaide, and she didn't believe what she said either. "Addy, someone set this in motion. Why was Peter suddenly there and pointing us toward Clara's tent? He wasna doing it to help Fergus."

"Do ye think he did this to weaken the Mathesons?"

Tate hesitated before he nodded. "If pressed, Peter will claim he was protecting his clan's allies, the Mac-Donalds."

"If ye were Fergus, could ye humble yerself enough to beg forgiveness once we all ken whoever it was in the tent?"

"I would never treat a woman the way Fergus treated Clara. It was like looking at a stranger. But aye, I could be that humble if it sets things to rights. But I dinna ken if Fergus can be. I pray he can, but I just dinna ken anymore. If ye were Clara, could ye forgive Fergus?"

"I dinna think I could, but I believe Clara can. As distraught as she was, she understood he lashed out from pain. She kenned it because she was feeling the same thing."

"If Peter and the Chisholms were involved in this, if they concocted and acted out a farce, there will be a battle."

"Is it one ye would ride into?"

"I dinna ken. I might as Fergus's friend, but I canna say I would as a Sinclair. I dinna think Grandda or Uncle Callum would agree that it's our fight. But if someone wronged Fergus like he did Clara, then I will stand beside him. But only if he will make things right with the MacDonalds. Mayhap Clara willna forgive him. Mayhap he will have to marry Agnes. I dinna ken. I willna ride into battle to support him if he willna admit and beg forgiveness for the wrong done to Clara. It willna just be the Chisholms who must make amends."

Adelaide nodded. She respected Tate's loyalty to his friend, but she also respected that it had boundaries. She was certain his faith and support would always be blind for his family, but that didn't extend to outsiders. He was no one's fool.

"I must get inside before anyone spots me out here. Tate, thank ye. I truly mean that."

"I'll do whatever I can to help ye, Addy. I'll stand beside ye."

Adelaide's heart hiccupped as she took in what Tate left unsaid. He had put no qualifiers on his support for her. "I'll see ye later."

She hurried away and signaled her guard. Tate watched her disappear through the postern gate before looking around. No one appeared to look in his direction, but when he entered the camp, he spotted Peter and Adam watching him.

$\mathcal{A}$ scream rent the air as Adelaide stood with her door open only a sliver. She heard voices in the Great Hall below, and people moving toward the stairs. "Da! Mama!"

She screamed for her parents, even louder and with more urgency than she had when Peter threatened her the last time they danced. She heard pounding footsteps coming up the stairs and a door slam down the passageway.

"Adelaide!" Madeline called out.

"Mama, hurry. It's Clara. Hurry."

"I'm coming, Ada!" Fingal bellowed.

She stepped aside as her parents burst into the chamber. Madeline's scream raised the hair on Adelaide's arms. If she didn't know better, she would think a dead body really lay on her bed from the way her mother sounded. Fingal nodded to his wife and daughter before turning on his heels.

"Where's the MacDonald?" Fingal roared.

A soft knock sounded, almost too hard to hear over Fingal's voice. "It's me. Davina."

Madeline opened the door to the older woman, who was also in on the plot. As Lady Grant, people would expect Davina to help with the crisis. The women stood together in silence until someone pounded on the chamber door. Madeline opened it and stepped aside as the MacDonalds and Edward entered. Yet another woman's high-pitched wail filled the room.

Adelaide had noticed Grant guards stationed at the top of the stairs, so no one could get past. A crowd of lairds and ladies gathered already. Laird MacDonald scooped his wife into his arms as she squeezed her nose to make it red. She blinked until tears welled in her eyes. Then Madeline opened the door for the couple.

"Ma lass. Ma lass," Lady MacDonald muttered over and over as her husband carried her up to their guest chamber.

"Do I go now?" Adelaide asked her parents and her aunt and uncle.

"Aye. Find Tate, then go to Fergus. If anyone asks why ye went to Tate first, tell them ye either feared telling Fergus alone and kenned Tate can control Fergus. Or ye believed Fergus deserved to have a friend there. Say whichever one makes sense for how Fergus reacts. Go."

Adelaide slipped from the chamber, gathering her skirts. "Let me through!"

She hadn't expected the number of people that gathered on the stairs, trying to peer into her chamber. She heard the whispers but couldn't make out what most people said. She soon realized there was no way she would make it down the main stairway with so many people clogging the narrow area. She changed course and sprinted to the servants' stairs, realizing it was better to be less conspicuous. She ran across the bailey, signaling Jamie to come with her.

With her guard beside her, she navigated her way through the tents to the Sinclairs' area. She wasn't sure where Tate was, so she stopped when she saw two of his aunts. "Ma ladies, have ye seen Tate?"

The women turned toward her; their expressions muted. They seemed neither surprised nor expectant when they found a young woman asking for their nephew. The woman with strawberry-blonde hair responded.

"He's with the Mathesons."

"Thank ye, Lady Siùsan."

Before she could leave, the woman with honey-colored, spiral-curly hair held up her hand. "What's amiss?"

"It's Lady Clara. She—she—I need to find Tate then Fergus, Lady Deirdre. It canna wait."

Adelaide noted the women's surprise, but she didn't wait to leave. She didn't want anyone else to tell Fergus what they might have heard. She spotted the men as Fergus bent over to retch.

"Fergus! Fergus!" She called out and waved her hands over her head. The man slowly stood, scowling at her.

"What the hell do ye want?" Fergus snapped at her.

"Fergus," Tate warned. He softened his tone to Adelaide. "What's wrong?"

Adelaide burst into tears she didn't know were just below the surface. Tate stepped forward, unprepared for Adelaide's response. He didn't think she pretended. He worried something really had happened to Clara. He wrapped his arm around her shoulders and pressed her against his side.

"Lass?"

Adelaide sagged against Tate, but she continued to watch Fergus. "She's gone."

Fergus's face drained of all color. "Who?"

"Clara. She said she didna want to live anymore. That since her heart was dead, she may as well be too. I didna think she really meant it. I never would have gone to sleep if I'd kenned she was serious. She's gone, Fergus. She's gone."

She turned into Tate's chest and clung to his leine. "Shh, Addy. It's all right."

"Nay, it's nae. It'll never be all right." She leaned away from Tate and looked at Fergus. Tears streamed down his cheeks. "Ye were so sure of something that couldnae have happened. I canna understand how ye could be so positive it was Clara without seeing it with yer own eyes. Nae through a tent but truly see her. Ye guessed at best, and now she's gone. Ye didna love her."

"I did," Fergus insisted.

"Nay, ye didna. If ye could turn from her so easily, accuse her of something so heinous before the whole Gathering when ye ken she loved ye, then ye didna feel for her what ye claimed. Now what are ye going to do? Find some other woman to marry?"

Fergus swayed as he held his head in his hands and shook it. "They want me to wed Agnes. I canna. I couldnae last night when Da told me, and I canna now that ma Clara is gone."

Adelaide wrenched away from Tate and stepped in front of Fergus. "Dinna ye ever call her yers ever again, ye bastard. Ye have nay right." Anger she didn't know she'd controlled the previous night and that morning when she spoke to Tate poured forth. "I would say I hope ye have a miserable life, but that means sentencing Agnes to the same misery. She doesnae deserve that, and ye dinna deserve Agnes any more than ye deserved Clara. I hope ye die feeling the same way Clara surely felt last night. A dirk in the back and an arrow through the heart."

"Addy." Tate pulled her away, but she fought him. He stepped forward, his chest pressing against her back as he wrapped his arms around her. The moment she felt his larger size engulf her, she spun around. He nudged her head to rest against his chest as he stroked her hair. He was certain she didn't pretend the pain she felt. This was no performance for Fergus's sake.

"Tate, I'm never going to see her again," Adelaide whimpered. She knew it was unlikely she ever would. She could think of no reason she would go to the Mac-Donald keep. Clara wouldn't be able to leave her clan's land, even if she could escape the keep from time to time.

"I want to see her," Fergus demanded.

"Nay. Stay away from her. Ye did enough to her in life. Dinna do aught more to her now that she's gone. Let her be in peace."

"Peace?" Fergus demanded. "She's in hell."

"Aye. Right where ye put her," Adelaide snapped.

"This canna be right."

"Miss her now?" Adelaide sneered.

"I've missed her since the moment I saw her in that tent."

"Ye didna fucking see her!" Adelaide twisted in Tate's arms, ready to strike Fergus if she could reach. "Ye are the dumbest mon alive if ye dinna think Peter Chisholm had something to do with this. He just appears and happens to send ye near Clara's tent. Where is he this morning? He isnae here consoling ye. Tate is. He wasna the one trying to keep ye from ramming yer cock wherever it'll fit. Tate was. Och aye, it doesnae take much to guess that's what ye were thinking to do in the alehouse last night. Where is yer great friend who cared so much that he had to show ye how the only woman who would have ever loved yer worthless arse was betraying ye? Where the fuck is he, Fergus?"

Tate stared down at Adelaide, shocked by the venom in her voice. She looked up at him, remorse entering her eyes as they stared at one another.

"I dinna usually curse like that," Adelaide whispered. Then she wrapped her arms around Tate and closed her eyes. His hand pressed her cheek against his chest again. Her eyes flew open when Fergus whimpered.

"I should be holding Clara right now, like Tate's holding ye. I should be loving her just as ye love each other. What have I done?" Fergus fell to his knees, his head once more in his hands, as he rocked back and forth.

Adelaide tilted her head back, and Tate wiped a tear from her cheekbone. He kissed her forehead, and she melted against him. He leaned over to whisper in her ear. "We'll talk later, lass. I need to deal with him, even if I dinna want to let go of ye. Are ye well enough to make it back to the keep?"

"I dinna want to let go either. Canna he sort himself out?" Adelaide sighed. "Aye. I can make it back. Tate, for Clara's sake, I have to ken what Peter did."

"I ken. Wait for me by the postern gate. Let me get him to his family, then I'll come to ye."

Adelaide nodded before she let go of Tate. "Fergus, if she were still with us, what would ye do?"

"Beg forgiveness until I breathed ma last. I thought the pain I felt last night was the most excruciating I'd ever felt. Far worse than any sword or knife wound. But this? I dinna ken that I can survive it. I'd rather be with Clara. I want to be with Clara."

"None of that," Tate admonished as he moved to help his friend to his feet. He and Adelaide exchanged a glance. Neither wanted Fergus to kill himself, even if Adelaide still wished for him to suffer a little longer.

"Do ye believe she would forgive ye, Fergus?" Adelaide pressed. She knew she hadn't actually said Clara was dead. She'd said Clara was gone. It wasn't a euphemism. Clara had left Freuchie Castle. She'd insinuated it but stopped just short of lying.

"I dinna ken. I want to believe she would. That she could understand why I was so out of ma mind with hurt. I just want Clara back. Why couldnae I have any sense last night? Ye're right aboot Peter being there but nae being here now. Why would I believe a bluidy Chisholm? I dinna believe Clara did this out of guilt. I shamed her and destroyed her just like Tate said. I may as well have slain her maself."

Tate lunged forward when Fergus yanked a dirk from his belt and pointed it toward himself. Adelaide feared one of them would die when Tate and Fergus wrestled over control. She covered her mouth when Tate's fist slammed into Fergus's temple, and the latter went limp. Tate rose to his feet with grace Adelaide didn't expect. He pulled the knife from his friend's hands and shoved it into the sheath on Fergus's belt. He bent forward and hefted the unconscious man onto his shoulder.

"Meet me at the postern gate in fifteen minutes." Tate watched Adelaide nod, then he headed to find Fergus's family. He wanted done with this mess, so he could concentrate on whether Adelaide might feel a fraction of what Fergus claimed. What Wiley claimed. What Ailish claimed. After holding her, he was certain how he felt. He just didn't think she reciprocated.

* * *

"LAIRD MACDONALD, I told Fergus. Tate was with him. Fergus—I dinna ken what's going to happen to the mon. He pulled a dirk and was ready to stab himself in the heart. He would have if Tate hadnae been there. He regrets what he's done. It's a shame regrets dinna undo the past." Adelaide stood in her parents' solar, next to her mother's desk. The clan council still met in Edward's solar, so this chamber wasn't as spacious. But there was still enough room for Edward, Davina, Fingal, Madeline, Laird and Lady MacDonald, and Adelaide.

"Regret willna heal ma daughter's heart or give her, her life back," Lady MacDonald hissed.

"Andrew, the lass asked over and over if she could come back if Fergus came to his senses." Fingal frowned before continuing. "She's a far sight more forgiving than I think I could be. She seems to understand why he acted that way and has even accepted it. I think she would reconcile with him. Nae because she's desperate to have him. Nae because she's blind to reality. I believe she sees her pain in him, and she doesnae want either of them to suffer."

"She might forgive easily, but I dinna." Laird MacDonald fisted his hands on the arms of his chair.

Adelaide rubbed her fingers over her left eyelid, her head hurting. She wanted to escape the chamber and meet Tate. Her grief over what had transpired in the past twelve hours had shocked her when she burst into tears. Her anger had been entirely genuine, and she needed Tate nearby, lest she dive too deep into those emotions.

"Are ye going to marry Agnes to him?" Madeline wondered.

"If I do, it'll be a long betrothal before aught happens to make the marriage binding," Laird MacDonald fumed. He hadn't wanted to agree to Agnes replacing Clara, and he certainly didn't think he owed the Mathesons anything, but he needed them to strengthen the MacDonalds' trade routes. He'd considered marrying Agnes to Adam to solidify his alliance with the Chisholms. He would have done that after allying with the Mathesons. He hoped he could broker a truce between them as well. It would bring his clan more income, and it would have ensured both his daughters would have been safe from their enemy raiding their new clans. Now he had only one marriageable daughter, and two candidates for her groom whom he despised.

"Mama," Adelaide whispered. "May I go?"

Madeline kissed her daughter's temple before she nodded. Adelaide slipped from the chamber and moved along the passageway that took her to the gardens. She slipped through the gate and along the wall to the postern gate. She spotted Tate immediately. She didn't realize how much she feared he'd change his mind until she spied him waiting for her. She had no warrior accompanying her when she was with her parents, and she hadn't requested one come with her.

"Tate, I dinna have a guard with me."

Tate looked past her to where he could see into the bailey. "Do ye wish to get one?"

"Nay. I feel safer with ye than I do with a slew of Grant men." She couldn't believe what she'd just admitted. Her cheeks flushed.

They walked toward the pasture where the archery tournaments had been. They'd suspended the games that day, so few people milled around. Adelaide steered them to the far side where an oat field met the wooden fencing. The grain was tall, so the crops disguised them as they wandered farther from the keep. Tate slid his hand into Adelaide's when he knew no one could see them. When they walked far enough into the field that no one would easily recognize them, he tugged her to a stop. Then they were in each other's arms.

"Addy, I want to kiss ye. I have since last summer. But if that isnae what ye want, then I will let ye go. If ye want only to talk, I willna pressure ye for aught more."

"I wanted ye to kiss me last summer just like I want that now. But I didna think ye were interested," Adelaide confessed.

"Wee one, I've been interested for years. Last year was when I thought I might let ye ken. But ye didna seem like ye'd welcome it, so I kept it to maself. Then ye told me when I arrived that yer da warned ye away from me. I didna want to do aught to get ye in trouble with yer da."

"I've been interested for a long time, too. But ye laugh and smile at everyone. I didna think ye saw me as anyone special."

"Ye are the most special." Tate cupped her cheek as his other arm tightened around her. "Everyone else seems to have seen what we couldnae."

"Aye. Clara said something last night aboot us. Ma sisters have hinted too."

"Same with ma family. I'm nae best pleased with Fergus right now, but mayhap it was a good thing someone finally said something in front of us both."

Adelaide slid her hands up his arms, over his shoulders, and up his neck until both cupped his cheeks. Their lips fused, and years of blossoming emotions poured forth. She wasn't certain how it would feel, but she'd seen how her parents kissed. She knew to expect Tate's tongue to touch hers, but she wasn't ready for how her body ached when he did. His arm was a steel band around her waist when she flicked her tongue against his. She was tentative, but she soon knew he enjoyed it. When they pulled apart, he kissed her forehead like he had earlier, then the tip of her nose before they shared a series of short kisses. Her hand slid down to rest on his biceps.

"I dinna make a habit of kissing lasses, Adelaide." Tate didn't know what to make of her body stiffening. But she relaxed with the next word. "Addy?"

"I'm nae used to ye calling me Adelaide. I dinna think I like it. It feels—distant."

"I dinna want that. Just the opposite. I only meant

for ye to understand how serious I am. I ken this is a horrible time for me to approach yer father, but I wish to ask his permission to court ye. Would ye want that?"

"Aye. Have ye asked yer da or grandda if ye can?"

"Nay. They ken ye. I dinna doubt they'll support us. It's yer da who is likely to say nay. I'd ask him in private to save maself the embarrassment if he says nay, but I dinna want to be alone, so he can run me through."

"Would ye let me go with ye? He wouldnae kill ye in front of me." Adelaide grinned.

"Och, cheeky lass." Tate's head dipped to kiss her again, and she welcomed him. "I wish I could stand here all day, kissing ye. But we also have to talk aboot Fergus and Clara. Do ye think Clara could forgive Fergus if we prove it wasna her?"

"Da said she probably would. She must have said something of the sort while he rode with her. He said she understood the pain he must have felt. I dinna ken how any couple comes back from such allegations and such public humiliation. But if they can, it's nae ma place to say aught."

"I feel the same. Addy, I would never do what Fergus did. If we ever had a problem, I would never air it before our clan or outsiders. I would speak to ye alone."

"I'd do the same. I kenned that aboot ye last night. I heard what ye said to him to make him stop, and I kenned it was those reasons why ye would never do what he had. Ye ken the damage, and I believe, even in a moment of rage, ye'd still respect me enough to nae harm me like that. Fergus's claims aboot Clara being loose endanger her, make her a target to men who wouldnae listen to her say nay. Ye would never do that to me or any woman."

"Ye're right. And I wouldnae ignore any mon who threatened ye or touched ye."

"I ken. Ye already proved that by trying to help with Adam."

"I only made that worse."

Adelaide's brow furrowed as she looked at Tate's chest. But her mind focused on a niggling thought. "Do ye think Adam and Peter caused trouble with me as a distraction from what they really planned? Do ye think they made me fear for maself, so I wouldnae be so aware of what they planned for Clara?"

"That's what I was just thinking. Assuming it was Peter who arranged last night's incident, did he do it because he thought to have Clara for himself somehow? Or does he really nae want the alliance between the Mathesons and MacDonalds?"

"The latter. The Chisholms have hated the Mathesons for generations. Mayhap Peter plays nice with Fergus now, but that doesnae mean they wish the Mathesons well. Allying with any MacDonald branch or sept strengthens the other clan. The Chisholms may nae want competition for the MacDonalds' favor."

"I suspect we saw one of the alehouse wenches with a MacDonald guardsman in Clara's tent. I think I ken which woman. She kept approaching Fergus last night, offering to ease his troubles. She came up to him as soon as we walked in. It was before the tent got crowded. I kept wondering how she already kenned he had any troubles when everyone within a stone's throw of here kenned the betrothal announcement was that night."

"Can ye describe the woman?"

"Dark hair, brown eyes, medium size. She has a scar on her shoulder."

"Silvia. Nae shocking." Adelaide curled her lip in disgust. She was the woman her brother had been ogling that day she entered the alehouse for the pint she thought to take him. She and Silvia had been oil and water since they were children. It hadn't surprised Adelaide when Silvia took work at the village's tavern. It wasn't a far stretch for her to become a whore after that. "Do ye ken which MacDonald mon it was?"

"Nae for sure. But I can think of a few who would duck into a tent, nae caring whose it was, just to tup a woman."

Adelaide nodded. "What's yer full name?"

"What's that, lass?"

"Yer full name. Tatum what Sinclair?"

"Rowan. Why?"

"Ye call me Addy. I canna shorten Tate. I wondered what else I could call ye. Mayhap Tatum or Rowan."

Tate swooped in and kissed Adelaide, stealing her breath. He lifted her off her feet and wrapped an arm beneath her backside. His other hand went to her hair, fisting it. His kiss was ravenous, and Adelaide gave as good as she got. Her hand clutched a handful of his leine, pulling him as though they could get any closer while clothed. Her other hand tunneled into his hair.

"Addy, call me whatever ye like. Just keep letting me hear yer voice and kenning ye're speaking to me."

"Gladly, Tatum."

They clung to one another, continuing to kiss until they heard a crow caw. They tilted their heads back to see a murder of ravens flying toward the far end of the field. Tate lowered Adelaide, and they beamed at one another.

"We should go back."

"I ken." Adelaide frowned.

"I dinna want to, wee one."

"Me neither, braw one."

"When ye say things like that, I might never let ye go."

"I wouldnae complain." Adelaide stretched to kiss his cheek, her lips landing just above his jaw.

"Let's deal with what awaits with Fergus. Then I'll speak to yer father. Stay away from Peter unless I'm with ye, Addy. Dinna dig for aught alone."

"I willna. I dinna trust any of them. And I admit it. I'm too scared to go near them without ye being with me. Even with someone else at ma side—a warrior even—I dinna feel safe without ye."

"I hate kenning anyone scares ye, especially on yer own land. There's naught I willna do to protect ye, Addy. Whether we wed or nae, ye always have ma protection."

"Wed?"

"That's why I wish to court ye. Is that nae what ye want?"

"It is. I just canna believe how good it sounds when ye say it out loud."

Tate's heart felt fuller than it ever had, and his cock ached for release after holding Adelaide against him. As she beamed up at him, he knew what he wanted most.

"I promise I'll do whatever it takes to prove to Fingal that I can be worthy of ye."

"Ye already are. Even if he says nay, I willna walk away. I believe we suit, and I wish to find out for sure."

"After the Gathering ends, I must go back to Dunbeath. That isnae within a day's ride. We could exchange missives."

"I'd like that."

They turned toward the keep, excited for the prospect of a future together, trepidatious that Fingal might stand in the way, and determined to discover what Peter Chisholm did to destroy their friends' lives.

CHAPTER 13

Tate stepped inside the Mathesons' tent and found Fergus huddled in a corner. As the clan's tánaiste, he could have claimed a chamber in the keep, but he'd refused the offer when his clan arrived. He'd said he would fare better on the ground than a married man and his wife. Now Tate wondered if it would be better to have his friend shut within a chamber and out of sight. Fergus's hair stuck out in every direction, and his face had a tinge of yellow to it. His red-rimmed eyes were from the after-effects of the alcohol and his tears since Tate left him to meet Adelaide.

"Ye should bathe and put on fresh clothes, Fergus. I passed yer father on the way here. Ye are to say yer betrothal vows to Agnes this eve. Before that, ye must sign the amended contracts."

"Nay! I willna marry Clara's sister. I dinna give a bluidy damn aboot the alliance."

"Ye dinna have the luxury nae to care. Ye are yer father's heir. Ye will be Laird Matheson one day. This is nay longer aboot ye or Clara. Ye will do yer duty to yer clan, even if ye couldnae do yer duty by Clara."

"What the hell does that mean? She didna do her duty to me."

"Ye claim to have loved her, but ye judged her with nay proof. I canna and willna swear it was Clara we saw. Neither can ye. Yer duty was to protect and defend her, nae be the first one to accuse her. Yer duty was to love her unconditionally. Nae assume she would betray ye. Ye daft bugger. It makes nay sense. She kenned yer fathers were going to announce the betrothal last night. She kenned people would be watching her. She kenned ye were waiting. Why would she jeopardize any of that for a rut with someone else?"

"One last one before she was bound to me for life." Fergus shook his head.

"That's shite, and ye ken it. Yer pride shall be yer downfall. As a mon, as a husband, and as a laird. Abdicate now, Fergus. Let one of yer brothers inherit."

Fergus lunged to his feet, his warrior agility still in place despite his hangover. "What did ye just say to me?"

"Ye heard me. I said give up yer title as heir and tánaiste. Ye dinna make sound decisions in times of crisis. Ye dinna wait to see all the evidence before passing judgment. Ye are too rash. Ye dinna pick yer words wisely before ye speak in public. Ye are too great a risk to yer clan's future. Step aside."

"Ye're goading me, and I willna listen." Fergus made to push past Tate, but Tate didn't budge.

"What? Ye dinna care to hear yer supposed faults listed aloud? I wonder how Clara felt hearing her supposed sins listed before every person in the Highlands. The only difference is, ye're guilty, and she isnae."

"Ye saw—"

"Fergus, neither ye nor I saw shite. We saw silhouettes. We didna see faces. We heard moans. We didna hear names. And ye lay all the blame at Clara's feet. What aboot the mon?"

"She lured him in."

Tate snorted. "Ye might think Clara is alluring, but she's the least beguiling lass we ken. She couldnae seduce the devil. She's more innocent than a day-old lamb. That mon wasna protesting or begging the woman to stop. Nay one forced him. He's as much to blame for this as whoever that woman was."

"Clara. That's who it was."

"I shall make ma recommendation to yer father."

"Ye wouldnae dare," Fergus hissed.

"Come with me and listen if ye dinna believe me. Fergus, ye're ma friend and have been since we were weans. But one day ma cousin is going to lead ma clan, and I dinna want him to think he can rely on ye to make sound decisions. I dinna want ma clan riding alongside yers when ye lead. If this is how ye behave when tested, then I dinna trust ye anymore. I never thought I would say it, but I willna risk ma family and ma people's lives with an alliance to yers once ye're laird." Tate crossed his arms and widened his stance until his feet were hip-width apart. He wondered if he was pushing Fergus too far, but he wasn't exaggerating either. When his cousin Thormud became laird one day, Tate would sit on the Sinclairs' clan council. He would advise Thor to think twice before following Fergus.

Perhaps this would be Fergus's only error in judgment. Mayhap his heart led him astray. But Tate didn't like Fergus's snap decision that Clara was guilty. He didn't like that Fergus wasn't questioning or investigating what happened. He had said nothing about Clara's supposed death. He'd talked more about how it affected him and what he wanted.

"I should have gone in the tent and confronted her

there. I should have been certain before I accused her. Now she's gone." Fergus mumbled to himself, but Tate heard him.

"Those are the first words of sense ye've uttered since last night. Mayhap there is hope for ye yet. What are ye going to do aboot it? Ye need to clear Clara's name since ye are the one who destroyed it."

Fergus looked around as though he only now recognized where he was. "I need to bathe. Then I will insist I see her. I need to see her."

"Her parents willna let ye within a hair's length of that chamber."

"But I was to be her betrothed. Everyone kens I loved her. I deserve—"

"Fergus," Tate warned. He shook his head. "Ye canna have it both ways. Get fresh clothes and yer soap."

Fergus put up no argument. Tate waited on the loch's banks while Fergus scrubbed himself, dunking into the chilly water several times before trudging to his clothes. Tate stood where he could watch his friend but also keep an eye on the keep. He wondered what Adelaide was doing. Had she done a normal day's duties? Was she upset again like she had been when she confronted Fergus? If she was, would he have any chance to console her? When his gaze landed on Fergus again, he tried not to glower. He wished to speak to Fingal, but he couldn't possibly express his wish to have a happy future with the man's daughter when another young woman allegedly killed herself only hours earlier. Resentment toward Fergus bubbled and threatened to leak in the form of real chastisement he wouldn't be able to take back.

"I wish to speak to Laird MacDonald. I want to see Clara," Fergus insisted as he stomped toward the path to the keep. He reminded Tate of a spoiled child.

They'd barely stepped into the bailey when Laird Mac-Donald charged toward them.

"Ye! Get out of ma sight. Ye broke ma lass's heart. Ye may as well have thrust a dagger into her. She didna wish to live after what ye did. *Ye* shouldnae be allowed to live. I challenge ye, ye bastard." Laird MacDonald pointed at Fergus with his left hand while his right pulled a dirk. "We ride off Grant land, and I challenge ye to single combat."

Tate knew the ruse, but the MacDonald's grief and anger were real. He'd believed the man was indifferent to his daughters, but sadness marred his face. Tate didn't believe the MacDonald issued his challenge merely out of duty to defend his daughter. It went far deeper than that. He wished to avenge his little girl.

"Laird MacDonald—"

"Nay, ye weak wee mon. Ye had the bollocks to ruin ma daughter's life. Now ye can have the bollocks to defend yer own." The older man came to stand before Fergus and Tate. Anyone who looked knew Fergus would likely defeat the laird. Andrew MacDonald was nearing his seventh decade while Fergus hadn't reached his third. An injury years earlier made the MacDonald unable to ride into battle anymore. While the man still appeared fit, it was unlikely he'd trained in the lists in ages. But he was willing to lose his life to defend his daughter's honor.

"I willna fight ye."

"Coward," Laird MacDonald spat. Fergus straightened and inhaled, expanding his chest. "Dinna puff up like a righteous rooster. Ye're lucky I'm even giving ye the chance to defend yerself. I ought to kill ye where we stand. It's only for the sake of ma daughter's memory that I dinna. She didna want ye dead, even if I do. I will give ye the chance for a fair fight."

"And I willna kill Clara's father. She would never forgive me for that."

"As though that matters," Laird MacDonald sneered.

"It does to me."

"She didna matter much to ye last night." Laird MacDonald's voice cracked on the last two words. His body did the opposite of Fergus's. It seemed to deflate as grief once more weighed heavily on him.

"I ken," Fergus whispered. "If only she hadnae done it."

Tate lurched forward, barely able to get between Laird MacDonald and Fergus before the laird wrapped his hands around Fergus's throat. "Nae here, ma laird. We're still at the Gathering. There canna be any violence here. Ye will lose people's respect, even if ye are a grieving father. He isnae worth that. Clara wouldnae want her clan to suffer because of her. It's bad enough they're suffering because of him."

Tate released the laird when the older man stepped back. He glowered over Tate's shoulder at Fergus before spinning on his heel. He marched away, but not without shooting Fergus a thunderous glare before reaching the keep's steps. Tate turned toward Fergus.

"I canna stand beside ye, Fergus. Ye continue to insist upon a truth nay one kens is real. One moment, ye bemoan Clara being gone. The next, ye insist ye're the victim in this. Nae once have ye said ye want to find out why she supposedly did this. Nae once have ye said ye wish to find out who was in there—whether it was a mon with her or a completely different couple. Until ye pull yer head out of yer arse, I canna defend ye or encourage ye to continue as ye are."

"Ye're taking Clara's side because ye're sniffing around Adelaide." Fergus jumped back, but he wasn't fast enough to avoid Tate's fist to his jaw.

"I ken ye're suffering right now. I ken yer anger

comes from feeling betrayed. But if ye ever speak aboot Adelaide like that again, I will kill ye. Ye dinna get to insult her to make yerself feel better. Ye ruined one woman's reputation. Ye willna do the same to another."

"I'm sorry. I—" Fergus's shoulders drooped. Tate shook his head before turning away. "Tate?"

"When ye wish to learn the truth, come find me. Until then, there's naught for either of us to say." Tate walked toward the portcullis just as Adelaide crossed the bailey toward the barracks. "Lady Adelaide?"

"Tate." Adelaide offered him a warm smile until she looked in the direction whence he came. She frowned as she spied Fergus staring into space. "I've already heard Laird MacDonald just challenged him."

"That didna take long to spread." Tate swept his gaze over the bailey.

"Nay one's gossiping. At least, nae yet. I heard Da and Uncle Edward. Neither sounded surprised."

"I wasna. I'm surprised he didna challenge Fergus last night or rouse him at dawn to do it. Fergus said he wouldnae kill Clara's father."

"He assumes he would win."

"Addy, he would. The MacDonald isnae the warrior he was only a few years ago."

"Dinna underestimate a mon defending his family. If anyone should ken that, it's ye. If yer da were in Laird MacDonald's position, would he nae do any and everything to defend Ailish? If ye'd been injured but someone defamed yer lass, wouldnae ye find it in ye to fight?"

Tate stepped closer to Adelaide and kept his voice low. "If we had a lass, there's naught I wouldnae do for her."

"We?"

"Aye, Addy. Ye ken I wish to court ye because I wish to wed ye. Who else would I be having a lass with?"

Tate offered her a devilish smile that made her pulse thrum. When he winked, she thought she might strip naked right there for all and sundry to see. "Addy?"

"Hmm?"

"Are ye picturing us having a wee lass?"

"Sort of." Adelaide flushed.

Tate leaned forward to whisper. "Are ye picturing how we—"

"Wheest!" Adelaide swatted at Tate but caught herself and yanked her hand back.

"Ye were." Tate chuckled and waggled his eyebrows.

"I wouldnae ken—" Adelaide was certain there would be nothing left of her cheeks but ash by the time they would finish their conversation. She'd stopped herself, but Tate inferred what she didn't say.

"I hope it's me, Addy. But if ye wed someone else, it should be a mon who listens to what ye want and teaches ye. It should be done *with* ye, nae *to* ye." Tate's gentle words made Adelaide tingle.

"I canna believe we're discussing this. Nae just here, but at all."

"Love and the marriage bed arenae something ma parents shied away from explaining. We dinna discuss it at the evening meal. But it's something ma parents, and ma aunts and uncles, made sure we all understand is sacred. I willna pretend I'm still an innocent, but neither am I that well tutored. I ken enough." It was Tate's turn to feel an inferno beneath his skin. And this time it wasn't just from lust. His cheeks radiated heat.

"I suppose it's good one of us kens what should happen." Adelaide hesitated. "Will I meet the women from yer past?"

"Nay. At least, I dinna think so. It's been more than a year since I last rode out with ma family to fight alongside Andrew Murray. It was during those campaigns. I was away from Dunbeath. Before that, it was while visiting other clans." Tate looked around, aware this was far too private a conversation to have in the bailey. And they would draw attention from standing together for so long.

"More than a year?" Adelaide's incredulousness made Tate laugh.

"I only need a wee bread and ale to survive, lass."

"And yer sword. Dinna forget that." Adelaide grinned.

"I carry them both, but I only swing one. Addy, when the time comes, only ma wife will ever see the one I dinna use in battle. Nay mon in ma family strays."

"Tatum, everyone in Scotland kens that."

Before Tate could respond, a deep voice rang across the bailey. "Ada!"

Adelaide leaned around Tate to see her father rushing toward them. Tate turned too, not surprised to see he displeased Fingal. He forced himself not to sigh or groan. He didn't want a confrontation, but if Fingal forced him, he would admit his intentions toward Adelaide.

"Sinclair."

"Grant."

"Ada, ye need to return to yer chamber. People will wonder why ye're clishmaclavering if yer friend just died."

"Da, everyone kens Clara was—is—ma friend. Everyone kens Tate is Fergus's friend. It canna surprise anyone that we would talk after what's happened to our friends."

"But ye arenae talking aboot Clara or Fergus, are ye?"

"Nay, we werenae," Tate admitted. He shifted to ensure Adelaide was at his side. "I ken this isnae the time nor the place, but I dinna think I should wait any longer. Fingal, I wish to court Lady Adelaide."

"It's Addy. And I want that too." Adelaide stared at her father, whose lips pursed before he nodded.

"At least ye did it in time to ask—tell—me in person and nae in a missive after ye left." Fingal skimmed his eyes over Tate from top to bottom and up again. "I worried ye would disappoint Ada last summer. I worried aboot it even more this year. But I've seen ye two together, and I ken ye defended her against Adam. I ken ye were ready to protect her against Peter. She looked to ye last night over and over. She trusts ye with what's happening. I've kenned yer da and his brothers since we were all lads. Ye are like yer da in many ways, but ye arenae him. At least, ye arenae how he was before he met yer mama. Ye are him ever since he fell in love with Lady Ceit. I dinna look forward to any of ma lasses leaving here. I ken it's inevitable, but it doesnae mean I'm eager. If Ada's going to Dunbeath, I will sleep easy every night."

"We have yer permission to wed?" Adelaide asked.

Fingal grinned. "Tate asked to court ye. He didna ask to marry ye. Give him a moment, lass."

"It's the same thing, Fingal. I wouldnae ask to court yer daughter if I didna mean to marry Lady Adel—"

"Addy," Adelaide interjected. "If ye're going to marry me, then I dinna see why ye should call me aught but that. It's yer name for me, and I like it."

"Ye are yer mother's daughter." Fingal laughed. "I wasna so sure aboot Madeline and Adelaide since they are similar. Now it'll be Maddy and Addy."

"Nay, it willna. Nay one but ye calls Mama Maddy. And nay one but Tatum better call me Addy."

"Tatum is it?" Fingal cocked an eyebrow.

"Aye. Addy calls me that. Ma mother only does when I'm within inches of a skelping."

"Ada, ye'll need a new name for him. I suspect ye'll

hear Lady Ceit using yer name for him quite a lot." Fingal smirked.

"I'm sure I'll come up with something, Da." Adelaide shifted her gaze up to Tate, who said a prayer of thanksgiving that his sporran hid his arousal. His cock had been at half-mast since he and Adelaide started talking about a future together. Now it was fully at attention. He didn't need Fingal to guess where his mind roamed.

"Should I speak to yer da and grandda aboot drafting contracts?" Fingal grew serious.

Tate looked down at Adelaide and raised his eyebrows. She nodded and beamed at him. "Aye. I think that would be a good idea. Most noble couples ken each other for far less time than Addy and I have. We've kenned each other since we were weans. Ma interest changed last year, but that's because I realized I could see a future with her as a woman I've kenned and cared aboot for ages. I'm even more convinced of that now than last summer." Tate brushed the back of his hand against Adelaide's, wishing he could hold it.

"Then I think ye should ask me something," Fingal stated.

"May I marry yer daughter?" He didn't think Fingal would suddenly laugh in his face and deny him, but he had a moment's trepidation.

"Aye."

Before Fingal could say anything more, Tate turned toward Adelaide and took both her hands. "Addy, what I said is true. Ma interest in ye has always been there. I've enjoyed being yer friend since we were weans. Last year, I wondered if ye might feel more for me than friendship. I feared ye didna. I wasna convinced ye did this year either. But I wish to make ye ma wife. I think ye wish to have me as yer husband. *Am pòs thu mi?*" Will ye marry me?

"Aye!" Adelaide's response was far more effusive than Fingal's. She flung open her arms, uncaring who watched. Tate wrapped his arms around her waist and lifted her off her feet until they were eye-to-eye. Both withstood the temptation to kiss, but they grinned at each other.

"Enough of that. Come, Sinclair. We should find yer da and grandda. I suppose yer mama will want to be there, and I ken Ada's mama will too. We need Edward as well."

"We're right here," Tavish stated as he and Ceit stepped out of the stables. He not so subtly pulled a piece of hay from Ceit's hair. "I'll find Da."

Tavish stepped forward and pulled Tate into his embrace, lifting the younger man off his toes. He clapped Tate on the back. "I'm so proud of ye, lad."

When he let go, Ceit encircled her arms around her older son's waist and squeezed. "I'm proud too. And we love ye, wee one."

Adelaide stifled her giggle. She could think of something she doubted would be wee. Ceit barely came to the middle of her son's chest. He had to lean forward to rest his chin on her head as she swatted at him. Ceit let go and turned around before opening her arms to Adelaide.

"Finally, it shall be even."

"Even?" Adelaide's brow furrowed as she exchanged a brief embrace with Ceit.

"Aye. Three to three. The men outnumber Ailish and me. Hopefully, Wiley will wed before Ailish. Then things will be set to rights."

"Mama, ye sound so aggrieved. Do ye really need four to three?"

"Nay. I dinna even need three to three to remind ye, yer da, and yer brother who to fear. But at least ma nose willna burn so badly when ye three are around." Ceit wafted her hand beneath her nose with a grin.

Adelaide enjoyed watching mother and son as Ceit teased her soon-to-be betrothed. She would miss her family terribly, but it was nice to see she would marry into one similar to her own. That gave her pause.

I'm getting married! But when?

CHAPTER 14

Tate held Adelaide a little closer than propriety dictated as they twirled together after the evening meal. When they moved through steps that had them hold hands, each squeezed a little tighter than necessary. They longed for more moments alone like they'd had in the oat field. They'd been fortunate no one spied them, and as far as they knew, no one gossiped about their brief tryst.

"Now that our fathers have signed the contracts, I wish we could tell the world," Tate whispered.

"Same. Mayhap after the Gathering officially ends with the feast. Nae all the clans will leave that evening. Mayhap the next morning." Adelaide kept her voice equally low.

"Do ye think yer da and uncle would let me stay on after the Gathering ends? I'd like more time with ye."

"We can ask." Adelaide prayed she didn't sound too excited. When Tate merely nodded, she realized she might have sounded more nonchalant than she intended. "I'll do what I can to convince them if they dinna agree right away. I dinna want ye to leave yet."

"Would ye like to go riding tomorrow? I dinna have any competitions left. Are there any ye wish to watch?"

"I'd love to go riding. Mayhap a picnic like we joined Fergus and Clara on."

They both remained silent for a moment. It felt like a lifetime ago, not barely a week earlier. The song ended just as they finished making their plans to ride out in the morning and spend the midday meal together. Tate promised to arrange for Sinclair and Grant guards to accompany them.

* * *

"Good morning, lass." Tate turned as he heard Adelaide walk into the stables across from where he stood, saddling his horse.

"Good morning. Ye already readied ma horse." Adelaide fed her mount an apple, then stroked the steed's long nose before stepping closer to Tate's stall. His horse nickered and nodded its head. She reached into her pocket and retrieved another piece of fruit. She held her hand out.

"Addy, nay." Tate hurried to reach Adelaide to push her hand away, but his horse gently lifted the apple from her hand before its crushing teeth crunched the fruit. "Ye could have lost a finger or five."

"He sniffed and already tried to nudge ma pocket. I smell like flowers, and I'm nae large and imposing. I'm nae a threat to him, so he was gentle."

"Ye couldnae be sure." Tate stepped out of the stall, being sure to loop the rope around the peg to keep his monstrous beast from following him. He scanned the surrounding area before leading them away from the door. There were no empty stalls, but he guided them to the end of the row. It made them difficult to see from the door. His right arm wrapped around Adelaide, and his left hand grasped her wrist. He placed her hand over his heart, and she could feel it racing. "Ye took at least five years off ma life. I dinna want our time together cut short."

"I didna mean to scare ye." Adelaide splayed her fingers until she could weave them through the laces of his leine. Her fingertips pressed against the heated skin, and it always mesmerized her how men could be warm year-round. Her father and brothers exuded heat, even during the dead of winter.

"Ye ken aught that might harm ye frightens me. Addy, I didna exaggerate yesterday when I said ma interest began before last year. The last Gathering was when I thought I could finally act upon it. I've had a tendre for ye for years. Ever since I was two-and-ten."

"That's more than ten years." Adelaide's fingers flexed and fisted the leine.

"Aye. At first, I thought it was merely calf love because I admit I didna think of ye often after each Gathering. But I couldnae stop thinking aboot ye when we saw each other every summer."

"I felt the same. But there are so many of us of an age that I didna think I was that special. We were often together because Sarah and Ailish are the same age, and so are several of yer cousins. Then we were just as often together because of Clara and Fergus. I admit I found excuses for Clara and Fergus to spend time together, telling her that I thought it would be nice for them. I really wanted to spend time with ye."

"I did the same. Addy, it's only been within the past few days that I've truly let maself accept how I've felt for ages. I didna think ye reciprocated, so I told maself that ma feelings were naught."

"I thought I was foolish."

Tate released her wrist and cupped her jaw. He lowered his head as she lifted her chin. Their lips brushed together before melding into one. Adelaide opened to him, catching herself before she moaned at the feel of his tongue invading her mouth. She didn't entirely know what to do, but instinct said to suck on it lightly. She immediately felt Tate tighten his hold, but she reached between them and tried to push his sporran out of the way. They had to pull their hips back for her to spin it farther to the right on his belt. Then his rod pressed against her mound. Her instinct spoke once again. She rocked her hips, rubbing her mons. This time she didn't stifle her moan. Tate's hand slid from her jaw, down her neck, over her collarbone, until he reached her breast.

"Tell me to stop if ye dinna want this."

"I want more," Adelaide breathed. She didn't know the woman she became in Tate's arms, but she was happy to meet her. She felt brazen but brave as her free hand roamed over his ribs and up his back. Neither wanted to pull away, but a horse stomping its hoof and the need to breathe finally necessitated it.

"It wouldnae be good to get caught in here. I ken the contracts are signed, but nay one kens outside our families. The gossip would be horrible, and I dinna want anyone to think I dinna respect ma bride." Tate kissed her cheek before they let go of each other and walked back to their horses.

"But mayhap being discovered would make it easier. Then we wouldnae need an announcement. We could tell the truth. We dinna wish to make it aboot ourselves given what's happened."

"If ye wish for people to ken we're betrothed, then we can arrive at the evening meal together and hold hands. Ye can sit with ma family," Tate suggested.

"It would say even more if ye sat on the dais with me." Adelaide stopped by her horse's stall and looked up at Tate.

"If yer parents agree, then I'll gladly sit beside ye at the laird's table. If they willna, then I hope they'll at least agree to let ye sit with ma family. Ye could always sit between me and one of the lasses. Then mayhap people would think ye're sitting with a friend."

"Do ye nae want people to ken yet?"

"*Mo leannan*, I would let the entire world ken. But I dinna want to make aught uncomfortable for ye if people start asking questions or talking aboot us." My sweetheart.

"Tatum," Adelaide sighed as she wrapped her arms around his neck. "*Mo ghràidh*." My darling.

"I can think of a couple more phrases for that. *Mo luaidh. M'eudail.* I plan to spend a lifetime calling ye each of them." There was more Tate wanted to say, but the stables—where anyone could walk in—wasn't the place to say it. Plus, they had guards waiting for them outside. They'd already saddled their horses and would soon guess what kept the couple. At the very least, they would speculate. He'd been serious about not wanting anyone to think he didn't respect his future wife. Trysting among smelly horses wasn't what he wanted said about Adelaide. His parents might have been in the hayloft the day before, which hadn't shocked him in the least, but at least that wasn't inches from dung heaps.

They led their horses outside, and Tate helped Adelaide mount. Then he vaulted into the saddle. With five Grant guards and five Sinclair ones, they rode out beneath the portcullis. It was still early, so members of the clans camped outside the wall barely stirred. Tate watched the tents, scanning for anyone who might spot them. He saw no one looking in their direction, but that didn't mean he hadn't missed them. They spurred their horses and charged north toward the Cairngorms, the majestic mountains not far from Freuchie.

When it was possible to hear over their horses' hooves, they chatted about what they'd liked best that year. They shared memories from previous summers before moving on to talk about how their families celebrated other seasons and events throughout the year. Adelaide shared that her mother and Uncle Edward, who'd also believed he would dedicate his life to a monastic order before becoming laird and marrying, were still very pious about many of the feast days. But she recounted tales of visiting the Isles of Lewis and of Skye to celebrate with her mother's brother and sister, and their respective families. She shared how she loved the Isle of Lewis the most since her mother's brother's wife made everything perfect for Christmas, Samhain, and Epiphany. All the decorations and foods were the best she'd ever had.

"Addy, yer aunt-by-marriage is ma father's cousin. Ye ken we've been to Lewis before." Tate grinned. He and his family had swarmed Stornoway on more than one occasion. It had felt like the Sinclairs were enough to amount an invasion, but when the Sutherlands and Camerons arrived too, there was little room for the MacLeods of Lewis, the MacKinnons of Skye, and the Grants. While the couples had their own chambers, the children from all the families often had five or six to a chamber to accommodate the enormous families. Because it was usually the dead of winter for Christmastide, the barracks veritably overflowed. Warriors slept at least four to a tiny chamber, rotating who had to sleep on the frozen floor.

"When I think aboot it, we've spent a great deal more time together than most couples who wed," Adelaide noted. "Many dinna meet until they're standing together on the kirk steps. We've kenned each other since we were weans."

"That's why ma feelings arenae new. Just ma courage to act on them is." Tate shot her his devilish grin, which made parts of her ache for his attention.

"I feared what Da said would be true. That's why I

was so wary of ye when ye arrived. But I should have kenned nae to fear aught with ye. Ye've always been sincere."

"Yer da isnae ready for his lasses to grow up. I ken ma da isnae ready for Ailish to leave Dunbeath."

Adelaide watched Tate unsure if she should voice an observation she'd made several times during this Gathering alone. When his smile fell, she kept her thoughts to herself. She suspected Tate already sensed what she might say, but he didn't look particularly pleased at the notion that Ailish might have taken an interest in a man, and that man clearly returned the sentiment. Instead, Adelaide pointed to a spot not far from the base of the first mountain.

"How aboot we stop there?"

It was a wooded area that would keep the sun from blazing down upon them since the morning quickly heated until their cheeks were rosy, not just from exertion, but sunshine. The only breeze was the wind they created from riding hard. When they were a hundred yards from the tree line, Tate signaled them to stop. Grant guards fanned out and rode ahead.

"Tate?"

"I'm nae taking ye into the woods without kenning if there's anyone else already there. This isnae ma land, but yer men ken it well. They'll ken where to look." Tate looked at his men, who were already shifting to encircle the couple. Adelaide noticed the movement and swept her gaze over the remaining guards. She nudged her horse closer to Tate's. He reached out his hand and covered hers on the reins. "Dinna fash, *leannan*. I dinna think aught is wrong, but I willna take any chances with yer safety."

"Thank ye. How'd ma guards ken that's what ye wanted?"

"Because the woods are ahead of us, and I made us

stop far enough away that we could ride away if they warned us, or I spotted any danger. They kenned that must have been why. Ma guards didna go because they dinna ken this land like yers do. I'm sure they arenae thrilled to leave ye with just Sinclairs, but I'm sure they'd rather they search thoroughly than have ma men accidentally miss something."

Adelaide again swept her gaze over the men surrounding them as a protective shield. It couldn't be a secret to any of them why they accompanied the couple. She twisted in her saddle and leaned toward Tate. She pressed a kiss to his cheek. "Thank ye for taking ma safety so seriously."

Tate brushed his lips against hers for barely a peck. "I always will. I canna stomach the idea that aught might happen to ye, especially if I can prevent it."

"Ye ken ye canna control everything in this life or the next."

"But I can do everything possible to protect the people who matter the most to me. Ye're at the top of that list." Tate's heart thumped behind his ribs. He had more to say, and he hoped they would have the privacy to do so in the woods, but he feared Adelaide wouldn't reciprocate to the extent he wished. He caught himself before he said more where his men could overhear. His words were for Adelaide's ears only. He noticed movement, so he shifted his focus to the returning men.

"It's all clear, Sinclair," one man called to them.

Tate and Adelaide nudged their horses, and the group rode to meet the Grants where they'd stopped. The group entered the tree line but went little farther. Tate swung his leg over his saddle and landed on the ground just as Adelaide moved to dismount alone. He rushed over and wrapped his massive hands around her waist. Hidden between their horses, he pressed her body against his as it slid down his length until her feet settled on the ground.

"If ye mount and dismount on yer own, I willna have much chance to touch ye. And I dinna want to let go."

Adelaide looked around. "Do ye think we could walk a little farther in and nae have anyone listening or watching?"

"If we do that, they'll ken for sure what we're aboot."

"Are ye worried they'll gossip?"

"Nae gossip, but report to yer da."

"Ma men wouldnae do that," Adelaide assured.

"But ma men will tell ma da." Tate pretended a terrified expression.

"Do ye fear yer da?"

"Ye've met him." Tate chuckled.

"Yer mother scares me more."

"Wise lass. But Mama will probably spoil ye while scolding me. Ye dinna need to fear either of ma parents, in jest or in seriousness. Ma da's bark is worse than his bite, and Mama had to be stern to wrangle three wild weans who went in all different directions. Da is fierce in the lists and on the battlefield, but naught means more to him than Mama and his weans. That'll include ye."

"Weans?" It was Adelaide's turn to laugh. Nothing about Tate spoke of a small child.

"Aye. Until I have the experience fighting and leading that Da, Grandda, and ma uncles have, I'm still a wean to them and everyone else. It's the same for all ma cousins too. Wee Liam will probably go to his grave in three score years still bearing that moniker since they named him for Grandda. He isnae wee in size anymore, but he still doesnae have the fierce reputation Grandda does."

"I've heard aboot yer cousin. He's been called a lion

before because of how he sounds when he roars the Mackay battle call and his tenacity during battle. I dinna think he's far off from being as legendary as any of the men in yer family. They call Blake a bear because of his size. Yer uncle Magnus and Tor are the same."

"And what should I be called?" Tate's dark eyes bore into her, and she feared she'd melt from the heat.

"Dark hair. Dark eyes. That smile. That intense stare. The devil most likely."

Tate pulled Adelaide closer and brought his lips to her ear. "Lass, that smile and that stare are only for ye. But I shall chase ye around our chamber like the devil is on yer heels. And when I catch ye…" Tate kissed the spot behind her ear. "I'll be the one begging for mercy."

Their gazes met, and temptation pushed them closer. They wrapped their arms around one another before their kiss combusted. Neither cared who might see them. Neither cared who might report their tryst. All they wanted was each other. When they stopped, Tate's tongue and lips trailed down her neck to her collarbone before Adelaide turned her head to nip at his earlobe. He entwined his fingers with hers and whistled. Adelaide's brow furrowed when she heard the men moving farther into the trees.

"Where are they going?"

"They'll set a perimeter aboot a hundred feet in all directions. Nay one comes near ye without passing at least two of them. That also gives us some privacy." Tate guided her several yards deeper into the woods until they found a massive oak tree. "I wish to kiss ye properly."

"That last one wasna proper?"

Tate snorted. "Hardly proper for any polite person's eyes."

"When ye look at me like that…" Adelaide dropped her gaze to the ground, unable to finish.

"When I look at ye how? Addy, there's naught we canna tell each other. If there's something ye desire, ye wish to try or do again, ye can tell me. I dinna think that makes ye immoral or less virtuous. I want ye to want me the same way I want ye. I want to bring ye pleasure when we're alone. I dinna want ye to fear it or be embarrassed by it."

"I think I ken enough, but I dinna ken everything a mon and woman can do together. I want ye to teach me. Then I'll ken what to ask for."

"Ye dinna have to ask, Addy. Ye can tell me what ye want, and if I can, I'll give it to ye. Asking implies ye need permission for yer feelings. Ye dinna need permission from me to want to touch me, couple with me, show me affection. I crave all of it and hope ye'll give it freely. I hope ye'll accept it, too."

Adelaide's chest couldn't expand enough to hold the whirlwind of feelings churning within. She released them the only way she could think of. She went onto her toes and pressed her mouth to Tate's. She reached for his hands, pulling his left arm around her so she could place his hand on her backside. She raised his right hand to her breast. When he squeezed with both hands, she rocked her hips forward. She mewled in protest when his hand left her breast, but it was only gone long enough for Tate to shift his sporran. Then it was back where it belonged, kneading the supple flesh.

Adelaide knew what else she wanted from Tate, and she wanted to ask because she knew he wouldn't think less of her for wanting it. But she wasn't certain if it was too soon to suggest it. For now, she was happy to follow Tate's lead, but he feared being too presumptuous. He'd told Adelaide that he wanted her to feel comfortable enough to participate in their intimate moments, and he hadn't lied. But he'd also said it, so that he wouldn't overstep and attempt something she didn't want or wasn't ready for. Between the two of them, their need and frustration grew when all they continued to do was kiss. When they were breathless, Tate stroked hair back from Adelaide's temple.

"If that's all ye're comfortable with for today, I willna push ye for more."

"Is it all right for me to want more? I mean, should I tell ye that we canna do more until we're wed?"

"Addy, I willna take yer maidenhead until ye're ma wife. If aught were to happen to me before we can wed, I willna leave ye unable to secure a noble marriage."

"Dinna tempt fate," Adelaide whispered.

"I'm nae. But I'm being realistic. I willna do aught to compromise ye, but there are other things we can do that willna end yer innocence."

"Can we do those things?"

Tate's smile stretched across his face. "Ye dinna want to try just one. Ye want to try 'those things.' We can do that for as long as ye wish, *leannan*."

"Tatum, I feel comfortable telling ye what I want. Or at least, telling ye the things I ken aboot and want to try. But I'm still worried I'll ask for too much, and ye will think less of me." Adelaide's confession made her want to cry. Tears pricked at the back of her eyes. She felt foolish and embarrassed, which is what Tate said he didn't want. And that only made her feel more foolish and embarrassed.

"Och, Addy. Dinna fash. I dinna think less of ye. It excites me, and that makes me worried I'll scare ye by how ardent ma desire for ye is. I'm scared I'll ask or do something that ye dinna want and ruin this for ye."

"For us. Ye said we do this together. And I dinna think there's aught ye could do to ruin this. I've trusted ye all along, and I trust ye now. If I didna think ye would care for me properly in all things, I wouldnae have told Da I wish to marry ye. I just dinna ken if what I want today is proper."

"I hope ye're thoroughly improper in all ye want. Today and every day for that matter." Tate's wolfish expression made Adelaide wish to strip herself bare, lie down on the ground, and open all of her for him to do with as he pleased. "Kiss me, wee one, and let me touch ye."

delaide gladly tilted her chin up to receive Tate's kiss, and she sighed when not only did their lips touch, but Tate's hands went back to her breast and bottom. Moments later, she felt warm air swirl around her calves, and she realized Tate was hitching up her skirts. His hand grazed the back of her thigh, and her knees knocked together. When his bare hand brushed over her bare backside, she wanted to wrap her legs around his waist.

"Once we wed, I shall pick ye up, wrap yer legs around me, and thrust into ye," Tate whispered. "Does that sound like something ye'll want?"

"That sounds like something I want now." The words tumbled from Adelaide, and she wished she could pull them back in and swallow them.

"Nae until we wed." Tate groaned. Mayhap giving her such ideas for her to agree to wasn't so wise. Now that was the only thing he could imagine. He forced himself to focus on the present. He inched his fingers between her thighs until he could sweep them along her seam. She shifted and opened her legs to him. He lifted his head so he could watch Adelaide. Her eyes were closed, but her expression was blissful. He could tell she reveled in every movement and moment they shared. As her dew dampened his fingertips, he pressed the pad of his middle finger into her entrance.

"Tatum," Adelaide sighed.

"Aye, wee one."

"I ache for ye there. Is that normal?"

"It means ye desire me to be joined with ye. Ma bollocks ache for me to be inside ye."

"It's so intense. It almost burns."

"I ken. I feel the same." Tate's other hand tugged at the laces at the front of Adelaide's gown. When they came loose enough, Adelaide pulled the kirtle down her left shoulder. Tate's hand slid beneath her chemise now that the gown wasn't so snug. He wrapped his hand around her breast, his thumb thrumming her nipple until it tightened to a peak. "Pull yer chemise down, Addy."

She loosened the ties and pulled that down her shoulder, too. Tate yanked until he uncovered her breast. He bent his head and laved her nipple before sucking it into his mouth. Their moans blended. His tongue swirled around before the tip flicked her nipple. Then he suckled. As he drew on the puckered flesh, his other hand glided over her hip until it could ease between her thighs. His thumb found her pearl as his middle finger dipped inside her again. He rubbed slow, deep circles over the bundle of sensitive nerves.

Adelaide couldn't help it. Her hips undulated, trying for more friction, mimicking what she already knew her body would do when they coupled. She tugged her other sleeve down until she could free her other breast. Tate immediately switched to his new target. Her head fell back, her hair brushing her backside. She no longer felt in possession of her mortal coil. She felt as though she left her body and floated above it, yet she experienced every sensation as need grew until it exploded.

She tunneled the fingers of her left hand into Tate's hair and pressed his head to her breast, encouraging him to take more and to suckle harder. Her other hand scrambled to hike his plaid high enough for it to dive beneath the wool. She wrapped her hand around his length and stroked.

"Bluidy hell, Addy," Tate groaned before switching to the first breast. He worked harder to bring her to release since he knew he could only last another minute or two. His cock had twitched with each breathy sound she'd made. Now the feel of her encircling his rod was divine.

"Tatum, this feeling is starting, and I dinna ken what it is. It's like it's in ma belly and ma sheath. It's an ache but a tightening."

"It means ye shall find yer release in a moment. Keep moving on ma hand, wee one."

She followed his instructions as she continued to work his cock, praying she was doing something at least a little right. As warmth and pleasure surged through her, radiating into her limbs until her legs shook, she stifled a scream. Instead, moaning, "Tatum."

The sound of his name and knowing he'd brought Adelaide to her first release were mighty aphrodisiacs, and before he could slow himself, he felt his cock twitch once more as his seed shot from the tip of his cock. He knew it coated her hand and likely felt strange, but he couldn't stop. He seemed to have an endless stream, and his entire body pulsed with satisfaction.

"Addy?" He pulled her against him as soon as his hand was free from her gown, and he'd wiped hers with his plaid.

"Hold me."

"I'm nae letting go."

"How long do ye think we can stay out here before people wonder where we are?"

"Probably two hours before we need to head back. We've already ridden for an hour. We have time for our picnic and to walk or talk—"

"Or stay right where we are?"

Tate grinned before rubbing his nose against Adelaide's. "Aye, *mo ghràidh*. We can stay right here for as long as ye'd like."

Adelaide's lit with surprise and happiness, and Tate hoped he could bring that brightness to her robin egg blue eyes until his last breath. He kissed along her neck, making his way to and across her jaw before moving back down the other side. His right hand went to her breast, kneading it with a groan. She pressed her other breast together, offering him what he seemed to enjoy. He covered her hand, bringing his mouth to them, licking the seam before smattering kisses over them. He suckled one, then the other as Adelaide thought she might faint. Her body discovered sensations she never imagined.

She reached for his leine, yanking at it, trying to free it from his belt. Tate reached back with his left hand to help. The moment his leine loosened enough for Adelaide to slide her hands beneath the material, he returned to focus on both her breasts. Her fingers tingled as they slid over smooth skin that covered his ribs, shoulders and back. Her fingers brushed the line of curls that led from his navel to his belt. She pulled one hand free and dipped it beneath his plaid, discovering the hair ran farther down his abdomen. Satisfying that part of her curiosity, she wrapped her hand around his lengthening rod. She tested what he enjoyed by brushing her fingertips over the length of his cock then its head. Her other hand roamed over his chest covered with the short, tight curls she'd seen when he competed without his leine. Her fingers splayed as she rested her hand over his heart.

"Ma sweet Addy, I'll be a raving bampot if ye continue to torment me. Yer touch is all I'll be able to think aboot from now until ma last day."

"Ye say such wild things." Adelaide laughed until Tate's teeth grazed her nipple before he gave it a soft bite and tug. "What are ye doing to me?"

Tate suckled harder, making Adelaide shift restlessly. She mewled her protest when he pulled away. He unfastened the brooch from his shoulder, dropping it into his sporran. He kneeled before her and spread the extra length on the ground. "Come here, wee one. Let me show ye more."

Adelaide sank to her knees, and he cupped her cheeks before pressing a soft kiss to her lips. He guided her to lie down, and she spread her hair out from beneath her. Tate's mind flashed an image of her arranged just so in their bed in their chamber in Dunbeath. He knew with absolute certainty that he'd share the room he'd occupied nearly his entire life with Adelaide before the season changed. He settled onto his forearms as he hovered above her.

"If ye dinna like what I do, stop me. But dinna be embarrassed by what I wish to do."

"Tatum, I want to try whatever ye wish to do."

"I'm glad ye feel that way, but never accept something because ye believe it's what I want. I dinna want to tup ma wife. I want to make love with her." Tate tested the last phrase, hoping Adelaide would notice his choice of words. She scooted closer, wrapping her arms around his waist before she responded.

"I dinna think ye use that phrase lightly. I dinna think any mon in yer family says that unless he means it."

"I've never said it aboot aught I've done in the past. I

told ye I've cared aboot ye for a long time, and I didna exaggerate. Mayhap it was calf love when it began when we were barely more than weans, but last year it became more, and this year has made me certain. I love ye, Adelaide."

"And I love ye, Tate. I didna ken what to call ma feelings since I've never felt this way before. But I wish to be with ye when I'm nae. I'm happier with ye than I am with anyone else. I feel better aboot maself with ye than I ever have. Ye make me laugh. Ye make me feel safe and precious. I want to make ye as happy as ye make me. I want these moments alone, but I also want the ordinary moments of sitting together for our meals."

"I promise ye, Addy, that I will always protect ye and cherish ye. I feel a kind of peace with ye that I havenae in years. Nae since I started riding into battle or became responsible for leading other men. Ye make me feel braw and confident when in the past I've been that way to hide how unsure I am of maself. Ye trust me and already rely on me, and I dinna take that lightly. I want to be worthy of ye."

"Tatum, ye dinna have to do aught, but keep being who ye are. I'm nay better than ye or anyone else, so worthiness isnae aught to worry aboot. But I canna think of a better mon to love and spend ma life with. I admit I've compared other men to ye for years, and every one of them doesnae compare. I thought I would have to consider men other than ye for a husband because I ken I canna remain unwed for forever. None appeal the way ye do. That means ye are the vera best."

Tate kissed her neck from her collarbone up to the tender skin behind her ear. "I wish to taste all of ye, ma bonnie bride." He shifted down, drawing her skirts up before settling on his belly between her thighs. His broad shoulders slid beneath her legs before his tongue swept over her seam. His thumb ran over her pearl as he finally tasted the treasure he'd fantasized about for a year while he eased his need alone. It was always Adelaide he pictured, whether he was alone or with someone. He'd hoped more than once that the experience he gained was training him for when Adelaide became his wife. His tongue laved her over and over before he moved his thumb and drew her nub into his mouth. His teeth grazed her, and she fisted his plaid beneath her. She lifted her hips to him, but his hand pressed on her belly. He would rush nothing.

"Tatum, I want to touch ye, too. I want ye to feel what I am. How do I do that?"

Tate's cock and bollocks ached with each of Adelaide's words. Her voice was so innocent, yet her words conjured lurid images that he worried would frighten her. So instead of answering, he sucked on her bud. She writhed as he teased her until she could barely form a thought beyond whispering his name over and over. When euphoria burst throughout her, she could do little more than rasp, "Tatum."

He shifted to bring himself over her again, careful his plaid remained between them. He knew the moment they touched skin to skin, he would have no resolve.

"Tatum, I still want to ken how to touch ye like ye did me. Is that possible? I mean, I've heard maids talking aboot it when they didna ken I could hear. But I dinna ken if ladies are allowed to do such."

"Addy, when we are together, we are just us. We arenae nobles. We arenae a tánaiste's daughter or a laird's grandson. We are a couple in love who will soon wed. Whatever ye wish to try, we will. It doesnae have to be today."

"Do ye nay want me to? Are ye being kind in yer refusal?"

"Lass, if ye move ma plaid out of the way to do aught more than wrap yer hand around me, I'll be inside ye, spilling ma seed. Ye are every temptation a mon could imagine. I'm nae refusing ye. I'm refusing maself."

"But I dinna want ye to refuse aught." Adelaide's eyes locked with Tate's. "What we said earlier... It sounded a lot like we pledged ourselves."

"Are ye saying ye wish them to be our handfast vows?"

Adelaide hesitated before she nodded.

"Ye must say it, Addy. I want to hear it."

"I wish for ye to ken they were ma handfast vows. What aboot ye?"

"I said what I did because I mean it, and in ma head, I meant them to be ma vows. I didna wish to push ye. I ken I asked if I could stay after the Gathering to get to ken ye better. But we've been honest aboot our feelings, and we ken each other better than we thought."

"Does that mean we are?"

"Aye, *mo chridhe*. Ye're ma wife." My heart.

Adelaide threw her arms around Tate's neck, and he lowered his body onto hers. She smattered happy kisses all over his face before their mouths melded. "And ye're ma husband. I didna want to hope, but I did. And I thank the angels because I couldnae be happier."

Tate shifted to his side, gently pulling Adelaide with him until they lay looking at one another. "Addy, ye ken I want to make love to ye, and mayhap one day we will somewhere like this, or even this vera place. But I am nae making love to ma wife for the first time on the ground. At least, nae in such an open place where someone might happen upon us. I canna strip ye bare and love every inch of ye."

"What does that mean for us, then? Ye're staying in a tent with yer parents, brother, and sister. I'm sharing a chamber with ma sister. And I dinna ken what Da will do when he finds out. I hope I'm nae a widow by morning."

"Ye willna be a widow, but I might be a gelding." Tate grinned and dropped a kiss on her nose. "I'll talk to Thor and Greer. Mayhap they'd stay with Blake and Cerys."

"Blake and Cerys have a bairn. Thor and Greer arenae going to want to stay with them since they're newlyweds too."

"Then Blake and Cerys can stay with Wee Liam and Elene."

"Tatum, that's two bairns and a wean in there if they do that."

"Aye. They're all used to nae sleeping through the night. It willna bother them." Once more, Tate grinned, and Adelaide tsked.

"I dinna think yer cousins or their wives will be so accommodating."

"I dinna want to consummate our marriage here and this way, but we can stay with ma family."

"I'm nae really yer wife until ye—"

"Ye are ma wife, Addy. Whether we lie together or nae, today or any day, ye are ma wife."

"Others willna think that without a sheet. People might even demand a bedding ceremony." Adelaide flinched at the ferocious mien that greeted her words.

"Yer father would never allow it, and even if he did, I wouldnae. Nay one is watching me with ma wife. That is for us alone. Yer mama would never agree either. And I ken ma mama and aunts would stand guard if they had to. None of them had to survive such embarrassment, and ma da and ma uncles would never expect ye to. Grandda—well, suffice it to say, the Gathering wouldnae end peacefully if someone pushed too hard for it. He willna even listen to the words put together."

"I ken Da and Uncle Edward wouldnae agree, but what if someone does make a fuss? They could cause a feud over it or reopen auld ones. We've seen it happen." The more they discussed their wedding night, the more anxious Adelaide grew. She didn't want anyone—man or woman—watching her fumble her way through pleasuring her husband. She definitely didn't want any women watching her husband strip bare. She could only imagine what would happen to any man who insisted upon seeing her in such a state. Tate would run them through with anything in reach.

"Addy, we'll figure it out when we return to the keep."

"Ye really willna consider it here?"

Tate hesitated. "Addy, I long to be inside ye right now. I ache to find ma release in ye, and I want ye to discover pleasure like ye've never kenned while we make love. But our men are too near." Tate smoothed hair back from her shoulder. "Wheest, wee one. They arenae watching us. They ken we're doing something, but if we remain here much longer, they'll guess. It also leaves us too vulnerable if we're nae clothed, and I plan to see, touch, and taste all of ye. If aught were to happen, we would be at risk. I'm nae willing to do that. I dinna ken this land like I do Dunbeath."

"But if we just do it quickly, this one time—just long enough to show proof on ma chemise..." Adelaide glanced around.

"Would yer parents insist upon the midwife checking ye?"

"Never."

Tate sat up as he pulled a dirk from his belt. He scanned their surroundings, even though he knew no one was in sight. He pushed down his stocking until the top of his calf peeked out. He pushed up Adelaide's kirtle and flipped the inside of her chemise out. "Stay still, Addy. I dinna want to nick ye."

"Tatum, what—Tate! Nay!" Adelaide reached for her husband, but he sliced a small cut along the back of his calf. It wasn't deep, but blood immediately trickled from the wound. Adelaide tried to twist, but Tate dropped the blade and held her away. He glanced at the chemise, guessing at the best place to smear his blood on it. He pulled his stocking back up and wiped his blade on the grass before sheathing it on his belt.

"There."

"Ye canna leave that cut like that. It'll get infected. The wool will get in it."

"I kenned where to cut to make it bleed, but it isnae a deep one. I made sure of it. Once the blood stops, it'll barely be noticeable to anyone." He kissed his bride's cheek. He rose to his feet and helped her to stand in front of him. He pulled up her kirtle until he could see a smudge of blood through the under gown. He breathed easier, seeing he'd managed to smear his blood mid-thigh. It would look like Adelaide was lying on her chemise when she lost her maidenhead.

Adelaide appeared doubtful, but she twisted and pulled up the white chemise. She spied the mark, and she decided it was likely a reasonable amount of blood. But she still worried about Tate's calf. She wanted nothing adverse happening because he tried to protect her. Her conscience would never be at peace.

"Come, wee one. Let's have our picnic." Tate held out his hand after he fastened the extra length of plaid over his shoulder, and she'd righted her gown.

CHAPTER 16

Tate girded his loins as he walked toward Fingal and Edward. He'd spotted Tavish, who'd read his son's expression. He followed without request, which meant his uncles Callum, Alex, and Magnus, along with his grandfather joined him. Fingal and Edward turned a wary expression toward the Sinclair hoard. Fingal stepped forward, casting his eyes over Tate before frowning and nodding at the same time.

With an aggrieved sigh, Fingal put his hands on his hips. "Ye've handfasted, havenae ye?"

"Aye." Tate answered without hesitation. He felt the men in his family groan more than he heard them.

"Following yer family tradition. I expected as much when I learned ye and Ada rode out for a picnic." Fingal rolled his eyes with the last word.

"And ye didna send men to fetch us." Tate fought the urge to cross his arms.

"Aye well, I figured I'd be too late and didna want any of ma men spying ma daughter."

"We need to move this to yer solar."

Fingal's brow furrowed but nodded. He glanced back at Edward, who nodded as well. Fingal led the way into the keep, spotting his wife. "Maddy, ye'd better come too."

While Fingal called out to his wife, Tate nodded to Adelaide, who stood with her mother and sisters. She and her mother joined the men, leaving Sarah and Finley to stare after them. Tate noticed the moment the group shifted, the young women whispered. Their smiles told Tate they'd already guessed. Instead of going to Fingal's solar, Edward gestured toward his. Since this was now both a family matter and a clan alliance matter, it would take place in Laird Grant's study.

The moment the door shut, Fingal glowered at Tate. "I suppose yer marriage is uncontestable."

Tate pulled a chair out for Adelaide at the oblong table where the Grant council met. Adelaide hesitated as she looked over her shoulder at Tate, but his reassuring eyes eased her fear enough to turn her back to Tate and look at her parents.

"Among us, it is. To everyone else, it's nae. But that is only a technicality. Nay one is separating me from ma wife." Once again, Tate fought not to cross his arms. He knew it would appear sullen or belligerent. That wasn't how he wanted this conversation to progress. "We were in the woods with only the ground. I dinna consider that acceptable for ma wife." He twisted his leg and pulled down his stocking. Blood smeared on his skin and stockings showed where he'd cut his leg. The wound was unnoticeable, just as he'd promised Adelaide. "There is proof others might want on Adelaide's chemise."

"Thank you." Madeline reached out to Adelaide, leaning past Liam but looking at Tate. "Da would have fought the king if he'd forced the matter when we wed." Madeline turned to look at her husband. "Ye protected me when ye kenned I couldnae manage something like that. Tate's done the same for our daughter. Nay one will even have the chance to suggest it."

"Do ye plan to keep it a marriage in name only?" Fingal looked like he might be sick as he asked the question.

"Nay." Tate and Adelaide answered together. His hand already rested on her shoulder, so he gave it a brief squeeze. He couldn't see her face, but he was certain her cheeks were the same color as ripened rowan berries. His thumb stroked the top of her spine, at her hairline. He felt the tension ease, so he continued. The gesture was lost on no one, and neither was Adelaide's reaction. He did it without thought. He knew this was a necessary conversation, but he wished it over to spare Adelaide further embarrassment.

"Sarah can stay with Finley, Mairi, and Amy." Madeline named her two nieces through her brother and his wife.

"There isnae that much room in Finley's chamber. Three is already uncomfortable." Adelaide felt guilty that Sarah would likely sleep on the floor.

"We'll make it work. Besides, she will be happy she won the wager against Finley. Sleeping on the floor will be a small hardship since she'll force yer sister to clean the chicken coop for a fortnight."

"They bet on us?" Adelaide couldn't keep the shock or hurt from her voice. Did Finley believe they wouldn't marry?

"Aye. Sarah said ye'd be married when ye came back from yer picnic. Finley said ye'd wed tonight when ye realized..." It was Madeline's turn to flush. Adelaide could guess what her mother left unsaid. When she and Tate returned and realized they didn't want to sleep alone. They didn't want to sleep at all.

"Can we just be discreet and nae announce this until the Gathering is over?" Adelaide looked around, wondering what the Sinclair men thought of this development. Their expressions were warm, but she couldn't tell anything beyond that. She fixed her gaze on Tavish. "I'm sorry. Lady Ceit should be here for this conversation. Should I fetch her?" She finished by twisting to look up at Tate.

"Ma wife already kens. We didna wager, but she was of the same mind as Lady Sarah. She's making space in the tent in case ye should need it. Wiley will sleep with Tor and Kirk. Ailish is going to sleep with Nessa, Mirren, and Keira," Tavish explained. Kirk and Keira Hartley weren't members of the laird's family, but their father, Dedric, was the clan's most trusted warrior. He and his wife, Isabella, fled to the Highlands from the Lowlands' border after being forced to be a spy at the royal court. "Ceit and I will stay with Alex and Brighde beside the lass's tent."

Fingal shook his head. "That willna be discreet. Someone is far more likely to notice Adelaide entering yer tent than they are to spy Tate going up the servants' stairs. We can wait until everyone leaves before the clishmaclaver starts. If anyone says aught before tonight, then we have Ada's chemise. If anyone says aught in the morning, then—we'll have what we need. Ada, I ken ye dinna want this merry time to overshadow Clara and Fergus. I dinna think any of us do."

It surprised Tate that Fingal should call this situation merry since he looked anything but. Then again, anyone who didn't know his relatives would think they didn't support the marriage either. They were—reserved, taking their cues from the Grants. But Tate saw the happiness in each man's gaze. It shouldn't have surprised him that his mother was already preparing for the eventuality that Adelaide would join them. That posed a question he'd been wondering since they exchanged their vows.

"Would ye allow me to stay on after the Gathering, so Addy can have time to say her proper goodbyes to ye?"

Sadness entered Fingal's eyes, and all he could do was nod. Madeline still held Adelaide's hand, but now she reached for her husband's. She was his strength, but Tate could tell Madeline was in no hurry to bid her daughter adieu. It was several days' ride from Freuchie to Dunbeath. It wouldn't be easy for them to visit frequently. But since Tate was so far down the line to inherit, he didn't fear being away from his family or traveling far afield.

"I ken it willna be as often as anyone wants, but Addy and I will visit whenever any of ye wish. Whether she asks or ye do, I will do ma best to always bring Addy home to Freuchie." He felt Adelaide stiffen at the word home, and she looked back at Tate. His eyebrows raised, but she gave a quick shake of her head. She wasn't ready to share that Tate calling Freuchie her home made her feel as though he and his family might not consider Dunbeath her new one. She knew it was ridiculous, but the fear was visceral. She turned back to everyone else.

"I would like that."

"Edward, Fingal," Liam spoke up. "We're glad to call ye family after all these years of fighting alongside one another. We dinna have the bride price with us, but we will send it once we are home. We dinna need Lady Adelaide's dowry. We dinna have the room to carry aught back with us. And it's obvious this isnae a political marriage. Save what ye'd give Lady Adelaide and add it to Lady Sarah's and Lady Finley's dowries. Ye ken there's more than enough land in Caithness to dower all ma daughters and granddaughters and their daughters too." It was clear Liam made no distinction between the members of his family who entered it by birth or by marriage. They were all Sinclairs.

Fingal hesitated.

It was Callum, the Sinclairs' heir and tánaiste, who spoke next. "Fingal, we ken ye're a prosperous clan. We ken ye have plenty ye can send with Lady Adelaide or to us. If there's aught ma new niece wants to bring with her, then we will make arrangements. But Da is right. There's naught we need, and all we want is Tate and Lady Adelaide to be happy."

"Could yer—" Adelaide stumbled over her words. "—Our family call me Ada instead of Lady Adelaide?"

"Of course, lass." Tavish smiled. While all the Sinclair men bore remarkable resemblances to one another, when Tavish smiled, Adelaide knew exactly how he must have looked when he was younger because it was like looking at her husband. It also gave her insight into what Tate would look like in nearly thirty years. Her husband would remain the most handsome man she'd ever seen.

"Welcome to our family, Ada." Alex, the quietest of the four brothers, beamed at her. He had three daughters, but his eldest had married and moved away. It was no secret he missed Saoirse, so while Adelaide wouldn't replace his eldest child, he would welcome her addition.

"I'm certain Cerys and Greer will be happy to have another wife join our family," Magnus chuckled. "Ye help make sure the lasses outnumber the lads. Together, the lads have aboot as much common sense as one of the lasses. The keep would fall down around our ears if it wasna for the women."

The four Sinclair brothers and their father nodded their heads with grins that finally signaled they believed Adelaide joining their clan brought good tidings. She'd worried, even though she could tell Tate hadn't.

Tavish rose from the chair next to hers and pulled Tate into an embrace that would have crushed a smaller man.

"Mama and I are so vera happy for ye. We're also so bluidy proud of ye. Ye will make an excellent husband and father when that day comes. We couldnae ask for a better son."

"Does that mean I'm yer favorite?" Tate jested.

"For this hour," Tavish teased back.

"But Ailish is still yer most favorite." Tate shot his father a playfully hurt look.

"Aye well, the lass is her mama. Ye canna blame me." Everyone knew Tavish didn't favor one child over another, but it was a running joke amongst them that Ailish scared Tavish too much to let Tate or Wiley take her place as the most favored child.

"Do ye wish for our kirking to happen here or Dunbeath?" Tate asked. "If it's here, I would ask that Mama and Da remain with me. I dinna want them to miss ma wedding."

"We could wait the year," Edward suggested.

"Nay." Tate and Adelaide responded together, but Adelaide's voice was more determined. She shrank back into her seat, but Tate leaned down and kissed the top of her head.

"Ma wife and I dinna need to wait a moment longer before we say our vows before a priest. I'm willing to wait until the other clans leave, but I willna leave Freuchie without ma wife, and I'm only bringing her back to visit." Now Tate did cross his arms. The men in his family sat back in their chairs and crossed their arms, too.

"Dinna get in a twitch," Fingal grumbled before he explained what he was certain Edward meant. "Ye can cease yer glowering. Nay one thinks ye'd leave without Ada. Having the wedding in a year means ye can travel to Dunbeath together before the weather changes. And we wouldnae risk being caught in a storm if we followed in a few sennights or moons. We can celebrate at next year's Gathering since the Sutherlands will be hosting. It wouldnae make anyone question ye having yer wedding there since ye're family. It would also leave an appropriate time of mourning for Clara after this Gathering ends."

"Da, I dinna want that." Adelaide's voice was less strident this time. She was still embarrassed that she'd barked her last answer. She looked at Liam. "Laird Sinclair, could yer clan stay an extra day, so we could wed with yer family here? Mayhap the MacLeods and MacKinnons could, too. Nay one would question them staying after the Gathering."

"It's Liam, lass." He wouldn't suggest Grandda yet, but he hoped one day Adelaide would think of him that way, especially as she'd never met either of hers since they'd been dead for years before her birth. "We can certainly do that. I ken ma family wouldnae want to miss yer wedding."

"If that's the case, ye may as well invite the Sutherlands and the Mackays," Fingal conceded.

"Ma cousins and I will hunt since there will be so many of us staying for the feast," Tate offered. Between his male and female cousins in the Sinclairs and the Mackays, they had some of the best hunters and trackers in the Highlands. Partly because of their skill, and partly because of the sheer number of them.

Edward watched the Sinclairs, knowing the men sitting across from him would ensure they contributed to the feast and celebrations. He didn't fear going into debt by having his soon-to-be in-laws stay, but he knew he couldn't house all of them. He would continue to have dozens of tents pitched outside his barmkin, or surrounding wall. He knew if he didn't offer an extended invitation, Davina would, and she did.

"Since we'll invite the MacLeods of Lewis, we should invite the MacLeods of Assynt." Tate's aunt Siùsan was a MacLeod through her mother. "And we should also invite the Mackenzies." His same aunt was the half-sister of the Mackenzie laird and their tánaiste. The latter, through no blood relation, married Tate's cousin Saoirse.

"Thank ye," Callum stated.

"And if we're inviting the MacLeods, MacKinnons, the Mackays, and the Sutherlands, then we should also invite the Camerons and Gordons." Lady Cameron was the elder generation of Sinclair brothers' cousin and a Sutherland before she married, just like Adelaide's uncle's wife, Maude. Adelaide's uncle was Madeline's older brother. Blair Cameron and Maude MacLeod were sisters, and their brother, Lachlan, was the heir to the Sutherlands. Liam's deceased wife was Laird Sutherland's sister.

Madeline's younger sister, Abigail, married Laird MacKinnon. Edward and Davina's elder daughter married one of the Gordon twins. Their other daughter, Fenella, married Laird Campbell's cousin. Between the Campbell laird's sons and his brother's—the tánaiste—sons, there were ten strapping young men to feed. They'd also have to invite the Rosses. The Sinclairs were connected to them through Liam's sister-by-marriage. His deceased wife's brother's wife was a Ross before becoming a Sutherland, and her niece was Lady Campbell. What a tangled web they'd woven, but it meant the alliance Robert the Bruce fought so hard to create was ensured by a handful of Highland women whose marriages truly allied the clans.

"At this rate, we may as well just extend the Gathering an extra day." Adelaide said in defeat. So much for keeping it discreet. "The only people nae related to us are the MacDonalds and MacDonnells, the Mathesons, and Chisholms. If we're inviting Lady Siùsan's family, then we must also invite Lady Deirdre's, the Frasers of Lovat. We must also invite the Gordons since Cairstine married Eoin. We canna have him without his twin, so that's Ewan and Allyson, and all their weans." These weans were the same age as Tate and Adelaide. "We canna nae invite Laird Gordon too."

The guest list was growing with each breath. Discretion seemed to be impossible unless they didn't celebrate the wedding at all. Tate didn't want to suggest it since he didn't want to rob Adelaide of such a special event. But he would have been content merely standing before a priest on the kirk steps with Wiley, Ailish, Sarah, Finley, Angus, and Harry as their witnesses. He wanted his parents too, but it would be enough with his siblings by birth and his soon-to-be siblings-by-marriage. They would one day help lead powerful clans across the Highlands, and he wanted to better his friendships with Angus and Harry, along with Adelaide getting to know Ailish better.

"Life doesnae stop because of tragedy," Madeline spoke up. "Clara is nae really dead, and she wouldnae want Ada and Tate to nae have their wedding. She's been trying to get them together for a year. She'd encourage their wedding. Fergus is too beside himself to think aught aboot ye marrying. But he was just determined to get ye together as Clara. We invite our families, and we celebrate."

Adelaide twisted in her seat as Tate squatted beside her. Keeping his voice so low that only she could hear, he asked, "What do ye want? We only do what ye wish."

"I'm nae waiting a year for us to marry at a kirk. That's what matters most to me. What do ye want?"

"The same. *Leannan*, if ye wish for the wedding and

feast, dinna feel guilty to say so. If ye dinna want the celebration, then we can keep the gathering small."

"I'd like to celebrate, but I dinna ken if that's what we should do." Adelaide felt torn but hearing that Clara had been engineering them together for a year didn't surprise her once her mother said it. She knew Clara wouldn't want her to forego a wedding for her, just like she wouldn't want Clara to forsake a wedding for her. "Ye still havenae told me what ye want. Just that ye'll do what I want."

"I'd like all of our family to be together, and our wedding is a good reason. I wish to dance and feast with ye, so I can show everyone how lucky I ken I am. I wish to dance with ma wife."

Adelaide turned back to look at her parents and nodded. Fingal smiled for the first time since the couple returned from their picnic. Madeline suggested she and Davina find Ceit to plan. Fingal and Edward needed to return to their duties with the games. Tavish, his father, and his brothers said they'd let the family know quietly about the new development. With a warning glare, Fingal was the last to file out of the chamber, leaving Tate and Adelaide alone. The moment they were, Adelaide pushed back her chair as Tate practically yanked her from it. Their mouths fused together as they clung to each other, relieved the conversation remained civil, and Fingal hadn't gelded Tate. Tate cupped Adelaide's cheek before he asked a question she was completely unprepared for.

"What do ye think aboot a double wedding, *mo ghràidh?*"

CHAPTER 17

"A double wedding?" Adelaide hesitated. "Ye mean Fergus and Agnes?"

"Nay. Fergus and Clara. We both ken Clara didna do aught wrong. We ken Peter did."

"Fergus doesnae deserve to marry Clara. Agnes shouldnae be sentenced to a life with a mon who loves her sister." Adelaide's lip curled as bile stung the inside of her cheeks.

"While I wouldnae have forsaken ye in a such a public way, I can understand his feelings. I did while he spoke because I kenned I would feel the same way if ever we were to marry, and I feared ye had betrayed me. I dinna think ye ever could, but neither did Fergus think that aboot Clara. I was with him. It was vera damning. If I didna ken Clara, I would believe it was her."

"But Fergus does ken her. Apparently, even better than I realized. He said such vile things."

"And if he can admit he was wrong and what he did was wrong?"

"That's up to Clara." If anything, Adelaide's gaze only hardened.

"And if she forgives him?"

"Then she's likely a better woman than I. Fergus has made much ado aboot naught because of his pride. What if he does this again? Accuses her without cause and judges her without evidence?"

"Then it will be his clan who decides whether he's fit to lead." It was the same thing he'd told Fergus.

"And it'll be Clara's life he destroys twice. There will always be people who will question her and refuse to accept she's the wronged party in this." That assumption was the same reason Fingal had warned Adelaide away from Tate and what she thought about now as she spoke.

"Then we must show it was Peter who caused this. I'm certain I ken why." Tate's jaw clenched.

"Because the last thing the Chisholms need when they're constantly feuding with the Mathesons is for the Mathesons to ally with a mighty clan like the Mac-Donalds. Even the smallest septs within the smallest branches are forceful because of their ties to the major branches. With eight branches, some even in Ireland, they're a bluidy spider."

The MacDonalds were one of the most dominant clans in Scotland, rivaling only the Campbells. The Sinclairs dominated most of the far northeast, but much of their power also came from the alliances formed through marriage, and Liam's role as the Earl of Caithness. The earldom was the combined earldoms of Sinclair and Orkney. The MacDonalds had branches in Antrim, Ireland along with Ardnamurchan, Clanranald, Dunnyveg and the Glens, Glencoe, Glengarry, Keppoch, and Sleat. That didn't even include lesser branches or septs, like the one to which Clara belonged: Clan MacDonald of Lochalsh. The MacDonnells were also closely allied to the MacDonalds, sharing ancestors and allies.

"Aye. That's what I believe too. I think Adam genuinely doesnae like ye because of the failed betrothal and yer aunt. He used that to distract us. He must have kenned what everyone else did. I'm in love with ye, and I wouldnae let him harm ye, whether by word or deed."

"Tatum, everyone seems to ken. Could our wedding really come as a surprise to anyone at this point?"

"I dinna think so. That's why I say we make it a double wedding." Tate grinned. He slid his hands down to cup her bottom, giving it a squeeze before resting them there. "We dinna actually need the double wedding. I dinna want to make ye share that day. But we get Fergus to believe we're having one. He'll balk again at marrying Agnes, which will mean he'll have to admit in public he would rather Clara still be his bride."

"We'll have to get Agnes to agree; otherwise, it willna work. I dinna want her to fear they will force her to marry Fergus."

"Before the wedding, we prove Peter conspired and caused their breakup. Once Fergus accepts that, and he believes he's aboot to wed, we bring Clara back for their wedding. Presumably, Clara still wants to marry him." While there were plenty of weak points in Tate's plan, that was the one that would create a gaping hole that made it all collapse.

"I canna trust that ma brother or even Da wouldnae muck it up if I sent them to talk to Clara. I need to see her."

"I'll take ye."

If Adelaide couldn't tell from Tate's tone, then his expression veritably yelled that he wouldn't let her go with only her guards. They both knew they would need to do it at night, so no one watched and wondered.

"Nae tonight."

"Definitely nae tonight, wife." Tate waggled his eyebrows, his expression now wolfish. He pulled Adelaide closer, though there really had been no space between them. "Tonight, I shall have ma own private feast and celebration."

"I wouldnae want ye to eat alone," Adelaide whispered before Tate brought their mouths together, fusing their lips into a kiss that made them both wish it was time to retire. Adelaide slid her hands over Tate's shoulders, down his arms to his elbows, then across his back. Tate kissed along her neck, nipping as he went. His hands roamed over her body until he settled them on her breasts. He kissed her cleavage as he pressed the mounds together, envisioning his rod between them.

"We should stop before we consummate our marriage on yer uncle's council table," Tate said. He spoke the words out of duty. He had no desire to live by them. Adelaide grasped his backside and moaned her disagreement.

"More, husband. I dinna ken what ye're doing to me, but I want more."

A knock on the door decided for them, making them leap back with guilt. Tate skimmed his eyes over Adelaide, ensuring she didn't appear like she'd been seconds away from being ravished.

"Aye," Tate called out.

Lady Madeline entered with a warm smile, but her eyes swept the chamber and the young couple. Satisfied that she had interrupted nothing untoward in the laird's solar, she came to stand with them.

"Lady Madeline—" Tate began, but Madeline shook her head.

"Ye're ma son-by-marriage. I'm Madeline."

"Thank ye, ma—Madeline." Too many hours of decorum being drilled into him would take a while to at least relax, if not undo, with his new mother-by-marriage. Addressing her as "ma lady" was as expected as calling her Lady Madeline. "Will yer priest expect us to post the banns?"

It was something that came to Tate as Madeline entered the solar. He hadn't thought about that as he and Adelaide hatched their plan. Since they had already read the banns for Clara and Fergus, that couple could marry immediately. But if the priest at Freuchie Castle insisted upon the banns for Tate and Adelaide, it would be another three sennights. No one had mentioned that consideration while rattling off the guest list.

"Nay. Since ye've handfasted and will be mon and wife by morning, I dinna think the priest will insist upon them." Madeline may have borne five children and been a lady-in-waiting to Queen Elizabeth de Burgh, but her years at a convent still made her reticent to discuss such private matters in public. She struggled early in her marriage with her self-imposed fears for her morality while falling in love and in lust with Fingal. "I came in to see if ye would like to dine together on the dais. We can announce a betrothal but nae make a fuss. Or Ada could dine with yer family and appear to sit with yer sister or the other lasses."

Tate and Adelaide looked at one another. They'd discussed it earlier, but now, it felt like they'd come to no resolution. They silently questioned which was better. Tate cocked an eyebrow, thinking he knew what Adelaide would choose. She nodded; fairly certain she agreed with Tate.

"Addy?" Tate prompted.

"We'd like to sit on the dais. Apparently, everyone else kenned aboot us before we did. It canna surprise many that we agreed to wed. It probably will cause less gossip than us continuing to deny how we feel now that we arenae completely oblivious to how we've appeared. I'm joining the Sinclairs, but I'm still the host laird's niece. And the Sinclair laird and tánaiste dine with us on the dais, anyway."

"I'm honored to sit at yer table, Madeline. I think it

would cause more of a stir if Addy sat at a lower table. People might think ye and Fingal arenae pleased with the match or that we're marrying with Addy in disgrace. I ken I'm never going to be laird, and I dinna aspire to be. But Addy is still a tánaiste's daughter, and this is still her home. I willna do aught to lessen the respect she deserves."

Madeline nodded with a smile that made Tate think she might be proud to call him her son-by-marriage. He looked down at Adelaide as she peered up at him. He entwined his fingers with hers, giving them a squeeze. Adelaide looked at her mother.

"Do ye ken where Fingal, ma da, and Laird MacDonald are?" Tate asked. "We have something else to discuss."

Madeline's smile dropped. "Laird and Lady MacDonald are in their chamber. Their grief isnae pretend. They miss their daughter and grieve the future she should have had. They also worry the Mathesons might insist upon the marriage between Agnes and Fergus. Laird MacDonald says he's remaining locked away to keep from murdering Fergus. Lady MacDonald is making sure he doesnae forget his promise."

"We think we might have a solution," Adelaide offered. "But it means Tate and I ride out to Clara after everyone retires. We need to tell Da and Tavish, so they ken where we are. I ken Da willna let me leave without guards, and I suspect Tavish will insist upon Sinclair men. If nae for Tate's sake, then for mine. We also need to speak to Agnes once we ken whether Clara would consider marrying Fergus if we set things to right."

"I dinna ken that meddling is best, Ada. We planned for Clara to remain hidden and for people to believe she's dead. We did that to protect her."

"Aye. But we've let people assume she died," Adelaide reasoned. "Nay one's actually said she is. We've said she's gone. We're mourning her nae being with us anymore. Those are all truths. If people interpret them to mean something else, that's their concern."

"Madeline, the more I've thought aboot it, the more certain I am that Peter and Adam Chisholm are responsible for this," Tate said. "There is nay other reasonable explanation for why Peter was there. That he was and told us to take another path that led past Clara's tent wasna a coincidence. Following Fergus was his way back into the keep when yer father already banned him. As Addy said to me before ye came in, the Chisholms dinna want the Mathesons and MacDonalds to ally. They fear their alliance with the MacDonalds will weaken in favor of the Mathesons.

"Ye plan to speak to Clara tonight?" Madeline looked at the newlywed couple, highly skeptical. She hid her smile when both faces pinkened, and neither wished to look at her when they both shook their heads.

"Tomorrow will be soon enough." Tate sounded half strangled as he made the concession. He would tuck his bride and himself away for at least a sennight in their chamber once they reached Dunbeath. He had a family tradition to uphold, after all.

Spoken aloud, Adelaide didn't care for the notion that she would spend her second night as a married woman riding in the dark—riding a horse, that is. She reminded herself that they were trying to help their friends, and that she could put aside her selfishness for one night when she had a lifetime ahead of her with Tate. She told herself that several times.

"Vera well. Ada, I came to see which gown ye wish to wear this evening. Do ye still wish to wear ma gray one?"

Adelaide's face softened, and Tate knew he'd never seen a lovelier sight in public. The way Adelaide's expressive visage responded to his touch was by far the bonniest thing he'd ever seen. He wondered why the gown made her smile. She looked up at him as she explained.

"When Mama returned to court after the king summoned her from the convent, she didna have courtly gowns anymore. Lady Campbell lent Mama a dove gray gown and eventually gave it to her. Mama loves the gown because it reminds her of Da's eyes, and he says nay one has ever been more beautiful that Mama when she wears that gown. When I was wee, I decided I wished to wear the gown at ma betrothal since it seemed lucky."

"Since ye look just like yer mama, I'm certain there willna be anyone more breathtaking than ye." Tate cupped her cheek and swept his thumb over it, ignoring Madeline. "I'm certain because gown or nae, ye already take ma breath away. If any mon looks too long, I'll take his breath away too."

Adelaide stared for a moment before she giggled. She shook her head before going on her toes to kiss his cheek. "Silly, sweet mon."

"Lass," Madeline whispered. "He isnae jesting." It was Madeline's turn to laugh. Tate reminded her of Fingal, even before her husband admitted he'd fallen in love with her. She recalled when Tate's parents fell in love at court. She'd only been there a few days when Tavish and Ceit met. While Ceit hesitated, Tavish's rakish reputation ended immediately because everyone realized he was enamored with Ceit from before he even knew her name. She could imagine how Tavish would have reacted if any courtier had lingered overly long around Ceit.

"Mama, may I wear yer blue gown at ma wedding?" It was another Laurel Campbell creation that the Campbells' lady of the clan gave Madeline, who wore it to her wedding. Adelaide, Sarah, and Finley expressed their wish to wear it to their own nuptials when each reached a marriageable age.

"Of course." When Madeline beamed at her daughter, Tate glimpsed Adelaide in twenty years. He knew she would remain the most attractive woman he'd ever seen. While their faces were so similar that it foreshadowed Adelaide's future, there was something unique and irreplaceable about Adelaide's soul that set her apart in Tate's mind. "I'll get the gray one out to air before ye prepare for the evening meal. Tate, I'm certain ye wish to find yer best plaid and leine."

Madeline's pointed comment made the new couple aware she believed their time shut away from the world had ended, at least for now. Adelaide frowned but nodded. Tate smothered his aggrieved sigh. Since they had proof through the signed betrothal documents and what he'd created on her chemise, he wasn't so worried about anyone discovering them locked away alone. But he knew Madeline protected her daughter's reputation, and his too. She wouldn't have anyone speak poorly of her daughter, and she wouldn't have Tate develop a reputation for causing brawls at the Gathering. She didn't doubt how he would react if anyone even whispered a word he might consider defamatory.

"Aye, Mama." Adelaide released Tate's hand that she still held. The trio left the solar, and Tate left the keep to return to his family's tent. He'd watched Adelaide and Madeline make their way up the stairs to the family chambers. He couldn't help the excitement that coursed through him as he imagined spending the night in Adelaide's chamber with her. By the time he arrived at his tent, he was fighting his body's response to picturing Adelaide naked and beneath him, over him, beside him, and in front of him. His mind generated vivid images of making love to her in every way they could conceive.

"Tate?"

"It's me, Mama." Tate ducked into the tent. His mother had a sixth sense about her children, always knowing who approached without seeing them.

"Ma felicitations, lad." Ceit wrapped her arms around Tate's waist as he returned the embrace. "I've made space for ye here if ye need it. I ken it isnae where ye'd like to spend yer wedding night."

"Madeline is sending Sarah to sleep in Finley's chamber. We will spend the night in the keep. Fingal pointed out that I'm more likely to slip into her chamber successfully without notice than Adelaide coming out here and entering our tent."

"That's for the best. But if aught changes, ye and yer bride will have privacy here. I canna believe I have a daughter-by-marriage." Ceit grinned at Tate, and he could only imagine what his mother and sister would draw his wife into. The two women were quick-witted, and Adelaide was no different.

"Should I say aught to Cerys and Greer aboot helping Addy become a Sinclair?" Tate asked. "I ken it wasna easy for them to enter such a large clan. They werenae the same situations since Addy's family supports us, and we dinna have any bad blood with them. But I dinna think it'll be easy to go from a family of nine living together to one with two-and-twenty. And that's just who lives at Dunbeath. Never mind Saoirse and her new family or Auntie Mairghread and hers."

"I think yer lass will do just fine, but I also think it would be a good idea to ask Cerys and Greer to help her. Cerys has her bairn to care for, but Greer is still new to the clan. I think it'll be good for Adelaide and Greer to have one another."

"Do ye think anyone will have aught poor to say aboot Addy?"

"Nae at all. Ye havenae been involved with anyone who thinks ye might wed them, and nay one has ever whispered of arranging a marriage for ye. The men of our clan ken better than to say aught untoward to any lass, let alone a member of the laird's family. They value yer grandda's and Uncle Callum's respect far too much. And if it wasna ye skewering them by the bollocks, it would be yer da."

"Nay, Mama. It would be ye."

"Well, aye. But yer da would be right behind me."

"Ye ken everyone thinks ye're far scarier than Da. He's all bark, and ye're all bite."

"Dinna come near ma weans, and there's nay reason for me to bite. Adelaide's one of mine now."

"I wouldnae say this to Addy since I dinna think any woman would appreciate it, but she reminds me a lot of ye. I think she'll be just as good a mama as ye are. I think she'll love our bairns and always do her best for them."

"Och, ye are a sweet lad when ye want to be." Ceit went onto her toes to kiss her son's cheek, but he still had to bend down for her to reach. Tate wrapped his arms around his mother and lifted her off her feet, giving her a smacking kiss on her cheek. "Ye are a big softie, just like yer da. Dinna tell him that since I dinna think any mon would appreciate being compared to a wean."

"A wean?" Tate straightened and pushed back his shoulders. "I got married today."

"Ye can be as auld as Methuselah with nae a tooth in yer head, and ye will still be our wean. And I wouldnae have it any other way. I'm so vera proud of ye, Tate. Ye have become a mon our clan respects. A mon our family trusts. And a mon Da and I couldnae admire more. Ye have proven yerself a mighty warrior, but as good as ye are at that, I think ye will make an even better husband. Adelaide is a vera lucky lass to have ye as her mon."

"I'm the lucky one, Mama."

"Aye. Well, ye remember that. Dinna muck it up. And when ye do—which all married people do from time to time—remember humility goes a long way to keeping a loving marriage a happy one."

"Mama, I ken I havenae really asked ye or Da for advice much lately, but would ye give it to me aboot being a good husband if I asked for it?"

Ceit hesitated, and Tate's heart rate spiked. "Da and I willna give advice that isnae asked for. There are only two people in yer marriage, and that's how it should be. If ye need advice, ye can always ask. But that doesnae mean we'll tell ye what to do. Only ye can ken what's best for yer wife and ye."

"Mayhap I'll just try to do what Da does."

"Good Lord, nay. The mon drives me barmy." Ceit chuckled. She shooed him toward his bedroll and belongings. "Tidy yerself up before ye sit on the dais. Make yerself bonnie for yer bride."

"Bonnie? Mama, ye wound me. First, ye call me a wean. Now, ye call me bonnie."

"Ye're both." She winked at him before ducking out of the tent. Tate wasted no time grabbing his best leine and his best plaid with the laird's family pattern before heading to the loch. He would make sure he looked his best for the meal. He knew Adelaide would accept him no matter how he looked, but he wished for people to think he made a good impression because he was proud of his wife. He wanted them to see that he saw her as worth his effort. He didn't know why it mattered so much to him, but he wanted his marriage to begin on a high note. He wanted Adelaide to feel as special as he believed she was. And he wanted to ensure no one had anything negative to say about him since announcing their betrothal on the heels of Fergus and Clara's disaster would already cause a buzz. He wanted nothing to ruin the evening for Adelaide.

When he arrived at the loch, he found a group of his Sinclair and Mackay cousins, so he whiled away the time with them. There were still a few hours before the evening meal, so when he could no longer linger in the water, he returned to his tent and bedroll for a brief nap. When he emerged, he felt fully rested despite sleeping on the ground. He eagerly anticipated the announcement that evening, finally admitting to the world that he loved Adelaide, and that they had a future together.

Unfortunately, when he arrived in the Great Hall, it was abuzz with people talking to and talking about Laird and Lady MacDonald, along with Agnes and Fergus's planned nuptials. Tate looked around for Adelaide and spotted her with her sisters and his. He caught Wiley's eye and titled his head toward them. It looked less questionable when both of Ailish's brothers approached and stood among the women.

"Do ye still wish me to sit at the dais tonight?" Tate whispered as he looked around.

"If ye do, then Da or Uncle Edward has to make the announcement. Right now, all anyone is talking aboot are Agnes and Fergus. We canna overshadow that. It will have to wait."

"I agree, though it disappoints me tremendously."

"Does aught else have to wait?" Adelaide whispered as her cheeks darkened.

"Nay, wife. Naught else aboot tonight changes. Ye will sleep in ma arms and nay where else."

"Sleep?" Adelaide's lips twitched.

"Eventually." Tate hesitated, and Adelaide's brow

furrowed. "I dinna ken that ye will wish for such a—a—an energetic—night since it might—ye might—ye may nae feel up to it. I dinna wish to harm ye."

Adelaide watched Tate flush as he stumbled over his words. He hadn't been tongue-tied earlier that day when they were alone. She wondered if it was the possibility that someone might overhear them or the subject that made him uneasy. Perhaps it was both.

"I ken I'm always safe with ye, Tatum. We'll see how things go. If it's only once tonight or it's ten times, we'll decide when we get there."

"Ten, lass?" Tate waggled his eyebrows. "Ye compliment me."

"I dinna think I'm wrong, though. Yer family didna get so large by chance."

Tate chuckled as he nodded, but he grew serious as he looked around. "When I leave, I'll be sure I do it with other members of ma family. But I will slip back in. Is there a door into the keep from the gardens or somewhere else?"

"Aye. The gardens. It'll bring ye in by the kitchen, and there are servants' stairs just inside the door. Take them to the second floor. Mine will be the fourth door on the left."

Tate shifted as though he looked around, but the back of his hand brushed Adelaide's before he wrapped her little finger with his. "The meal will be interminable, but it willna be long, *mo ghaol*." My love.

"I ken. I wish the priest would bless the food, so we can begin."

"Why dinna ye sit between Ailish and one of the other lasses? I'll sit across from ye."

"I'd love that. I didna fancy watching ye from the high table."

"Nay more than I fancied watching ye from one of the trestle tables."

The couple made their way to the table where the Sinclairs gathered. Tate wished he was sitting beside Adelaide, so he might hold her hand beneath the table or rest his hand on her thigh. But alas, that was not meant to be for that meal. However, with his long legs, he could touch hers beneath the table. He captured one of her knees between his. Her other leg pressed against the outside of his. It was the most contact they could have, and they found comfort in it.

When the music began, neither moved toward the dancers. They only joined them when songs began that would keep them together throughout the set. They didn't fancy dancing with anyone else. Tate knew he held Adelaide a fraction too close, but he enjoyed the sensations of having her nearly pressed against him. He figured, since everyone else recognized their attraction, there was little point in pretending it wasn't there. However, he was mindful not to do anything that would jeopardize her being the subject of vicious rumors.

"I'm tired, Tate," Nessa said as she came to stand beside the couple. She shot them a quick wink. "So are Mirren and Shona. Would ye and Wiley walk us back? I'm certain Ailish is ready to go, too."

None of his cousins nor his sister would dare walk back to the camp alone at night. It was the perfect excuse for Tate to leave with them. However, he wouldn't put Wiley in the position of having to choose who to guard if something happened. In the light of day, Tate wouldn't worry whether his younger brother could protect all the women on his own. But the dark complicated everything.

"Ask Tor and Kirk to come with us. Keira and Maisie too." It was all the unwed cousins and friends.

"Aye. I'll let Da ken ye and the others are walking Mirren and me back." Nessa turned away in search of

Alex. As the only older generation sibling with only daughters, he was vigilant about their safety. The young women's cousins knew without being asked to protect Nessa and Mirren, and before she'd married, Saoirse too. But Alex always did when other clans were present. He wanted to ensure no one thought his daughters would make good targets.

"I'll find Finley, Sarah, and ma cousins. We can all retire too. They'll understand." Adelaide released Tate's finger, and they both paused.

"I'll be there soon. Lock and bar the door. Dinna open unless ye hear ma voice."

"I ken, husband. But thank ye for the reminder." Adelaide flashed a grin before she signaled her sisters, and Tate and Wiley walked away with Ailish.

ate swallowed several times as he tried to tamp down his eagerness and nervousness. He wanted the time alone with Adelaide, and he longed for the intimacy they would share. But he felt anxious that he would somehow fail her or not impress her. He wasn't the most experienced young man, but he was hardly ignorant of what happened between a man and woman. He knew what to do. He just didn't know how well he would do it. The women he'd been with lied for a living, moaning and sighing to earn more coin.

"Addy," Tate's hushed voice felt like it boomed in the passageway just like the three raps on her door. He knew she would be certain it was him since no one else called her that. She let him in and stepped back. Tate's gaze swept the room before settling on his bride.

"I didna ken if I should already be undressed or if ye'd want to—" Adelaide snapped her mouth shut and looked at the floor.

"Addy, I didna have a chance to tell ye how bonnie ye are in this gown." She wore the dove gray one her mother lent her. "If ye'd undressed, I might nae have had the chance to tell ye and let ye see just how much I admire ye in it."

He wrapped his right arm around her waist while his free hand drew hers to his chest. He bent his head forward and kissed her knuckles since her fingers curled around his. He brushed his lips against hers for a whisper of a kiss.

"Thank ye. I feared the moment was lost for it to matter since we couldnae let everyone ken."

"It wasna lost on me. Will ye let me undress ye?"

"Aye. I dinna have a lady's maid, and I didna want to ask ma sisters. It was too embarrassing."

"Ye will never need a lady's maid. Ye have me." Tate moved her long raven-colored hair out of the way as he kissed the back of her neck after turning her away from him. As the laces loosened, he smattered kisses over her shoulder. "Addy, ye ken I have a sister and half a dozen female cousins. We've traveled together and have swum together. I ken how to help with a gown because of them."

Adelaide looked over her shoulder and smiled. "I might nae have thought of that tonight, but I would have wondered."

Tate paused with only half the laces undone. He considered whether they should have the conversation that swirled in his mind. He decided in favor of it, but he wondered if Adelaide should remain dressed for it. With her gown sagging around her shoulders and halfway off, he figured it was easier if she removed it. Once it pooled on the floor, and she only wore her chemise, he encircled her waist with his arms, drawing her back against his chest.

"*Leannan*, let's talk for a moment."

"I ken what happens, Tate. Ye ken I do."

"That's nae what I wish to talk aboot." He led her to the bed and waited for her to sit before he took the spot beside her. But he changed his mind and lifted her onto his lap. His arms hung loosely around her hips. "Ye ken I'll always be faithful."

"That's like saying the sky is blue. It doesnae need stating."

"But I am nae a virgin."

Adelaide didn't like where the conversation was going. She moved restlessly and considered getting up.

"Wait and let me start. If ye dinna like what I have to say, then I'll stop."

"All right."

"Ma da and ma uncles all had more experience than I do when they wed. Ma da is a third son. He never expected to inherit the lairdship, so he wished to remain unwed. I will share a secret with ye that I dinna think half ma family kens. He didna want to fall in love and commit to one woman in case she died like ma grandmama. He'd seen how Grandda mourned and how he swore off all other women for the rest of his life. It scared him to love someone that much and to grieve so hard. King Robert decided for Da that marriage was a requirement. But ma parents fell in love before they wed. But Da's past hurt and humiliated Mama several times when they were newly married and at court. Similar things happened with Uncle Tristan and Uncle Callum. It only happened once or twice to Uncle Alex. The point I'm eventually going to reach is that ma generation of men have enough knowledge to ken up from down, but we dinna have the experience Da or ma uncles had when they wed. None want our wives to experience what our mamas and aunts did. I've been with three other women, Addy, and none are at Dunbeath."

Adelaide wasn't sure she enjoyed knowing the exact number. She supposed it was better than thinking half a dozen, a dozen, or even a score. It made her wonder who the other women were, but she was certain they weren't anyone Tate harbored any feelings for.

"I kenned I'd marry one day, and I wished to ken how to pleasure ma wife. I was also curious, and men are allowed to indulge that curiosity. I'm also telling ye this, nae to hurt ye, but to reassure ye that I dinna have some sordid past. I never spilled ma seed in a woman's sheath, so I dinna have any bastards." Tate cleared his throat, not sure that the next part would go over any better than what he'd already said. "Do ye ken there are other ways for a mon to find his release within a woman?"

Adelaide blinked owlishly before the answer dawned on her. "Aye. Two ways."

"Aye. Both ways nae only ensure a mon doesnae sire a child, but they also protect a mon from catching aught. I would never forgive maself if ma past harmed ye, Addy. If it made ye ill. I canna stomach the thought of it, so I'm glad that I dinna have much experience."

"Ye havenae been tempted?"

"Ye've been tempting me for years." He nuzzled the spot just below her ear. "Aye. I have been. But like I said, I've always kenned I would marry, and Da made sure I understood his wisdom before I could get up to aught. The temptation didna seem worth it if it could ruin ma marriage or hurt ma wife. The only people Da loves more than Mama are Wiley, Ailish, and me. I ken it's the same for Mama. Nay one has ever questioned his devotion to Mama, and nay one will ever have cause to question mine to ye. But I dinna want aught that could come between us. That's why I'm telling ye all of this. I dinna want ye wondering and worrying. I dinna want ye to question us because ye simply didna ken ma past."

Adelaide sat motionless except for her shallow breaths. Conflicting emotions of resentment, relief, embarrassment, and love warred within her. "I dinna like kenning for certain that ye have a past. I kenned it existed, but I didna ken specifics. Kenning there was someone else doesnae feel good, but kenning it was only three is a relief. I never thought ye might have any bastards. As for disease, I did ken that. Mama explained it when she explained everything else. I just wasna thinking that fast a moment ago."

Tate tightened his arms around Adelaide's hips, sensing something went unsaid. She rested her head against his chest and closed her eyes. "Is there something ye wish to ken? Some question I havenae answered with what I offered?"

"Those two other ways—since ye only did them with wenches, do ye believe only they should do those things?"

Tate tried not to let his surprise show, and he tried not to laugh. He didn't want to embarrass her further, and he didn't want to make her shut him out. "They are nae meant just for wenches. Men and women, lairds and ladies, nobles and peasants can enjoy those things regardless of their stations. They were practical in the past. If ye wish to try aught, then we will. It's aboot sharing this and the feelings that go with it with only ye that make it different and special."

"So, it doesnae make me a whore to want to take ye in—" Adelaide could only whisper the end of her sentence. "—Ma mouth and arse?"

"Ye arenae that word. I willna say it when I'm talking aboot aught that has to do with ye. Some of those women do what they do because they want to. But most of them do it to survive. Yer life will never depend upon what ye let me do to ye. I will never make ye trade pleasuring me for food, clothes, shelter, or ma attention. I will never withhold yer pleasure to control ye or ignore its importance. So, nay. Ye arenae that word. What we do together is only our business. I certainly will never share it with anyone else, and I dinna think ye'll be shouting it from the rafters or whispering aboot it in the kirk."

"Definitely nae. Will ye teach me how ye like a woman to pleasure ye?"

"We'll discover it together. I dinna ken yet what I'll enjoy with ye, but I strongly suspect there willna be aught I dinna want to do over and over. I love ye, Addy. That makes all this new. I dinna ken what to expect aboot how it'll feel. But I'm pretty bluidy certain it'll be better than aught I've fantasized aboot."

"Ye've pictured us together a lot?"

"Aye. Nay other woman has ever caught ma interest."

"Ye're the only mon I've been curious aboot. Nay other mon has ever caught ma interest." Adelaide twisted to look at Tate and wrap her arms around his neck. Their kiss began slowly, both savoring the connection they felt through their bodies after such a vulnerable conversation.

Tate's hand slid along the outside of Adelaide's leg, over her chemise, until it came to her backside. He rested his hand there for only a moment before he bunched the material high enough to move his hand back down to her knee and slide it beneath the cloth. His hand glided up the side once more, his fingers wrapped around the back of her thigh.

"Help me undress, Addy. I want to feel yer hands on me."

They rose together. Tate unfastened the brooch on his shoulder, dropping it into his sporran before Adelaide unfastened his belt. Its weight surprised her as she caught it. She noticed more dirks in sheaths than she expected. She glanced at the door then the bedside table where she imagined his sword would rest once their marriage became public. Only the laird's family carried their swords within the keep unless they were the guards assigned to the keep that day. Tate was now part of her family.

"What are ye thinking aboot, wee one?" Tate unraveled his plaid before folding it in half, then half again. He laid it on the bed. As Adelaide answered, he removed his boots and stockings.

"That one day, yer sword will rest beside the door or against the table beside the bed when we visit here because ye're now part of ma family, too. It seems so intimate to ken that. I dinna ken why."

"Because a warrior is almost never without his sword. It's a part of me, and I only take it off where I ken I'm safe. I'm safe with ye, *mo ghaol*. Ye give me respite from ma duties, ma family, ma clan's name. It's intimate because it will never rest in a bedchamber that I dinna share with ye. But it will never be too far for me to reach and protect ye."

Adelaide reached beneath her chemise and rolled down her stockings, then placed them and her mother's gown over the back of a chair. She'd kicked off her slippers before he arrived. They stood together, Adelaide in her chemise and Tate in his leine. He drew her closer, and she gladly stepped between his legs when he sat on the end of the bed. His hand slid along silky bare skin this time when he drew up the back of her chemise. When his hands reached her backside, he squeezed before kneading the supple flesh.

Her moans spurred him to wrap his hands around her waist and lift her until she straddled him, only two pieces of material keeping his sword from her sheath. He continued to run his hands over her legs and bottom as her hands explored his upper arms, shoulders, chest, and back. With no sporran, or even a plaid and gown in the way, Adelaide felt Tate's arousal. She gasped as her mound rubbed against him.

"Do ye feel what ye do to me, wife?"

"Mmhmm," Adelaide murmured with excitement.

"Shall I feel what I do to ye?" He didn't wait for an answer, instead trailing his left hand from her backside to her seam. The back of his index finger ran along her netherlips before his thumb pressed on her pearl. He felt her dew coating his finger. He withdrew his hand and licked his finger. "Did ye enjoy this last time?"

"Aye." It was more of a sigh as she kissed along his neck after watching him slide his tongue over his digit. Knowing he wanted to taste her spurred Adelaide to nip and nuzzle his neck as she rocked her hips.

"Are ye ready for me to see ye bare?"

Adelaide didn't miss the seductiveness in Tate's tone, but she also heard concern. She leaned back, her right hand cupping his jaw. "I'm ready for all of it. If we do something I'm nae comfortable with, then I promise to tell ye. But I want everything. Ye dinna need to ask me for permission or to be sure it's something I want. I promise ye, it is."

She reached down and whipped the chemise over her head. She'd gathered every ounce of courage she had to be so forward with her comments and to strip before her husband. As she flung the gown away, she watched Tate. Hunger filled his eyes as his gaze swept over her. She clung to him when he suddenly rose and turned them before crawling onto the bed. The moment her back touched the mattress, he devoured her breasts. He alternated sides, suckling like a starving man finding an oasis. His hands roamed everywhere he could reach.

"Tate, take off yer leine. I want to touch ye, too."

"Nay." He practically barked his answer. His eyes locked with hers when he looked up. "If I take it off now, then I willna stop maself from entering ye and being far too rough. I want ye to discover other things, and I need to calm down."

"What if I dinna want those other things right now after all? What if I want ye inside me because I feel like I might crawl out of ma skin if ye dinna? What if I dinna want ye to be gentle? The way ye look at me—ye make me feel more beautiful than aught else in the world. It makes me ache for ye in a way I still dinna understand. But I think the only way to stop that ache is to join with ye."

"There is naught more beautiful than ye. I desire yer body as much as I do yer mind and heart. But I'm bigger than ye. I weigh more. I'm stronger. And I'm nae small anywhere. I want to be sure yer body is as ready as mine."

"Can ye check?" Adelaide's brow furrowed. Her simple question made Tate pause and chuckle. It was so innocent but practical. He inched down the bed and brought his mouth to her entrance. He swiped his tongue across her netherlips before using his fingers to peel them back. He swirled the tip of his tongue along the shimmering skin before flicking her bud. She writhed on the bed, unsure if she wished to get away from his probing tongue or have Tate hold her closer. When he sucked on her pearl, her back arched as her head fell back. She could no longer hold it up to watch him. Her eyes squeezed shut with too many sensations to master or distinguish. Her body felt like it was aflame, and she would happily go up in smoke.

Tate watched his responsive bride as her hips lifted off the bed in offering to him. Her face showed every emotion—need, confusion, frustration, pleasure. He wanted to see bliss. His fingers and tongue continued to run along her entrance, heightening her eagerness.

"Tatum, please. I need ye. I told ye. I dinna understand this. The ache—it's like a burn now. It doesnae feel as good as it did before. I..."

Tate heard the hitch in Adelaide's voice as she

trailed off. He was pushing her too far, too fast. He knew she didn't have any reference to explain how she felt other than what her mother likely described and the sample she'd had in the woods. If it were anything like he was feeling, there weren't words adequate to articulate his need for her. He didn't want to send her from the point of arousal, past frustration, into desperation. He didn't want her to withdraw and give up. He whisked his leine over his head as he spoke.

"Move up the bed until ye're comfortable." She shimmied backward, then reached for him as he prowled closer. She marveled as the muscles bunched with each move. She looked down between his arms and spied his rod for the first time. She wasn't certain, but she thought she licked her lips and even purred. The way Tate pounced made her think she had. She had nothing with which to compare Tate's cock, but she was fairly certain most men weren't made like him. He came to rest his weight on his forearms as his body hovered over her. He pressed gentle kisses along her temple and cheeks as he lowered himself to press a fraction of his weight onto her, giving her the chance to get used to the first of a series of new sensations.

Adelaide wasn't feeling nearly as patient as Tate appeared. She tugged on his shoulders, pulling him closer so she could wrap her arms around his neck. When their chests brushed, she sighed. As more of his weight pressed her into the mattress, she had a sense of feeling untouchable. That she had a giant shield that would always protect her from the world outside the bedchamber door.

"Are ye scared that it'll hurt me, and I'll tell ye to stop?"

"Aye."

"*Mo ghràidh*, I ken it hurts more for some women than others. I dinna ken what it'll be like for me. But I also ken that it's passing. If it were miserable every time, then I dinna think I would see so many women leave their crofts with smiles every morning before they kiss their husbands when the men leave to work."

Tate grinned. His practical and philosophical wife set some of his worries at ease. When their lips met, their need swelled just as his rod continued to do. Adelaide wasn't the only one who ached to consummate their marriage. His cock twitched, and his bollocks tightened as his body demanded relief. They continued to kiss as the tip of his rod slid between her netherlips, her dew coating him just as it had his finger and tongue. While he'd intended to bring her to release and seize the moment when her body relaxed, he was just as eager as she was. When the head of his cock aligned with her entrance, he drew back his hips and thrust forward.

Adelaide tensed in anticipation of pain, trying to prepare herself for what she was certain would feel like a battering ram bursting through a postern gate. But the intensity she feared wasn't there. She suspected her discomfort came more from her channel never having been stretched before, rather than the breaching of her maidenhead. She shifted her hips. She found a more comfortable position as Tate groaned. She watched his face, just as he did hers. She moved her hips again, watching Tate suck in a hissing breath.

"I'm all right. It smarts, but it wasna excruciating like I've heard told. It's more getting used to the feeling of being so—full. Please, can we do more? I ken there is more."

"There willna be if I dinna calm down for a moment," Tate muttered.

Adelaide grinned. "Ye like it that much?"

"Holy St. Columba. If I liked it any more, then it would surely be a sin. I dinna need to go up in the flames of hell on ma wedding night." Tate eased back before thrusting slightly harder than he had before. Their sounds of appreciation mingled in the air. "I shall be saying ma prayers morning, noon, and night because I shall commit gluttony for the rest of ma days."

"Gluttony?"

"Aye, because I will never get enough of how this feels. Being with ye, Addy. Kenning ye're ma wife, and I'm making love to ye is even more incredible than I could imagine. And the way we fit together. The Lord made us for each other. Ye're perfect."

"Will ye hold me closer? I dinna want even air between us. When ye say things like that, I dinna ever want to let go of ye."

Tate gladly slid his arms beneath Adelaide, his hands wrapping over her shoulder as he surged into her again and again. He could tell she'd grown self-conscious of the noise she made when her breath hitched over and over, but she made no sound.

"Let me hear ye, wee one. I see it in yer face that ye're enjoying this. Ye move with me, so I can tell from yer body, too. But I would hear it. It does something to me."

"Do ye mean ye wish for me to tell ye what I like?"

"Good God, aye. I'd meant moan, but if ye wish to tell me, then I'll listen raptly."

Adelaide giggled again, and it tightened her core. Tate grunted as his hips moved of their own volition. He'd worried he would be too rough if he didn't give himself a chance to calm down before they coupled. That patience he'd found while he pleasured her with his mouth vanished when she spoke again.

"I imagined what this would feel like, and I wasna entirely wrong. But ye feel so much bigger than I thought ye would. I thought I would feel like I was being ripped in two, yet yer size only makes it feel perfect." Adelaide wasn't sure if that's what he meant about telling him how she felt. It was the truth, but it didn't sound very alluring to her own ears.

"I want to make it better than ye ever dreamed."

"It is. I like how hard ye feel." That earned her a more demanding thrust, and she realized that was the sort of comment Tate wanted. "Faster, Tate. I need more."

Her wish was his command. Watching her, looking down between their bodies reminded him of how much smaller she was than him. His good intentions hung by a thread, but it wasn't one that would fray completely. He wanted to drive into her harder, faster, more urgently. But he knew he would hurt her, regardless of whether it was their first time or their hundredth. The notion that she could ever associate anything unpleasant with their coupling made Tate's mind buzz with fear. He wanted each time to be as perfect for her as it was for him.

"Ye feel so good, wee one." He drew her left leg over his hip, rolling her to give him deeper access as he drove his rod into her over and over. Sweat beaded along his brow, and he felt it between his shoulder blades. When he shifted, Adelaide gasped. He watched her eyes drift closed, but her brow furrowed. She was suddenly concentrating harder than she had before. He wondered if he'd elicited a new sensation for her. One she wanted again. One that was leading her to release. He mimicked the move he'd just made, and he felt her arch her back into him. "Is this what makes it feel good for ye?"

"Aye." Adelaide's tone was one he couldn't describe. It was as though she answered his question simply to get it over with because she was too entrenched in what she was doing to say more. He allowed himself to move with a little more force as he felt his pubic bone rub against her pearl. Each new surge of his rod into her sheath made her dig her fingers deeper into his back. When her eyes opened, her gaze was pure seduction. It wasn't the look of a woman who knew what she was doing. It wasn't speculative or manipulating. It was innocent wonder, and that made her more alluring than any woman Tate had ever seen.

"Is this what ye like? Do ye want more?"

"I want it all. I want ye."

The sound of their bodies moving against each other filled the chamber, and Adelaide could no longer stifle her moans. Each appreciative sound drove Tate wild, and she realized she needed his evaporating self-control to disappear altogether. It made her mind and her body feel something she hadn't experienced before: unadulterated desire. It was what she felt for him, and what she knew he felt for her.

"Tate, I still ache for ye. It's nae enough. Harder. I need ye to stop worrying ye'll hurt me."

"But I will."

"Ye dinna trust yerself, but I do. I ken in yer heart, ye'll never let yerself lose all control to the point where ye'd hurt me. But I dinna want ye to keep holding back. I need to ken—" Adelaide released a moan, hoping it would distract Tate from what she'd almost admitted.

"Ye need to ken that I need ye so much that I have nay control, that I willna stop maself from taking what I want."

"Aye." Adelaide feared it made her sound egotistical, but it was what she craved. It's how she felt about him as she moved beneath him, trying to meet each thrust with as much force. She wanted to pleasure him as much as he did her. She thought she'd ruined the moment when he reared back onto his knees, but he grasped her hips and hammered into her. She couldn't tear her eyes away from the picture he created as his washboard stomach flexed and his chest muscles strained beneath his skin. The gleam in his eyes would have scared her if it was any other man, but with Tate— she wanted to be as alluring as he made her feel.

"Is this what ye want, Addy? Ye want me to show ye just how much I want to make ye mine?"

"I am yers. That's why I want it."

Those first three words. They did something to Tate. They filled his heart to bursting, but they also set off every possessive and protective instinct he had. There was nothing he wouldn't do for his wife. And that included making her enjoy their coupling so much that she craved it in her soul like he did. He didn't fear she would ever stray, but he never wanted her to want another man, wonder what it might be like to be with another man.

"Oh, Tate... Aye... Aye... Dinna stop... Please, just dinna stop."

"I'm nae stopping until ye find yer release."

"Neither will—Tatum!"

Adelaide's body shuddered, and her core tightened around his cock. She clawed at him, so he leaned over her, not slowing his pace. She yanked him down, their bodies once more pressed together. Her kiss pushed him over the edge. It was passionate, possessive, and added to the most sinful delight he'd ever experienced. He felt his rod twitch before streams of his seed shot forth, filling her until he was certain it would drip from her sheath while he was still buried inside her.

Her arms dropped to the mattress as though she had no strength left to hold them up. Her eyes had squeezed shut in the midst of her release because it was too intense for all her senses. With her sense of sight gone, her sense of touch took over. Now, her chest heaved as she fought to catch her breath. Her heart hammered behind her ribs so hard that it burned.

"Kiss." It was the only word she could muster. Tate obliged and pressed a soft one to her lips, pulling back before their mouths melded together. These kisses were tender and languid, no longer demanding. Affection flowed between them as Tate once more settled a fraction of his weight on top of her, and she found the energy to wrap her arms around him. "Tatum."

She had no more words. She gazed into his eyes, and she saw all her love reflected in his whisky-hued orbs. She cupped his jaw, brushing her thumb over his cheekbone several times before brushing hair back from his forehead. A moment of sadness flashed brighter than she expected when Tate pulled away, but she was unprepared for him to roll them, so her weight rested on him. He wrapped his arms around her as she rested her head against his shoulders. She drew up her legs and hugged him like a bear climbing a tree. His hands moved lazily over her back before one cupped her backside.

"I love ye, wee one."

"I love ye, braw one." She tilted her head back as Tate tucked his chin to see her. His smile made his already handsome face breathtaking. He appeared more relaxed than Adelaide had seen him since they were children. "Ye look happy."

"What's beyond happy? Blissful? Whatever it is, that's how I feel." Tate closed his eyes as he tightened his hold. But he wanted to see his wife. Her flushed cheeks, her plump rosy lips, her dreamy blue eyes. She was too magnificent to miss. "Are ye happy?"

"Blissful."

"Would ye let me hold ye for forever? I dinna want to let go."

"I dinna want ye to let go. Aye. Ye can hold me until ma last breath." She tucked her chin and sighed. Her eyes drifted shut as her heart finally stopped racing.

Contentment replaced arousal. The tenderness juxtaposed with the primal desire left them both feeling complete.

"Do ye wish for me to call ye a bath? Mayhap a soak in hot water will keep ye from getting too sore. I dinna want ye to regret—"

"Dinna finish that thought, Tatum. Naught aboot what we just shared is or will be regrettable. At least, nae for me."

"Ye canna think for a second I would regret any of that. But I willna be the one who is uncomfortable later. I worry aboot ye."

"I ken ye do, and it makes me feel precious. Mayhap in a bit. Can we just stay like this for a while longer?"

"Of course, *mo ghràidh.*"

The air in the chamber remained warm since the window was open and the hide was pulled to the side. As their bodies cooled, exhaustion swept in. Comfortable as they were, they both drifted off.

CHAPTER 19

It was the middle of the night when Tate and Adelaide woke. She insisted it was far too late for them to summon anyone to bring her a bath. He offered to do it himself. He just needed to know where they kept the tub and the buckets. She shook her head and insisted he would wake the entire keep trying to maneuver the copper tub up the stairs alone. She compromised and appreciated Tate when he brought a cool, wet compress to her. He was gentle as he cleansed her, then pressed the linen to her sheath, easing some of the inevitable discomfort about which he'd feared. His ministrations were so considerate and gentle that she felt no embarrassment when she spied the evidence of her lost innocence on his rod.

That attention to her needs led to attention to other shared needs. Their lovemaking wasn't as frantic as their first time. They lingered with subtle caresses and unhurried kisses before their bodies joined. Compared to their first time together, their rhythm was painfully slow. But it accentuated each move and emotion that passed between them. Their two experiences couldn't be more opposite in their actions, but the sentiment was the same. Neither could love someone else as much as they did each other.

It was nearly dawn when Tate sighed and climbed out of bed. The servants would soon be up, so it was time to leave. His wish to tend to his bride made him forget their plan for discretion when he wanted to summon a bath. Now that the sun was preparing to peek over the horizon, he remembered they weren't prepared to announce their marriage to the world yet.

Adelaide crawled to the end of the bed as Tate pleated his *breacon feile*. She knew how to do it since she'd seen her brothers do it when they swam together or traveled, but it was more personal watching her husband in the chamber where they'd spent most of the night making love. She had the sheet wrapped around her and tucked beneath her arms, but the modesty seemed entirely ridiculous. She let it drop.

"Put that sheet back where it was, Addy, or I willna leave. Everyone in the keep will hear us this time, and I willna feel a moment's remorse when yer family and all the servants hear ye scream ma name."

Adelaide's cheeks burned. "I think ma family may have already heard me at least once. I'm certain they heard ye. I'm surprised nay one came to ensure ye werenae screaming because I was dead."

"Nay one thought either of us was dead if they heard aught before we cried out our releases." Tate waggled his brow before focusing on wrapping his great plaid around him and belting it. He rose to his feet and strode to the bed. He tilted Adelaide's chin up before kissing her. "When we arrive at Dunbeath, we are locking ourselves in our chamber for a fortnight. Ye will see the light of day, but it will only be through our window. I shall keep ye naked every moment of every one of those days. I will feast on ye and enjoy every minute."

"And if I wish to feast on ye?" Adelaide's eyes dipped to Tate's sporran, knowing what lay behind it. She'd yet to explore him with her mouth, but she had every intention of doing so soon.

"I'm sure we can make certain neither of us goes hungry." Tate dropped a smacking kiss on her cheek before growing serious. "Addy, please call for a bath this morning. Ye ken I worry."

"And I dinna want ye to feel guilty either. Whether I end up sore or nae, last night was perfect. I would do it all over again and hope we do tonight."

"Would ye ride with me again this morning? We can share a mount, so ye dinna have to ride astride."

"Aye. I'd love that. I'll call for a bath now, and we can ride out after we break our fast." Adelaide's shoulders drooped.

"It's one meal, *leannan*. We have plenty to sit together in the many years to come."

"I ken. But it means I must deny ye're ma husband, and I dinna like that feeling."

"It means enjoy the meal with yer family without distraction."

Adelaide snorted. "Without distraction. Daft mon. Ye ken I willna have ma eyes or ma mind anywhere but on ye."

"Same for me." Tate pressed a final, wistful kiss to her lips before moving to the door. "We'll ride out together in an hour. It willna be that long."

Adelaide nodded. She climbed off the bed and met him at the door. She wrapped her arms around him, going onto her toes. He lowered his head and accepted the kiss she proffered before she let go, and he disappeared. She picked out her gown for the day and the underclothes she needed before sticking her head into the passageway. She heard servants stirring and caught one's attention. She requested the tub filled before shutting the door and donning her robe. She gazed out the window, watching Tate cross the bailey and leave the front gate just as it opened. She lost sight of him twice as he wound his way through the tents, but she was certain he looked back before ducking into one.

When a soft knock sounded, she expected it to be the maids, but she found Madeline on the other side of the portal. Her mother offered her a knowing smile that made Adelaide run her hand over her hair. Madeline had explained many aspects of married life several years ago, and it included a frank conversation about love and intimacy. It made Adelaide understand things she'd seen pass between her parents that she hadn't comprehended or paid much attention to before that. Now she realized she and Tate would share those knowing looks and little touches. It embarrassed her all over again to think about her parents that way, and it especially embarrassed her that her mother knew that she now knew those things, too. But it wouldn't dampen her joy.

"I was aboot to see if ye wished for a bath, but I heard Mary mention it in the kitchens. Ma guess is ye and Tate will ride out again this morning. Should I have another picnic packed?" Madeline's teasing smile made Adelaide flush all over again.

"Aye. After we break out fast, we're going for another ride." The moment the words left Adelaide's mouth, she flinched.

"I wasna thinking that, but I am now. And I will push that thought out of ma head. Ye're married now, Ada. There's naught wrong with what happens between the two of ye. I dinna doubt Tate made ye happy last night, but I still wished to check on ye. Do ye need aught but the bath?"

"Nay, Mama. Thank ye." Adelaide couldn't meet her mother's gaze. "Um, nay one heard..."

"Nae that I ken of." Madeline sucked her lips in since she knew she had heard no one over Fingal and her making love. It was her turn to blush. Adelaide's nose wrinkled. "The servants should be here any moment. I'll arrange for that picnic."

"I appreciate it." Adelaide kissed her mother's cheek before a train of servants hauled the tub and buckets into her chamber. When it was ready and she was alone, Adelaide slipped beneath the water. The warmth soaked into her skin, then into her weary muscles and bones. She laid her head back and relived the night before. Desire surged back to life, and it tempted her to ease her need as she ran the soapy linen over her mound. Tate had explained and taught her how husbands and wives could pleasure themselves when they had to be apart. But they weren't apart. Tate wasn't riding on patrol or traveling. They were merely in different places at the moment. She didn't want to find pleasure without him, so she continued to scrub her skin then her hair.

She poked the fire alive once she dressed. She combed out her hair until it was mostly dry. She considered braiding it or wrapping it in a chignon, but she hadn't worn her hair like that during the Gathering. Since she wasn't laboring over anything, it would stand out as the hairstyle of a married woman. She considered the kertches her mother and Aunt Davina wore. She'd given little thought to it until now. She was proud to be Tate's wife, and she wished she could wear the head covering. She hoped her mother, Ceit, and Davina would conduct the ceremony where she received her first one.

People were already trickling into the Great Hall when she arrived belowstairs. Since she'd had dinner with the Sinclairs the night before, she didn't dare share a second meal in a row with them. She took her place on the dais, only to find her sisters grinning at her. When she shifted her focus to her brothers, neither knew where to look. That made her smile. They returned her mirth with scowls, which only made her laugh harder.

The morning meal passed faster than she expected, so she was soon crossing the bailey toward the stables. She spotted the Sinclair guards before she spotted the men she'd known her entire life. When she looked at their plaid, she had a sudden pang of longing. She'd taken for granted that her arisaids always made her blend in among the Grants. She suddenly wished to blend in among the Sinclairs. She wanted to share that sense of community with her new family and people.

"I brought ye something, *leannan.*"

Adelaide jumped when Tate stepped behind her on silent feet. She followed him into the stables and to his horse's stall. They both looked around before Tate withdrew a Sinclair plaid swatch of wool. Adelaide practically snatched it from him, and Tate's heart swelled to see her excitement. She ran her thumbs over it and stared.

"Thank ye."

"I ken ye canna wear a Sinclair arisaid or sash yet, but I want ye to ken ye're part of ma family and ma clan. I wish I'd thought to give it to ye yesterday when we handfasted or last night when I came to yer chamber."

"I dinna mind that ye didna. I ken ye were still thinking aboot us." Adelaide looked down at the front of her gown. It was one that laced in the front, so she swept her gaze around the stables before hurrying to loosen her kirtle. She tucked the piece of Sinclair plaid under the top edge of her gown. When she pulled her laces tight again, the kirtle swallowed it. "If Da announces our betrothal tonight, then I could wear a sash in the morning. The only thing that really keeps a betrothal from being a marriage is the consummation. I'd be as good as married to ye if the announcement was all that happened tonight."

"People will stare if ye wear a sash tomorrow."

"Good. Let them. I've always been proud to be a Grant. I'm nay less proud to be a Sinclair. And since I call the finest of all the Sinclair men ma husband, why shouldnae I boast?"

"The finest, is he?"

"Aye. The brawest. The bravest. The best of all the men. And there are a mighty lot of them at that." Adelaide beamed at her husband before he lifted her off her feet and brought her up to eye level.

"All I ken is that I'm the luckiest mon in ma family." They kissed as Adelaide wrapped her arms around Tate's neck. However, Tate's horse stomped his hoof, and it signaled an alarm that someone approached. He put her down, and they stepped apart. Adelaide breathed easier for a moment when she recognized Grant stable hands. But the Gordon twins and their wives entered right after them.

"Ada." Cairstine Gordon walked over to her distant cousin who felt more like a niece than anything else. She was Davina and Edward's older daughter, so Adelaide had known the woman since her birth. "Tate."

Adelaide watched as Cairstine's gaze shifted from her to Tate. The woman glanced over her shoulder to where her sister-by-marriage, Allyson, waited with Allyson's husband, Ewan, and her own husband, Eoin. She flashed her extended family a quick smile before turning her attention back to Tate and Cairstine.

"Are ye riding out? Together?"

"Aunt Cairstine, Da's announcing our betrothal this evening."

"Felicitations." The older woman had once been a

friend of sorts to Madeline when they both served as ladies-in-waiting to Queen Elizabeth de Burgh. She'd grown up at Freuchie with Fingal as though they were close cousins, not ones many times removed. There was little she didn't know about Adelaide. "Ye handfasted, didna ye?"

It wasn't accusatory. It was more amused.

"Um."

"Lass, ye married a Sinclair. They canna wait to get to the kirk. Everyone kens that. Patient in battle. Impatient in love. Besides, ye ken Eoin and I did the same. So did Ewan and Allyson. I'm nae passing judgment. I'm happy for ye. It's aboot time. I told Fingal last year that his griping would be for naught."

"Ye talked to Da aboot us?"

"I heard part of what he said to ye, warning ye away from such a dashing young mon. I told him it was pointless. Ye two might nae have kenned ye loved each other yet, but I said ye would by the end of this Gathering."

"We didna ken we were in love. At least, we didna accept that we were. I thought I was—intrigued—by Tate."

Tate remained quiet as he listened to Adelaide and Cairstine talk. His eyes darted to the others, but his focus was on Cairstine. Yet another person who seemed to know what stood between Adelaide and him before they did. He knew he'd harbored strong feelings for Adelaide for ages, but he'd thought he'd finally fallen completely in love with her during this year's Gathering. Apparently, he was the last to know that he was already enamored.

"Would ye like to join us? We're going out too." Cairstine's lips twitched. She'd offered partly out of politeness but more so to watch the young couple squirm as they tried to find an excuse to be alone. Finally, Tate spoke up.

"Thank ye, but nay. I wish to have all of ma wife's attention."

"Canna fault yer honesty. Enjoy." Cairstine gave Adelaide a quick squeeze before returning to her husband and in-laws.

Tate hurried to prepare his horse before walking the beast outside. People milled around, but there weren't that many since plenty were outside the walls in the camp. He helped Adelaide onto his horse, then mounted behind her. The same men who'd ridden with them the day before joined them again. They traveled the same route, and Tate called a halt in the same spot. This time, Adelaide nestled against him and listened to his steady heartbeat while they waited.

They'd ridden much farther that day and the one before than they had with Clara and Fergus. With the foot of the mountains nearby, there wasn't as wide an expanse to walk as the meadow where they'd picnicked with their friends. But there was enough room for the guards to spread out around the couple as they strolled hand-in-hand.

"I ken ye've always lived in a keep. So have I. There's plenty of space in Dunbeath, and I've always had ma own chamber. But if ye find it's too much, I'm certain Grandda would let us have a croft within the walls. I dinna feel comfortable having ye live in the village when I'll be on patrol for several nights at a time. There's naught unsafe aboot being in the village. It's just—ye're ma wife. I dinna like it."

Adelaide smiled to herself as she leaned against Tate's arm and wrapped her free hand around it. "I like the idea that we could live in our own home. I can cook and clean, so it wouldnae force us to share every meal in the keep if we didna want to. Mayhap we might prefer a croft, but I'd like to live among yer family first. I dinna want them to think I'm taking ye from them. Even if it is only to the bailey. I dinna want them to think I'm demanding all yer attention or that I dinna wish to be part of the family."

"They willna think that. Until Cerys and Blake's bairn arrived, they lived in a croft within the walls. The birth wasna easy for Cerys, and it terrified Blake. It was less challenging for Cerys to have help if they lived within the keep. But I think she would have managed. She agreed to move back into the keep because she knew Blake worried himself sick when he had to be away. I ken Thor would like to live alone with Greer, but he feels obligated to remain since he's second in line for the lairdship and now captain of the guard. Grandda and Uncle Callum have told him it wouldnae be a problem if he and Greer did. Uncle Callum said they could live in one until Thor became laird if he wanted. If he didna worry so much aboot anyone thinking our family doesnae completely accept Greer since she was a Gunn, I think he would. He doesnae want anyone to think the laird's family shuns her. Daft mon. Everyone would ken they need the privacy."

"Is that the real reason we might need a croft?"

"Aye." Tate leaned over and kissed her cheek. "It's part of it. Ye ken there's a lot of us. It's nae exactly noisy, but it's never quiet. It's nae that ye canna be alone, but there's usually someone around the corner. I ken it will take some getting used to it since ye're family is so much smaller. Mine is more than twice yer family's size, and it keeps growing."

That last thought had them both imagining their own family with bairns and weans running between them. They stopped, and Tate stepped to face Adelaide. Neither said anything. They both knew they needed the kiss they shared. She wrapped her arms around his neck as one of his arms wrapped around her waist and the other beneath her bottom when he picked her up. Her feet dangled against his shins, but they both enjoyed how much easier it made their kiss.

"Ye ken I desire ye, and now that ye're ma wife, I dinna have to keep ma hands off ye. If last night was what our marriage bed will be, then I imagine we will have a large family of our own. Do ye wish to have bairns as soon as we can? Or do ye wish to wait?"

"I never thought a husband would ask me that. I dinna ken. I hadnae thought aboot it. I suppose I figured I would fall pregnant at some point and likely—hopefully—far more than once. But I hadnae thought aboot waiting. Are ye nae ready for bairns?" Adelaide's brow furrowed. Was there a part of bachelorhood he wished to hang onto?

"I'm ready for whatever family fate has in store for us. I can only imagine what it's like for a woman to leave the home she's kenned her entire life to move to nae only live under a new roof, but among people she doesnae ken. Ye ken ma family, but ye dinna ken ma clan. It'll take time to meet people and to sort out whose company ye enjoy. Even with so many people around ye, I ken a person can still feel lonely. Some might say a bairn would be a good distraction or even a way to meet more people. Mayhap it is. I just never want ye to be overwhelmed by yer decision to marry me. I dinna want ye to feel trapped in a strange place with strange people with a bairn to care for on top of it."

"Do ye worry this much aboot everything?" Adelaide wondered.

"Hardly. But nay other person matters as much as ye, and nay other thing matters as much as our marriage. What ye want is important. If ye arenae ready for bairns, we can be careful. I can pull out."

"Nay." Adelaide shook her head as she spoke. "I like how it is after we both find our release. I dinna think it would be the same if we arenae still joined. I dinna think it would be as enjoyable for ye either. And I dinna want to only do it that other way."

"We will never do it that way if ye dinna wish to. I will never expect ye to couple with me like that to prevent having bairns. If ye wish to try, then we can. But the only reason to do it is to satisfy us both." While bending Adelaide over the side of the bed or a table or anywhere often crossed Tate's mind as he imagined the more conventional way to couple, he wouldn't expect Adelaide ever to agree to him entering her back passage.

"I could take penny royal then."

"Is that safe?" Tate knew of the plant, but not much beyond its capability to prevent conception.

"Women have used it for generations. I dinna think wives usually do, but I'm certain some do." She'd heard of tavern whores drinking tea from the leaves and even some of the unmarried serving women who anticipated their weddings. "I could ask Mama before we leave. Or I'm certain Lady Ceit would ken once we're at Dunbeath."

"Lady Ceit." Tate chuckled. "Hearing ye call her that now that ye're ma wife sounds odd. I dinna ken if ye'd ever think of her as yer mama—a second mama, that is —but I ken she'd prefer ye call her Ceit without her title. We never use the women's titles amongst ourselves; only amongst our clan members."

"I dinna think it would hurt ma mama for me to call yers that. I think mine would hope I feel that close to yers since I willna be around ma own anymore. Do ye really think Ceit would want that?"

"Naught would make her happier."

They resumed walking in silence for a few minutes

before deciding to turn back. They enjoyed the companionable quiet, and it relieved them both that neither felt the need to fill the void with constant chatter. They'd strolled for longer than they realized, and the midmorning sun beat down on them when they returned to their horses. They both looked toward the copse of trees; the same ones where they'd handfasted the previous day. Tate met each guard's gaze before canting his head toward the woods. Just like the previous day, the men fanned out and entered the trees.

Adelaide and Tate made their way back to the enormous oak they'd stood beside when they pledged themselves. Tate's hands cupped Adelaide's bottom as she pushed the sporran out of the way. When they stepped closer, she felt the insistent press of his rod against her mound.

"We've barely touched," Adelaide observed.

"Ye've been breathing."

"What?"

"All ye have to do is breathe in ma direction, and ma body is ready. Hell, all I have to do is breathe, and I'm ready." Tate tugged her closer and swayed his hips to rub his length against her.

"It wouldnae be our first time together." Adelaide's expression showed Tate her anticipation.

"True. I did say one day we might couple here."

Their kisses grew fevered until Tate backed Adelaide against the tree trunk and raised her hands above her head. She arched her back, pressing her breasts toward him. His hand cupped her ample flesh and kneaded. When their impatience grew, he pulled her kirtle's laces loose, careful not to lose the piece of wool he'd given her. He kissed along her neck as he fumbled to slide his hand down the front of her gown. They both sighed when her breast fit into his palm.

She nipped at his earlobe and rocked her hips. She

enjoyed the control Tate had by restraining her hands over her head because it forced her to find other ways to enjoy the feel of his body against hers. When he slid a thigh between hers, she ground her mons upon it. It was Tate who grew impatient. He released her hands and snatched handfuls of her kirtle as he drew it up to her waist.

"Ye feel divine, wee one." His hand slid around her waist beneath the layers of material until his thumb could rub her pearl. His other hand rested on her bare backside, guiding her to rock against him faster. One slight nudge was all it took for Adelaide. She rode his thigh while she fisted the front of his leine. Their kiss pushed her over the edge.

"Tatum," she moaned. His kiss swallowed any cry she might have made as her body shuddered with release. She clawed at his plaid, pulling it up and tucking it into his belt. He tried to do the same with her skirts, but he couldn't find the ends. Adelaide scooped up the lengths of material to her kirtle and chemise to place over her shoulder. Then he was inside her.

Neither noticed Tate lifting Adelaide or her legs wrapping around his waist. It was only the moment of relief before the flood of arousal when their bodies joined. Nature took the lead, and Adelaide moved along his cock, intuiting what she needed to do. Tate guided her hips, helping to bear some of her weight. He was careful not to pin her against the rough bark.

"I ken we canna take our time. Dinna hold back, Tatum."

Her words released the levee, and Tate's need to bring his wife to completion as well as the ache in his bollocks for his own release pushed him into a speed that made Adelaide cling to him. His strength to hold her and flex his hips with such vigor lit another roaring fire within her. Their kisses were all that kept the entire world from knowing what they were doing.

"God that feels good," Adelaide panted.

"Make… it… feel… better." Tate punctuated each word with a thrust.

"Better might kill me."

Adelaide watched the concentration settle over Tate's features, and she knew it wasn't just his own satisfaction upon which he concentrated. She knew he would always put her first. She was attentive as she moved, finding what made his brow furrow more or dig his fingers into her bottom harder. What things made his nostrils flare, and what made him move with desperation. She wanted to remember it all. She wanted to learn what Tate enjoyed as much as he enjoyed teaching her what she enjoyed.

"Och, aye, *mo ghaol*." Pleasure began low in her belly as his rod pressed against the sensitive spot within her core. The sensation spread warmth through her as she tensed, as she cleaved to him. His brawny hands gripped her hips and held her in place as he thrust twice more before his cock pulsed with ropes of his seed spurting forth.

Tate was unconvinced his legs could hold him upright. His knees shook worse than when his father made him run laps around the lists if he dropped his sword. He turned them, so his back rested against the tree. It wasn't enough support. He wobbled but lowered them to the ground. Adelaide sat, straddling his lap, as they both recovered.

"Could we have our croft right here? Tucked away where we're alone."

"Would that we could, wee one." Tate gazed toward the mountains barely visible among the trees. "If I could remain on Grant land, this would be perfect. We could find a special spot on Sinclair land where we can sneak away to. But I would never live somewhere so isolated as a member of a laird's family. It wouldnae be safe for ye."

Adelaide's lips twitched. She recalled Tate had a vivid imagination from the stories and jests he would tell when they were younger. But his mind seemed incapable of playing along with any image where she might be at risk. She found it endearing.

"We should have at least brought the picnic basket with us. I'd vera much like to dine just as we are, husband."

"With me buried deep inside ye, wife?"

"Exactly."

They remained, cuddling together, until Tate's body no longer agreed with his mind. Several light kisses later, they stood and fixed their clothing. Tate whistled as he and Adelaide moved toward the tree line. The men appeared like wraiths, and Adelaide had a moment's trepidation.

"I kenned where they were, wee one, but I couldnae see them. They couldnae see us, but they kenned where we were. They were never so far that they couldnae get to us, but they werenae close enough to ken how I pleasure ma wife. That isnae something any other person will ever ken."

"Thank ye."

They spread out the Grant plaid Adelaide brought and handed out food to the warriors who accompanied them before they shared the leftovers from the previous night's meal. Then they laid side-by-side and watched the clouds. They continued to chat about everything and nothing until they couldn't avoid having to return to the keep. It was well into the afternoon, and they were certain people would put two and two together and realize they'd both left the Gathering.

"I shall go to the loch before coming in for the

evening meal. I'm nae at ma best right now." Tate waggled his eyebrows as they stood alone in the stables.

"I'd say ye were at yer best against an oak tree this morning." Adelaide jumped away and gathered her skirts as she pretended to run from Tate. He snagged her around the waist and tapped her backside.

"Cheeky, wife. I like it."

"I like ye."

"I'd say ye did against an oak tree this morning." Tate kissed her cheek and released her. He watched as she left the stables and made her way into the keep before he left the bailey through the postern gate. It didn't take him long to bathe. He returned to his family's tent to polish his dirks and his boots. He wished to look his best for that night's announcement. When he stepped out of the tent, ready to make his way back to the keep and look for Adelaide, he knew his best laid plans were about to go up in smoke when he saw Peter and Adam flanking Fergus. Nothing good could come of two Chisholms and a Matheson stumbling, drunk, together toward the keep.

What the bluidy hell is Fergus going to do next?

CHAPTER 20

Tate followed the three men, knowing they'd just left the alehouse tent together. Fergus appeared more morose than he had since his catastrophic betrothal announcement. Peter and Adam appeared far smugger than they should. And the trio looked like a walking disaster. Tate knew they hadn't seen him, so he waited for them to pass the Sinclairs' cluster of tents before he set off after them. He knew they were still just sober enough to sense if someone followed, so he walked parallel to them and kept his head turned slightly away. Since none of them tried particularly hard to keep their voices low, Tate had no trouble hearing them.

"Peter, I canna thank ye for helping me see the truth. Ye saved me from taking a wanton home to ma clan."

Tate narrowed his eyes. He'd heard Fergus drunk only a few nights earlier. He'd drunk with his friend before, and he never sounded like he did now. Fergus's words slurred together, and his brogue was almost unintelligible to even a fellow Highlander. Either someone had drugged him, or he was putting on a show for the Chisholm brothers. Tate prayed it was the latter. He continued to listen to the men.

"I ken our clans dinna get along, but one day, ye and I shall lead. I dinna wish to feud with ye or anyone else. It isnae good for either clan."

Tate nearly snorted. Peter Chisholm barely cared about his own clan beyond what they could do for him. He hardly cared about any other clan. And the only care he had for the Mathesons was their destruction. But he sounded as intoxicated as Tate was used to.

"Ma brother is right. We dinna wish to keep losing men and cattle by feuding with ye. Mayhap, ye should marry our sister instead of Lady Agnes." Adam sounded casual, but Tate didn't think there was anything specu- latory about his comment. He was planting the seed for the Chisholms to subjugate the Mathesons. Tate knew immediately that if Fergus was ever fool enough to marry a woman from Laird Chisholm's family, the Mathesons wouldn't stand a chance against them. That was one reason Fergus's father supported his match with Clara. The alliance with the MacDonalds would keep the Chisholms at bay. It's why Laird Matheson still wanted Fergus to marry a MacDonald, albeit Agnes instead of Clara.

"I canna marry yer sister. I thought she was mar- rying a Rose."

"Naught's been agreed upon," Peter explained. "Ye could stake a claim tonight. Dance with the lass."

Every ounce of Tate's intuition screamed Fergus was being set up for a forced marriage. Either Peter and Adam's sister would accuse Fergus of doing something untoward, or the brothers would force Fergus into a situation that trapped him into marrying the woman.

"I dinna dance. I only did for Clara because she en- joyed it."

"Our sister enjoys it," Adam prodded.

"Nay. I'm set to marry Agnes."

Tate could see Fergus's profile, and he was certain his friend was intoxicated. But he wasn't nearly as drunk as he sounded. Tate continued to pray it was a ruse to lure something out of the Chisholms.

"But she isnae who ye want," Peter hinted.

"Nay, she isnae."

"So, if ye dinna want her and ye canna have Clara, then our sister is a fine choice. It would end our feud," Adam insisted.

"Nay. If I canna have Clara, at least Agnes reminds me of her."

Tate's nose curled. He felt horrible for Agnes. It was just what worried Adelaide. The two clans would compel Clara's sister to marry a mon who wished she were someone else. But he reminded himself that Fergus wasn't as drunk as he appeared, even if the Chisholm brothers were. He wondered what Fergus wished to weasel out of them or what idea he wished to plant with them. He continued to walk just a few steps behind them and parallel with a tent column between them. When Tate had to stop short because someone stepped out of one, Fergus glanced over his shoulder and winked at Tate.

"Are ye nae fearful Agnes will turn out to be just as loose with her favors as Clara? They are much alike," Peter pointed out.

"Nay. They arenae that similar at all. They couldnae be more opposite in temperament."

While Tate knew there was some truth in that, he also knew neither sister would ever be promiscuous like Peter implied. He wished Fergus would reach the conclusion of this farcical conversation, so Tate could understand its point.

"I wish I'd never seen what I did," Fergus lamented. "I would be only days away from marrying Clara. But, alas, ye showed me who she really was." Fergus clapped his hand on Peter's shoulder.

"Like I said, I dinna want to continue this feud."

And there it was. Fergus glanced back at Tate, who nodded. Peter hadn't admitted outright that he arranged for Fergus to see the couple in Clara's tent, but he'd made it clear he had. He could no longer claim it was a coincidence. But it made Tate wonder what Fergus thought he would accomplish by getting Peter to indirectly confess. To Fergus, Clara was dead. And even if he didn't believe that, he hadn't renounced his accusations. For all Tate knew at this point, Fergus might have wanted a confession of Peter's role, but still thought Clara was guilty.

They'd reached the keep and where members of the various clans gathered for the most current results. All the games were nearly over, with only two more rounds of finals the next day. The majority of the clans would leave in four days since there would be two days of feasting and merriment after the last competition. Tate couldn't wait to leave Freuchie, so he could get Adelaide to her new home and the privacy of their chamber. But he knew she might not be as eager, so he would keep that idea to himself.

Fergus walked to the center of the gathered crowd, finding a place beside Fingal. Edward was mid-sentence when Fergus's voice boomed through the bailey. Tate's stomach likely hit his backbone as he sucked in a breath.

Hell and the devil. Now what?

"That mon confessed to me—" Fergus pointed to Peter. "—That he intentionally led me to Lady Clara's tent to see what ma former betrothed was aboot. His actions forced me to renounce her, and now she's dead. And Tate Sinclair heard him."

Fuck.

Tate knew he had no choice but to step forward. Peter and Adam glowered at him, but he maintained an impassive mien as he walked toward Fergus, Fingal, and Edward. This was the last thing he wished to be drawn into, but there he was.

"Tell them what ye heard, Tate. All of it," Fergus demanded.

With a silent sigh, Tate responded. "I saw them walking toward the keep and happened to be close enough to hear their conversation since none kept their voices down." That gave Tate pause. He watched the Chisholm brothers, and neither of them seemed nearly as drunk as they had minutes ago. Intoxicated but not sloshed. They were the same as Fergus. "They suggested Fergus marry their sister to end the feud. Fergus insisted he's already arranged to marry Lady Agnes since Lady Clara is nay longer with us. Fergus thanked Peter for showing him Lady Clara's *supposed* perfidy. Peter responded by saying a second time that he doesnae wish to continue the feud. That time made it clear he wished to destroy Fergus and Lady Clara's betrothal, so that he could push his sister into Fergus's arms instead. Supposedly, for an alliance or to end their bad blood."

"Liar!" Peter bellowed.

The crowd murmured throughout Fergus's accusation and Tate's explanation. But now everyone held a deathly silence. Eyes darted between Peter and Tate while others searched for Tate's relatives among the onlookers.

"Say that again," Tate challenged, his voice barely more than a whisper.

"I will. Ye are a liar."

Fear hung heavy in the air as people expected Tate and his family to retaliate for the slight.

"Prove that I am," Tate stated. "Prove that ye didna say it. Prove that I didna hear it."

"Ma father would never consent to ma sister marrying a Matheson," Adam interjected.

"That doesnae mean neither of ye wouldnae force yer sister into a compromising situation that would force what ye want. Ye would leave neither Fergus nor yer sister any choice. Ye were willing to ruin Lady Clara's life. What would stop ye from ruining someone else's?"

"Ye lie!" It was the only refrain Peter had.

"Nay, he does nae." A deep voice emerged from the crowd. Everyone turned to stare as an enormous man stepped forward. Monty Campbell, second son of Laird Brodie and Lady Laurel Campbell and Laird Ross in his own right, emerged. The Campbell men were among the few who rivaled the Sinclair men in size. "I went to ma brothers' tent to find Craig, who wasna there. I heard them talking as they walked by. Sinclair doesnae lie, but the Chisholms do."

Tate widened his stance until his feet were hip-width apart. He crossed his arms and glared at the brothers. His expression was nothing short of menacing and threatened retribution for the slight. "Recant yer accusation."

"Or what?" Peter snapped.

"Ride out with me in the morning and find out," Tate proposed. "Ye're mon enough to gossip like a fishwife. Are ye mon enough to defend yer blather?"

"We arenae ruining the Gathering, Sinclair. Ye ken the rules. Nay fighting here," Peter sneered.

"That's why I said ride out with me. We take this away from the Gathering." Tate knew where Adelaide stood when she joined the crowd. Her eyes couldn't be wider, and she shook her head. He was certain she didn't trust Peter or Adam to fight fairly if it came to that, but Tate knew they would never accept the challenge. "Are ye worried ye'll shite yerself instead of swinging yer sword?"

"Dinna be a fool, Peter." Monty stepped beside Tate and stared out at the crowd. "Recant. Or are ye calling me a liar, too?"

This was rapidly spiraling out of control. The Campbells were one of the two most dominant clans in all of Scotland. Monty Campbell would inherit the Earldom of Ross from his uncle who never had children. It was one thing to insult and accuse the Earl of Caithness's grandson. It was another, entirely different thing to accuse an earl-to-be himself. Brodie and Laurel stepped out of the crowd to stand to the side where everyone could see them. Montgomery Ross—Laurel's brother, and the previous laird and current earl—moved next to his sister.

"What shall it be?" Fingal interceded.

"Mayhap Tate misheard. He believes what he thought he heard and has repeated that," Peter prevaricated. Tate's narrowed eyes bore into him, and he chose to remain silent after his weak concession.

"Do ye accept that, Tate?" Fingal turned toward the younger man.

"Aye, I can accept that. After all, mayhap I didna mishear, but he believes he didna say aught, so he willna repeat it." Tate shrugged.

"They will serve the evening meal shortly. Let us move to the Great Hall," Edward boomed.

"For an announcement, I suppose." Adam's comment made everyone hesitate. When eyes turned toward him, he gloated. "After the way Sinclair was pawing Fingal's daughter, they must be announcing their betrothal."

Tate's arms unfolded as though he were in slow motion. Fingal leaned forward, his hands on his hips. The

Sinclair and Sutherland women, along with the Mackays, pushed through to encircle Adelaide, who now stood alone.

"Did ye follow me?" Tate's voice was harder than the steel of any sword a warrior carried.

"We were headed in the same direction."

"Where was that?" Tate knew no one followed that morning or the day before. He was certain of it. He knew the Sinclair men he took with him, and the Grants had impressed him. Adam spoke out of his arse, but his accusation would have the same effect as Fergus's allegations about Clara. It would ruin Adelaide.

"West."

"West? That's a vera large part of Scotland. Where did we stop?"

"In a place where ye thought nay one would see ye tossing her skirts."

"Tell us exactly where that place was that ye saw me with ma *wife*."

A murmur rippled through the various clans. More people had entered the bailey since the showdown began. Nearly everyone attending the Gathering was now congregating in one place. Many arrived for the evening meal, while others came because they learned of the confrontation.

"Wife?" A woman's voice emerged above the whispers.

"Aye. Lady Adelaide and I handfasted yesterday, but didna wish to make it public since we didna believe it was the right time. We wished to respect Lady Clara, but it's obvious neither of the Chisholms are capable of that." Tate turned his attention back to Adam. "Why did ye follow me and *ma wife*?"

People shifted nervously, more worried about the Sinclair, Sutherland, and Mackay women who all had a hand in their pocket. Everyone knew they carried knives—not in the singular for any of them. Tate's aunt Mairghread drew hers. She walked up to Adam with her dirk resting lightly in her hand. Gazes shifted to Tristan, who only shrugged and remained quiet, happy to let his wife have her say.

"Ma nephew asked ye more than one question, and ye havenae answered. Mayhap ye didna understand them. Do ye need me to explain?" Beyond her reputation for knife throwing skills, it was no secret Mairghread would speak out on behalf of any woman who feared doing it herself. With four older brothers, she'd grown up fearless. The Mackays were commanding in their own right, and she'd risen to the occasion as Lady MacKay when clans thought to harry them when Tristan rode out to support King David. No clan made the same mistake twice.

Adam remained silent. Fear flashed in his eyes for a heartbeat before his arrogance returned. Mairghread tsked.

"Ye arenae a wise lad, are ye? Ye wish to humiliate ma nephew and his wife. Do ye nae understand that makes her ma niece? Do ye nae understand that makes her the Earl of Caithness's granddaughter? Do ye nae understand, ye bluidy eejit, that makes her the Earl of Sutherland's grandniece? How bluidy stupid are ye?"

"Vera!" Someone in the crowd bellowed.

"Leave. Yer clan. All of ye. Leave," Mairghread commanded.

"Ye have nay authority—"

Mairghread merely cocked an eyebrow. Clans allied with or terrified of the Mackays surrounded the Chisholms. The largest clan that neighbored them to the north and west were the Mackenzies. They were her sister-by-marriage's—Siùsan's—clan of birth. Siùsan's half-brother married one of Mairghread's nieces. The Frasers neighbored the Chisholms to the east, and they were Mairghread's other sister-by-marriage's—Deirdre's—clan of birth. Siùsan and Deirdre were close with their families. The MacDonnells to the south had a poor history with Mairghread and Tristan through his late stepmother. Frankly, Mairghread terrified the pish out of their laird, and Tristan wasn't a far second.

"Do I really need 'the authority?'" Mairghread queried. "Think of ma warning as advice. If ye wish to live long enough to return to yer land without having yer entire clan slaughtered by the three I belong to, then ye would move yer arses. Be gone by dawn."

"Ye—" Peter snapped his mouth shut.

"Aye?" Tristan stepped behind his wife and rested his hands on her shoulders. "What were ye going to say?"

"Naught," Peter hissed.

"Ma wife is a wise woman. She offers sage advice. Ye should heed it. If ye dinna, who will ye whinge to? King David in France? He's ma father-by-marriage's godson. Laird Keith, the Great Marischal, who happens to be in France with the king? He's ma niece's father-by-marriage. Andrew Murray? He's ma friend along with ma brothers-by-marriage's."

While people believed the Campbells and MacDonalds were the most formidable clans, the alliances the Sinclairs made over three decades meant they were undefeatable. With allies in nearly all the Highland clans, they had the true power, even if their clan lands weren't as sizable as the Campbells and MacDonalds, even if they didn't hold seats in the government.

"What is going on?" Laird Chisholm demanded. Everyone looked at him and snickered. His leine was barely tucked in on his left side and not at all on his right. He was winded, and his cheeks were ruddy. No one thought it came from him running to the bailey.

Everyone knew he'd been tupping a wench. His mistress-turned-wife standing in the crowd confirmed it.

"Ye'd be late to yer own wake, Lathan." Fingal stepped up to the man he loathed. He got so close their boots practically touched. "Yer blight of a son insinuated ma daughter behaved inappropriately when it turns out she was with her husband. Yer other son admitted to forcing Fergus to see whatever happened in Lady Clara's tent, making him responsible for all our loss. And he was aboot to call Lady Mackay a profane word. I warned ye aboot yer son. Gather yer clan and go."

Lathan possessed more sense than his sons. He gestured for them to follow him, and the members of their clan separated from the rest. None needed to announce they were leaving. It was clear from Lathan's resentful glances that he opted to lead his clan away from battle, even if he despised everyone in sight.

Once the Chisholms left the bailey, the Sinclair women and their female relatives stepped aside. Adelaide rushed forward, and Tate pulled her into his arms. Aware they weren't alone, he settled for dropping a kiss on her crown. She trembled against him, and she heard his racing heart as her ear rested against his chest.

"This isnae the announcement ma daughter and ma son-by-marriage deserve. But since it isnae a secret anymore, I would introduce ye to our most newly wedded couple. Tate and Lady Adelaide Sinclair."

Well wishes passed through the crowd, and cheers went up among many. It wasn't the way Tate wished for the news to spread, feeling like they cheated Adelaide of the momentous occasion. Even if it had been subdued and inside, it would have been done in the proper way at the evening meal. He continued to stroke her back as they stood together, accepting people's kind words.

Tate could see some clans were less enthused than others. The Sinclairs weren't previously directly linked to the Grants, but now they were formally. Not everyone in the Highlands was thrilled the Sinclairs continued to grow in power and position. But he pushed aside his worries as his family congratulated them. Adelaide stepped away, and he missed the feel of her beside him. However, it made him happy to see how his sister and cousins drew her in as though she'd always been part of their inner circle. It eased many of his earlier fears.

"I ken this isnae how ye wanted people to learn of yer marriage." Liam draped his arm around his grandson's shoulders. "But nay one will dare repeat what those arses said aboot ye and Adelaide. Even if anyone believes them, which some may, none are daft enough to say such aloud. Between Fingal's protectiveness of his children, and our family's protectiveness of each other, people ken they willna be long for this world if they slight yer wife."

"Thank ye, Grandda. And I ken that. But it still doesnae take away the humiliation for Adelaide or her fear that people saw us."

"I ken, lad. But it wasna a poor reflection on ye or yer bride. The only ones who looked bad were the Chisholms, and that isnae new for them. People ken them and their sort. There's a reason only Clan Mac-Donald of Lochalsh and Clan Rose will ally with them. Their list of rivals was far longer even before ye married a Grant. The Chisholms are their own worst enemy right now, and that did naught to move them toward peace. The Grants are well connected themselves, so the Chisholms kenned even before yer marriage that any battle with the Grants is also a battle with the Gordons, the MacKinnons, the Campbells, and all their allies. One can hope Peter and Adam both die without issue and a new family line becomes their lairds."

"I hope it's that simple, but I doubt it. Things arenae resolved between Fergus and Peter now that Fergus has called out Peter. There's still the matter of Lady Clara. More things are unsettled than they were before. The only thing resolved is that I married the woman I love."

"That's what matters most to ye and our whole family. The rest will sort itself out."

"Aye, Grandda. But I dinna think I'll be locking maself away with ma bride at home any time soon."

Grandfather and grandson looked at each other as Liam squeezed Tate's shoulder. They both knew the younger man spoke the truth. There was little chance they'd resolved things, and it made Liam wary about traveling all the way north with his family while the Chisholms were in a snit. It made them unpredictable.

CHAPTER 21

delaide stood at the front of the dais with Madeline, Ceit, and Davina. Each woman held an end of the kertch they would bless and place upon her head. After the commotion in the bailey, Adelaide and Tate, along with their families, agreed that a small service at a kirk would take place after the Gathering to ensure no one doubted the validity and permanence of the young couple's marriage. But they would go forth from that day as a truly wedded couple. That meant Adelaide would wear a kertch to cover her hair.

Her mother stood to her left and began the ritual. "If there is righteousness in the heart, there will be beauty in the character." She placed her hand on Adelaide's shoulder.

"If there is beauty in the character, there will be harmony in the home," Davina recited. Standing behind Adelaide, she let go of the tail of the kertch and placed both hands on Adelaide's shoulders, one of hers covering Madeline's.

"If there is harmony in the home, there will be order in the clan," Ceit finished as she placed her hand over Davina's. As much as they welcomed Adelaide as a married woman, the women's actions solidified it wasn't just the Grant and Sinclair men who stood together. The women did too.

"If there is order in the clan, there will be peace in the land." The three women spoke the final words of the blessing together.

The gathered clans cheered, "So let it be!" as Madeline, Davina, and Ceit placed the kertch over Adelaide's head, and Davina made sure it would stay in place.

The women stepped away, and Tate came to stand beside her. While their lovemaking made them man and wife between them and in the eyes of the law. The kertch was a symbol to the world. Tate cupped Adelaide's cheek before leaning forward.

"Wife." He pressed a kiss to her lips that they both intended to keep appropriate for polite company. But it shot past that when Adelaide opened her mouth, and Tate's tongue slipped past her teeth, caressing the velvety inside of her cheeks. Their arms went around each other as people stomped and banged their tankards on tables.

"Husband," Adelaide sighed.

"I love seeing ye wearing a kertch in public, but that wretched thing is coming off the moment we're alone. Here and at Dunbeath. I love seeing yer hair and touching it. I'll burn the hideous thing if ye have it on in our chamber."

"And I'll only have to make another. What a waste." Adelaide's eyes twinkled. She knew Tate didn't jest, but she would.

"Ever practical. Heed ma warning, wee one." Tate brushed a kiss against her lips as he grew serious. "I will have a ring for ye, Addy. I promise a kertch isnae what will signify ma pledge."

"Tatum, I ken why it matters that I wear one. But that isnae something I care aboot right now. I dinna even care aboot the kertch that much. I'm just happy it isnae a secret anymore."

"I feel the same. But I'll still have a ring when we marry at the kirk."

Adelaide's hands ran along the outside of his upper arms. She nodded before bouncing onto her toes to kiss his jaw. They held hands as Tate joined Adelaide, her family, and the leaders of the clans at the high table. The priest blessed the food and offered a special one for their marriage. As the servants passed around platters, Tate leaned to whisper in Adelaide's ear.

"We canna wait to speak to Clara. It must be tonight. The Chisholms may appear to have left, but I dinna put it past Peter to accept Fergus's challenge."

"What aboot the one ye made to him?"

"That, he isnae daft enough to accept. He kens at least one of his limits. But he would be evenly matched with Fergus, so I canna guarantee the outcome."

"Since everyone kens we're married, they'll expect us to retire together. We do, but we take the servant's stairs down to the bailey. We ride out while most people are still here."

"Aye. Can ye tell yer brother?" Harry sat to Adelaide's left. "And I'll arrange for guards once the dancing starts."

"After our first dance."

"Of course. And nae because people will expect it. But because ye have been out of ma arms for five minutes, and it'll be a bluidy eternity before this meal ends, and ye're back in them."

Adelaide giggled as her hand slipped beneath the hem of his plaid and up to the middle of his thigh. She whipped it away when Tate reached for it. He snagged her wrist and brought her hand to rest on top of the table, where they entwined their fingers.

"If ye dinna want me to carry ye over ma shoulder

with ma hand on yer arse on the way to our chamber, I'd nae tease me."

"Ye'd never."

"Mayhap nae on yer arse, but ma arm would find its way just below yer vera shapely and vera alluring backside."

"Promise?"

"Och, aye. Then nay one would see us till morning, and our plan would go awry."

"Or we could sneak in a few moments together before we leave." Adelaide's speculative expression made Tate wonder if they could. But he sighed and frowned. Adelaide's smile slipped before she conceded. "I ken. That isnae the responsible choice, and we need to figure out this business with Clara once and for all."

"The sooner we leave, hopefully, the sooner we'll be back. Then we can have the rest of the night to ourselves."

"Do we tell Laird and Lady MacDonald? I told Mama and Da just before we came inside." Adelaide glanced down the table.

"I did the same while ye talked to ma sister and cousins. We should tell them or have someone do it for us."

People congratulating them drew their attention in separate directions. Much like the reaction in the bailey, some lairds, ladies, and tánaistes were more celebratory than others. But none dared show any disapproval. Despite feelings some harbored, the meal progressed smoothly. It wasn't as interminable as Tate and Adelaide feared. The musicians tuned their instruments as servants cleared away the tables and benches. The couple took their place among the dancers and moved together. They remained for four sets before Tate drew her away from the crush.

"I spoke to ma men and yer brothers. They're arranging for Grant men. There will be a score of us riding with ye. I also asked Grandda to tell the Mac-Donalds."

"Did ye insist on that many?"

"I suggested it and yer brothers agreed. I dinna like the idea of any of us riding in the dark, and I definitely dinna like ye riding in the dark that far from a keep. But it's necessary, so we'll bring adequate protection."

Adelaide felt more at ease knowing so many men would accompany them, but she also appreciated Tate always prioritizing her wellbeing. She didn't think he was being overprotective with that many guards. He understood what would allay her worries. They made their way to the dais to say their goodnights. Several people noticed them moving toward the stairs, so bawdy suggestions filled the air. When Fingal stood, the comments ceased.

"Get yer arisaid before we go," Tate whispered once they reached the landing. He stood outside their chamber door as Adelaide hurried inside. She reappeared only a moment later, wrapping the length of wool around her as they walked. Tate led the way down the narrow, winding stone servants' steps. He often marveled at how the servants carried anything abovestairs when the steps were barely wide enough for half his foot. He descended first, in case Adelaide should trip in their haste.

When they were outside and had reached the end of the keep's eastern wall, Tate put out his arm to hold Adelaide back for a moment. He peered around the corner, then swept his gaze over the battlements. It was dark enough that no one would recognize his plaid's pattern or Adelaide's. But he was certain the guards stationed on the wall walk would recognize members of their own clan leaving on horseback.

"Dinna fash," Harry whispered as he emerged from the shadows. "They ken nae to ask questions. Let's go."

They crossed the bailey with Adelaide between the two men, her identity hidden by their larger frames. It wasn't long before the group filtered through the main gate, walking with their horses in pairs and trios. When they were beyond the camp, they mounted and rode toward the cottage where Clara hid.

It took nearly three hours to reach their destination. They'd stopped to rest their horses twice, but they hadn't dawdled. They were nearly to the Grants' border with the Mackintoshes. Their ride across so much territory already had Tate's situational awareness heightened. But drawing close to another clan's land made him hypervigilant. His head was on a swivel, even looking behind them several times. Angus rode at the head of the line, and Harry rode at the rear. Tate was to Adelaide's right, and his most senior Sinclair warrior was to her left. He'd glared at Angus and Harry when the men moved into formation. The brothers relented, but not before a tense moment passed.

"There," Adelaide whispered as she pointed to a cluster of four crofts. "The one second from the left."

They slowed their horses while men fanned out to make a perimeter around the crofts. The Grant siblings and Tate continued forward with five guards. When they reined in, Adelaide waited for Tate to help her from the saddle. She knew it would make him anxious if she didn't, but she pulled on his arm when he intended to approach the croft first.

"At least let me be at yer side. If two women open the door to a hoard of warriors, they'll panic. Let them see me. If for any reason, there's a threat, ye have yer sword and targe."

"Vera well. One step back, Addy. They'll see ye, but I can shift in front of ye if I must."

Adelaide could live with that. "All right." When they reached the door, her arm shot out to knock before Tate could. It was a soft rap rather than a pounding. While she didn't think Tate would make the door rattle, she knew it would sound like a determined male knock. "Clara."

Between her soft call and light knocking, it made the inhabitants comfortable enough that they heard a bar being lifted, then a bolt sliding back. The door opened a crack, but Adelaide recognized Clara's eye peering through.

"It's me, Clara. I'm with Tate and ma brothers. Let us in, please."'

The door opened wider, and Clara stepped aside. Tate shifted to block Adelaide, silently insisting that he inspect the home before she entered. Only a moment later, he moved, and Adelaide and Clara collided with each other. The women embraced, silent strength and relief passing between them. When they pulled back, Clara looked at Tate, then grinned at Adelaide.

"Aboot bluidy time ye two wound up together."

"Everyone is making such an ado aboot us, and it's naught more than two people marrying," Adelaide reasoned.

"Marrying, as in already, or in the future?" Clara cocked an eyebrow.

"As in yesterday. We handfasted."

"That's wonderful. But I dinna think ye're here to spread those good tidings."

"We're nae. Can we sit with ye?"

The cottage's owner was already filling mugs with drams of whisky. It was still summer, but the nights were brisk. Riding into the wind had made everyone's noses and cheeks red. The woman remained quiet and out of the way once the Grant siblings, Tate, and Clara sat at the table in the center of the croft.

"What's happened now?" Clara wondered.

"Peter admitted he led Fergus to yer tent with the intent that he should see someone inside," Tate explained. "He didn't say it in so many words, but…"

"But what?" Clara looked at her friends. "Is Fergus still accusing me?"

Tate wished he weren't the messenger. "I dinna ken how deeply he still believes that. He pretended to be drunker than he was as he walked with Peter and Adam toward the keep. I overheard them. Fergus thanked Peter for helping him to see who he *thinks* ye are before a wedding. Adam suggested Fergus marry his sister to end the feud. Peter said he didna want it to continue, but Fergus insisted he was bound by the agreement to marry Agnes."

"Agnes?" Clara gasped. Clearly, she remembered little of what happened after she reached Adelaide's chamber.

"Aye. The Mathesons still want the alliance," Adelaide interjected.

"Neither of them wishes to marry the other," Angus reassured. His dark expression made Adelaide wonder if there was something more to this situation than she realized.

Tate picked up the explanation once more. "Fergus didna back down, saying he would marry Agnes now. He repeated his thanks, and Peter responded with 'like I said, I dinna want to continue the feud.' It was clear he meant he'd engineered Fergus seeing whatever was happening in yer tent to break the betrothal. He wants his sister to marry Fergus and supposedly make the alliance between the Chisholms and the Mathesons rather than between the MacDonalds and Mathesons."

"It wasna me in there," Clara insisted.

"Nay one believes it was," Adelaide assured her.

"I'm sure plenty of people do. I want to ken who the hell was in ma bluidy tent."

Tate ran his hand over his face. "I think I may ken."

Four shocked faces turned toward him. Adelaide spoke up. "Ye do?"

"I'm nae certain, but something has stuck with me. I followed Fergus to the alehouse that night. I kept him company there to make sure he didna—" Tate caught himself. "—Get too drunk." Everyone knew what he really meant: To make sure Fergus didn't bed a woman.

"Aye," Clara prompted.

"There was one woman who was more persistent than the others. Fergus turned her away each time, preferring his whisky. But she offered at least five times, and only to him. She didna bat an eye toward me. It seemed odd to me then, but I wasna completely sober. Now that I've had time to consider it, I think someone put her up to it. If Fergus had bedded her, whoever arranged this believed ye wouldnae marry him because of his betrayal. They wished to make sure neither of ye wanted the marriage. They couldnae have kenned ye would leave."

Clara ran her hand over her face several times before her elbow rested on the table, and her fingers covered her mouth. The strain of this ordeal was clear on her face. She appeared exhausted and haggard. It was obvious the croft had plenty of food within it, and its owner had already silently offered them bread and cheese. Clara's weight loss hadn't come from lack of sustenance.

"So, I'm to believe Fergus nae tupping a whore means all is well from ma perspective."

"Nay," Tate responded. "Naught is well from any perspective. But I think it was part of the plotter's intentions. Clara, if we can prove that it wasna ye, would ye come back? Nay one has actually said ye're dead except for Fergus when he blamed Peter today. We've said ye are nay longer with us and the like, but nae deceased."

"I would come back if ma name were cleared."

Adelaide leaned forward and twisted to see her friend's face beside her. "What if Fergus apologized? Took responsibility for what he did and how that nae only hurt ye but endangered ye?"

"I'd speak to him alone before I make any decisions. But I understood his anger from the beginning. Kenning that he might have been with another woman that vera night—well, I ken now the hurt and fury he must have felt. I didna even see aught, but just hearing that he might have taken another woman to bed makes me feel like I'll be ill while ma heart stops. If I can live with what he says, then aye. I'd marry him."

"Will ye return with us? We can get ye into the keep and up to our chamber without anyone seeing ye." Adelaide's eyes darted to Tate. If they hid Clara in the chamber they'd planned to share, they would put their lovemaking on pause. He dipped his chin, even though Adelaide could tell he wasn't thrilled. It wasn't obvious, but she realized she knew Tate well enough to understand.

"It'll be nearly dawn by then. Mayhap I ride out tomorrow night and arrive in the dark." Clara tensed, and Adelaide didn't blame her friend for the apprehension.

"Nay. It's best if we ride together with all the men. There is a score of them. We canna leave them here, and it would defeat the point if they had to ride here tomorrow night."

"True. I wouldnae want ye to ride back unprotected, and I can tell Tate and yer brothers willna agree to that." Clara shot Tate a smirk. It relieved everyone at the table to see Clara could still find things about which to laugh. "Vera well."

"When do ye wish to speak to Fergus?" Harry had said nothing since they arrived, but he'd wondered that single question the entire time.

"Nae until after he's proven wrong. He willna believe me now any more than he did that night. I dinna want him to have a chance to say something he canna take back. I'm forgiving, but I'm nae a fool. I love him, and that's why I can accept his reaction. But I willna marry a mon who proves he can treat me that way more than once."

"Will ye push for ye and Fergus to marry instead of he and Agnes?" Adelaide wanted to be sure they brought Clara back for the right reasons.

"Aye. If a marriage between Fergus and me isnae possible, then I will speak against it being with Agnes. They would be miserable together. They arenae well suited." Clara looked at Angus, her stare unwavering. Adelaide shifted to look at her brother.

"Angus?"

"Aye. I wish to marry Agnes and have for some time. She kens that. We spoke to our fathers, and they agreed I could court Agnes. But then all of this happened, and yer father announced his plan to marry Agnes to Fergus before anyone in ma family could object."

"Harry, did ye ken this?"

"Aye. Ada, when Angus becomes laird, I'll be his tánaiste if he doesnae have a son auld enough. I only ken because of that. Angus didna share his feelings with me for any other reason. Sarah and Finley dinna ken either." Harry grinned at his older brother. "Until the day he told me, I didna ken he had any feelings."

"Ye ken I feel anger, little brother. I shall remind ye of that in the lists." Angus raised a smug chin, but everyone could tell it was in jest. However, he soon grew serious. "Even if Clara agrees to marry Fergus, and assuming Fergus would agree once he kens the truth, we dinna ken that Laird Matheson will agree. He might still insist that it's Agnes. Yer sister told me they plan to make her marry Fergus at Freuchie. They arenae even going to wait until they reach the Matheson keep or yer home. They want the wedding over and done with, so the gossip ends."

"That's tomorrow!" Clara swept her gaze across her friends.

"Nay. They cancelled the games the morning after ye left," Adelaide explained. "That pushed everything back. The games ended today, and there are still two days of feasting. Have they already made the wedding arrangements?" Adelaide turned to Angus.

"Aye." He spat the word as though it were acid on his tongue.

"Then we must hurry to discover who was in that tent. There may nae be time for ye to speak to Fergus in private. If there isnae, what aboot at the wedding?" Adelaide looked around. "What if he believes he's confessing to Agnes that he doesnae wish to marry her after we convince him nae to? Yer father isnae pushing for the marriage. If he thinks Agnes is unwilling, then mayhap he'll admit the same. If he admits it's ye he'd rather marry, then ye'll be wed that night. If he refuses ye, then he continues to think he's refusing Agnes."

"How?"

Adelaide focused on a spot on the tabletop as she thought aloud. "Fergus already kens what Agnes looks like, but she could still wear a veil. Or rather, ye wear the veil. He willna ken it's ye unless he lifts it."

"What if he denies me again and says he wishes to marry Agnes instead of me?" Clara couldn't imagine anything worse after what she'd already experienced.

Adelaide shook her head. "A priest willna marry an unwilling woman. If Agnes doesnae wish to marry Fergus in truth, then her allowing ye to go in her stead proves her protest. Even if he accepted ye as Agnes, ye can still refuse before the ceremony begins. It will infuriate the Mathesons, but I dinna think yer father would force ye or Agnes."

"This could start a war with the Mathesons. Is it really worth the risk?"

"Do ye want Agnes to marry Fergus? Can ye live with yer sister marrying the mon ye've already..." Tate's unspoken words hung heavily in the air.

"We never actually did. He said that out of spite," Clara whispered.

Adelaide frowned. She shifted her focus to Tate, and he knew what she was thinking. She couldn't remain quiet. "Clara, if that's how he handles getting his feelings hurt, and if that's how he treats ye now, I dinna think ye should marry him. I willna stop being yer friend, and I will accept it. But I canna nae say this."

Clara covered Adelaide's clasped hands on the table. "Ye ken Fergus and I have loved each other since we were barely auld enough to ken what love is. That's why he reacted the way he did. He has never led me to believe he would mistreat me or hurt me intentionally. Before this, I dinna think ye had any doubts. I'm nae going to blindly accept a reconciliation. Like I said, I need to speak to him before I decide. If this truly is the mon who has always lurked within him, then I willna subject maself to a miserable marriage to him. Thank ye for being honest. I ken ye'll support me nay matter what, but sometimes people need to hear exactly what nay one wants to say."

"Then we should go," Tate stated. The women thanked the croft owner before the group slipped back into the night. The women rode in the center with the men always vigilant. Tate and Adelaide had much they wished to discuss with one another, but it was impossible. Since they would forsake their chamber, they knew they would have to sneak into the camp and into the tent Ceit set aside for them. Then, at best, they could whisper to one another.

When they stopped to water their horses, Adelaide slipped over to Tate and signaled for him to lean forward. She cupped her mouth and spoke into his ear. "Is this the most absurd thing I could ever suggest? Tricking Fergus into marrying Clara."

"This entire situation is absurd, but it's where we find ourselves. Naught more reasonable seems likely. If Clara decides to marry him, she can reveal herself before they exchange vows. Then the real truth, nae any more half-truths, will be there. They both agree, or one of them refuses. Either way, this is done."

"Hopefully, the implausible is plausible. If this doesnae work, we could still have our own wedding." Adelaide dropped a kiss on Tate's cheek. She was only half joking.

CHAPTER 22

$\mathcal{A}$ group of unmarried men eased their way into the crowded alehouse tent the night after Clara returned with the Grants and Tate. Tor and Wiley, with their cousins Alec and Hamish, walked alongside their friend Kirk. The five men parted the crowd just as Moses stood before the Red Sea. They found a table and promptly ordered a tankard of ale and a dram of whisky each. They stretched out their long legs and ran their hands through their hair. They grinned at the wenches and challenged each other to arm wrestling. There wasn't an average-looking man in the group. Tor and Wiley had inherited the chestnut hair from their fathers. Alec and Hamish inherited their father's jet-black hair, and Kirk had inherited his mother's white-blond locks. They stood out.

It didn't take long for them to have the working women cozying up to them. With a wench on each lap, they began chatting. Tor wrapped a lock of mousy brown hair around his finger as he grinned at the woman with a scar on her shoulder pressing her breast against him.

"Where do ye go if a mon wishes for some privacy?" Tor tried not to choke on his words.

"There's plenty of space behind the tent for a swive," the woman answered.

"And if I wish for something more than just a hurried tupping?" Kirk asked the woman on his lap as he stroked her hip.

"Then ye tell the bugger interrupting to shove off," the wench on Wiley's lap answered.

"Are ye worried someone will see ye dinna have much?"

Kirk tried not to jump when the woman he held suddenly flipped back his plaid and wrapped her hand around his cock. Tor's eyes narrowed, but Kirk was just as quick to yank her hand away. He winced when she tightened her grip until he held her wrist tightly enough for her to yelp and let go. Kirk scowled back at Tor, silently warning his friend to keep what just happened to himself.

"We dinna fear that for a moment, lass." Wiley grinned and winked. "Where do ye sleep? Canna we go there?"

"We sleep in here," the woman on Tor's lap answered as she leaned forward to expose half her breasts, her nipples more than peeking over the neckline of her blouse.

The one of Alec's lap shrugged. "Or we slip into tents that are empty. For a quick hump, we take our chances."

"And have ye been caught? I mean, I canna imagine anyone would be happy to find a couple in their tent ravishing each other," Alec responded.

"Nae yet."

"Ye should be more worried that someone accuses ye of filching their belongings. Ye could have yer ear pinned to the village post," Alec pointed out. It wasn't an uncommon punishment for an accused person to have their ear nailed to the post where the village crier made announcements or the arrested were held for public hearings. If they acquitted the accused, they were free to go. But not until they ripped their own ear free. Guilty or not, the allegation ensured punishment.

"Like I said, we havenae been caught, so nay one's had reason to accuse us."

The men looked at one another. The women were careless with their words, which was exactly what they wanted. They'd report the possible thefts to Edward and Fingal, letting them sort that out.

"I canna imagine picking a tent next to here is wise. Too easy for someone to see ye," Hamish stated. The woman on his lap ran her hand over his chest. When she leaned forward to kiss him, he shifted and gently pushed her away. His stomach couldn't handle the stench from her breath. She leaned back and sighed before speaking up.

"We pick tents in the center of the camp, usually a tent where we're certain the owner will remain in the Great Hall until the end of the evening. We only do it at night when nay one can see us."

"Dinna ye worry aboot warriors coming back to their tents and demanding what they find without paying?" Alec pressed.

The woman on his lap grew tired of the questioning, so she rolled her eyes. "We dinna go to the warriors' own tents or even those of other men unless we ken they'll pay. They're the ones who already paid to tup us out back."

"Ye go to nobles' tents?" Hamish leaned forward and whispered.

"Aye. Far more comfortable."

Tor's hand slid along the ribs of the woman he held. She'd grown quiet, and he wanted to hear what she had to say since he suspected he'd found half of the infamous night's culprits from the way she withdrew. He whispered in her ear. "If I wanted to leave with ye right now, where would we go?"

"I dinna ken."

"What aboot that MacDonald tent that's been empty? I hear the other woman is sleeping in the keep now." Tor felt the woman stiffen. "Ye dinna like that idea. Is it because someone would ken we were there, and it's supposed to be empty?"

"Nay. I can be quiet. Nay one would ken."

"Quiet or nae, I like a candle lit. I enjoy seeing what I paid for." Tor tweaked her nipple before dipping his fingers toward her neckline. He knew his father would kill him if he saw what Tor was doing, but he was certain he was making headway. He returned Kirk's earlier warning glare, knowing he was the guilty party this time. The other men reached for their drinks, making them appear distracted from the women for a moment.

"We couldnae do that in Lady Clara's tent. People would see us and ken someone was in there who didna belong. I almost got caught there the last time."

Tor and the other exchanged glances. If it wouldn't draw too much attention for the five of them to leave with one woman, or if it wouldn't scare the wench into silence, they would have dragged her outside to demand an explanation.

"Caught? Who were ye in there with?" Wiley waggled his eyebrows and leaned forward as though he wanted to hear the latest gossip.

"A Chisholm. He kenned Lady Clara and Lady Agnes would be in the Great Hall already."

"How'd he ken that?" Wiley prompted.

"I dinna ken. I suppose someone told him to use the tent. I'm nae going back there. I heard what happened to Lady Clara."

Tor's fingers bit into her hip. "That was ye that night, wasna it?"

"Aye," the woman yelped. He eased his hold. "The Chisholm guard suggested it and said he enjoyed having a candle lit, too. I didna ken anyone saw us until the next afternoon, when I heard what happened to Lady Clara."

"And ye didna think to speak up." Alec's voice was flat, but his disgust shone in his eyes.

"And be put out? Left to fend for maself in this clan without a job? Face Laird Grant and ken he'd banish me or take the lash to me? Mayhap both. Nay. I didna decide to forfeit ma life for some noblewoman who was fool enough to take her life over a mon like that Matheson. More fool was she."

Tor kept his voice low, but the commanding tone wasn't one the woman could ignore. "Get up. Ye and I and Laird Grant are going to talk. Make one sound of protest, and I will tell the entire alehouse what ye did."

The other men put coins on the table, moving the remaining women aside. The wenches cursed and grumbled. Only enough to pay for the drinks was on the table. They'd wasted their time with men who'd never intended to pay them for more. They moved away, looking for better, more reliable customers. The woman was short enough that the men surrounded her, and no one could tell who left with them. A few grins broke out as the other patrons watched the men leave with the woman. None of the Sinclairs, Mackays, or the Hartley looked anywhere but straight ahead.

Once outside the tent, the woman stopped. She balked when Wiley nudged her forward. Tor grasped her arm in a vise-like grip. "Dinna make me drag ye because I will. By the hair if I need to."

"Ye're a Sinclair. Ye dinna hurt women."

"Ye look like the sturdy sort. It wouldnae hurt ye." Tor yanked her forward. "Walk."

The men marched her to the keep and inside.

People stared and whispered, but the group didn't stop until they were outside Edward's solar. Kirk knocked, then opened the door when they were bidden to enter. They filled the chamber to the brim with the Grant laird, lady, tánaiste and his wife. The MacDonald laird and lady sat beside Fingal and Madeline. Adelaide and Tate tucked themselves away in the far corner.

"Is this the woman?" Laird MacDonald demanded. Tor nudged her again when she didn't answer. She still refused to speak. "I shall take yer silence as a bellowing admission of guilt."

Edward stepped forward. "Silvia, I'd answer if I were ye." With her laird standing before her, she nodded. "I must hear yer answer."

"Aye. I was in the tent that night. I didna ken anyone was meant to see us. I didna ken until after that someone arranged for the Matheson tánaiste to walk by and think I was Lady Clara."

"Why did ye pick that tent?" Edward asked evenly. He shot the MacDonald a warning glance when the other man opened his mouth to speak.

"I didna. It was the mon I was with. He was a Chisholm. He said he'd seen the sisters leave for the evening meal, so it was empty. He said ye—" She nudged her chin toward the MacDonald. "—Wouldnae find out."

"Do ye ken which Chisholm it was? Could ye recognize him?" Edward continued his questioning.

"Och, aye. I willna forget. Once I kenned I was a part of what happened, I kenned I wouldnae go near him again. He asked for the next night, but I refused."

"What was his name?" Laird MacDonald couldn't remain silent.

"He said it was Simon, but I heard another mon call him Niall."

Edward locked gazes with Laird MacDonald as he spoke. "Could he have been Laird Chisholm's nephew?"

"I believe so. I'd seen him with Peter and Adam each time they came to the tent. Peter was the one who told Niall to pick me. I didna understand at the time, but he told Niall something or other like Niall would win the bet that he was mon enough once it was done. I thought he meant once Niall finished tupping me." Silvia appeared to shrink with each word. It wasn't either of the lairds or even the group of young men who made her wish the ground would swallow her. It was Lady Davina.

"Silvia, I've kenned ye since the day ye were born. I helped bring ye into this world. I offered ye a place to work in the keep when yer parents died, but ye were too stubborn. Ye wound up working in the alehouse for it. I offered ye a position again, but ye were too proud to admit it was a better choice. Now, ye have gone so far past disgracing yerself that I canna even name where ye've wound up. Nay one would be more disappointed in ye than yer mama and da." Lady Davina came to stand before the woman. Her voice held a note of regret rather than accusation. "Ye assumed we'd lash ye or banish ye, didna ye?"

Silvia nodded.

"Yer mother was one of ma first friends when I arrived here to marry the laird. Ye played alongside our lasses. If we allowed that and offered more than once to help ye, why would ye assume we'd banish ye or lash ye?"

"What else could ye do, ma lady? I ruined an alliance."

"Did ye do it intentionally?" The MacDonald demanded.

"Nay, ma laird. But I was in yer daughter's tent. That alone…"

"Confessing what ye heard would have redeemed ye," Laird MacDonald stated. "But ye didna. What are ye going to do with her, Grant?"

"I'm undecided. It could have been anyone caught up in Peter Chisholm's plan. She didna intentionally get involved in that. But I will punish her for entering the tent and for nae being forthcoming. That I can assure ye." Edward peered down at Silvia, who could only nod. "I willna imprison ye in the dungeon while I decide. But ye will have a guard assigned to ye while ye serve drinks. That is all ye will do."

Silvia turned to Laird MacDonald, the severity of her situation sinking in. "Ma laird, I am sorry aboot what happened to yer daughter. If I'd kenned how she would react, I would have spoken up that night, ma punishment be damned. I got too scared after she..."

Laird MacDonald looked at his wife, who'd remained silent the entire time. She nodded and rose. Without a word, she walked to the door. Her husband followed her out of the solar. Edward was two steps behind, signaling a guardsman to come and take Silvia back to the alehouse with strict instructions that he was not to let her out of his sight until Edward sent the man's brother to relieve him.

The Sinclairs, Mackays, and Hartley had remained quiet too, having moved to stand near Tate and Adelaide. The couple suggested the unmarried men seek the information, and they'd all agreed not to speak during the meeting. Tate and Adelaide clung to each other's hand, both having plenty they wished to say. It was Adelaide who broke the silence.

"What now? Laird and Lady MacDonald will tell Clara what we learned. What aboot the Chisholms? They left. Does Tate move forward with suggesting the double wedding to Fergus? The MacDonalds and Clara have already promised Agnes that she doesn't have to marry Fergus if she doesn't want to, and Agnes made it vera clear that was the last thing she wanted."

"Silvia confesses to Fergus," Edward responded. "We go from there. But naught more will happen until morning. I suggest we all retire. I suspect it shall be a vera long day."

* * *

FERGUS'S already ruddy cheeks flamed dark enough to match his hair. His ears practically glowed as he listened to Silvia recount what happened that fateful night and why she hadn't confessed. Tate stood beside his friend, not only as moral support but to ensure his friend didn't wrap his hands around the woman's throat. It had tempted him to do that very thing the night before.

"Ye sneaked into Lady Clara's tent to couple with a mon. Then ye realized what ye were a part of, but ye didna step forward to admit that ruining a marriage and an alliance was all part of a farce. Then ye learn the woman whose life ye helped ruin by this is dead, and ye still didna think ye should speak."

Tate could guess what Silvia thought as her expression grew mutinous, but she remained silent. She clearly blamed Fergus for the ruining of anyone's life. Tate wouldn't disagree if she said as much, but she kept her lips pressed firmly together.

"Get out of ma sight," Fergus barked. Silvia backed away, then spun on her heels. Edward signaled guards who led her out of the Great Hall. Edward had ordered Silvia to confess her role in front of everyone gathered for the evening meal. She'd done it haltingly with tears streaming down her cheeks, but she'd admitted everything.

"What do ye have to say for yer actions now that ye

ken the truth?" Tate asked. Only the people on the dais could hear him.

"Never could I have been more wrong aboot aught. I destroyed Clara. It should be me burning in the flames of hellfire." He dropped his voice to a whisper, speaking only to himself, but Tate heard him. "I will join her."

"Why were ye so quick to believe it was her? Why couldnae ye even consider there was another explanation?" Tate asked what everyone at the Gathering wished to know.

Fergus closed his eyes and shook his head. "Because she saw Lady Melissa Oliphant in ma arms and kissing ma cheek. The woman tripped, and I caught her as I went to meet Clara. She gave me the kiss on the cheek to thank me, then tried for more. I put her aside, but I ken it appeared incriminating. I explained to Clara, and she said she saw enough to believe me. When I saw the couple in her tent, I thought she did it out of spite. That if I thought I could get away with it, that she could too."

"But she didna see ye coupling with Lady Melissa, so why would ye imagine she would go so far as to couple with another mon?" Tate pressed.

"I dinna ken. I saw the hurt on her face even though she said she'd seen Lady Melissa appear to trip. She believed the lass pretended in order to flirt with me. The shock and memory made me assume the worst. I said things before I had time to realize what flew from ma mouth. The more I said, the angrier I became, and the more convinced I was. I ruined everything. They may as well name me Clara's murderer. I did that."

Tate lowered his voice to little more than a murmur. "Mayhap ye will fall in love with Agnes."

Fergus's nose curled. "That would be like falling in love with ma own sister. I will do ma duty, but it's Clara I will always love."

"Do ye think Clara would forgive ye if she were here?"

Fergus's shoulders drooped. "That's the worst part. I ken she would. This time. She wouldnae if I mistreated her like this again. I never would. She wasna naïve nor a fool. But she felt for me what I felt for her. I ken she'd understand. She didna believe the situation could ever be fixed. I forsook her, and she couldnae bear the shame of what I said. I dinna blame her. I've wished I was dead since the moment it happened. I wanted Peter to confess he'd had some part in this. I have. Now there's nay reason for me to live."

Tate looked over his shoulder at Adelaide and shot her a worried glance. His friend's moroseness concerned him. He wasn't sure Fergus would live to see his wedding day. He would need to make sure Laird Matheson didn't allow his son to be alone. As Tate turned back to look at Fergus, his friend took a deep inhale before speaking once more for the crowd to hear.

"I wronged Lady Clara in the most grievous of ways. I did far more than just slight her. I did more than accuse her of heinous things I kenned all along she could never do. I broke her trust, and I broke ma pledge to always protect her. To always stand beside her. There is naught I will ever regret more than pushing her away." Fergus twisted to look at his father who sat among the lairds on the dais. Then he looked at Laird MacDonald before facing forward and finding Agnes in the crowd. "Lady Agnes, I ken ye dinna wish to marry me. I dinna wish to make ye wed me when ye ken I love yer sister. I dinna want ye to go through life thinking the mon ye married only took ye as a substitute for yer sister. Ye canna marry me any more than I can marry ye. I willna force ye to."

"And if it isnae Lady Agnes, then who? Ye need an

heir," Laird Matheson boomed as he rose. His ruddy complexion matched Fergus's from moments earlier.

"I have enough brothers to give our clan an heir."

"Ye will marry. I will pick who this time."

"Nay, ye willna." All eyes turned to see Clara descending the stairs, her skirts gathered in her hands. "I'm nay more dead than any of the rest of ye. I left, and now I am back."

Fergus shoved Tate in his hurry to get to Clara. He leaped from the dais and pulled her into his arms. He stared at her, uncertain that he wasn't dreaming or in a fit of hysterics far from reality.

"Clara?"

"Aye. Nay one but ye ever said I was dead. I ken people said I was nay longer with them or had left ye or was gone. Which was all true. I left the keep and the Gathering. I returned last night."

"Ye let me think ye were dead. Everyone let me think ye were dead. Ye deceived me."

Clara pushed at his chest, but he wouldn't loosen his hold. "Nay, I didna. Ye made another assumption based on only part of the evidence. I was prepared to retire to ma home and never leave or retire to a convent for the rest of ma years. Ye gave me only those two options besides taking ma life. I may nae have told anyone to disabuse ye of yer assumptions, but nay one deceived ye, Fergus. Ye deceived yerself."

Fergus remained silent as he considered what Clara said. For once, he truly considered his words before uttering them. "What did ye hear before ye came down?"

"All of what Silvia confessed, and yer admission of guilt. Naught else until yer father started bellowing."

"I thought ye did it because of Lady Melissa."

"What?" Clara reared back. "Did more happen than I saw? Did ye think I kenned something else far worse, and that I did it to punish ye?"

"There was naught else, but I did think ye were punishing me. It made so much sense at the time. Now, it was naught."

"It was the Chisholms trying to prevent our clans' alliance. That's what it was." Clara looked around the gathered diners who sat below the salt, then everyone at elevated positions on the dais. "I planned to wait before I revealed maself. I wanted to ken if ye wished ye could still marry me. If ye had, I would have agreed right then and there. If ye hadnae, I would have tried to convince ye nae to marry Agnes, anyway."

"Ye wished to ken all that before ye revealed yerself?" Fergus's brow furrowed.

"Aye. If I'd gone through with it, I would have deceived ye. I dinna want that. Believing I had is what caused this. Doing it for real ensured our marriage—if there ever were one—would be doomed from the start. Neither of us would have ever trusted the other. I was going to pretend to be Agnes before the wedding ceremony. I would have worn a veil and questioned ye before the priest began. But I couldnae keep maself from hearing what was happening tonight. I couldnae hear what ye said to Tate, but I could see yer face. I ken what ye would have done."

Fergus rested his forehead against Clara's. "Because nay one kens me better than ye. I always said that aboot ye, but I was wrong."

"Nay, ye werenae. Ye kenned in yer heart that I didna do it. That's why ye wanted to ken why Peter got involved."

"I love ye, Clara. Will ye still wed with me?"

"Aye. I love ye, Fergus. And I will marry ye, but nae at the end of the Gathering. I need more time to put aside ma fear that ye could act like this again. I never imagined ye could, so it's been a shock."

"Understandable. I will give ye all the time ye need."

Fergus dropped a peck on her nose. Clara tilted her head back, and the couple shared a tender kiss that made the entire Great Hall furrow their brows since only the couple and Tate and Adelaide—who'd hurried to them but stopped short of interrupting—could hear what Fergus and Clara said to one another. Then a collective sigh passed through the diners.

"Did ye ken they married?" Fergus asked when they pulled apart.

Clara grinned as she looked behind Fergus and up to the dais. "Aye. Who'd have imagined they'd have an easier time than we did? Sinclairs never have easy marriages." Clara grimaced as the last thought slipped out.

"Ye arenae wrong," Tate muttered. His arm rested around Adelaide's waist, and she looked up at him. He whispered to her, "There's more family history to share at another time."

"Ye can have yer chamber back." Clara grinned at Adelaide.

Clara and Fergus turned toward the dais, both knowing they couldn't put off the inevitable. They might have made peace between them, but they had two irate fathers to placate and the Highlands' nosiest people's curiosity to appease. While everyone's attention was on Clara, Fergus, the MacDonalds, and the Mathesons, Adelaide and Tate slipped away to the kitchens. They gathered food and smuggled it up to her chamber, where they locked and barred the door.

"We have plans to make, wife."

CHAPTER 23

"*P*lans?" Adelaide asked as she and Tate placed their repast on the table near the fireplace. With no thought of modesty, she turned her back to Tate, and he undid her laces.

"Aye. The most immediate are all the ways we wish to make love tonight. Then aboot when our wedding will be. Do ye wish to have it here or at Dunbeath? We never decided aboot that. There was just talk but nay real resolution." Tate pushed the gown down Adelaide's arms as he smattered kisses over her shoulders, neck, and jaw. His hands remained on her hips after the gown dropped to the floor.

"All of yer family and mine are already here. Since it's nay secret, we dinna have to fear excluding anyone. It makes sense to do it here, but since I'm entering yer clan, would they prefer it at Dunbeath?"

"It willna matter to them. They wish us to be happy, so that means we choose. I'd like it to be at Dunbeath because it's familiar to me. It'll be our home. But I love the idea of being lawfully and irrefutably married within a day or two far more."

"There will already be a feast tomorrow. Why nae do it before the evening meal?"

"If yer parents agree, then I say aye. I'm sure ma family wouldnae object." Tate pulled up Adelaide's chemise and lifted it over her head. She turned toward him, and his hands rested on her breasts as he kneaded them.

"What other plans do we need to make?" Adelaide reached to unpin the brooch at Tate's shoulder. He leaned forward and stole a kiss while making it easier for Adelaide to reach. When they pulled apart, he took the brooch and dropped it into his sporran. He quickly removed his belt, clothes, and boots while Adelaide kicked off her shoes and took off her stockings.

"Ye need to decide what ye wish to take with ye to Dunbeath when we leave and what ye wish to send later."

"How many carts did yer family travel with?"

"Enough that we could likely fit two chests." Tate ran the back of his fingers between her breasts and up to her collar bone as he spoke. He nipped and kissed her neck while she responded.

"I dinna think I have more than that, that I wish to take. Ma clothes and what-nae can fit in that chest." She gestured absently toward the trunk at the foot of her bed. "Second, albeit a wee larger, would hold ma dowry items." She turned her head to capture his lips. Tate lifted her, and she wrapped her legs around his waist as he carried her to the bed.

"Do ye have any tapestries or loom ye wish to take?" Tate supported himself on his hands as he gazed down at her. It surprised him when she pushed hard enough on his chest to signal she wished him to move. She followed, still pressing until he was on his back.

"I dinna have tapestries I've made or inherited. Besides, there are already so many women who live in yer keep. I'm certain it doesnae have space on any walls for more."

Tate drew back her hair that hung down over her breasts as she straddled his abdomen. "There will always be room for yer possessions or aught ye make. Dunbeath is as much yer home as it is any other person in ma family. Besides, if we decide to live in a croft, all the walls shall need tapestries." Tate grinned. Crofters didn't have the resources nobles had to create such luxuries. But Tate would be sure Adelaide felt at home anywhere they lived.

"Thank ye. I still dinna have any, but mayhap one day." Adelaide rocked her hips, allowing Tate's rod to rub between her globes as she felt him grow even harder. "Any other plans, husband?"

"Only how we wish to make love tonight, wife."

He reached for her, but she inched backwards until she kneeled between his legs. She wrapped her hand around his length and stroked tantalizingly slowly. She leaned forward and swirled her tongue around the tip, flicking the small opening. She shifted her gaze to watch Tate draw the pillows behind his head. She reveled in his heated concentration on everything she did. She once again swiped her tongue over the bulbous head but paused a moment later.

"I dinna ken what else to do. Ye put yer tongue in me. Do I put ye in ma mouth?" Adelaide felt foolish since she'd heard maids talk about sucking on a man's rod, but she didn't know how much of it she was supposed to take. She doubted she could manage all of him, but she didn't know if she was supposed to manage any of him.

"Only if that's what ye wish."

"Do ye wish me to?"

"Wee one, can ye nae tell I'm practically panting for ye? Slide yer mouth down it as far as ye feel comfortable. Ye can lick and suck, even graze yer teeth over it."

He grinned. "*Lightly*. Just dinna bite, or we may nae have bairns."

"And these?" Adelaide cupped his bollocks.

"Ye can do what ye have in the past." She'd discovered how responsive they could be the first time she'd asked to try bringing him to release with only her hand since he did it with just his fingers. "If ye wish to, at some point, ye could do the same to those as ye're aboot to do to ma cock. I willna complain."

"If I get this right, I dinna think ye'll complain aboot aught."

Tate sat up and took her hands in his before pressing a soft kiss to her lips. "There isnae right and wrong in aught we share. There are things we might enjoy more than others. But ye being here with me and touching me at all is heavenly. Do what feels right to ye, wee one. I love ye."

"I love ye, too. Ye ken I wish to please ye. I'm just nervous."

"I understand, and if ye pleased me any more than ye do already, ma heart would give out. Ye make it race and pound nearly out of ma chest just looking at ye. Ye touching me—like I said—it's heavenly."

"Thank ye." Adelaide appreciated the boost to her confidence. She gave him a quick peck on his lips before pressing on his chest again. He laid back, and she lowered her head once more. She ran her tongue along his length, from root to tip. She flicked her tongue on the underside of the mushroom-shaped head and felt as much as saw him twitch. She did that three more times, eliciting a deep groan each time. She inhaled before opening her mouth as wide as she could and lowering it onto his cock. She sucked with each inch she covered. When he grazed the back of her throat, she stopped despite there being more of him left. She wrapped her hand around what she couldn't manage and began bobbing her head in rhythm with her hand.

"Addy," Tate sighed. He couldn't believe how sensual the experience was. The ones he'd had in the past brought him to release as quickly as possible. There was no savoring the moment. Adelaide's eyes drooped closed, and she hummed her appreciation. The vibration nearly made him spill. He knew he wouldn't last long, but he wished to linger in tortured bliss for just a few more moments. He forced himself not to thrust like he wished. He didn't want to terrify Adelaide if it pushed his length too far into her mouth. He clutched the sheets when he could no longer hold back the flood of pleasure. "Aye... I canna stop."

He sat up and tried to pull Adelaide off, but she swatted at his hand and redoubled her efforts until she tasted him. She gagged, then reflex made her swallow. She wasn't sure what she thought of what just happened, but she knew she'd pleasured Tate, and it hadn't taken very long. She licked him as she straightened. She yelped when Tate's hands wrapped around her waist and spun her until she laid beneath him. His kiss was fiercer than any she remembered. He nudged her legs wider before reaching between them. He slid his fingers into her slick channel.

"Ye enjoyed that, didna ye, *mo ghaol?*" Tate whispered. He swept the satiny skin within her, finding the spot that made her hips jerk off the bed. "Ye enjoyed teasing me, then making it so that ma eyes crossed, and I saw stars."

"I dinna ken aboot that last part, but aye. I loved pleasuring ye. I loved kenning I did that for ye. That ye didna last long. It satisfied ma heart and aroused ma body." Adelaide arched her back, pressing her breasts toward him. He shifted so he could suckle them. She knew how he loved her responses as they coupled, so she moaned. Her pants came unbidden as need coalesced in her core before it tightened. She felt the wave of pleasure building until it crested. She contracted around his fingers as he continued to slide his digits in and out while his thumb rubbed her pearl.

Tate pulled back, loving the sight of his sated wife. She reached between them, stroking him, and moving him toward her entrance. He glided the tip between her netherlips until his rod had recovered enough for another round. He eased into her painstakingly slowly as she tried to roll and flex her hips to take more sooner. He chuckled.

"I've caught ma breath and fed the beast by making ye climax. Now, I shall give ye the same torment ye gave me."

"Beast, are ye?" Adelaide grinned.

"Aye. I could have swallowed ye whole while I kissed ye." Tate slid the last inch into Adelaide before withdrawing nearly the entire way and thrusting hard. He kept that rhythm as Adelaide gripped his chiseled backside. Each time his muscles flexed, he pressed into her. The double sensation made her moans longer and louder.

"I'm close," Adelaide murmured. She shifted and ground her mons against his pubic bone, setting off a maelstrom of emotions: need, urgency, relief, and satisfaction. The need for more battled the satisfaction she already felt. Tate continued, knowing he could bring her another release before they stopped. He surged forward harder, having already learned just what his wife preferred. "It's happening again. Mmm… Ahhh… Aye."

Tate pistoned his rod into her over and over until his back arched, and he wished to roar like the devil himself possessed him. But he stifled his bellow instead, dropping onto his forearms and once more devouring

Adelaide with his kiss. She gave in equal measure as they clung to one another.

"Tate!" Pounding sounded at their door just as they caught their breath. They looked toward the portal. "Tate! Now!"

"Wiley," Tate explained as he rolled off the bed. He grabbed his plaid from the end as he yanked the bed curtains closed on the side toward the door. He covered his groin before opening the door a crack. "What?"

He tried not to sound irritated since he knew it must be urgent for Wiley to intrude.

"The Chisholms razed three fields and slaughtered a score of cattle. Grant guards said they saw more riding north. We think they're riding to Dunbeath and hoping to get there before we can."

"I'll be down in a moment. Where?"

"The Great Hall for now." Wiley spun on his heel and hurried toward the stairs. Tate could hear movement belowstairs, and he saw his uncle Callum step out of his chamber, his aunt right behind her husband. Tate ducked back into his chamber as he heard Adelaide yank open the curtains. She scrambled off the bed and ran to the clothes she'd discarded earlier. She donned the chemise but tossed the gown onto the bed. She pulled one she could lace herself from a peg on the wall while Tate hurried to pleat his plaid. In any other circumstance, she would have marveled at his speed and accuracy.

"Addy, I wish ye to stay here until I ken the danger, but this is still yer home and yer people. I just ask that ye promise to come up here and lock yerself in if I fear ye're in danger. Even if ye dinna agree, please promise me."

She gazed at him for a moment as he pinned his plaid in place. She knew what he wasn't saying. He wouldn't be able to focus if he feared for her. She didn't want her husband dead because she couldn't oblige his one request.

"Aye. I'll come back here."

They slipped on their shoes and bolted from the chamber. He grasped her hand as they descended the stairs, terrified she would trip. But she was surefooted, having taken the stairs her entire life. As they entered the Great Hall, they found people already awake and rushing around. Servants hurried into the kitchens when Davina ordered them there. It was too early to begin preparations for the new day's meals. She wanted them out of earshot as the Grants and Sinclairs, along with their allies, rallied around the dais.

Adelaide and Tate stepped onto the raised platform but stood off to the side. Davina came to join Edward, Madeline, and Fingal at the center of the table, each taking their regular seat. Callum, Magnus, and Tavish stood behind the chair in which Liam sat. Thor stood beside his father, Callum. Tristan Mackay sat beside Liam with his sons Wee Liam, Alec, and Hamish behind him. Laird Hamish Sutherland and Lady Amelia sat to Liam's other side. Their son, Lachlan, stood behind them with his oldest son. The lairds of several other clans hurried to take seats. Adelaide swept her gaze around and spotted the MacLeods of Lewis at the opposite end from the MacLeods of Skye. Kieran of Lewis sat beside his brother-by-marriage, Hardi Cameron. She watched her uncle Kieran as he looked at his wife who stood in front of the dais. Andrew Gordon sat beside Fingal with Ewan and Eoin behind him. Their wives, Allyson and Cairstine, stood beside Kieran's wife, Maude.

Moments later, Brodie Campbell and his son Rick arrived on the dais. Rick was his heir and tánaiste while his second son, Monty, arrived to take his place as Laird Ross. Brodie's brother, Dominic, stood between

Rick and Monty. The Keiths were on the far side of the Sinclairs. Callum's oldest child, Rose, perched on her husband's lap. Blaine Keith rested his hand on her swollen belly. Her aunt, Abigail, stood beside her as her husband, Ronan MacKinnon, took a seat next to Kieran, his brother-by-marriage.

Adelaide watched the most commanding lairds in the Highlands gather around the table where she'd sat since her birth. Marriage and blood allied them all to one another. Lairds and tánaistes who weren't part of the strongest alliance in Scotland hadn't been roused from their slumber. She noticed the Mathesons and MacDonalds were missing.

"Edward will summon the Matheson and the Mac-Donald to join us once there's a plan in place. Neither of those men need to be here sharing their opinions since they're part of what caused this," Tate explained, guessing what Adelaide wondered.

"But the MacDonalds rival the Campbells. Shouldnae *a* MacDonald be here?"

"Aye. Look." Tate jutted his chin toward John Mac-Donald of Sleat, Lord of the Isles, as he walked toward the dais with Archibald "the Grim" Douglas. The latter was a near mirror image of his dead father, James "the Black" Douglas. It was said that neither father nor son had ever smiled except over their enemies' graves.

"We have word from one of ma chieftains that the Chisholms razed three fields on Grant land beside Loch Ness," Edward explained. "Lathan couldnae have crossed Mackintosh and Fraser land this quickly with the size of his entourage. He must have sent riders ahead days ago."

While the distance between Freuchie and Castle Erchless wasn't more than a two-day ride, the clan would move slower with the carts and walking guardsmen.

"But why yer land?" Hardi Cameron asked. "To have

sent men ahead of him with enough time to do this speaks to more than being in a snit for being sent away. He still needs to get his people across that Grant land before he can get to his own. This canna be aboot Lady MacKinnon. Everyone kens none of yer family gets along with the Chisholms, but there hasnae been violence between any of ye and the Chisholms in more than a score of years."

"Aye," Ewan Gordon agreed. "I could understand them setting ablaze MacDonald lands to make it look as though the Mathesons retaliated for what happened last eve, but there wouldnae have been time."

Adelaide realized then what Tate meant about needing neither the MacDonald nor the Matheson lairds present. If they'd been present, the moment they came up, there would have been arguments about their roles.

"Ye ken Peter does as he pleases," Wee Liam Mackay spoke up. "He has since before his father legitimized him by marrying his mistress. It wouldnae surprise me if Lathan had nay clue what was happening."

"Lathan is a greedy fool, but Wee Liam is right," Kieran agreed. "It's more likely Peter acted on his own. The Chisholms have learned their reach isnae as long as they thought. Nae when our family surrounds them."

"I agree with Hardi. I dinna think this is aboot ma wife," Ronan MacKinnon interjected. "Lathan's bitter aboot having to return most of Lady MacKinnon's dowry to Kieran and that I received it when I wedded ma wife. But he kens nay one is interested in a handfast from more than a score of years ago that didna last. It's his smug bastards who dinna like their wishes thwarted." Ronan turned his attention to Adelaide. "Lass, there isnae a kind way to say this, but ken that I dinna blame ye at all. This is aboot ma niece and her husband."

Adelaide froze. Tate drew her closer, then wrapped both arms around her.

"Wheest, wee one," Tate whispered in a soothing tone before addressing everyone else. "I believe Laird MacKinnon is likely right. Adam is still openly hostile to ma wife aboot their betrothal that never happened. He and I exchanged words more than once when I warned him away from Lady Adelaide. Now that we're married, and there's absolutely nay possibility Adam could marry ma wife and secure an alliance with the Grants, he's petty enough to want revenge. Add to it that Lady Adelaide and I helped figure out Peter was responsible for what happened. It'll only be worse when they learn we brought Lady Clara back. Both brothers are furious. They canna reach Sinclair lands before ma family could overtake them, so they opted for land that's closer."

"What do ye wish for us to do?" Liam asked. While the other clans would support the Grants and the Sinclairs, this was a matter for them to address before anyone offered or was called upon.

"Take ma daughter safely to Dunbeath," Fingal answered. "Ye dinna need to pass through that portion of Grant land or go near the Chisholms. If ye wish to ride ahead, I can arrange for yer carts along with Adelaide's belongings to follow ye."

"If that's yer wish, then we will do that." Liam nodded.

Adelaide looked up at Tate then over to her father. Now that her impending departure was upon her, fear of the unknown crashed over her. She would miss her family and everything she'd known since her birth.

"Would ye marry me at dawn instead of dusk?" Tate whispered.

"I'll marry ye anytime." Adelaide shifted her gaze back to Tate.

"Laird Grant, Lady Adelaide and I wish to say our vows at dawn. I ken ma family will leave this morning. It's important to both of us that ye and yer family be with us when we exchange our vows."

Edward smiled at the young woman who'd been more like a granddaughter to him than a distant cousin. "Of course."

"Ye ken we and the Keiths travel the same route as ye, Liam. We'll ride with ye," Hamish Sutherland stated to his brother-by-marriage. Liam hadn't believed he'd warm to Hamish after he learned about his late wife's family. But it hadn't taken long for the two men to become the best of friends. They were more like brothers than allies.

Everyone looked at Tristan, who shrugged. "We have to cross Sutherland to reach our land, so why wouldnae we travel together? We'd need to spend at least one night camping in the Sutherlands' territory, so why nae do it in a proper bed? Ma lads need their beauty sleep, or they're positively beastly."

Wee Liam, Alec, and Hamish were the spitting image of their father. Raven-black hair, deep emerald eyes, shoulders so broad they turned sideways in most doorways, and height that rivaled all their Sinclair cousins, uncles, and grandfather. Rugged barely touched on the men's appearance and disposition. Tristan winked at his wife who'd come to stand beside Tristan but now occupied his seat. Their sons grinned while a female voice near the dais huffed. Wee Liam winked at his wife, Elene, confirming he was his father's son.

"Ma clan must travel the same route, too. I'd like time with ma great-uncle and great-aunt," Monty Campbell said as he nodded toward Hamish and Amelia Sutherland.

"Since we dinna wish to set eyes on a single

Chisholm, we will skirt their land." Seamus Mackenzie looked at his sister-by-marriage, Saoirse, who'd been a Sinclair before she married Seamus's younger brother. "We'll travel with the Sinclairs. Magnus Óg and I would like to visit more with our sister."

Yet another complicated branch on the Sinclair family tree. Magnus Óg—or the younger—Mackenzie bore the moniker after fostering with the Sinclairs and training under the Sinclair brother, Magnus. The latter became known as Magnus Mòr—or the greater —to lessen the confusion. Magnus Óg and Seamus were Siùsan's half-brothers, and she'd married Callum.

At this point, the Sinclairs, the Sutherlands, the Mackays, the Keiths, the Rosses, and the Mackenzies would all travel together. Seamus and Monty shot each other warning glares. Just because alliances existed among the group didn't mean alliances existed between all the members.

Silent nods from Kieran MacLeod of Lewis and Michail MacLeod of Assynt confirmed they would travel with the larger group, too. Michail was Siùsan's cousin through her mother, and Seamus and Magnus Óg were his second cousins through their mother. The MacLeods of Assynt were a sept of the MacLeods of Lewis and shared ancestors. Kieran MacLeod was also Hamish Sutherland's son-by-marriage, which made him Liam Sinclair's nephew-by-marriage.

The other Highland clans, like the Gordons and Campbells, would travel in opposite directions. The larger caravan would resemble an army sweeping through the northern Highlands, whereas the other clans could travel relatively inconspicuously. That suited most of them well.

"There are a few hours left before dawn. I suggest we all rest. Grant men will ride out at dawn to check our land while everyone else gathers for the wedding." Edward offered Adelaide a tight smile.

Everyone trickled out of the Great Hall, but Tate and Adelaide walked over to the Sinclairs. It was Ceit who engulfed Adelaide in a tight embrace. She rubbed her new daughter-by-marriage's back several times before they pulled apart.

"Those eejits caused this, nae ye. They made their choices, and they will have to live with what will inevitably happen. They are nay match for Edward and Fingal. They may have gotten their noses out of joint because of ye and Tate, but nay one told them to have a fit of temper. Neither ye nor Tate made Lathan a weak laird who canna control his weans. Dinna fash, lass. All will be fine." Ceit kissed Adelaide's cheek before letting go. Tate stepped forward and slid his arm around Adelaide's waist. Everyone bid each other good night for what was left of it.

"Tatum, I dinna think it's going to be that easy," Adelaide said as they climbed into bed and cuddled together.

Tate trailed his fingers over her back as Adelaide nestled closer. "Neither do I. Dinna go anywhere I canna see ye. Something is going to happen."

CHAPTER 24

*T*ate's chest surely couldn't expand enough to hold his heart as it filled with pride as Adelaide approached where he stood on the kirk steps. She wore a shimmering blue gown anyone would believe was made just for her. But Tate knew it was the same dress Madeline wore to marry Fingal. He watched as Fingal walked alongside Adelaide as they processed to the kirk. Adelaide reached out and gave Lady Laurel Campbell's hand a quick squeeze since she'd made the gown all those years ago.

Tate was taller than most in the crowd, so he could see over them as Adelaide approached. At her shorter height, she'd only been able to see Tate's hair and eyes as she walked toward him. When the gathered people moved to let Fingal and her pass, she thought she might melt into a gooey puddle. She'd never seen a more handsome man, and she couldn't be prouder to call him her husband.

Tate stood in his best leine and his plaid made with the laird's family pattern. The hilts of his sword and dirks shone even in the muted dawn light. His smile made everything right in Adelaide's world. She had her left arm wrapped around her father's arm, but she reached her right hand out to Tate when he came to meet them at the base of the steps. She smiled at her father as he joined Madeline and her siblings. Wiley stood beside Tate, a welcoming smile plastered across his expressive face. But it was Tate's expression that took her breath away. He'd made her feel special, precious, and loved ever since they confessed their feelings.

The way he looked at her now made the rest of the world disappear. No one else existed except for the man who led her to the top of the kirk steps. She barely noticed the priest as her gaze locked with Tate's. She could tell that just like Tate was her entire world in that moment, she was the same for him. Watching the priest wrap a length of Sinclair plaid around their wrists and clasped hands entranced her. She knew she spoke her vows and heard Tate recite his, but the blissful haze didn't fade until Tate slipped the ring on her finger. Everything snapped into crisp reality as she officially became Tate's wife under the law and before everyone's eyes.

"I love ye, Addy," Tate whispered as he drew their bound hands between them to cover his heart.

"I love ye, Tatum. Is this real?"

Tate chuckled. "Aye. I wasna sure for a moment since it's so perfect. I thought I was watching us from heaven, but it's real. Ye're ma wife forever."

As they came together for their kiss, they knew they'd both experienced the same surrealness as the Grant priest married them. When they finally pulled apart to catch their breath, neither heard the crowd cheering. Adelaide only heard the steady beat of Tate's heart as she rested her ear and cheek against his chest. He only heard her sigh as they relaxed against each other. Neither knew how long they stood like that, and neither cared that they kept anyone waiting.

When they couldn't ignore their families or spectators any longer, they turned toward the crowd, who cheered again. They took turns embracing Ceit and Tavish, and Madeline and Fingal before members of both extended families came up to share their well wishes. After they moved into the Great Hall to break their fasts, Adelaide slipped abovestairs when the priest finished blessing the meal. She hurried to change out of the gown both her sisters hoped to wear too. She and Tate had risen early, so they could pack what she wanted with her to begin her life as a Sinclair. She swept her gaze over her chamber one last time, her eyes resting on the bed where she'd laughed and traded stories with her siblings. The same bed where she and Tate made love for the first time. Once she'd closed the door, she hurried back downstairs, sliding into her place beside Tate. A bowl of perfectly prepared porridge awaited her.

"Thank ye, *mo ghràidh*. For some reason, I'm always starving." After they'd finished packing and before Madeline came to help her daughter get ready, they'd built up an appetite with a hurried, but oh-so-satisfying coupling.

"Ye ride with me, *leannan*." Tate's devilish smile made Adelaide's toes curl. But they both knew it would be several days before they would be alone and able to indulge in their desire to make love without hurrying. Tate knew they wouldn't be the only couple slipping away each night, but he knew it would mortify Adelaide if he mentioned it now. He grew serious a moment later. "Once we leave Grant land, I want ye to ride yer own horse. Nae because I want ye out of arm's reach, but because I want ye able to ride away if ye need to. I need to swing ma sword without making ye a target in front of me. I ken ye ken, but I canna nae say it. Ye stay in the middle of the circle nay matter what. Ye only leave it if I tell ye to."

"I ken, but I dinna mind hearing it from ye. It's reassuring."

"There's naught I willna do to protect every member of ma family. But ye will always come first. Ye and our weans."

"Tatum," Adelaide rested her hand on his wrist. "Once we have weans, they come before me. I may nae be a warrior, but if our weans are in danger, I will fight. They come first."

"Aye, Addy. They come first, but ye and the weans come before anyone else. Always. The rest of ma family understands. It's that way for every parent." Tate kissed her temple before they turned back to their meals.

* * *

ADELAIDE PUSHED her sopping hair out of her eyes as she adjusted her arisaid for the hundredth time. The wind off the North Sea dislodged it the instant she got it in place to cover her head. It began raining the moment they passed Inverness and turned toward the coast. It hadn't relented in two days. Tate had amended his rule and now held her in his arms with his extra length of plaid wrapped around them both and over his own head. When he noticed her fingers and lips were blue, and her teeth chattered, he plucked her from her saddle and placed her in front of him. She protested, saying none of the other women rode with a man. They were all surviving, and she didn't need coddling. Tate had stared straight ahead until she pinched his ribs. He shot her a stare that made her sigh and relax against his chest. He'd tightened his arm around her as she rode sideways and pressed kisses to her hairline. She felt him sigh when she stopped protesting. She realized she hadn't irritated him. He'd been scared for her.

Now she thanked God that he'd insisted she continue to ride with him since it was not only raining but windy, too. Once she'd acquiesced to Tate, she'd looked around and seen Alec take his brother Wee Liam's oldest child onto his horse, wrapping his plaid around the toddler. Elene rode with her husband and their infant as Wee Liam did the same to buffer the wind and rain. She hadn't seen them from her position when the rain began, but Magnus Óg lifted his wife and infant onto his steed, and Blaine lifted his pregnant wife onto his horse, too. Neither man was happy to have his wife riding while one had a newborn and the other was pregnant, but both women refused the cart, saying the vehicles rattled them so badly that it scared them more to be on them than horseback. As their third day trudged along, Adelaide curled tight against Tate's chest.

"How are ye nae cold?" Adelaide whispered.

"I'm perishing."

"What? Tatum!"

"Haud yer wheest, ma wee devil. There's naught we can do but push on. We all ken that. This isnae the worst weather I've been in. It's miserable but bearable."

"If ye're freezing, how are ye still putting out so much heat?"

Tate chuckled. "Because the bonniest woman alive is pressing against ma rod and making the front of me overheat. It's the rest of me that's chilled."

Adelaide reached down and touched Tate's leg where it was exposed between the hem of his plaid and the top of his stocking. It was an icicle. "How do ye nae have frostbite? How do the lot of ye nae have frostbite? There isnae a mon with us in trews."

"It's nae quite that cold. It's just rain, nae snow. Like

I said, ma bonnie wife keeps most of me quite toasty." Tate pressed his hips forward. Since his sporran was on his side, so it wouldn't bite into Adelaide's hip, she could feel his hardened rod nudge her.

"If ma hands werenae so bluidy cold, I'd wrap one around ye and watch ye try to concentrate with nay one kenning what I'm aboot." She stroked his thigh. "Then again, mayhap it's hot enough to warm ma hand."

She pretended to reach between them, but Tate squeezed her against him. He tsked as she wriggled a little.

"Yer hand's cold enough to make ma bollocks hide inside me. If ye want bairns at some point, we will need them in place."

Adelaide nodded, keeping her laughter to herself. She'd discovered on the first night that all the other couples found ways to sneak away. She'd seen surreptitious touches and kisses throughout the journey, which made her realize the rumors about how much the Sinclairs loved their spouses wasn't exaggerated. The older generation couldn't keep their hands to themselves.

"We make camp here," Tavish called. He led that day, so Wiley rode between his mother and sister toward the middle of the group. Each husband rode beside his wife unless it was his day to lead. The announcement trickled back to the other clans. The Sinclairs wouldn't always be at the front of the veritable army. The clans took turns just like the leaders within the groups did. Adelaide stifled her groan as Tate lifted her off his horse and steadied her as she put weight on her legs for the first time in hours. She'd ridden several times a week since she was old enough to control a horse on her own. But she hadn't spent hours in the saddle like the men. She worried she wasn't hardy enough to live so far north, which meant more days of travel to just about anywhere. But she'd seen the other Sinclair women rely on their husbands and brothers in the same way.

The clans fanned out in the meadow beside a copse of trees. It wasn't ideal, but with so many people traveling en masse, it was the only way to keep everyone together. It also meant very few people would foolishly attack such a large entourage. Adelaide watched as everyone set to work, so she made her way to Siùsan for an assignment. It wasn't long before they erected tents, built fires with tarps protecting the flames, crafted spits, and men went hunting. The women moved around the camp, setting out bedrolls for their families and the warriors.

Tate and Adelaide shared a tent with Thor and Greer, so the two women ducked inside to help peel their gowns off each other. With her chemise sticking to her, Greer's secret made Adelaide's eyes widen.

"Shhh. Only Thor kens right now. It's still early, and I dinna ken if I will lose the bairn." Greer's past was one filled with violence and mistreatment. She'd lost one child already, and she feared she might never carry another to term.

"I willna share yer secret, but felicitations."

"Thank ye. We're vera excited." Greer whisked off her sodden chemise and donned a fresh one before helping Adelaide remove her gown. Once both women were in dry clothes, they huddled together, waiting for their husbands. It wasn't long before Thor and Tate returned. It still made her smile to see the cousins together. While their faces were similar, Thor had a shock of strawberry-blond hair he'd inherited from Siùsan instead of the Sinclair dark hair. He was the only male to inherit his mother's hair color instead of the chestnut all the sibling shared from Liam.

"I feel like a drowned rat," Thor grumbled as he

gathered fresh clothes. Tate did the same before both men disappeared without another word. They would change in Tor, Wiley, Alec, Hamish, and Kirk's tent. The four cousins and their close friend always gravitated toward one another when they traveled. They were the remaining bachelors. Their Sutherland male relatives also gravitated to one another. Lachlan's, Maude's, and Blair's sons used to all cram into one tent when they were weans. Now they occupied three. The lasses stayed with their parents, the fathers sleeping next to the flap.

"If this rain would cease, we could stretch our legs," Greer mused. "Thor barely lets me hold ma own gown up to relieve maself. And he'd be like this even if I wasna carrying."

"Tate's the same. I appreciate the sentiment, but it's embarrassing. Even after everything we've—" Adelaide flinched as she blushed.

"Ada, I didna get in this state by Thor merely looking in ma direction. Ye're married. Hell, ye married a Sinclair."

"True," Adelaide giggled. "Even with how well we now ken each other, it's still embarrassing to have him hover so nearby when I relieve maself. I dinna go traipsing into the woods when he needs a moment of privacy."

"Shh. Dinna tell anyone this either." Greer leaned close to whisper. "Thor canna if I'm close enough to hear, let alone see." It was Greer's turn to giggle.

"St. Columba's bones. Tate is the same!"

Both women were nearly in hysterics when their husbands returned. The tent wasn't tall enough for both men to stand completely upright, so they hunched as they stood with their feet hip-width apart and arms crossed. That only made the women laugh harder.

"I canna… catch… ma… breath," Adelaide wheezed.

"Why do I think ye're laughing at ma expense, wife?" Tate huffed. "Even before—especially before— we came in."

"Because we were." Adelaide snorted as she laughed. She covered her mouth, which only made Greer laugh hard enough to snort too. Both men had the same solution. They pulled their wives into their arms and kissed them breathless. Both women responded immediately, practically ready to climb their husbands like a bear up a pine tree. When the two couples pulled apart, panting, the women still smiled. Neither would reveal their shared secrets.

"Some of the women are going to the stream to refresh themselves. Do ye wish to go?" Tate asked Adelaide.

"Aye. I already put dry clothes on, but I'd like a chance to clean up." She gathered the lump of soap and a drying linen from her saddlebag. Greer did the same before the two couples walked toward the stream. They heard women's voices, so the men stopped and swept their gazes over the surrounding area before encouraging their wives to join the others.

"Our das are still as protective of our mamas as they were when we were weans. I dinna think they'll ever stop being like that. But when does it get easier kenning yer wife is safe even if ye arenae with her?" Tate asked.

"I havenae figured that out. With all that Greer survived and things still nae being completely resolved with the Gunns, it makes me nervous. They contested the king's decision to allow ma mother's cousin to take the lairdship. They canna stomach a MacLeod of Assynt as their laird, but I dinna think they'll have a choice in the end. And with the Chisholms being the reason we're all so anxious right now, I dinna think either of us will stop worrying aboot our wives being out of our sight." Thor looked at his cousins as he rubbed his hands together and blew warm air on them. They stood together, their backs to the stream where the women bathed and laundered clothes.

"Addy!" Tate called out to his wife.

"Aye?"

"It's getting late and will grow dark soon. Everyone needs to hurry up," Tate responded.

"We ken. We're almost done. We're just gathering everything."

Before Tate could say anything else, he and Thor whirled around, sensing someone approached. Both drew their swords, but all they could see was tall grass in front of them, the stream now to their right, and trees to their left and behind them. They shifted positions, so they stood back-to-back.

"Do ye see aught?" Thor whispered.

"Nay." Tate whistled and a response came from the tall grass. They knew at least one Sinclair guard was nearby. Tate whistled again, but nothing came from within the trees. There should have been an immediate response; something was very wrong. The cousins shifted again, so they could both see into the woods but in different directions.

"Greer! Get back to camp! Now!" Thor bellowed as ten men charged toward them from the woods.

"Addy, go! Mama!" Tate yelled as he swung his sword at the first man. He and Thor had trained their entire lives together, less than a year's difference in age. They knew each other like they knew themselves. They moved with synchronicity drilled into them by their fathers who'd learned from their own father.

Thor turned his head too late to see the man five feet away from him. He couldn't duck in time when the enemy hurled a rock at his face. It struck him in the temple as he tried to push Tate out of the way of the man he had seen coming. He crumpled to the ground, knocking Tate sideways. Another rock flew, colliding with the back of Tate's head. It propelled him forward as the hilt of a sword was jammed into the left side of his neck, then a fist plowed into his cheek. He saw stars as he fought back, but the unrecognizable enemy drove his fist into his temple. Tate lurched forward, falling to the ground and into blackness.

"That bitch shot me," one attacker muttered with an arrow in his shoulder.

"Kieran!" Maude MacLeod screamed for her husband. She watched as men attacked her cousins' sons. "Callum! Tavish!"

She fired another arrow into her victim, embedding it in the man's throat. She twisted and launched an arrow toward the man who dragged Thor toward the trees. He moved just in time for the deadly projectile to only land in his arm instead of his throat.

"Callum! Tavish!" Maude screamed again as her sister, Blair, came to stand beside her. Both women were master archers, the best in all their families. Blair's first shot went through the eye of the man hoisting Tate onto his feet. When he fell, Tate followed him, pushing the arrow deeper into the man's skull. One by one, eight of the ten men fell from the women's arrows. But two survived to get Thor and Tate over their shoulders, the men's heads banging off the enemies' backs. Neither Maude nor Blair could fire their arrows without risking the young men.

"Maude! Maude!"

She pointed toward the trees as Callum barreled toward them, Tavish and Kieran just behind him.

"Blair?"

"I'm here, Hardi." She waved in the dimming light to her husband. "Men just attacked Thor and Tate. They took them." She pointed to the same place as Maude. "Ten came, two survived."

"Tate? Tate!" Adelaide rushed forward, but Tavish caught her around the waist. While he did that, he couldn't stop Ceit, who charged past him, dirks drawn. Ailish was beside her mother. Both women were fleet footed, and Ailish could run for hours. They were almost to the tree line when they both hurled dirks. A deep bellow filled the air. Both women raised their remaining dirk, but neither launched it.

Sinclairs soon surrounded Ceit and Ailish as others drew closer, hearing the commotion. Ceit wilted against Tavish, who'd let go of Adelaide when they ran to catch Ceit and Ailish.

"They have ma lad," Ceit sobbed. "Ailish and I hit someone, but we couldnae see well enough to ken where or who he carried."

"Where's Thor?" Siùsan and Greer demanded together. Neither had her kirtle laced all the way closed, and neither wore their kertches. It was clear they'd been in the middle of bathing when the cry went out. Adelaide turned huge, tear-filled eyes to them and shook her head.

"Dead?" Siùsan demanded.

"We dinna ken," Maude answered. "I only saw what was happening after Thor collapsed. It was just as a mon knocked out Tate. They took the lads."

"Auntie Siùsan, Mama and I hit at least one of them," Ailish whispered. The older woman drew her niece into her arms.

"Ye and yer mama are so brave. I ken ye tried. It's nae yer fault those men didna stop." Siùsan released Ailish, who turned to Ceit and Tavish. Her parents engulfed her as Callum pulled Siùsan and their youngest child, Shona, into his arms. They watched as Wiley, Tor, Blake, Kirk, Alec, Hamish, and Wee Liam darted into the woods; their swords drawn. Alex, Magnus Mòr, Tristan, and Dedric—Ric—Hartley followed their sons. Mackay, Sinclair, Sutherland, and Cameron warriors did the same, spreading out to cover more ground as they wove among the trees.

"What happened?" Monty Campbell asked as he arrived with the elder Hamish and Amelia.

"Men took Tate and Thor," Adelaide mumbled.

"Thor and Tate were taken," Callum answered more clearly. He released Siùsan and Shona as Tavish released Ceit and Ailish. Certain their wives were safe, the brothers looked at one another. A loud whistle rent the air, then the sound of two horses neighing in response. A moment later, two unsaddled horses charged toward the group. Tavish's horse raced toward his owner while Callum's did the same. Both men mounted with ease, grasping the reins someone had hurriedly tossed over the horses' backs when they released them from the hobbled group.

"Ride south," Tavish announced. He and Callum spurred their horses, backtracking the way the group had come in order to ride around the far end of the trees where they'd been sparser. Lachlan and his three sons appeared moments later on horseback.

"Ride north," Hamish commanded to his son and grandsons.

"Aye, Da," came one voice.

"Aye, Grandda." Three younger voices responded in unison with their father.

"Hamish." Liam came to stand beside his friend as he watched all but two of the men in his family charge after the attackers. They stepped aside, only Amelia joining the men, her hand clasped in Hamish's. "We ken they're Chisholms without seeing their plaids. If our lads dinna find Thor and Tate in the woods, ye ken where Peter and Adam will take them."

"Aye. The firth." Hamish looked in the direction that Cromarty Firth lay. The large body of water connected to the North Sea. Further inland were steep cliffs that dropped sharply into the water. Those cliffs were rife with caves that would suck people in with the currents that swirled around them. There was little likelihood either Tate or Thor would survive being tossed over the cliffs while unconscious, which Liam and Hamish were certain the Chisholms would ensure. Awake, both men were robust swimmers used to the biting temperatures of the North Sea.

"Da?" Mairghread approached the trio and stopped beside Liam. She kept her voice just as low. "They'll take them to the firth. Can we get there first? Spread out, so we dinna miss them?"

"That's what we were aboot to discuss," Liam stated.

Mairghread looked back over her shoulder at the women clustered together as the rain began again. She turned back to her father, aunt, and uncle. "Rose canna go in because she's with child. Ye ken I'm the only one who can manage."

Mairghread and her niece Rose had both inherited Kyla Sutherland Sinclair's endurance and tolerance for the temperature and waves of the North Sea. No one could explain why the seals called to both women just as they had Kyla when Mairghread was a child. They could both read the waves and currents as intuitively as Kyla had. But they were both still human. Mairghread wouldn't survive the frigid waters indefinitely.

"Ma guess is they'll head to North Sutor," Amelia spoke up. "The caves will make them assume nay one will find them. If the lads enter the water there, they have a better chance to survive. They've been swimming in and out of that cave at Dunbeath since they were weans."

Amelia didn't say what everyone else thought: they

had to be alive to save themselves or at least uninjured enough to swim once the freezing water revived them. The risk wasn't only the tides and rocks. The shock of entering the water would naturally make them both gasp, inhaling saltwater.

"It's there or likely Invergordon. That's the easiest cliffside to approach since it's farther inland. The North Sutor side of the firth means the lads could wind up in the Cromarty or the North Sea," Hamish reasoned.

"If they come back without Thor and Tate, Tristan and I will take our lads and warriors to North Sutor. Da, take Ainsley with ye. Tristan will worry himself into a grave if I have to swim. Nae being able to reach me but also having to protect Ainsley if the bastards attack will tear him in two. Tristan will need Hamish and Alec to help command the men. Only Wee Liam and a handful of men will stay with Ainsley, Elene, and the weans. If Elene's children werenae so young, I ken she'd come with me. She's used to the water too. It's even colder in Orkney. But she needs to be with them and her brother and sister."

Mairghread's son met her daughter-by-marriage on Orkney, where Elene grew up. While she wasn't as natural in the water as Mairghread, she tolerated the cold better than most and was a strong swimmer.

"We'll go to Invergordon," Liam stated.

"What do ye want to tell the others?" Hamish asked. "Lachlan and I can take our men inland and south with the Rosses and Camerons. We can head toward Chisholm territory. It'll be easier for both clans to return home if they search in that direction. The Mac-Leods head west once they're on the other side of these woods." Both the MacLeods of Lewis and of Assynt would need to cross the breadth of Scotland to reach Ardvreck on Loch Assynt before the Lewis branch continued on to The Minch to cross over to their island home.

"Aye. I'm nae going to ask Blaine to leave Rose nor Magnus Óg to leave Saoirse. The Keiths and Mackenzies will protect the women here." Their grandfather wouldn't demand their husbands leave their wives unless it was absolutely imperative. Liam lowered his voice to a whisper. "Adelaide and Greer. Ye ken they'll demand to go with us. There's nay way we'll convince them to stay with the Keiths and Mackenzies. If they ken we believe the lads are most likely headed to North Sutor, they'll do whatever they must to go with ye, Mairghread. We need them to stay with Ceit and Siùsan, so they canna ken ye're more likely to find them."

"Da," Mairghread looked around. "I dinna ken for sure, but I'm pretty sure Greer is with child. I've seen how tired she gets, and it isnae because of the weather. She's asking for a moment of privacy whenever we're cooking meat, and she gets a whiff. If aught happens to Thor... Just be near her, Da."

"I will, lass." Liam offered Mairghread a soft smile. She reminded him more and more of Kyla with each passing year. Her face, her mannerisms, her speech, her thoughts and actions were as much a mirror of her mother, Kyla, as his sons were a mirror of him.

"We should go back," Amelia suggested. "Monty and Hardi need to ken the plan along with Kieran, Michail, Blaine, and Óg."

Mairghread pulled aside Blaine and Magnus Óg to talk about staying with the women while Liam and Hamish spoke to Monty, Hardi, Kieran, and Michail about their assignments. Amelia gathered her daughters, daughter-by-marriage, and nieces-by-marriage. She also called Michail's wife, Blythe, and Isabella Hartley over. The women were sisters. They left the younger generation to wonder what was happening. Maude's and Blair's children gathered with the Sinclairs while Isabella's and Blythe's children stood huddled nearby. Eventually, as the conversations among the clan leaders drew on, all the younger generation stood together, mostly in silence as they waited for the inevitable announcements of who would fight alongside one another if it came to battle.

Adelaide and Greer clung to each other as Siùsan and Ceit embraced them between the two of them. The four women were raised to watch their men ride off to battle. They were all too familiar with the fear that they would never see the men they loved again. None had tears to shed, instead too numb to do more than stare and pray.

Lord, bring them home, please.

CHAPTER 25

Tate's eyes fluttered open in the dark, his vision blurry as the haze slowly receded from his mind. He quickly lowered his lids halfway, looking out from beneath his lashes. He wanted none of his captors to know he'd woken. He sat on the ground with someone's back pressing against his. The memory of the attack flooded back to him as his bound wrists brushed against rope that wasn't around his extremities. His fingers tapped the other person's hands. The fingers curled around his. He knew Thor was awake.

Neither moved as they listened to the surrounding silence. Wherever they were, the men holding them captive were mostly asleep. They both strained to hear anything that might give them a clue to their location. A breeze wafted over them, and they both immediately knew where they were. The sea.

The briny scent mixed with the malodorous signal of nearby seals told them what they couldn't hear. Tate opened his eyes slightly more, so he could see the stars. The rain had stopped again, but thick clouds hid most of the sky. He could see just enough to get a sense of where they were.

"Cromarty," Thor whispered.

"Aye."

But which side? Both men wondered if they were near North Sutor and the North Sea or across the firth and closer to the village of Cromarty. This time the wind came as a gust, icy and strong. Only exposed headland would garner an air current that felt like needles pricking their faces.

"The cliffs?" Tate murmured.

"In the morning. They'll want to watch," Thor responded, barely moving his lips. Anyone not standing within a foot of the men wouldn't know they were awake and conversing.

"We dinna ken this coastline like we do farther north, but we ken caves and tides. As long as we are awake, we stand a chance of surviving. If we're unconscious, we willna be able to keep from sucking in water. We'll have to pray the shock revives us before we're pulled under too far."

"Even if we dinna go over the side at the same time, we'll go in at the same place. When we surface, we look for each other." Thor prayed they would both emerge.

"Aye. We risk them shooting arrows if they see us emerge, but the distance should be too great and the waves too strong for them to strike us." Tate dared to open his eyes all the way and surveyed their surroundings.

"And they willna have an easy way down to the water to go after us. But we can climb the rocks up."

"We'll have to. Do ye feel any of yer dirks?" Tate could feel his.

"Aye. The one inside ma belt."

"Same." Both men carried dirks anyone could see sheathed to their belts. They carried *sgain dubh*, short bladed but deadly sharp knives, in their boots. They also had garters with sheaths around their thighs. They could feel all those knives were missing. However, they also had knives sheathed on the inside of their belts that lay horizontal, so completely hidden. They weren't the easiest to reach, so they were a last resort. But they were meant for moments like this where their swords and all their other knives were confiscated.

As they spoke, they were both working to untie the ropes binding their hands behind their backs. Their voices were barely loud enough to hear each other. They planned for what would happen in the morning, but they didn't intend to be there when the sun rose. They fell back into silence as they concentrated on working together like they'd been trained. Liam's father insisted all his men learn how to escape bondage, and Liam taught his sons, who taught their sons. Each Sinclair warrior trained not only with weapons to defend himself and others but to escape if they were ever captured. Thor and Tate had spent hours in similar positions with each other, their relatives, and fellow warriors. They worked efficiently at untying each other's bindings since they didn't have the flexibility to untie their own.

It was a slow process, and they had to stop when the guards rotated. They pretended to be asleep, even though they sensed where each man was as they traded positions, and some left their posts to sleep while others came to take their turn at watch. There were far more than the two who kidnapped them. Tate estimated it took them nearly two hours to work the stiff and coarse rope out of the knots, drawing no attention to themselves. It was neither their fastest nor their slowest time for such an endeavor. They'd once been tied together for four hours when neither could figure out their uncle Alex's series of knots and twists. The man finally had to come and release them, then show them how he'd done it.

The ropes dropped to the ground between them,

but neither pulled their hands away. Instead, they slowly straightened their backs, pressing their shoulders against each other while leaving space between their lower backs. Tate sucked in a deep breath, pulling his stomach in as far as he could, creating a gap between his body and his belt. Thor's hands slipped under the leather and felt around until they touched the dagger hilts. His concentration focused solely on not slicing Tate as he removed the *sgain dubh* and drew his hands down and away. Tate repeated the same process as Thor but had to tug the belt a little to get his hands underneath.

"Too many meat pies," Tate grumbled.

"Ham hocks for hands," Thor muttered.

They both went still as they heard two guards abruptly stop talking. Both men let their heads sag and their shoulders droop, knowing the guards would check on them.

"Nae so strong after a wee tap on their heids," one warrior snickered.

"Aye. How the mighty Sinclairs have fallen. They arenae the gods they pretend to be. Nay different than any mon. Now they're defenseless and without their das to save them." The second man kicked dirt at the cousins. Neither flinched when debris hit their faces. With no reaction from their captives, the men eventually sauntered away.

"Did ye see what I did?" Tate whispered.

"Aye. They werenae Chisholms."

* * *

ADELAIDE RODE beside Greer and behind Ceit, but in front of Siùsan. All the Sinclair women barely had enough room between their horses for their legs. Callum, Tavish, and Magnus Mòr, along with their sons, formed a tight circle around the women. Alex was the only Sinclair sibling to only have daughters. He rode between them with his wife in front of him. The Sinclair warriors who accompanied their laird and his family rode two abreast around the nobles. Liam, alone, rode outside the family circle. He led the riders as they charged across the pastures toward the Cromarty Firth.

Adelaide and the others had waited for an agonizing two hours before the search parties returned without either Tate or Thor. Callum and Tavish could barely speak and only held their wives when they returned without their sons. Adelaide and Greer clung to each other until their parents-by-marriage drew them into their embraces. All six had given in to their tears for a few minutes before determination straightened their backbones and brought forth their resolve.

Now, Adelaide called upon the resilience she'd discovered the previous night as she listened to the plans the clan leaders agreed upon. She knew there were things no one told her despite her husband being one of the kidnapped men. It irritated her, but she understood they wouldn't tell her for two reasons. She wasn't the lady of any clan nor a tánaiste's wife. And they didn't want her to panic if the plans went awry or to argue their merits. She accepted the first, but the second aggravated her. She was old enough to marry and be a wife, but it felt like they treated her as a child they couldn't trust to hear adult information. She was certain Siùsan knew because she was a tánaiste's wife, but she was also certain Ceit knew too.

When they stopped to rest their horses, Adelaide confronted her mother-by-marriage. "Ye ken the plan. I want to ken too." She saw no reason to prevaricate, especially since they wouldn't linger long.

Ceit looked over at her daughter-by-marriage and smiled. She took one of Adelaide's hands and squeezed it. "I do, but nae because anyone told me. Lass, I've been a Sinclair for nearly five-and-twenty years. I ken how ma husband thinks better than he does himself. And he thinks just like his father and brothers. Before I met Tavish, I was a spy for King Robert. Ye ken I was a Comyn before I wed. The king and ma uncle used me against each other, forcing me to be a messenger for them both. I didna spy on the lairds' meeting last night, so dinna think that's why I'm telling ye this. I ken because I've helped Tavish and the others strategize before because of ma experience moving between two enemies and keeping ma head on ma shoulders. I wasna a part of this one, but I'm confident in ma guess."

"Which is?" Adelaide appreciated the family history since she'd never guessed about Ceit's past, but that wasn't what she wanted to hear at that moment.

"The Mackays will probably go to the coast while we stay farther inland along this firth. The Camerons and Rosses rode with the Sutherlands because that's the direction the Cameron and Ross lands lie. Hardi is Hamish's son-by-marriage and Monty is Hamish's great-nephew. The MacLeods rode west since that's also the direction they need to travel. Magnus Óg and Blaine would leave their wives behind if they had to, but nay one wishes to make them do that, so they will guard all the women when our men decide they must split off from us. The Keiths and Mackenzies will also guard us because the Sinclairs have the most women in their family. There are enough guards to protect the few women that ride with each of the other clans."

"Why couldnae anyone tell us that? What is there for Greer or me to argue aboot or fear? Every warrior traveling with us is among the best in Scotland."

Ceit drew Adelaide away from where Greer stood with Siùsan, likely having a similar conversation. She kept her voice to barely more than a whisper. "Because it's most likely Tate and Thor are being taken to North Sutor or the area around that. There are caves beneath the cliffs, which are far taller than the ones in Invergordon and that area. The Mackays are going there because of Mairghread."

Adelaide's brow furrowed. She didn't understand why her new aunt determined where any clan went.

"Mairghread is likely part selkie. The woman belongs in the water more than she does on land. I've never seen anyone else wade into the North Sea and nay shiver even once. While seals keep their distance from most people, they'll bark and slap their fins when Mairghread is near. She doesnae swim close to them, but they'll draw nearer to her than anyone else. Apparently, her mama was the same. She's nae as fast a swimmer as her brothers, husband, or any of the lads in a loch. But she's the best in the sea. I dinna ken how, but she reads the waves. She kens when to dive beneath the surface and when to let them carry her. If Thor and Tate survive the fall, she's the one who'll be able to lead them out of a cave or to a part of the cliffs they can climb."

"She throws knives better than any mon, swims in the sea better than anyone else, and doesnae flinch when she tells an entire clan to get off land that doesnae even belong to her. What kind of woman is she?" Adelaide wondered aloud.

"The kind who had aulder brothers who included her in everything because their parents raised them to always put family first and to never take any of their siblings for granted. Parents who encouraged Mairghread to do whatever the lads did and were within her ability. Parents who raised their sons to respect women and never underestimate or undervalue them. She married a mon who kens her worth and loves her for every bit of her stubbornness and independence. A mon who relies on her to lead their clan as much as he does. She's a woman who could lead an army to victory. She likely would if Andrew Murray werenae such an arse."

The man commanded Scotland's forces as they continued to fight the English to maintain their independence and to return King David to his rightful throne. He wasn't a man known to tolerate women in general and loathed ones with intelligence. While he was a friend of Tristan's and the Sinclair brothers, he'd once made a disparaging remark about Mairghread needing to learn her place. He learned his lesson when Tristan broke his jaw and Alex dislocated his shoulder.

"Is Ainsley as strong a swimmer as her mother?"

"Nae. She's stronger than most of the lads, but she doesnae have the same intuition as Mairghread. Rose is the one most like Mairghread, but she's with child. If she werenae, she'd go with her aunt. Rose led Thor into a cave beneath Castle Clyde when the Gunns took Blaine."

Adelaide nodded as she looked toward Greer and Siùsan. "Do ye think she's telling Greer what ye're telling me?"

"Probably."

"Why doesnae anyone else trust us to ken?"

"For the same reason Tavish didna tell me. He kens naught will stop me from getting to ma wean if I ken where to go. Siùsan only kens because she's Callum's wife and has basically been Lady Sinclair since the day she married Callum since Kyla passed so long ago. Rose likely kens because Blaine is their tánaiste, but while his father is in France with the king, he's their clan's laird. The other women ken because their husbands are lairds, and they lead their clans when their husbands ride out. If aught happens to any of the lairds, the ladies must ken what must be done next."

"What will ye do if we find out Tate and Thor are at the coast and nae where we're headed?"

Ceit's gaze darted to Siùsan, who looked over at the same time. Both women turned back to the younger woman to whom they spoke. Ceit's pointed gaze told Adelaide what the woman would do, even though she refused to put it in words.

"I go with ye, Ceit. If I dinna, I'll find ma own way," Adelaide warned.

"We ken. That's why nay one's told either of us and why Callum and Tavish have been stepping between Siùsan and me every time we get near each other. It's why Callum's nae let Siùsan out of his sight. He kens she'll bolt given the chance. Tavish kens I'll follow."

"What aboot Ailish and Shona?"

"All the more reason Callum and Tavish dinna want Siùsan telling me aught. Ailish has a wild streak, but Shona will put Callum in his grave. The lass doesnae have an ounce of fear aboot aught."

Adelaide had sensed that about Rose and Thor's younger sister. She'd won all the women's horseback races during the Gathering because she and her horse were as closely bonded as any warrior and his steed. Obstacles the other riders avoided, Shona and her mount leaped and traversed without a moment's hesitation.

"None of the rumors aboot the Sinclairs are exaggerated, are they?" Adelaide asked as she looked around, her gaze sweeping over everyone assembled.

"They dinna even scratch the surface, lass. *Familia prima, semper familia.* Family first, always family. Naught means more to us than family. It's our creed, and we'd each die protecting it. Pair that with how a mama feels aboot her weans, and there's a reason people fear ma sisters and me. There are things even our husbands wouldnae do in battle. There's naught

Mairghread, Siùsan, Brighde, Deirdre, or I wouldnae do to protect our weans or to avenge them." Ceit took hold of Adelaide's other hand. "Ye're as much ma child now as the ones I bore. I promise ye that I will defend ye and stand by ye just as I would Tate, Wiley, and Ailish. I dinna wish to replace yer mama, but I willna love ye any less than I do ma other weans."

Adelaide blinked as tears stung her eyes. She nodded because the lump in her throat kept any sound from passing. She leaned into Ceit's embrace as the older woman stroked her hands up and down Adelaide's back. She wiped her new daughter's tears away before she offered a maternal smile.

"And I care aboot ye for ye, nae just because ye're ma son's wife." Ceit gave Adelaide's arms a gentle squeeze before they rejoined the group. Tavish and Callum watched Siùsan, Greer, Ceit, and Adelaide exchange a glance. The brothers exchanged their own look before going to find Magnus Mòr and Alex to warn them.

* * *

"Can ye see where they put our swords?" Tate whispered as he looked around as best he could with Thor behind him in the dark. While two men carried them away, nearly a score more made camp around the cousins.

"Aye. They're in front of me. Daft eejits. We can reach them before anyone can reach us. We inch closer, so they have less time to react when we stand."

Thor pulled away slightly, indicating they should move. Tate leaned back to fill the gap as he followed his cousin as they scooted along the ground. After they'd moved three inches, they stopped. It wasn't much, but it was three inches closer to their weapons, and three inches farther from their enemy. They waited ten minutes before they moved again, having to pause when they heard a guard sneeze. They likely would have felt each other's hearts pounding if their own weren't racing. When they were only three yards away, they paused to reassess.

"Once we have them, which way do we go?" Thor asked.

"They'll expect us to either run back the way we came or in the opposite direction. We need to head northeast, so we go west," Tate suggested.

"That means circling the camp either to the north or the south since we're on the wrong side to do that. We split up, both heading west but apart. Four leagues from here, we meet up."

"Aye. I'll go north. Ye go south. Once we're a couple leagues from here, we change course and meet in the middle. Then we can continue in the right direction. How far from the coast do ye think we are?" They really needed to travel north, past the firth before they could continue east.

"Nae even a league from the stench," Thor answered. The wind had shifted while they hatched their escape. The seal odor was even more pungent. "We must get away from the cliffs. In the dark, it'll be too easy for them to press us over the edge. If we survive the fall, we'll be disoriented and likely slammed against the rocks. We willna make it into one of the caves."

"If we survive the fall, we do everything we can to get to a cave once the tide is out. We cling to the rocks till then. Ye ken Auntie Mairghread will get us. Among the men, there'll be enough rope. She'll reach us." Tate was as certain about that as he was that the sky was blue, and snow was white.

"I love ma mama and would die on the cross saying

there isnae a better mother alive. But is there aught Auntie Mairghread canna do?"

"I dinna think so." Tate shook his head. They continued to scoot a few more inches at a time, then paused before moving again. Both still whispered barely loud enough for the other to hear, but talking kept them focused as they thought about their family coming to their aid. They knew in the dark no one could see their lips moving. "Even with what she may nae be naturally good at, she's determined enough to find a way. Even if she's nae the best at something, she's still better than most because she simply doesnae give up until the task is done."

"Do ye think it was because of our das and how they always encouraged her to do what they did, except for going into the lists?"

"There's that." Tate grinned in the dark. "But I dinna ken anyone who understands duty better than her. Ye ken the story. She would have married Uncle Tristan's stepbrother because of the alliance Grandda and Uncle Tristan wanted. She would have been miserable, but she would have done it for the sake of our clan. We're lucky the bastard got himself killed and that Auntie Mairghread and Uncle Tristan were already in love by then."

"She's one of the most loyal people we ken." Thor paused as he considered the other women in their family. "Our mamas didna come from clans who treated them properly, but they did what they had to, to survive. It meant they also served their clans. But we both ken our mamas and Auntie Deirdre and Auntie Brighde put our clan before all others. They are Sinclairs and naught else. Auntie Mairghread is as much a Mackay as she still is a Sinclair. There's naught she wouldnae do for either clan. That makes her unlike anyone else we ken."

"It doesnae hurt that she's kind and beautiful. People still underestimate her."

"And that's to her advantage. Do ye remember how Peter looked like he would pish himself when she pointed that dirk at him?" Thor stifled his chuckle as they rested for a few minutes before continuing their progress toward their weapons that were two yards away.

"And how his eyes kept begging Uncle Tristan to make her stop." Tor's shoulders shook with his silent laughter.

"Ye ken how we used to say 'Auntie Mairghread will save us' when Uncle Tristan would try to capture and tickle us? We're both more than twenty summers, and I still feel that way."

Both men pictured those memories as they scooted the last few inches from the guards and closer to their weapons. There'd been struggles for their family and clan. Failed crops and foul weather. Their fathers riding out to fight battles against other clans and against the English. Illnesses that swept through and threatened to steal their kin and clan. But it was love that they both remembered most. They'd had happy childhoods filled with duty and obligation but also affection and laughter.

"Tate, ye ken ye're more like a brother than a cousin to me. Ye're nae even a year younger than me. Ye'll be ma tánaiste one day. Ye're a husband now too. I dinna wish this situation on anyone, but I'm glad I'm with ye."

"Aye. Ye ken we've all been raised more like brothers and sisters than cousins. I wouldnae be so confident we'll survive if I wasna with kin."

"Are ye ready?"

"Aye."

With their *sgain dubhs* in hand, they both rose with ease. Neither needed the other to get on their feet in one agile movement. Tate took four steps backwards, watching the camp before turning to sprint the last few feet alongside Thor.

"Four leagues," Tate whispered as they scooped up their weapons. They stuffed their knives into sheaths but carried their swords and their tiny, razor-sharp knives. They took off in opposite directions as the hue and cry went up as a guard spotted them. They both sprinted around their respective end of the camp before setting off to the west. Neither could see anyone when they looked around. Clouds obscured most of the stars now. There was just enough light to see a few feet in front of them.

The stars they'd seen while plotting and talking had oriented them during their escape. Now they had to rely on intuition to keep them going. They'd run miles upon miles as part of their conditioning from childhood until just before they left for the Gathering. They both had stamina and speed. After sprinting at least a quarter mile from the camp, they both settled into paces they could maintain. Tate knew he would reach their meeting point a couple minutes before Thor, which meant he'd hear his cousin's approach. If they were both running, they might miss each other or collide, unable to hear over their own labored breathing.

The minutes passed, and Tate's chest burned as he sucked in lungfuls of crisp air. His brawny arm carried his heavy, two-handed broadsword with ease. Hours of training to use the sword in either hand or both meant he could wield it with more ease than most men. Part of his running endurance came from the many laps his father made him run as an adolescent any time he dropped it. He might have been good at running, but he didn't enjoy it. He soon learned to keep the claymore in hand.

When he was certain he'd reached their meeting

point, he released a soft hoot. With few trees nearby, a real owl's call was unlikely. But it was the only nocturnal bird in the area. He heard one in return. He waited for approaching footsteps, and when he heard them, he hooted again.

"Put yer bluidy sword down before ye spear me," Thor panted as he came within sword's reach of Tate.

"Anyone following ye?" Tate whispered as they both caught their breath.

"Aye. Ye?"

"Aboot a league behind me."

"Half a league for me. We need to move." Thor looked over his shoulder before the men took off again. Each pointed out directions as they zig-zagged while heading north. They remained far enough inland that they could no longer hear or smell the sea. They ran for another hour before slowing then stopping. "I havenae heard aught in the last half an hour."

"Me neither. They either lost our trail or gave up running that far."

"Mayhap. But it also means they could be going back for their horses."

"Where do ye think we are? It's too dark to see any markings," Tate grumbled.

"We're either on that small patch of Campbell land or in Mackintosh territory. If we truly were right on the tip, we were over the Moray Firth out to the North Sea. That's the small patch of Campbell land. If we were farther into the Cromarty Firth, then it's still the Mackintoshes," Thor reasoned.

"We need to get into those trees until daybreak when we can get our bearing. If we're on Campbell land, we're safe. They willna do aught to us if they're the ones who find us. The Mackays are likely to pass near here, either after checking the firth or on their way to meet the others."

"If we're on Mackintosh land, we dinna breathe a peep," Thor advised. While the Sinclairs had no direct quarrels with the Mackintoshes. Things were still foul between the Camerons and Mackintoshes. That meant, things were unpleasant between the Sutherlands and the Mackintoshes. Both of those clans drew the Sinclairs in by blood and by marriage.

The men crept forward as they approached a cluster of evergreens. They would be sticky by the time they climbed down, but the thick branches and needles would offer them the best cover. They sheathed their swords across their backs and put their dirk hilts between their teeth. Tate scaled the trunk first, Thor only a couple feet behind him. When they were high enough to have a clear view in the morning and unlikely to be struck by arrows, they found branches to settle upon. They both leaned against the trunk and breathed easier.

"I'll take the first watch," Thor offered.

"Thank ye." Tate whispered; his eyes already closed. He was as deeply asleep as he ever became while outside. It felt like no time had passed when Thor nudged him two hours later.

"I can barely keep ma eyes open," Thor confessed.

Tate looked up at the sky, his mouth twisting from side to side. "I'd say we have three hours till daybreak. Sleep. I'm all right."

"Ma thanks." Thor was no different from Tate, slumbering the moment his eyes shut.

Tate's scanned their surroundings, sweeping over everything he could see with the limited visibility. His ears strained for any sound that wasn't flora or fauna. He breathed deeply in case he should catch a whiff of horse. But all remained calm. While he remained vigilant, his mind wandered to Adelaide.

She must be terrified. What must she think if men car-

ried Thor and me out of such an enormous camp? She'll believe we're all useless. Will she still trust ma family? Or will she regret it and wish she remained at Freuchie? I canna remember anyone being kidnapped from Clan Grant.

Tate rubbed his left thumb back and forth over his left eye while his finger rubbed his right eye. He pinched the bridge of his nose before sighing and returning to surveilling the area.

Is she safe? That should have been ma first thought. But I'm certain, despite what happened to me, she's safe with ma family. I just hope she kens that. I ken Thor willna give up. He'll die trying to get to Greer before he accepts defeat. We may nae ken where we are, how many men pursue us, or where our family is, but there's nay way either of us will stop trying to get to our wives. I understand the depth of that pledge now that I have Addy. All I want is to feel her in ma arms and ken we're together. To reassure her that I'm there with her, just like I promised. I willna give up for Thor's sake either. I refuse to even consider for a moment that this situation is hopeless. He deserves to go home with his wife, and I willna be the reason he doesnae. I ken he'd do the same for me.

But why? Why the fuck did they take us? It makes nay sense.

CHAPTER 26

*A*delaide watched from the safety of a hilltop as Sinclair and Mackay men crept across a clearing. They'd met up with the other clan that morning after they'd checked North Sutor. They'd found evidence of a camp, but no evidence that told them who or whether her husband and Thor were even there. Adelaide remembered the crushing sensation when she recognized her new Mackay relatives, but she didn't spot a thatch of strawberry-blond hair. She knew if Thor wasn't with them, neither was Tate.

Now the combined forces eased their way through a clearing that lay a few leagues north of where the Mackays found the camp and where they met the Sinclairs. The men were on foot, hunched low, with swords in hand.

"We can see them, but we canna see any hint that they'll find anyone. Why are they searching there?" Adelaide whispered to Ceit. When she turned to look at her mother-by-marriage, she knew the answer. They were looking for Thor's and Tate's bodies without disturbing any animals or clans that might camp nearby. Her grip tightened on her reins, and her horse sidestepped. She eased her hold to keep the steed quiet. She didn't want to be the one who gave away their vantage point.

She shifted her attention to where Tristan sat, watching his sons and relatives. She looked in the opposite direction and spotted Alex. He had no sons traversing the clearing, but his father, brothers, and nephews were out there. He kept a hawkish gaze on the men. The Keiths and Mackenzies rode with them. Blaine, Magnus Óg, and Seamus sat upon their steeds at the rear of the group, facing away from the clearing as they kept watch for any threat that approached from behind. Sinclair, Mackay, Keith, and Mackenzie guards surrounded the group of women.

Adelaide leaned forward as she saw a man raise his fist in the air. She suspected it was Liam, but she couldn't be sure. A moment later, Tavish and Callum burst into a sprint toward a cluster of evergreens. She didn't know whether to breathe easier because the men found their sons alive or whether her world ended because they spied their sons' bodies.

"They're alive, Ada," Mairghread said.

Adelaide looked down the row of women until she could see Mairghread, who sat upon her horse next to Tristan. "How can ye tell?"

"Because only Tavish and Callum went. Look." Mairghread pointed as four figures emerged from the trees. "If they werenae, then more men would have gone to investigate."

Adelaide turned to Greer, who waited beside her on the other side. Ceit was to Adelaide's right, and Siùsan was to Greer's left. Adelaide and Greer's gazes met before they looked at their mothers-by-marriage. The four women spurred their horses as they barreled downhill. Adelaide heard Tristan tell Mairghread to come along but to stay behind him. She caught sight of Alex just past Siùsan. Adelaide nearly toppled out of the saddle in her hurry to dismount. She kicked her foot free before she could fall.

"Addy!" Tate practically shoved his father as he broke free of Tavish's embrace. The couple sprinted to each other, and Tate lifted her off her feet as his arms engulfed her. Tavish moved no slower toward Ceit than Tate had toward Adelaide. Ceit hadn't waited for her horse to stop before she was out of the saddle. She wrapped her arms around her husband's sturdy figure as she watched her son with her new daughter.

"Wheest, *seillean beag*. Dinna buzz." Tavish had called his wife little bee since they met. He usually meant it in jest when she disagreed with him, but this time he reassured her.

"Is he truly all right?" Ceit whispered, knowing she had to let Tate and Adelaide have their reunion, but she wanted nothing more than to hold her son.

"Aye."

"Mama?" Tate opened his right arm while still holding Adelaide off the ground. It was Ceit's turn to practically shove Tavish, who chuckled. Tate lifted his mother as she smattered kisses on his cheek.

"Ma wee laddie," Ceit sighed.

"I'm hail. So is Thor." Tate nudged his chin to where his cousin was having the same reunion with his wife and mother. "We spent half the night in the tree."

"Is that why ye smell so good?" Adelaide asked, finally able to put a thought together and even able to smile.

"Aye. Though I have sap all over me and wish to bathe to get the scent out of ma nose. It's far better from a distance." He lowered both women to their feet, but he didn't let go of either. The rest of the family had hung back to allow the men to reunite with their wives and parents, but now they flooded forward. Wiley walked up behind Tate and clapped him on the back.

"Ye did always need to be the center of Mama's attention. Always jealous of me because I didna need to do aught for Mama to watch me."

"Didna do aught," Ceit snorted. "All I could do was watch ye, ye wee beastie. Ye were always in trouble. Ye and Blake."

"Well, Thor and Tor were worse," Wiley huffed with a grin.

"Haud ye wheest," Tate chided. "Ye ken Ailish is Mama's favorite."

"That's right." A female voice came from behind Wiley. "Move."

Wiley pretended to hold his ribs with a pained expression as Ailish elbowed him. Tate didn't loosen his hold on Adelaide, pressing her against his side so tightly no air passed between them. He opened his other arm, so he could wrap it around his mother and sister. Ailish's strength as she wrapped her arms around Tate's waist surprised him.

"Wheest, *piuthar bheag.*" Little sister. "Ye canna have all ma haggis so easily." Tate kissed the top of Ailish's head, but she didn't loosen her hold. He'd been angry with her only days earlier when she embarrassed him in front of Adelaide. But he didn't wish to let go any sooner than she did. Tavish and Wiley walked around to face the women and Tate. They stepped into the embrace, forming a huddle as the family breathed easier.

"Tate? Thor?"

They broke apart when they heard Liam's voice. Adelaide peered past the others to where she saw Greer, Callum, Siùsan, Rose, Blaine, and Shona embracing Thor the same way she and the others clung to Tate. The two young men stepped forward to see their grandfather. Liam's arms surely popped a couple vertebrae in each of his grandson's backs as he drew them against him. He cupped the back of their heads, and the three of them brought their foreheads together.

It was one of the most endearing things Adelaide had ever seen. The renowned warrior who'd fought alongside Robert the Bruce with his sons flanking each side of him was famous for his strength and his diplomacy. But at that moment, he was a grandfather relieved to have his grandsons with him. He was a man who'd always put his family first, who'd become the patriarch of a family undefeatable because of their bond.

Familia prima, semper familia. Family first, always family.

The family creed echoed in Adelaide's ears as she watched two younger versions of their fathers and grandfather embrace, none hurrying to end the moment. She looked at Siùsan and Callum as they held each other, watching their son and nephew with the man they both called Da. She shifted her gaze back to Ceit and Tavish as he continued to soothe his wife as they watched their son and nephew with the man they both called Da. Greer came to stand beside her, along with Rose, who'd had a brief but heartfelt embrace from her twin, both clinging to one another before Thor walked over to Liam.

"Ye're both one of us now," Rose whispered. "Dinna doubt that love includes ye both. Ye'll ken how our parents feel when yer times come. I'm almost there, and I never fathomed just how deep and abiding our family's commitment is to one another until I felt ma bairn move for the first time."

Rose grasped Adelaide's hand and squeezed it tight. She and Greer had been best friends for more than a decade, but she wanted Adelaide to know she meant her sentiments as much to her new cousin as she did her sister-by-marriage.

"Rosie?" Thor called. Only he called his twin that.

"What are ye saying to make ma wife smile while crying?"

"The truth." Rose stepped into her brother's embrace again, neither rushing the unique connection that they'd had since the womb.

"Three minutes," Thor grumbled to his older twin. "Always bossy, big sister."

"Ye need it, wee brother."

Tate and Thor looked at one another before looking at the others. "Ye'll never believe it," they said in unison.

"Who was it?" Liam asked.

"Mathesons," Tate and Thor answered.

"What?" Tavish bellowed.

"Ungrateful bastards," Siùsan muttered.

"Aye," Tate responded. "We dinna ken why. We thought it was Chisholms, but the attack happened so fast and in the twilight that neither of us saw their plaids clearly at first."

"Why would Fergus do this?" Adelaide wondered.

"We didna see Fergus in the camp," Tate responded. "But, then again, we didna see Laird Matheson either."

"So either could have sent men to do this," Adelaide surmised.

"What happens now?" Siùsan asked.

"We need another meeting amongst ourselves to decide that," Liam answered. "Did either of ye hear aught aboot what was to happen to ye or where they were taking ye? The Mathesons dinna live anywhere near here. They're on the other side of the Frasers and Chisholms."

"Because they're the least likely to be considered the culprits," Tate suggested. "They could have reached their land by travelling south to avoid the Chisholms. Now their most direct route home is across Chisholm territory. They're assuming nay one would believe they'd do that."

"They assumed we'd figure it was the Chisholms after what happened and because they're closer to the firth," Alex supplied. He and his wife had joined the others alongside Magnus Mòr and his wife while Liam embraced his grandsons.

"They're angry that the Chisholms interrupted the alliance, but they ken they arenae in a position to defeat the Chisholms on their own. Since they dinna have the MacDonalds at their back yet, they decided to have us fight on their behalf." Magnus Mòr stood with his feet hip-width apart and arms crossed, just like his brothers, father, Thor, Tate, and Wiley. But he was the broadest of the men gathered, more like a mountain than a man.

"Wiley, fetch Tristan, Mairghread, Tor, Blake, Ric, and Kirk," Liam instructed. The conversation paused until the other men arrived. Much like the lairds' gathering on the dais at Freuchie, the older generation and Liam formed the inner circle while the sons stood behind their parents. Ric and Kirk Hartley weren't related by blood, but Ric and his wife had joined the Sinclairs not long after they married and escaped the border region. Kirk had grown up as part of the Sinclair family. Ric was the most trusted warrior outside the laird's family, and Kirk was a natural leader just like the other young men. Their opinions were valued and included when strategizing.

"Should I..." Adelaide trailed off, uncertain where she belonged. Tate kissed her temple.

"Ye stay beside me, wee one. I willna let go for at least a decade." Tate kissed her again. "Normally, only Mama and ma aunts are the women who attend clan council meetings. But because this is aboot Thor and me, ye and Greer belong here too. Auntie Mairghread and Uncle Tristan are part of this because their clan will fight alongside us, and they've just always joined the council for meetings when they're at Dunbeath. Auntie Mairghread's still as much as Sinclair as she is a Mackay." Tate shrugged at the end.

"Do we march to them?" Alex asked, always the most direct in the group. "If it's just the warriors going, we can likely catch this band before they rejoin their clan. Depending on what they say, we either ride on to Loch Achaidh na h-Inich to confront them there or kill the men who did this and go home. If it wasna sanctioned, then Da sends a letter to Monty Mòr, since he's still the Earl of Ross, even if Monty Óg is laird. Da lets him ken what happened in Ross-shire. If it was sanctioned, then the Rosses ride alongside us."

"We could send riders ahead of us to see if they can catch the Rosses. If they can, then they ride with us. Uncle Hamish can go home," Callum suggested.

"In the meantime, we still have to cross Fraser land to get to either the Chisholms or the Mathesons," Magnus Mòr pointed out. "Let's get off Mackintosh land."

"Ye'll follow the River Beauly anyway to reach Shiness, so we can ask for ma relatives' hospitality at Dounie," Deirdre suggested the castle in which she grew up. She'd left the royal court and her tenure as a lady-in-waiting no longer on speaking terms with her parents when they were Laird and Lady Fraser of Lovat. But since their deaths, Deirdre had reunited with her cousin Thomas. She knew Thomas would offer them accommodations without hesitation. "The Keiths and Mackenzies can return home if they want."

"Nay," Rose interjected after having listened silently. She peered toward where her husband now stood with Seamus and Magnus Óg Mackenzie. "Blaine willna want me traveling to Ackergill until we resolve this. We have to pass Dunbeath to get there. He'll worry that the Mathesons lie in wait along the way. If Laird Fraser will allow us to stay, I ken it would make him feel much more at ease."

"That's fair," Liam agreed. "Since the Mackenzies border the Chisholms and Mathesons, ma guess is Magnus Óg willna be thrilled to have Saoirse and their bairn travel across Chisholm territory. Seamus will probably agree to Óg and Saoirse staying at Dounie with some of their men while he and the rest of the clan continue on."

"I canna blame ma son for wanting to keep his wife safe," Alex said as he looked toward where the younger of the two Manguses stood with his hand rubbing Alex's daughter's lower back as she cradled their child. It hadn't been easy to accept a man who'd been like a much younger foster brother but who was much older than his daughter. It had eventually worked out, and Magnus Óg treated Saoirse as though she were the most precious Highland jewel.

"We need to decide who goes where now that we've found the lads. It changes our original plan to separate. To be clear," Thor spoke up. He preferred conciseness when discussing strategy. "The women, along with the Keiths and some of the Mackenzies, will go to the Frasers at Dounie. They'll stay there until we return for them."

"Aye," Liam answered.

"We send a group of riders out to the Rosses and Sutherlands," Tavish continued. "Do we tell the Camerons to continue home and the Sutherlands to turn north?"

"If we find these bastards before we reach the Sutherlands and Rosses, and the attack wasna sanctioned, we deal with them," Liam responded.

"If we dinna meet up with the Rosses to tell them in person, then Grandda sends a missive to Monty Mòr, informing him of what happened to the Matheson men," Tate suggested. "If Laird Matheson did sanction it, we catch up to Uncle Hamish, Monty Mòr, and Monty Óg. The Rosses ride with us to the Mathesons since the Mathesons live in their earldom. What aboot ye, Uncle Tristan?"

"Why nae have the Sutherlands accompany the Keiths back to Ackergill? It isnae that far past them. We accompany the Mackenzies back to Eilean Donan before we head to Castle Varrich. The MacLeods will go home just like the Camerons, since nay one will summon them back. This way means nay one has to double back to Dounie to get the rest of our family."

It wasn't long before all agreed, and they dispatched riders to seek the men who took Tate and Thor. The rest of the Sinclairs and their extended family mounted and followed the same route as the scouts, but slower. While they rode, Thor and Tate recounted what happened during their captivity and their escape. Adelaide rode in front of Tate, and she trembled with each added detail. She sat facing forward with Tate's left arm wrapped snuggly around her middle while his right hand steered the horse.

"I'm here now, Addy. I'm safe."

"For now. Ye'll be riding into battle soon. I kenned this would happen one day. I'd just hoped to make it a sennight into our marriage before that. This reminds me too much of Mama and Da."

"What do ye mean?" Tate glanced down at his wife as she huddled beneath her new Sinclair arisaid.

"Horrible, vile men kidnapped Mama while she and Da were on their way to Freuchie right after they married. They were going to sell her, make her a whore. She got far enough away from them for Da to rescue her and take her home. But it wasna that long after they arrived he had to ride out. He was determined to get the men who hurt Mama. She'd almost died when one of them struck her, and she fell, hitting her head against a rock. But it was Da who came even closer to death."

Adelaide's fingers pressed Tate's arm tighter around her. He caressed her ribs as she continued.

"He was wounded and fell into a ravine. His men searched but couldnae find him. To this day, nay one kens how Mama kenned where he was. She's devout, so I really believe God spoke to her. He told her where to look, and she rode out. She didna care if anyone came with her. Uncle Edward did, but she wasna going to let anyone stop her. She found Da, and they brought him home. Obviously, he survived, but he was vera ill first. Someone already took ye, Tate. I dinna want the rest of history to repeat itself. We canna guarantee ye'd survive it."

"I canna ever guarantee aught."

"I ken. But I dinna want to lose ye before we even reach home. Ye promised me a sennight."

Tate chuckled as he nuzzled Adelaide's neck. "I am going to do everything I can to always come home to ye. This willna be any different. Ye will get that sennight and another after it."

She could only nod as she struggled to keep her imagination from conjuring scenarios where Tate's body was left beaten and battered before his family laid him over a saddle. They would bring him back to her, but he'd already be dead.

"We dinna ken for sure what's going to happen yet. Rest back against me, Addy. I'd feel ye sleep in ma arms and ken I'm here to protect ye. That's what bothered me more than aught else. I wasna with ye to protect ye."

Adelaide knew what Tate didn't say. She shifted awkwardly, but she drew her right leg over the horse's neck to sit sideways. She nestled close to him. "I will always feel safe in yer arms. I will always trust ye enough to close ma eyes and sleep when ye hold me.

Naught has changed and naught ever will. Now dinna talk, husband. Yer chest rumbles, and it shall keep me awake."

Adelaide sighed as she drew her arms up and between them, her chest against his chest, her hair against his shoulder. It was as close to content as they would get as they rode into the unknown.

CHAPTER 27

$\mathcal{A}$delaide listened silently as the two Montys spewed curses she'd never even heard before. Uncle and nephew took turns as they fumed. The Sinclairs had caught up with the attackers, beaten the truth out of them, and taken them as prisoners before riding to meet the Sutherlands, Rosses, and Camerons. The Matheson men would have died if they'd taken it upon themselves to capture Tate and Thor, who'd just finished explaining what happened during their ordeal.

"Why?" Monty Óg demanded to anyone and no one.

The clan leaders once more gathered. Liam sat beside Amelia and Hamish, who sat beside their daughter Blair and her husband, Hardi. Both Montys sat across from Amelia, Monty Mòr's aunt and Monty Óg's greataunt. When they caught the older woman's eye, both frowned, ducked their chins, and blushed. Blair snickered at Monty Mòr, who shot her a glare that only made her cover her mouth. They all knew she laughed at him, not with him. But it wasn't malicious between the cousins, so the meeting soon moved on.

"Since it was sanctioned," Liam started. He didn't have an answer to Monty Óg's question, so he'd offer a solution to a different question. "We ride to Shiness in the morning. Hamish, do ye ken where Kieran and Michail are?"

"Aye. I sent them home. It seemed unlikely we would need them. Now I wish I hadnae."

"Dinna fash," Magnus Óg interjected. He looked at his brother, Laird Seamus. "I dinna like ma wife and bairn traveling while this is unsettled, but we have plenty of men to protect all of us. We'll be fine to travel on without any of ye. They have to live with us as neighbors. They willna do aught to us. Neither will the Chisholms. It's nae worth their inevitable losses if they do."

"We'll take the Keiths to Dunrobin," Hamish offered. "Rose and Blaine can stay there until ye're ready to keep going up the coast. Ye can decide who travels the rest of the way with them to Ackergill once ye're at Dunbeath."

Blaine looked in Rose's direction before he nodded. He and Magnus Óg, along with Seamus, excused themselves since they would no longer be part of the plan. Hamish and Amelia remained because of their role in their families. Their son, Lachlan, stood behind Hamish. Much like Alex, he was an observer and spoke only when he felt he had something to say that no one else would. Lachlan posed the question, "How far ahead of us do ye believe they are?"

"Two days," Callum estimated. "The time we lost yesterday and today. It'll put them close to home but still on Chisholm land. I dinna think any of us want to deal with them while dealing with the Chisholms. We dinna do aught until we're on Matheson land."

After hashing out the details multiple times before connecting with the Sutherlands, Rosses, and Camerons, it was easy to explain the plan. With nothing left to discuss, the clan leaders returned to their clan members to explain the new development. It was a somber evening as warriors prepared for the possible impending battle. Families huddled together for their evening meals and the time they had left before husbands, fathers, sons, and brothers rode or marched toward the Mathesons.

"Are ye hungry?" Tate brought over two rabbits from the spit where Ailish prepared what she and their cousins Maisie and Nessa hunted.

"Nay. I ken I should eat since it'll be another long day in the saddle, but I just have nay taste for aught." Adelaide moved over to make room for Tate on the plaid she'd laid out for their family to sit upon while they ate. She accepted the meat Tate offered, blowing on it before taking a bite. She would eat because she would need the sustenance for the next day's long ride, but the food had no flavor and held no appeal.

"I dinna wish to send ye away, but ye ken it's for the best." Tate kept his voice hushed, not wanting their conversation overheard by his siblings and parents who sat near them on the plaid.

"I dinna wish to leave ye, but I ken it's for the best. I pray this is over soon, and we have some sort of resolution. All we ken so far is that Laird Matheson sent those men. We dinna ken why." Adelaide didn't hide the frustration in her voice. She wanted answers just like everyone else.

Tate sighed as he considered what they didn't know. "It's obvious the Matheson is angry aboot how things worked out. Is he fashing over Clara wanting to wait for the wedding and is blaming us? Is he upset Clara and Fergus are still getting married? He was the one who wants and needs the MacDonalds."

"Mayhap he's angry Fergus almost had to marry Agnes instead of the elder sister."

"But that wasna our fault. Peter is the one who ruined the betrothal."

"But we helped hide Clara," Adelaide countered.

"Could he believe those accusations? Is he angry that Fergus will marry Clara after all because he thinks her unchaste? If that's the case, then he did want Fergus to marry Agnes. It would anger him that Clara wasna really dead, and we helped Clara and Fergus reconcile."

"We're assuming Thor wasna the reason for them taking ye. Could he be?" Adelaide wondered.

"I canna think how. He has naught to do with the Mathesons, Chisholms, or the MacDonalds. Ma family doesnae have any direct connections—or even any solid indirect ones—to any of those clans."

"So, Thor happened to be in the wrong place and wound up taken because of ye." Adelaide flinched. She hadn't phrased that very sensitively.

"Ye arenae wrong. Those men only targeted Thor and me. They didna try to get past us to anyone else. They kenned they had to take both of us."

"I just realized something." Adelaide considered the scene she'd found when she ran after Blair and Maude. "We didna ken it was the Mathesons. Maude and Blair killed those men. We saw the plaids they wore. They didna have a clan pattern. They were just black wool."

"They're raiding plaids," Tate explained. "Some clans wear them to disguise themselves when they reive cattle. They think it'll provide anonymity. It doesnae. It might buy them some time, but people figure out who stole from them. Those men wanted to confuse us aboot who took Thor and me. They wanted to hide that they were Mathesons and likely hoped it would confuse us into believing they were Chisholms."

"The most plausible reason seems to be that the Matheson is angry that the alliance was delayed, and he blames ye for it."

"Which is horse shite. If aught, I helped make sure it wasna ruined," Tate grumbled. He tossed his rabbit bones into the fire after finishing it. "Do ye need a moment of privacy or a chance to wash at the loch?"

Adelaide looked around as she shook her head vigorously. She didn't realize she clutched Tate's sleeve until he pried her fingers loose. He shifted and drew her to lean against him. Fear had torn through her like a tornado, wreaking havoc on her already frayed nerves. She hadn't predicted its onset and underestimated its ferocity. Now there was nothing but calm as Tate held her.

"Ye're exhausted. Let's retire for the night," Tate suggested. They rose and bid everyone goodnight before entering the tent they would share with Thor and Greer. Their bedrolls were already side-by-side, so they slipped beneath the spare plaids. Tate ran his hand over her hip and leg as he spooned her, crooning to her. She rolled toward him.

"Ye're the one who's been in danger, yet ye're soothing me. I should be comforting ye, nae the other way around."

"Wheest. Holding ye and kenning ye feel safe is comforting to me. I told ye that. It makes me happy to touch ye and feel ye fall asleep next to me. It helps me sleep."

"I love ye, Tatum." Adelaide cupped his jaw as they kissed. It was the first one they'd had in private since Tavish and Callum found their sons. Tate's hand slid down to rest on her bottom. When they heard people approach, he gave it a quick squeeze before Adelaide rolled over.

"I love ye, Addy."

I pray I'm saying that for many years to come and nae having that be ma final thought on some field that belongs to the bluidy Mathesons.

* * *

"THERE THEY ARE." Monty Mòr pointed toward specks in the distance as the Sinclair and Ross warriors scouted from atop of a hill. The other clans had broken off two days earlier. Now, only men rode together. The Sinclairs rested in their saddles as they followed Monty's finger. "What do ye want to do? I want to wring the Matheson's bluidy neck for being a bairn and making me have to deal with his fits of temper."

"Much as I wish to do that too," Liam admitted, "there are women and bairns with them. If the entire force descends upon them, they'll attack, thinking they're defending themselves. Ye and Donan ride with me. I take Callum, Tavish, Thor, and Tate. We ride with ten guards from each clan. Monty Óg and Craig go with the others and surround them."

Donan Ross had been Monty Mòr's closest confidant since they were children. He'd served as Monty's second-in-command until Craig replaced him and Monty Óg took over the lairdship. They'd always been inseparable, but few people knew why. As far as anyone outside the Earl's immediate family knew, they were as close as brothers.

Monty Mòr twisted to see his nephews, men in their mid-twenties who'd ridden into more battles at their age than Monty Mòr had. "Dinna get even a wee scratch on either of ye. Yer mother's still a hellion and will blister ma ears, if nae ma arse, if aught happens to ye." He smiled and nodded with affection before watching the younger men break away from the group to pick out the guards who would accompany his relatives and those who would follow him.

Alex and Magnus Mòr did the same with the younger generation of Sinclair men flanking them on horseback. The men assigned to follow their leaders waited patiently. From the hilltop, they could watch as the Rosses and Sinclairs rode away. They would have to wait close to an hour for the men to encircle the slowly moving Matheson entourage. When the time came, Liam gave the signal. They'd lost sight of the Mathesons, but they soon spotted them as they raced toward them.

"Where are the women and bairns?" Tate called out as they came within sight of their enemy. All he could spy were warriors. The carts had straw, but no one riding on them. They hadn't been able to distinguish that detail from a distance.

"Good question," Tavish bellowed. "There."

Tavish recognized both Laird Matheson and Fergus from their red hair. It shone like ripe tomatoes in the sun, even though it was closer to carrots when seen up close. Their horses' pounding hooves alerted the Mathesons. They responded immediately, moving into a formation.

"They expected us," Callum growled. There was no hesitation or organized chaos when the Mathesons spotted the combined Sinclair-Ross force. Instead, the Mathesons drew their weapons while forming a circle, their targes raised. The Sinclairs and Rosses drew their swords and charged forward.

"Matheson!" Liam roared as he rose in his stirrups. "Cease! We shall speak, or I shall slaughter ye. Choose."

No one in that valley thought Laird Liam Sinclair, Earl of Caithness, exaggerated. But the Mathesons did nothing but raise their targes higher. Monty Mòr pushed ahead of the other riders, Donan emerging from the pack beside him. They rode until they were within a distance where Monty didn't have to yell to be understood.

"Matheson, ye will lower yer weapons, or I will destroy yer entire clan, nae just the men here now. Ye canna begin to afford the taxes I will levy, and ye canna keep land I refuse to allow ye to have. Ye are in Ross-shire, and I am the Ross." Montgomery Ross, Earl of Ross, might have abdicated the lairdship in favor of his nephew since arthritis made it difficult to train daily, and his vision grew cloudier by the year. But he was still fit and imposing. He struck fear in many of the Mathesons' hearts. "Do ye wish to wind up like the MacGregors? I can make that happen."

The MacGregors were pushed off their land by the Campbells, the clan of Monty Óg and Craig's birth, after King Robert the Bruce granted the Campbells a larger territory. It left them with few options but to encroach upon the MacFarlanes and MacNabs, which hadn't gone over well for the past twenty years. They survived by reiving and farming plots of marginally arable land.

Laird Matheson pointed his sword toward the Rosses and Sinclairs they could see. "*Fac et spera!*"

"Do and hope," Tavish snorted. "They need to do a far sight more than hope. They need to pray now that they've done themselves in."

The Sinclairs had signaled all the riders to rein in while Monty Mòr warned Laird Matheson. Now they nudged their horses into a canter as Laird Matheson commanded his men and their horses to charge. The battle wouldn't last long since the hidden Sinclair and Ross warriors would soon join them, but there was no avoiding the fight.

Tate maneuvered his horse once he spied Fergus. He would either discover why his friend's father did this, or he would slay Fergus to keep his own head upon his shoulders. There was little chance of anything in between.

"Why?" Tate demanded when he was certain Fergus could hear.

"Sod off." Fergus spat a wad of saliva in Tate's direction.

"What have I done to wrong ye? I stood by ye despite the pathetic arse ye made of yerself. Ye made much ado aboot naught, and now ye're angry at me."

"Ye ruined ma life." Fergus broke away from the men who surrounded him and dismounted. "Fight me."

"Why? Until ye give me a good reason before I kill ye, I will nae fight ma friend."

"Fight me, damnit!"

Tate looked around and spotted Laird Matheson fighting Liam. It took little to realize Liam offered the Matheson laird the opportunity to defend himself with a shred of honor. But when Liam decided the fight was over, Fergus's father wouldn't be the victor. His gaze shifted to where Fergus's brothers tried to corral the skittish horses. One of them was more likely to be trampled than keep the horses at bay. It was easy to see the Rosses and Sinclairs had the upper hand, and the Mathesons struggled to hold their own. Tate watched as though in slow motion as men converged on the battle. He recognized men from his own clan along with the Rosses. But there were Mathesons ahead of them, rushing to defend their laird and his family.

Tate looked back down at Fergus, who seethed. Once they made eye contact again, Fergus charged. Tate's horse reared, but he controlled his steed with his knees. Once all four hooves were on the ground, he kicked his feet free of the stirrups. He already had his targe on his left forearm. He shoved Fergus's arm away when his friend tried to strike him. He drew his right foot up and onto the saddle before pushing with all his strength. He rammed Fergus with his targe, making his former friend's head snap back before they collided and landed on the ground. Tate drew back his sword and brought the tip to Fergus's Adam's apple. He released the longest and loudest whistle he could.

"Ma son!" Laird Matheson bellowed as he tried to

run toward Fergus. But Liam and Alex blocked his path. Even if he'd gotten past them, Magnus, Blake, and Tor fought together and were an impenetrable mountain. Laird Matheson spun around as the battle halted. He shook his head when he spied Tavish fighting back-to-back with Wiley, and Ric fighting back-to-back with Kirk. The two Montys and their seconds were behind him, but he was certain what he would see if he looked.

Tate didn't move. His knees pinned both of Fergus's arms to the ground. His larger mass meant no matter how Fergus struggled, he couldn't dislodge Tate. "If ye dinna want ma sword to slice yer own throat, be still."

"Fuck ye." Fergus made to spit at Tate again, but the latter's fist plowed into the restrained man's cheekbone. Fergus's howl came as pain from a likely shattered bone radiated throughout his head.

"Fergus!" Laird Matheson tried once more to get to his son. Alex reached forward and drove the hilt of his claymore down on the wrist of Matheson's sword arm. The man's reflexes caused him to drop his weapon. Before he knew what happened, he was disarmed when Magnus yanked the targe from him. Suddenly, hands reached everywhere on his belt, confiscating dirks. He watched helplessly as Wiley, Blake, and Tor left him feeling more naked than if he didn't have a stitch of clothing on.

"Why did yer men take ma son and nephew?" Callum demanded.

"What?" Laird Matheson asked as he watched Tate hold Fergus hostage.

"Why did ye send men to attack us and take Tate and Thor?" Tavish spoke as though he talked to a fool.

"I didna," the Matheson snapped.

"Och, aye. Ye did." Liam pointed to where Monty Óg had jogged and joined some of the Ross men who held the captured Matheson men. They were the ones who told the Rosses and Sinclairs that it was a sanctioned attack.

Laird Matheson tore his gaze away from Fergus to look back over his shoulder. "What the bluidy hell?" He muttered before his already ruddy face went crimson. "I sent ye lot on ahead to inform our housekeeper of our return. What the fuck are ye doing with the Rosses?"

As a Ross warrior propelled the guilty Mathesons forward, none of the captives spoke.

"These men entered our camp and attacked Thor and Tate. They took both men and held them hostage until they escaped in the middle of the night," Liam explained. "Yer men said their actions were sanctioned."

"By whom? Certainly, nae me. Ye traveled with yer entire bluidy family. How there are only two clans trying to massacre us is beyond me. I wouldnae send ma men to their deaths. Though, ye've apparently discovered some mercy, Liam. They're breathing for now."

"Dinna think it was mercy. I plan to watch ye execute yer men before I kill ye. Ye claim ye didna send them, then it must have been Fergus. He's the only one with the authority. Why did yer son do it?"

"I dinna ken." Laird Matheson stood slack jawed as he shook his head. He watched as Tate rose, pulling Fergus onto his feet. Tate nudged Fergus toward his father, stepping behind him, so his sword poked Fergus's upper back. Fergus stumbled before stopping in front of his irate father. The Sinclair and Ross men didn't move, knowing their demands would get them nowhere. It was now between father and son.

"It's his fault," Fergus hissed as he looked over his shoulder.

"What is?" Laird Matheson demanded.

"He put that idea in yer head, and now ye've disinherited me. That piece of shite made ye believe I canna lead."

"He didna," Laird Matheson denied. "It was yer actions that did that."

"But ye heard Tate warn me. Ye heard him say he would suggest it to ye," Fergus insisted.

"Nay. Yer actions shamed our entire clan. First, ye accusing Lady Clara. Then yer sniveling and whining because ye made yer life a pile of shite. And finally, yer pathetic whimpering when ye realized a whore and a Chisholm fooled ye. Yer begging and groveling for forgiveness to Clara, the MacDonald, and me made me want to vomit. Ye arenae fit to shovel shite let alone be a laird. Ye're an embarrassment. Even Lady Clara kens that. She wanted her life back, but she didna want ye. That's why she refused to marry ye at the Gathering. She did that in front of everyone. Ye're worthless." Laird Matheson lunged at his son, but Magnus and Tavish restrained him.

Fury swirled within Tate as he listened to the accusations. He'd warned Fergus, but he never spoke to the Matheson. The man had drawn his own conclusions. He grabbed a handful of Fergus's hair and yanked it, making his head snap back at an awkward angle. He brought his sword to Fergus's throat. He brought his face next to Fergus's injured cheek as he hissed each word.

"Ye endangered ma wife, ma mother, ma sisters, ma aunts, and ma cousins. Ye would have had ma cousin and me killed. Ye have wasted our time and separated me from ma wife again. For what? Something ye believed happened but didna. Sounds bluidy familiar. Aye, I told ye mayhap yer father should pass ye over. Clearly, I was right to think that. Ye canna make a sound decision to save yer life. Truly. Ye stand here with ma blade to yer throat. I have every right to kill ye, Fergus. But I willna. I have a demand, Laird Matheson."

Tate shifted his attention to Fergus's father. He tugged on Fergus's hair and pressed his blade hard enough against Fergus's throat to draw blood but not wound him.

"Clara was prepared to retire to a convent after what Fergus did. She would have gone home and been a shut-in within her own keep after what Fergus did. If ma wife and I hadnae protected Lady Clara, she would still be hiding. Yer son sentenced her to a life of isolation. I sentence him to the same. Eynhallow Monastery."

"Where?" Fergus croaked.

"Orkney. It's on a wee, wee island between Mainland and Rousay. All that is there is the monastery run by Cistercians. Ye shall live a life of solitude imposed by nature and the order. Ye will have naught to look at but the wide-open sea. Ye will have nay one to talk to but the fish. Ye will toil all day with naught to show for it at the end. Ye will waste away with the life ye would have subjected Clara to. And I will be sure that ye live just this way. Do ye ken why I'll be sure of it?"

"Because yer grandfather is the Earl of Caithness."

"Aye. Orkney is under Sinclair control. Once a year, I will visit ye. I will bring ma wife and our weans. Ye will see the life ye forsook because ye were never fit to lead yer clan." He had no intention of ever taking Adelaide anywhere near Fergus or that monastery, but his former friend didn't need to ken that." He would let the idea fester in Fergus's mind.

"He's ma son! I decide what happens to him."

Monty Mòr stepped so close that his chest bumped the Matheson's. "Ye decide naught. Ye seem to have forgotten yet again. This is Ross-shire, and I am the Earl of Ross. Ma aunt is Laird Sinclair's sister-by-marriage.

That makes us family. I'm happy to hand yer sack of shite over to Laird Sinclair. If he sees fit to indulge his grandson, then who am I to stand in his way? Push me one more time, and ye will find yerself rowing the same boat as yer son."

Monty Mòr's strawberry-blond hair caught the sunlight and glowed around him like an avenging angel. Coupled with the primarily red Ross plaid, he appeared to rise out of flames. He was not a man with whom people trifled and survived. Laird Matheson snapped his mouth shut and shifted his gaze to Fergus, who still stood with Tate at his side. Fergus's scowl appeared out of place when humility would have done him some good.

Liam looked at Tate and nodded before his gaze fell on Fergus. "Yer actions nae only endangered ma grandson but everyone who traveled with us. Yer men entered our camp where ma daughters, nieces, and granddaughters were bathing at the stream. Ye're lucky that I dinna skelp ye and them. Ye're lucky that ye've lived long enough to give yer pitiful explanation. Ye're lucky Tate and I are so benevolent. Ye travel with us as our prisoner. Ye will be taken to Eynhallow at ma convenience. If that means ye reside in ma dungeon until I care enough to send ye, then so be it."

"He and Thor werenae harmed. Ma men didna go anywhere near yer women. Ye're all just in a snit that someone so lowly as a Matheson could kidnap two of the almighty Sinclairs. Ye're humiliated. That's why ye would banish me." Fergus smirked before lifting his chin in dismissive arrogance.

"That's what ye think?" Tate interjected. "Ye daft bugger. The only reason I didna kill ye is because Lady Clara is ma wife's friend. Yer betrothed loves ye, and ma wife is fond of her. I dinna want ma wife caught in the middle. For Lady Adelaide's sake, I am sparing ye. If Lady Clara had rejected ye, then ye'd be dead."

"Still doesnae mean ye arenae humiliated men carried ye off, and nay one stopped them," Fergus sneered.

With so many commanding men and skilled warriors at the ready, it baffled Tate how Fergus didn't know when to cease. It was clear his father couldn't control him. He clearly didn't have a healthy fear of the Sinclairs or the Rosses.

"Aye, yer men did snatch Thor and me. But we left with ease. Now yer army stands defeated, yer father disinherited ye, and ma grandfather has banished ye. I'd say the scales tip in yer favor for humiliation. Yer brother is only three-and-ten, and he is now yer clan's tánaiste. A child takes yer place because ye werenae mon enough to keep yer gob shut. Say yer goodbyes. I tire of this and wish to return to ma wife."

Fergus's eyes darted around until they landed on his brothers. Hate oozed from every pore. The boys took a collective step back, unfamiliar and terrified of the animosity the brother they'd worshipped directed at them. The oldest brother, now tánaiste and heir, straightened his shoulders, lifted his chin, and spat in Fergus's direction. Then he smirked. But he said nothing. Tate was nearly proud of the lad for his gumption and wisdom.

"Strip his plaid," Tate ordered.

"What?" Fergus and Laird Mathesons squawked.

"Either ye don one of the black plaids yer men wore or ye go without. The Earl of Ross and Earl of Caithness sanctioned yer banishment. Ye are nay longer a Matheson. Ye are a mon without kin or clan. Ye dinna deserve to wear any clan's plaid. Remove it."

Laird Matheson opened his mouth to object, but Tavish stepped next to Monty Mòr. Tavish had inherited his father's barrel chest. Even though he stood a hair's breadth shorter than his three other brothers, his physique was threatening without knowing his reputation.

"I wouldnae whisper a sound if I were ye," Tavish warned. "Yer worthless spawn attacked ma lad by sending men to our camp. Yer men came near *ma family*. They took *ma family*. I am the least patient mon in *ma family*. Ye have worn the little I have into dust. Yer son obeys mine, and we leave. I have been away from ma wife and daughter, and *ye* will pay for that if I'm kept waiting another moment."

Tavish wrapped his bear paw of a hand around the Matheson's throat, pulling him onto his toes, and shaking him as though he expected fruit to fall from the man's arms. He squeezed until all the other man could do was gurgle as he gestured to Fergus. When the younger man made no move to obey, the Matheson motioned men behind him to step forward. Warriors Fergus had once led stripped him of his plaid and his identity.

Thor handed Tate a length of rope he'd gathered from his saddlebag. Once Fergus stood without his plaid, dirks, and sword, Tate made quick work of hogtying Fergus with the rope around his ankles and wrists.

"Bring his horse," Tate commanded, and one of the Matheson boys hurried forward. Between Tate and Thor, they hoisted Fergus across the saddle. Tate tightened the rope, forcing Fergus to bend his legs and bring his feet closer to his bound hands that were behind his back. Each step the horse took would be excruciating. Fergus's only hope was that he passed out soon. Tate used the remaining rope to secure Fergus to the horse.

There was nothing left to say, so they left the Mathesons speechless as the defeated clan watched the Sinclairs and Rosses mount, then ride away. The two forces regrouped once they were away from the impromptu battlefield. Monty Mòr and Monty Óg shook Liam's and Callum's hands, and the rest of the men exchanged nods. Then the Rosses rode away toward their home. The Sinclairs headed north toward Dunrobin to reunite with their family. The next three days only made Tate's anger fester by the hour. Rather than be relieved that they'd resolved the strife between the Sinclairs and Mathesons, the responsible party was still within reach. He forced himself to remain at opposite ends of the formation and the camps lest he kill Fergus on the spot.

It wasn't just his own kidnapping that fueled his anger. It was being blamed for Fergus's actions when he'd been nothing but a loyal friend. It was watching Fergus hurt Clara, then hurt her even more by foolishly attacking the Sinclairs. The woman was without her betrothed again. It was the selfishness of him acting without his father's approval and risking anyone's life. It was the time taken from being with Adelaide. It was the betrayal and disloyalty. Those were two things he couldn't forgive yet. He would with time because he refused to allow Fergus to steal anything else from him. He wouldn't allow his former friend to steal any time or energy that he could spend loving Adelaide and building a life with her.

The bells tolled as the Sinclairs approached Dunrobin, and the bailey filled as Tate's family passed beneath the portcullis. Tate didn't need to look around. Adelaide was a lodestone, and she drew him to her without effort. He dismounted as she flew toward him. He met her halfway and lifted her off her feet as she wrapped her arms around him.

"Wife."

"Husband, I've missed ye. There's so much to tell ye."

CHAPTER 28

ate lowered Adelaide to her feet as his stomach clenched. What else could there be? Hadn't they been through enough in the last few days? His captivity had been brief, and the battle was over before it really began, but that didn't mean there hadn't been moments when he feared never seeing Adelaide again, feared never seeing his family again, feared losing a member of his family.

"Rose had her bairn!" Adelaide bounced onto her toes and clapped. Tate could only stare before he picked Adelaide up again and smothered whatever she was about to say with a kiss that stole their breath. When they pulled apart and each sucked in a lungful of air, Tate dove in for a second and third kiss, holding Adelaide so tightly that she finally had to tap her husband on his shoulder. "Breathe."

Tate didn't understand for a moment, then realized he was suffocating his petite wife. He lowered her to her feet once more and looked around. Rose, Blaine, Callum, and Siùsan were noticeably missing. Callum must have gone into the keep to see his daughter and first grandchild. He watched as Liam took the steps by two, so Tate assumed he ran to see his newest great-grandchild. Thor was beside their grandfather as he hurried to see his twin, Greer barely able to keep up with her husband's longer legs.

"Tate?" Adelaide cupped his cheeks, worried about why he said nothing.

"Aye. I'm all right. I expected bad news. Between needing to see ye, touch ye, taste ye and ma relief that naught more was wrong, I couldnae think aboot aught else. But her bairn is here? I thought she still had another moon."

"We thought that too, but the midwife here said the Keith midwife was off by a few sennights. The bairn is a healthy and vera loud wee lass. I've never seen a father prouder to hold his bairn than Blaine."

"Give us a few months, then ye will," Tate nipped at her neck. He slid a hand between them to rest on Adelaide's belly. "Truly. When the Lord sees to bless us, nay mon will ever be prouder than I am to hold ma bairn because we created that life together. I'll have another piece of ye each time we have a child. I canna think of aught to be happier or prouder of."

"Ye say the sweetest things, *mo ghaol*." A lump rose in Adelaide's throat, and her eyes prickled with tears because she could see and hear Tate's sincerity. The way his hand rested gently on her middle was protective and reverent. "I love ye."

"I love ye, too." This kiss was softer, more languid than the previous ones. When they broke apart, Adelaide rested her head on Tate's chest. He hadn't moved his hand as they looked around the bailey. It teemed with Keiths, Sutherlands, and Sinclairs as the families blended so seamlessly that only the plaids identified them.

"How have ye been?" Tate wondered.

"Lonely the few nights we were apart. I missed feeling ye beside me. I missed the warmth of cuddling with ye. I missed a few other things, too." She tickled his ribs, and he shied away. She giggled before wrapping her arms around him again. "Having the bairn arrive the night we arrived helped make the time pass and made it tolerable as we waited for ye to get here. What happened?"

Tate sighed. "Are ye sharing a chamber?"

"Nae. Only the unmarried people are sharing. Every couple has one for when the husbands returned."

"Let's retire to ours, and I'll tell ye everything. I dinna ken that ye'll be pleased with me."

Adelaide gazed up at Tate, worried about what he could have done. He didn't appear guilty, just fatigued. She nodded and let go of him, but before she could turn back to the keep, movement caught her eye. "Is that Fergus tied to that horse? Where's his plaid?"

"That's what I need to tell ye. This was his fault."

"Really?"

"Aye. Grandda and ma uncles will tell their wives and the Sutherlands. Ma brother and cousins will tell the lasses. I suppose Uncle Callum will tell Rose and Blaine. I wish to tell ye alone."

"Ye're scaring me, Tatum."

Tate paused and gazed down at her upturned face. "I dinna mean to. I decided Fergus's future, and I dinna think ye'll be pleased with me. I'd rather have ye angry with me in private."

Adelaide nodded as she slipped her hand into his. She walked beside him until they reached the keep's third floor. She led him to a chamber he already knew.

"This is where I've always slept here, but Wiley is usually with me."

"That's what Amelia said. She hinted I would make a much better person to share a chamber with." Adelaide sucked her lips in, but she couldn't repress her smile.

"Ye do. Shall we sit?" Tate gestured toward the

hearth where no fire was lit but two chairs sat before it. He didn't release her hand when she let go of his, instead guiding her to sit on his lap. She stroked back hair from his forehead as he rested his head against her breast.

"Tatum, what happened?"

"Fergus happened. Apparently, on their way home, Laird Matheson announced he disinherited Fergus and relieved him of his position as tánaiste in favor of Fergus's younger brother. The Matheson said he couldnae trust Fergus's decisions after what happened with Clara. He said her refusal to marry him right away was another sign Fergus isnae fit to lead. Because I warned him that I questioned his fitness too, he believed I told his father, or someone influenced the mon. I didna. I never spoke to him. But Fergus wouldnae let go of the idea. He sent men to take me without his father's knowledge. They captured Thor too because he was with me."

"How'd ye learn all this?"

"We tracked them after capturing the men who held Thor and me hostage. They told us it was sanctioned. The Rosses rode with us since the Mathesons' land is in Ross-shire. Neither Monty was pleased, but Monty Mòr ensured Laird Matheson kenned he continued to have land to live upon because of Mòr's largesse. I'm certain that only confirmed the Matheson's decision to strip Fergus of his place."

"Tate, ye didna just nashgab with the Mathesons. Was there a battle?" Adelaide wanted to know everything that happened, but only because she could tell Tate was unharmed.

"Briefly. Our joint army severely outnumbered the Mathesons. They stood nay chance, even when they had men charge us once the fight began. We had men behind them. It didna take me long to find and engage

Fergus. The fight was over the moment I pinned him to the ground. I held him at sword point and even had ma blade against his throat. He explained what I just told ye. There was some going back and forth until I grew fed up and announced what I wished for his punishment. I didna want to stand in that field clishmaclavering when I could ride closer to ye."

"How'd he wind up trussed up like an Epiphany goose?"

"Since his actions could have caused Clara to live the life of a recluse in her own home or isolated at a convent, I decided he should live that life instead. I announced I wanted him to go to Eynhallow Monastery."

"Where's that? I've never heard of it."

"Nae surprising. It's a Cistercian monastery on one of the tiniest islands in Orkney. It's between Mainland and Rousay. The only thing on that tiny rock is the monastery. There's little else. He will have a life of scarcity and labor, isolated from everything and everyone. I was angry when I said it, and I expected someone to talk me out of it. But Monty Mòr agreed if Grandda agreed. As the Earl of Caithness, it was Grandda's decision since the Earl of Ross turned his vassal over to us. Grandda accepted ma suggestion. He announced Fergus's banishment to Orkney."

"Banishment? Officially? That's why he doesnae have his plaid."

"Aye. I said he could wear one of the black plaids the men who took me wore or he could go without. Ye saw him in only his leine."

"To suggest such a lifetime of servitude, ye must have been furious."

"I was. I'm nay longer that angry. I refuse to waste the emotion on him because that is space in ma heart and ma mind that belong to ye. But I'm still disgusted with him. Ye ken duty, honor, and loyalty are among the most important values to ma family. Living by those is what makes ma family so strong. I dinna expect everyone else to place as much store in them as we do, but he broke all of those. There was naught honorable aboot the way he treated Clara or how he thought to punish me for ma perceived wrong."

"What did he plan to do with ye?"

"I dinna ken. I didna bother to ask because I didna care. It wouldnae have made me less unforgiving. And short of killing him, which I threatened with all honesty to do more than once, there wasna a more severe punishment than banishment. I dinna want him living in our dungeon. I dinna want ma family to do aught to keep him alive. Nae even bread and ale. He defied his father and put his clan at risk. He didna do his duty by his family or his clan. He was disloyal to them to put his wants ahead of them. And he was disloyal to me after how I stood beside him before, during, and after the fiasco with Clara. He betrayed me. Mayhap if I hadnae been able to offer a punishment in the heat of the moment, I would have thought of something more benevolent, but I wasna feeling that generous. I'm still nae, even if I'm nae as angry and hurt."

"What part of this did ye think would anger me?"

"Do ye nae realize his banishment means he canna marry Clara? She's lost the mon she loves twice."

"That's what ye're worried aboot?" Adelaide's eyebrows shot up. "I didna think she should marry him after the first time he loused things up. I thought he was without any honor then, but she loves him. I told her I disagreed, but there was naught else I could do. She kenned ma opinion, and I'm glad she opted to wait to marry him. He showed himself for who he is again. Better that happened before he trapped her."

"If he'd married Clara or Agnes, or anyone else for that matter, I would have killed him. I wouldnae force a woman to remain wed with nay chance for a proper marriage and family just because I wanted him banished. Would ye believe I was a murderer if I had?"

"Nay. I ken ye wouldnae have acted without yer grandda's permission. He would have been judge, and ye the executioner. If yer grandda didna think that would be the appropriate punishment, he wouldnae allow it. If ye'd killed him, it would have been because he deserved it. It would have set any wife free of such a mon. I'm nae angry at all. I'm sad for Clara, and I can accept that this will likely end our friendship. But Fergus put ma family in danger. Our clan comes first before ma friendship with anyone who isnae a Sinclair or a Grant."

"Do ye ken how ye fill ma heart to near bursting?" Tate brought her palm up to his chest and pressed it over his heart. "Do ye really think of ma family as yer family already? That it's nae ma clan but our clan?"

"Of course, I do. I wear the Sinclair plaid with pride. Yer family and people have been kind to me the entire journey. They've made me feel like I belong. That I dinna just wear yer colors. They make me feel like I deserve it because I'm welcome. I havenae felt like an outsider for even a moment without ye with me. Just the opposite actually. Nae having ye with me meant I had to get to ken people nae in yer family. They see me as me, nae as just yer wife. I hated worrying aboot ye, and I hated missing ye. But I told maself it was nay different than ye being on patrol. Yer mama and the others make it so much easier to nae miss ma family and have it hurt. I miss them, but I dinna feel empty."

"Ye dinna have any regrets leaving Freuchie?" Tate asked the question he'd wondered since they rode away from her clan of birth.

"Ye've really worried aboot that, havenae ye? Nay, Tatum. I dinna have nor have I ever had any regrets aboot marrying ye and leaving ma family to be part of yers."

"Did ye ken ye're perfect?" Tate kissed her neck and up to the spot behind her ear.

"We'll see if ye think that once we settle into our real lives. But for now, I'll take yer compliment. Did ye ken ye're perfect?"

"Aye." Tate waggled his eyebrows.

Adelaide pushed away from him and rose. She darted across the chamber, and he followed. They played chase until neither of them could wait any longer. They stripped each other and fell onto the bed.

"I may nae be the perfect mon, but we're perfect for each other." Tate settled between Adelaide's legs.

"It doesnae hurt that we fit together perfectly too." Adelaide grinned, but it soon turned into a moan as her husband thrust into her and spent the hours until the evening meal showing them how right she was.

EPILOGUE

*A*delaide pushed her hair back from her eyes as she watched five figures stand off to the side of the lists. They were mirror images of each other, except two of them had long chestnut braids hanging down their backs. She watched as her children observed Tate and Tavish practice drills, pausing every few minutes to give the twelve- and ten-year-old girls and the eight-year-old boy time to practice. She couldn't hear Tate and Tavish, but she knew their comments would be serious but patient.

She'd smiled when their oldest child asked for a wooden sword after seeing her cousin carrying one when he came to visit with his parents, Saoirse and Magnus Óg. She hadn't imagined Tate would carve one himself that night. It hadn't surprised her when their middle child asked for one two years later. But it had shocked her that Tate insisted upon training their older daughter the morning he gave her the sword. She was prepared when their second child followed them into the lists when she received her sword. And she'd choked on her giggles when their youngest child received his first sword and staggered, trying to follow his older sisters while keeping it from touching the ground.

Adelaide turned when she sensed someone step next to her. She looked over at Mairghread as the older woman stopped beside her. Her hair was graying, and there were faint laugh lines around her eyes and mouth. But those were the only signs the woman had entered her fifth decade. She still looked like a young woman from a distance.

"When ma brother finishes playing, I will teach yer weans how to properly defend themselves with dirks." Mairghread's tone was so serious it would have fooled anyone who didn't know her.

"He's a wonderful grandda to them."

"He is, but he only kens as much as he does because Da had to tell him so many bluidy times."

"Dinna pick on yer brother, *nighean*." Daughter. Both women turned to watch Liam approach, moving apart to make room for him to stand between them. "Ye already won the dirk from him yesterday after teaching Isla where to land her sword hilt on her grandda's wrist to make him drop it."

The older generation of Sinclair siblings had a dirk they wagered with. When Mairghread reached three-and-ten, her brothers no longer knew what to give her on her saint's day, so they gave her dirks each year. The first one they gave her became the one they passed amongst themselves when they wagered. Mairghread was the most observant and most patient of the five siblings, so she won it most often and kept it the longest each time. She'd wagered with Tavish the day before that the ten-year-old could knock his sword from his hand. Then she'd taught the child exactly what to do.

It resulted in a proud Tavish chasing his squealing granddaughter around the lists before lifting her onto his shoulders to charge around as her trusted steed as she held onto handfuls of his chestnut mane. It was the same thing Liam had done with his children and his grandchildren. Nearing his eighth decade, he no longer charged around, but he still played monster with his great-grandchildren, letting them hang from his arms and cling to his legs as he stomped around the Great Hall.

The bells tinkled, signaling the evening meal. Tate, Tavish, and the three children crossed the lists with Tavish carrying the three wooden swords and his grandson while Tate carried his two daughters. Adelaide couldn't imagine a more perfect picture of family. But all she had to do was look around the lists. The men had finished training hours earlier, so Tate and the men of his generation, along with their fathers, trained the youngest members of the Sinclair family. It mattered not if the child was a lad or lass. The lads would learn to become warriors. The lasses would learn to become independent.

"What did ye learn today?" Adelaide asked as Tate kissed her on the cheek.

"Everything, Mama!" Angus chirped. They'd name the boy after Adelaide's older brother.

Tavish and Tate put the children down, and they darted off with their cousins. The adults found their partners, wrapping arms around each other's waists and sharing kisses as they turned toward the keep. Liam led, his children and their soulmates following. Behind them were Liam's grandchildren with their soulmates. It often made each of them sad that Liam no longer had Kyla by his side, but he swore she was each time he looked out as his family and counted each of his blessings, which numbered almost a hundred.

"Dinna fall asleep so early, husband," Adelaide whispered to Tate as they sat at one of the long trestle tables.

"Blame yer weans for wearing me out. They have more energy than a fluffle of bunnies." Tate leaned over to murmur beside her ear. "Dinna wake the weans this time as I chase ye around the croft. I dinna want to answer any more of those questions when I should be making love to ma wife."

"That's yer fault for loving me so well." Adelaide grinned and gave Tate a smacking kiss on the cheek. Tate wrapped his arm around Adelaide's waist, and she leaned her head on his shoulder.

"Aye, I love ye, wife. I have since before I kenned it."

"I love ye. And I ken I will forever."

Celeste Barclay, a nom de plume, lives near the Southern California coast with her husband and sons. Growing up in the Midwest, Celeste enjoyed spending as much time in and on the water as she could. Now she lives near the beach. She's an avid swimmer, a hopeful future surfer, and a former rower. When she's not writing, she's enjoying the California sunshine with her family.

Visit Celeste's website, www.celestebarclay.com, for regular updates on works in progress, new releases, and her blog where she features posts about her experiences as an author and recommendations of her favorite reads.

Have you read *Their Highland Beginning, The Clan Sinclair Prequel?* Learn how the saga begins! This FREE novella is available to all new subscribers to Celeste's monthly newsletter. Subscribe on her website.

www.celestebarclay.com

Join the fun and get exclusive insider giveaways, sneak peeks, and new release announcements in

Celeste Barclay's Facebook Ladies of Yore Group
Celeste Barclay Facebook
Celeste Barclay Instagram

THE CLAN SINCLAIR LEGACY

Highland Lion
BOOK 1 SNEAK PEEK

Liam Mackay gazed at the bustling Orcadian village of Skaill, on the isle of Rousay. He thought of how it reminded him of his clan's village, outside the walls of Castle Varrich in the Scottish Highlands. As he crossed the dock, he noticed the massive longboats that Norse traders sailed to conduct trade on the island. With his father's jet-black hair and emerald eyes, few would believe Liam had Nordic heritage, but it had connected his family to Orkney for ten generations. He swept his eyes over the crofts nearest the marina of sorts. He watched as a tall blonde woman stormed out of a house and slammed the door shut. The fury on the woman's face made him think of his mother when she was angry with Liam and his younger brothers and sister. But the woman before him, statuesque and voluptuous, couldn't resemble his petite brunette mother any less. Her tall stature belied her curves until she leaned forward to fill a bucket at the well.

"Elene, come back here. We are not through speaking," an older woman called from the doorway to the croft

Elene Isbister left. The younger woman continued to fill the bucket as though no one spoke to her, but Liam watched her face grow red, and it wasn't from exertion. His path carried him toward the well, but he could have continued past to reach his destination. Instead, intrigued by the stunning blonde and the scene playing out before him, he stopped at the well as the woman finished raising the bucket. She poured the contents in her own pail before letting it drop back into the cavernous pit. Unaware of Liam, she jumped when he stepped forward and grasped the crank.

Liam's emerald eyes met deep sapphire, the shade of the Highland sky in autumn. Liam observed the surprise, then wariness, in her gaze as she stepped away. He drew the full bucket to the ledge and dipped the community ladle into the cool water. As he sipped, Elene took two steps back before turning away, disconcerted by the handsome stranger. However, her feet grew roots as the older woman stormed toward her. Liam kept his head down as he lowered the bucket, chiding himself for his nosiness but unwilling to move away. The older woman glanced at him dismissively before settling her attention on Elene.

In Norn, the language of Orkney, the woman continued her chastisement. "I didn't tell you that you could leave. We were in the middle of talking."

"No, Mother. You were in the middle of talking, and I was in the middle of not wanting to hear any more. I cannot believe you're considering marrying him."

"Not considering. I've already decided. When Gunter returns in a sennight, we will wed. Then we will all move home with him."

"Home?" Elene scoffed. "Norway hasn't been our people's home in ten generations. And you are a fool if you believe he will allow me to remain."

"You're old enough to marry."

"Getting married is a far sight different from being sold!" Elene made to step around her mother, but the older woman was just as quick.

"You exaggerate."

"And you believe a slave trader over your own daughter."

"Gunter is not a slave trader. You would smear his name because you aren't getting what you want, you selfish child."

Clearly not a child, Elene stood to her full height as she gazed at her mother, who was at least two inches shorter than her daughter. "Selfish," she repeated her mother. "I hadn't realized Katryne and Johan raised themselves."

"I am their mother."

"But I raised my brother and sister. I lost my chance to marry while you lost yourself in barrels of mead." Elene swung her glare at Liam, who'd remained near the arguing women while he spoke to his two ship captains. Despite speaking Gaelic, Liam sensed Elene knew he understood her conversation with her mother. It explained her accusatory glare.

"That was my grief."

Elene released a dismissive puff of air. "That was your habit. You haven't missed Father in years. You welcomed Petyre into our home almost every night, and Father hadn't been dead two moons."

"We need a man to provide for us," the older woman sniffed defensively.

Elene gawked at her mother before she laughed. "We do not need a man to provide for us. You might need one because you can't stand to be alone for more than a day. But I work our fields and hunt out supper. Petyre, and now Gunter, come into our home and eat the food I provide. I should have accepted Duncan's offer before he grew fed up with waiting."

"You didn't love him."

"You mean like you love Gunter?"

"I do love him," Elene's mother insisted.

"More fool are you," Elene muttered.

"Come inside. You're causing a scene."

"I'm not the one yelling. And I can't. I must bring Bess this water, feed the chickens, muck out the stalls, then milk Bess. I haven't time to argue when I know you refuse to believe me."

"He is not going to sell you!"

"He will. Or he'll force me to bed him. He will not feed and clothe another adult without getting something in return. He told me."

Highland Bear
Highland Jewel
Highland Rose
Highland Strength

THE CLAN SINCLAIR

His Highland Lass
BOOK 1 SNEAK PEEK

She entered the great hall like a strong spring storm in the northern most Highlands. Tristan Mackay felt like he had been blown hither and yon. As the storm settled, she left him with the sweet scents of heather and lavender wafting towards him as she approached. She was not a classic beauty, tall and willowy like the women at court. Her face and form were not what legends were made of. But she held a unique appeal unlike any he had seen before. He could not take his eyes off of her long chestnut hair that had strands of fire and burnt copper running through them. Unlike the waves or curls he was used to, her hair was unusually straight and fine. It looked like a waterfall cascading down her back. While she was not tall, neither was she short. She had a figure that was meant for a man to grasp and hold onto, whether from the front or from behind. She had an aura of confidence and charm, but not arrogance or conceit like many good looking women he had met. She did not seem to know her own appeal. He could tell that she was many things, but one thing she was not was his.

His Bonnie Highland Temptation **BOOK 2**
His Highland Prize **BOOK 3**
His Highland Pledge **BOOK 4**
His Highland Surprise **BOOK 5**
Their Highland Beginning **BOOK 6**

THE HIGHLAND LADIES

A Spinster at the Highland Court
BOOK 1 SNEAK PEEK

Elizabeth Fraser looked around the royal chapel within Stirling Castle. The ornate candlestick holders on the altar glistened and reflected the light from the ones in the wall sconces as the priest intoned the holy prayers of the Advent season. Elizabeth kept her head bowed as though in prayer, but her green eyes swept the congregation. She watched the other ladies-in-waiting, many of whom were doing the same thing. She caught the eye of Allyson Elliott. Elizabeth raised one eyebrow as Allyson's lips twitched. Both women had been there enough times to accept they'd be kneeling for at least the next hour as the Latin service carried on. Elizabeth understood the Mass thanks to her cousin Deirdre Fraser, or rather now Deirdre Sinclair. Elizabeth's mind flashed to the recent struggle her cousin faced as she reunited with her husband Magnus after a seven-year separation. Her aunt and uncle's choice to keep Deirdre hidden from her husband simply because they didn't think the Sinclairs were an advantageous enough match, and the resulting scandal, still humiliated the other Fraser clan members at court. She admired Deirdre's husband Magnus's pledge to remain faithful despite not knowing if he'd ever see Deirdre again. Elizabeth suddenly snapped her attention; while everyone else intoned the twelfth—or was it thirteenth—amen of the Mass, the hairs on the back of her neck stood up. She had the strongest feeling that someone was watching her. Her eyes scanned to her right, where her parents sat further down the pew. Her mother and father had their heads bowed and eyes closed. While she was convinced her mother was in devout prayer, she wondered if her father had fallen asleep during the Mass. Again. With nothing seeming out of the ordinary and no one visibly paying attention to her, her eyes swung to the left. She took in the king and queen as they kneeled together at their prie-dieu. The queen's lips moved as she recited the liturgy in silence. The king was as still as a statue. Years of leading warriors showed, both in his stature and his ability to control his body into absolute stillness. Elizabeth peered past the royal couple and found herself looking into the astute hazel eyes of Edward Bruce, Lord of Badenoch and Lochaber. His gaze gave her the sense that he peered into her thoughts, as though he were assessing her. She tried to keep her face neutral as heat surged up her neck. She prayed her face didn't redden as much as her neck must have, but at a twenty-one, she still hadn't mastered how to control her blushing. Her nape burned like it was on fire. She canted her head slightly before looking up at the crucifix hanging over the altar. She closed her eyes and tried to invoke the image of the Lord that usually centered her when her mind wandered during Mass.

Elizabeth sensed Edward's gaze remained on her. She didn't understand how she was so sure that he was looking at her. She didn't have any special gifts of perception or sight, but her intuition screamed that he was still looking.

A Spy at the Highland Court
A Wallflower at the Highland Court
A Rogue at the Highland Court
A Rake at the Highland Court
An Enemy at the Highland Court
A Saint at the Highland Court
A Beauty at the Highland Court

THE HIGHLAND LADIES
ALWAYS

A Sinner at the Highland Court
BOOK 1 SNEAK PEEK

I hate him. I hate him. I hate him. How can he do this to me? How could he pick her over me? That fat sow. Kieran will regret this till the day he dies. He and she both. This is her fault. All her fault. I hate her too.
Madeline MacLeod felt the four walls of her tiny convent cell closing in upon her. Her brother, Kieran, had dragged her from Robert the Bruce's royal court at Stirling Castle and dumped her at Inchcailleoch Priory earlier that week. She refused to accept that any of her words or actions had caused her fall from grace. She'd only spoken the truth each time she told Maude Sutherland how unconventionally curvaceous she was. Why her brother wanted to marry a woman who looked more like a tavern wench than a lady was beyond Madeline.
He just wants a good rut. He'll realize what a dreadful mistake he's made when he takes her home to Stornoway. He will realize that tupping her won't be worth the humiliation of having such a plain-faced, round as a barrel, heifer for a wife. He could have had Laurel Ross!

As Madeline listened to the bells toll for yet another Mass, she grimaced. All she seemed to do was pray these days, but God certainly wasn't listening because she remained at the priory despite her fervent appeals. She kneeled among the other novices, postulants, and nuns eight times throughout the day and night as they followed the Liturgy of Hours. The bells in the background signaled Prime, so she knew it was still very early. She'd already attended Matins in the middle of the night and Lauds at sunrise.

Madeline glanced out the narrow window set high in the wall, thinking that the masons must have designed it so the women couldn't escape. The sunlight, weak and dismal, matched Madeline's mood. When she lived at court, six o'clock in the morning was an hour she'd never seen. Now that she lived at the convent, she'd already been awake for an hour and a half.

Madeline dragged herself from her cot and her introspection. She could feel her anger simmering below the surface, and if she wanted to avoid another outburst—which would result in two days of wearing a hair shirt for penance — she would do well to calm herself. She splashed freezing water from the washbasin onto her face. It was refreshing, but it only reminded her of the austerity she now faced daily. Already dressed in her postulant's dark gray gown, she'd tucked her roughly shorn hair beneath her wimple, and a large wooden cross hung around her neck. The undyed wool of the dress made her skin itch, and it chafed the open cuts upon her back. But it was far better than the hair shirt they forced her to wear the third day she arrived. She'd lashed out at another postulant who bumped into her as they entered their pew. The postulant was formerly a lesser noble, and Madeline reminded her that she, Madeline, was the sister of a laird and a former lady-in-waiting to Queen Elizabeth de Burgh. Madeline's voice carried, but the other woman was more discreet in her own set-down, as she pointed out that Madeline's brother was the one to banish her from court.

A Hellion at the Highland Court
An Angel at the Highland Court
A Harlot at the Highland Court
A Friend at the Highland Court
An Outsider at the Highland Court
A Devil at the Highland Court

PIRATES OF THE ISLES

The Blond Devil of the Sea
BOOK 1 SNEAK PEEK

Caragh lifted her torch into the air as she made her way down the precarious Cornish cliffside. She made out the hulking shape of a ship, but the dead of night made it impossible to see who was there. She and the fishermen of Bedruthan Steps weren't expecting any shipments that night. But her younger brother Eddie, who stood watch at the entrance to their hiding place, had spotted the ship and signaled up to the village watchman, who alerted Caragh.

As her boot slid along the dirt and sand, she cursed having to carry the torch and wished she could have sunlight to guide her. She knew these cliffs well, and it was for that reason it was better that she moved slowly than stop moving once and for all. Caragh feared the light from her torch would carry out to the boat. Despite her efforts to keep the flame small, the solitary light would be a beacon.

When Caragh came to the final twist in the path before the sand, she snuffed out her torch and started to run to the cave where the main source of the village's income lay in hiding. She heard movement along the trail above her head and knew the local fishermen would soon join her on the beach. These men, both young and old, were strong from days spent pulling in the full trawling nets and hoisting the larger catches onto their boats. However, these men weren't well-trained swordsmen, and the fear of pirate raids was ever-present. Caragh feared that was who the villagers would face that night.

The Dark Heart of the Sea **BOOK 2**
The Red Drifter of the Sea **BOOK3**
The Scarlet Blade of the Sea **BOOK 4**

VIKING GLORY

Leif
BOOK 1 SNEAK PEEK

Leif looked around his chambers within his father's longhouse and breathed a sigh of relief. He noticed the large fur rugs spread throughout the chamber. His two favorites placed strategically before the fire and the bedside he preferred. He looked at his shield that hung on the wall near the door in a symbolic position but waiting at the ready. The chests that held his clothes and some of his finer acquisitions from voyages near and far sat beside his bed and along the far wall. And in the center was his most favorite possession. His over-sized bed was one of the few that could accommodate his long and broad frame. He shook his head at his longing to climb under the pile of furs and on the stuffed mattress that beckoned him. He took in the chair placed before the fire where he longed to sit now with a cup of warm mead. It had been two months since he slept in his own bed, and he looked forward to nothing more than pulling the furs over his head and sleeping until he could no longer ignore his hunger. Alas, he would not be crawling into his bed again for several more hours. A feast awaited him to celebrate his and his crew's return from their latest expedition to explore the isle of Britannia. He bathed and wore fresh clothes, so he had no excuse for lingering other than a bone weariness that set in during the last storm at sea. He was eager to spend time at home no matter how much he loved sailing. Their last expedition had been profitable with several raids of monasteries that yielded jewels and both silver and gold, but he was ready for respite.

Leif left his chambers and knocked on the door next to his. He heard movement on the other side, but it was only moments before his sister, Freya, opened her door. She, too, looked tired but clean. A few pieces of jewelry she confiscated from the holy houses that allegedly swore to a life of poverty and deprivation adorned her trim frame.

"That armband suits you well. It compliments your muscles," Leif smirked and dodged a strike from one of those muscular arms.

Only a year younger than he, his sister was a well-known and feared shield maiden. Her lithe form was strong and agile making her a ferocious and competent opponent to any man. Freya's beauty was stunning, but Leif had taken every opportunity since they were children to tease her about her unusual strength even among the female warriors.

"At least one of us inherited our father's prowess. Such a shame it wasn't you."

Freya **BOOK 2**
Tyra & Bjorn **BOOK 3**
Strian **VIKING GLORY BOOK 4**
Lena & Ivar **VIKING GLORY BOOK 5**

www.ingramcontent.com/pod-product-compliance
Lightning Source LLC
Chambersburg PA
CBHW011914130726
47903CB00016B/2817